Torpedo Bomber
Lugus Publications

Torpedo Bomber

by

Norman Emmott

Lugus

Canadian Cataloguing in Publication Data

Norman, Emmott
Torpedo Bomber

ISBN: 0-921633-59-9

1. World War, 1939-1945 - Aerial operations, British -
Fiction. 2. Great Britain. Royal Air Force - Fiction.
3. Beaufort (Bomber) - Fiction. I. Title.

PS8509.M56T6 1993   C813'.54   C93-094255-8
PR9199.3.E66Y6 1993

Dedication

To Pat

CHAPTER ONE

Pilot Officer Edward Douglas leaned forward as the lorry rounded a last curve before the main gate of the air station, and caught sight of a Beaufort aircraft parked on a hard-standing amid a clump of trees.

"So that's one of them," Douglas said to the man beside him.

"Maybe we'll be flying in it," Pilot Officer Henry Snow responded.

"Maybe." Douglas squirmed on the hard bench. There were two crews seated on planks in the back of a canvas-covered lorry. Douglas and Snow would have called it a 'stake truck.' Sergeant Trevor Williams and Sergeant Gordon Kitto, sitting on the other side of the vehicle, called it a 'lorry,' as did the four men of the other crew. The eight men, by a stroke of unusual luck, represented the statistical average of aircrew flying out of Britain during the dark days of 1941—four Britishers, two Canadians, an Australian and a New Zealander.

The lorry jerked to a halt at the main gate. The stocky, plain Leading Aircraftwoman of the Women's Auxiliary Air Force, who was driving it, responded to the raised hand of the Service Police corporal of the gate guard. She handed the man a piece of paper, and got the lorry into protesting motion again.

"Those WAAFs always grind the gears," Douglas told Flying Officer Philip Heathcote, sitting two places down.

"She didn't have all Saskatchewan to practice in, the way you did," Heathcote replied.

Douglas peered through the open back of the vehicle at the buildings they were passing. He had been in the service long enough to be reassured by the familiarity of the Air Force scene; the guardhouse, station headquarters, the parade ground, the RAF ensign flapping at the naval-style mast. The brick guardhouse and the stone-fronted Station Headquarters building were different from

1

their wooden opposite numbers at the Canadian stations where he had completed training, although their function, their general set and purpose, was the same. Everything else, here in this Lincolnshire setting, was poles removed from Valenby, Saskatchewan.

Everything in Britain was old. It had been old when a surveyor had hammered a stake into the prairie bunch-grass in 1902 and named the site Valenby. The name had to start with a "V," since the planners for the Canadian Northern Railway, as the lines of steel crept across the prairies, named each of the stations they laid down at ten-mile intervals alphabetically. The previous station was Uxbridge, and the next would be Wellington. Now it was thirty-nine years later. Valenby had five thousand people, six churches, two elementary schools, and the high school Douglas had attended.

He had graduated when he was eighteen, and had gone to work in a drug store. A year later the war had broken out and he had volunteered at once—anything to get away from the bald-headed prairie; Valenby, where the big event of the day was the passenger train pulling into the station. Especially from the drug store. Its carping, criticising owner, with all his joy and sparkle ground out of him by the depression, complained about the way Douglas served the customers, swept the floor, counted the change, or dusted the shelves. If Harley S. Dymock, Pharmaceutical Bachelor, hadn't been such an old bastard perhaps Douglas would have waited longer than October 1939 to volunteer.

Now it was October 1941, and Pilot Officer Edward Douglas had just arrived at RAF Station, Lower Lexington, Lincolnshire, wearing pilot's wings on his chest. He and his crew were recent graduates of the Operational Training Unit at Chivenor, where they had learned to fly Beaufort aircraft and drop torpedoes at enemy ships. He and Heathcote, with their crews, were replacements posted to No. 842 Squadron.

They neither knew nor cared whom they were replacing. All squadrons needed to be brought up to strength continually. They knew they were heading into danger, but they scarcely thought of it; this was squadron life, the culmination of all their training. The training grind was over, and they were full-fledged operational aircrew now, entitled to swagger and be careless about their uniforms.

2

The station buildings were brick, seven years old or so, built when Britons began to rearm in the Thirties. They were new, compared to the village of Lower Lexington, outside the perimeter fence. The village looked just as it had when half a dozen villagers had marched off to carry muskets to Quebec for Brigadier General James Wolfe in 1759. One of the men had stayed in Canada, and his great-great-grandson had helped to survey the site of Valenby and had settled there. Later he had married Douglas' mother. Douglas had no idea he had any ties to the village. He knew his father was from Toronto and his grandfather from Montreal. In any case the descent had stepped down through a maternal generation, with a name change. Douglas thought his roots were in Scotland, on his father's side, with distant cousins on his mother's side, in Lancashire.

Douglas' navigator sat beside him. Henry Snow hailed from British Columbia, a hamlet in the West Kootenays called Castleford, even smaller than Valenby. Both his parents had been born in England, his father in Manchester, his mother in Scarborough. His father had gone to Canada out of sheer wanderlust after having served in the South African War with the Lancashire Fusiliers, in search of wide skies and wider opportunities, of which he had had a taste in the Transvaal. He had liked Africa, but when someone asked him why he had not stayed there he would answer, "Too many blacks, me lad." Now he was a conductor with the Canadian Pacific Railway, and a man of solid worth. Snow's mother had been a teacher, inveigled to the far West by prospects of better pay.

As a well-paid railwayman Snow's father could afford to send his son to university. Snow was in his second year of engineering when he left school to enlist. He had wanted to become a pilot, but his depth perception did not pass muster, and he was trained as a navigator, a trade about which he soon became enthusiastic. He was twenty-five years old.

The two sergeants were wireless-operator air-gunners, who were to take turns manning the rear turret and the wireless set. Trevor Williams was a Welshman from Llandudno. Short and slight, he had been a busboy at a restaurant after leaving school at fourteen. He was a good gunner and a mediocre wireless operator. Gordon Kitto was a tall, rangy, sandy-haired Australian who had been an electrician in Perth, a good radio-operator and a mediocre gunner. Williams was nineteen and Kitto was twenty-seven, with a son and a daughter in Perth. He wrote his wife every other day.

3

He was in love with a girl he had met in Winnipeg, where he took his radio course, among the first Australians to graduate from the British Commonwealth Air Training Plan. She was a tall, beautiful redhead with an Icelandic background, whom he had met at a dance put on for the Australian trainees by a service club. He had never told her that he loved her, and he intended to return to his wife, to whom he had sworn to cleave until death did them part. He wished he had never met Thora Gustavson, and could not stop thinking about her.

Everybody else in the crew was fancy-free.

The crew had formed itself by accident, as most crews did, at the Operational Training Unit. Douglas and Snow had met at the General Reconnaissance School at Charlottetown, Prince Edward Island, and found themselves on the same liner taking them overseas. When they were posted to torpedo bombers they had ridden to Chivenor, where the OTU was situated, on the same train. They had fallen into conversation, and by the time they reached the OTU they had formed a tacit agreement that they would crew up. Kitto had been the one that had selected Douglas, not the other way around, not so much because Kitto respected Douglas' skill as that he respected Snow's. Williams had followed Kitto's lead because he admired the Australian's knowledge of radio. Snow, older that the others, found more in common with Kitto than with Douglas or Williams, though he opened their first conversation for the banal reason that he had known a family called Kitto in Castleford B.C. which was always getting into fights because they were being accused of being Italian rather than Scottish.

The men were beginning to speak the same language now. Snow refused to use the word 'petrol,' but he called a 'truck' a 'lorry,' while Douglas had forsaken the word 'gasoline,' because he had to discuss fuel consumption with the other pilots, but clung to the word 'truck.' They all called their aircraft a 'kite.' What Snow called a battery Kitto called an 'ack'—short for 'accumulator;' Snow and Douglas had got around to calling flashlights 'torches.' They were agreed on terms like 'port' and 'starboard' and `undercarriage'—the arcane jargon of a learned profession.

Flying Officer Charles Heathcote was an Englishman, as were his two gunners. His navigator was a New Zealander, a tall, smiling

4

round-faced sergeant called Eric Tinline. Sergeant Robert Thomas Brown was a Cockney. Sergeant John Hewlett-Curtiss was a public-school boy who had proved unable to land a plane, and hated mathematics too much to face the thought of becoming a navigator. His father was the president of a quarrying firm in Worcestershire, and 'HC,' as the crew called him, always had plenty of money.

The lorry stopped in front of Station Headquarters and the men climbed out of it, heads bent beneath the canvas top. Williams and Hewlett-Curtiss handed out the kitbags and suitcases. The eight men, carrying their gear, filed into the building entrance and looked around for the sign, *Orderly Room*, which they entered. A middle-aged sergeant handed them forms to complete. Pens scratched busily. An officer and a sergeant, both wearing red arm-bands, approached them. "Hello there," the officer greeted them. "I'm the orderly officer. I'll take the officers to their quarters. Sergeant Jefferson will look after the NCOs. What squadron are you posted to?"

"842," Heathcote replied.

"That's splendid, chaps. You can report to the squadron orderly room tomorrow. It's too late today."

They were shown to their quarters. The sergeants shared a room in the aircrew sergeants' quarters, while the officers shared a similar room, a little better furnished, in the officers' quarters. They stowed their gear away, and had supper in their respective messes before turning in for the night. Snow and Douglas were together, as they had been at OTU.

The next morning the two crews entered the office of Squadron Leader Jeremy Clifton. A tall, straight-backed man with a clipped moustache, he rose from his chair as the eight men filed in and saluted him.

"At ease, chaps," he said. "Sorry there aren't enough chairs for you to sit down. We're jolly glad to get you at 842, and you're jolly lucky to be reporting to the best torpedo squadron in Coastal Command."

"We think so too, sir," replied Heathcote.

"I'm sure you'll fit in splendidly. How many hours have you?" he asked Heathcote.

"Six hundred, sir," replied Heathcote. "I was on a transport flight for a while."

"Splendid, splendid. We need experienced people. And you?" he asked, as he turned to Douglas.

"About three hundred, sir."

"Very good, very good indeed." Clifton sat down. "I rather expected to see more of you chaps, though."

"You were supposed to, sir," Douglas replied. "We lost a couple of crews on course."

"Oh yes, yes. Hard cheese, don't you know, but we have to expect losses, don't we? Well, you'll go to A Flight. Flight Lieutenant Peterson will be your flight commander. Good luck, chaps, and I'll be seeing a lot more of you."

"Yes sir." They saluted him and filed out of the office, to seek out A Flight.

Flight Lieutenant Peterson was a tall man with a long, thin face, a big jaw, arms hanging from rather narrow shoulders, and a hint of a stoop. He had joined the Royal Air Force in 1935, and had become a torpedo-bomber pilot as soon as he gained his wings. A student of war, as most of his fellows were students of flying, he was known as a conscientious, somewhat pedantic officer and a mediocre pilot.

"Well, here you are, chaps," he greeted them. "We need you. Pity it's only two crews."

"We'll do the best we can," Heathcote answered, assuming the post of spokesman for the group. "The OC's away for the day, I suppose."

"You just met him, didn't you?"

Heathcote's brows lifted. "We were told the Officer Commanding is Wing Commander Harrison."

"Wing Commander Harrison did not return from a trip yesterday. Squadron Leader Clifton is acting OC."

"Oh, bad luck!" Heathcote murmured.

"That's the luck of the draw," Peterson answered. "Well, let's see what you know. We'll go up tomorrow morning for a few practice runs on a Navy trawler we play with. Take-off is at ten. I'll brief you at nine. Now go and draw your equipment—parachute, navigation equipment, and all that. Dashed glad to see you." Peterson ceremoniously shook hands with all eight of them before they left the office.

6

The two crews trooped out to go about their individual affairs. Heathcote and Douglas prowled about the pilots' crew room, while Snow and Tinline sought out the navigation section, where they drew dividers and hand-held computers, navigation watches, protractors, straight-edges, astronomical navigation tables and 'Air Almanacs,' maps and log-sheets, and sloppy canvas bags to hold them. The wireless air gunners drew log-books and handbooks on the radios they used, and repair-kits for their machine-guns. It was comfortingly familiar, since they had done the same at each new station during their training. They introduced themselves to the men they met, and were greeted with the reserve that all veterans greet rookies.

Douglas, Snow and Heathcote met in the officers' mess at tea-time. The building, a permanent one as opposed to the Nissen hits they had grown used to at the temporary stations they had seen so far, had a spacious ante-room with a high ceiling, a carpet on the floor and comfortable chairs. Snow reached for a rock-cake, and poured himself a cup of tea. "Rough do about the Wingco—you think he'd have stayed around until we got here."

"Wonder what it was—fighter get him?" Douglas said.

"Perhaps. Or maybe it was engine failure. A Beaufort needs both engines to keep it in the air—it won't hold height on one engine. And if you're down to fifty feet already you have no height to lose." Heathcote munched a bun. "The damn kite's underpowered, you know."

"Underpowered. You said it," Snow nodded. "That's how Jackson's crew got it at OTU. Lost an engine at take-off, and went in off the end of the runway."

"Well, we're stuck with the Beauforts now. Anyway, they're better'n those open-cockpit Swordfish the Navy has to put up with. Must be bloody awful in a rainstorm. And slow,you know, they cruise at ninety-bloody-knots!" Douglas said." At least they hold height on one engine," Snow said.

"Yeah. They only have one engine," Heathcote nodded.

"And we do have enclosed cabins," Douglas observed.

Heathcote munched at his rock-cake. "Peterson seems a rum chap," he said at length.

7

"He's lasted quite a while. It's probably about time for him to go to greener pastures," Snow said.

"He proves you can survive after all," Douglas mused. "If he can, we can."

"Wonder if we'll get a new wingco, or whether they'll just promote the squadron leader," Snow said.

Heathcote pursed his lips. "Somebody told me he's only had his scraper ring a month. They'll probably send in somebody else."

"Don't know if they have anybody," Douglas said. "They're kind of short of senior officers in this racket."

"Yes. Hopes for fast promotion," Heathcote laughed grimly. One by one they finished their tea and went to their barrack rooms.

Meanwhile, in the office of the Officer Commanding, Squadron Leader Clifton looked at Peterson. "Well, what do you think of them?"

Peterson shrugged. "Run of mill, I guess. Douglas looks an awful kid. Fresh from the wilds of Saskatchewan, with straw still behind his ears. Heathcote looks a little more mature. I looked at their log books. They're both rated as average pilots." Clifton nodded. "I thought Canada sent the better ones to General Reconnaissance School."

"The ones with good ground-school marks. Not necessarily the best fliers."

"I guess not. We should be grateful we got anybody. Losing two crews out of six was a bit of a shocker."

"That only leaves us one crew up, what with the wingco going for a Burton yesterday."

"You don't make money trading wingcos with ten years' service, who used to be in the aerobatic team, for pilot officers."

"No," Peterson nodded. "He was a fine pilot. I never agreed with him on tactics though. This rover business is bloody silly, I've always thought."

"I know, Peterson. You keep saying so. But Coastal Command Headquarters says it makes sense. A single aircraft, patrolling a given area, looking for an enemy ship to drop a torpedo on, keeps harassing the Huns. Gives their coastal traffic something to think about."

Peterson snorted. "Something to think about? Can't you see we're wasting our Beauforts, splitting them up into penny packets the way we do? We only get a ship by luck! If we catch a convoy off the Dutch coast by surprise we can sometimes get close enough to do something—but if they see us, even a merchant ship can comb the torp just by turning towards it—if the fish doesn't break in half when it drops, and if it runs true—and we lose too many aircraft. There are always fighters about, you know, and Jerry flak from the escorts is getting better. It was always good, anyway. We shouldn't operate in flights less than three, and all drop at the same ship."

"You keep saying that, Derek, but you know it just isn't policy. We all have to do what we're told, you know."

"The policy is bloody stupid. I'll bet that's how Harrison bought it. Some fighters caught him alone." Peterson's eyes darkened. "Or maybe it was those bloody engines again."

Clifton stood up. "Look, Derek, you're getting to be a common scold. The engines are getting better since those factory representatives came here and modified them. And the Rovers do give new crews experience in operational conditions where the pilots use their initiative."

"Initiative hell! We're playing at war sending individual lads out and hoping. We should use them as a team."

"I know—I know. But you're getting bloody-minded about it. We have our orders." Clifton put his hand on Peterson's shoulder. "You're only doing yourself harm with this bitching."

"Yes. I suppose so." Peterson subsided. A corner of his mind pounced on the word "bitching." Clifton had been around Canadians too long. An Englishman would have used the word "grousing." The Canadian word sounded affected. But then everything sounded affected until you got used to it. "A ropey do—a piece of cake—" had sounded pretentious once. But now they were just part of the language. He shrugged and left the office. He'd see how well the sprogs would fly tomorrow. Maybe they'd last long enough to learn their way around.

And maybe they wouldn't.

CHAPTER TWO

In the bar that evening, Douglas, Heathcote and Snow stood a little uncertainly, hesitating to make any approaches to these hardened aviators who had long since received their baptism of fire. They sipped at their tankards of beer and looked around them. At their OTU the instructors had let it be known that mere students were distinctly lower class, whose place was to do what they were told and not to presume upon their inconsiderable and temporary rank, and to treat their combat-tested betters with the greatest of respect. They backed away from the bar, looking at the photographs on the wall of an ancient *Wildebeeste* aircraft and an even more ancient *Atlas*, both strutted-and-wired biplanes that the RAF had flown between the wars. As Douglas stepped back he collided with a tall man who was hurrying to the bar, slopping a little of his beer on his shoes.

"Oh—excuse me! I'm sorry!" he hurriedly said, taking in the man's two rings that marked his flight lieutenant's rank, his wings, and beneath them the diagonal blue and white stripes of the ribbon of the Distinguished Flying Cross, that rare mark of distinction. Appalled by his clumsiness, Douglas stood rooted to the spot, waiting for the lightning of the hero's wrath to strike.

"Not to worry, old chap—no harm done." The man fixed his dark blue eyes on Douglas' face and tossed back his thick thatch of dark brown hair. "I say, I don't think I know you. Just visiting?"

"We've just been posted in today. To 842 Squadron."

"Jolly good. Have you been posted to a flight yet?"

"A Flight, sir."

"Dashed bad. I've got B Flight, and we could use a crew or two. By the way, I'm Hedley Westover." He put out his hand. "Welcome to Lower Lexington." He smiled. "Dash it, you look a little lost. Something on your mind?"

"Well, we were rather wondering what it's like on operations these days. The staff at OTU didn't seem to be too sure."

Westover laughed. "It hasn't been bad lately. Just remember to stay low, and jink like mad when you're coming up to the drop point. Don't stay on the same course any more than a minute or two. The Jerry gunners will be computing the deflection angle by your relative speed, so don't be where they're aiming at. Alter about twenty degrees, hold the course for not less than twenty seconds, then off on a new course. Then settle down for the torpedo drop, let the fish go, and start jinking again."

"Thank you sir," Douglas said as Heathcote nodded. Westover made a deprecatory gesture with his hand. "Don't bother to call me 'sir'—I'm not a squadron leader. Hedley is good enough. Lots of luck, chaps, and I'll be seeing you." He moved toward the bar, leaving the two with their eyes following him.

"Friendly guy, isn't he?" commented Douglas.

"Very much so. He's got a DFC too." The two turned to sit down near the fireplace beside another pilot officer, as young and fresh-faced as Douglas.

"Hello," Heathcote introduced himself. "We're new here."

The man smiled. "I'm an old-timer. Been here a month. Harry Hobhouse."

Douglas cocked his head toward the flight lieutenant. "Who's the flight looey with the DFC?"

"That's Hedley Westover—OC of B Flight. A real ace—a little too reckless for my taste, but a beautiful flier. Got his gong for picking an ammunition ship out of a convoy."

"Seems a nice chap."

"Oh he is—a real glamour-boy type though—public school and all that. He's a good cricketer—played for England once."

"He sure looks the part."

"The boys in B Flight think a lot of him. He shouldn't be here much longer, though—he's been here over a year, and he should get his scraper ring and go on to greater things."

"You in B Flight?"

"Yes. I hope the next flight commander is as good as Hedley."

The next morning they gathered in the briefing room while Flight Lieutenant Peterson told them what he wanted from them. "And

11

remember," he told them "none of that stupid jinking while you're on the run-up—your job is to sink ships, and you'll never do it if you spend your time throwing your aircraft around the sky like a cat on a hot tin roof. Keep it straight and level, and give yourself a chance to make a hit. And don't drop too soon." He looked around him. "That's what I want you to do. We're here for just one purpose—to sink German ships. It doesn't matter whether we survive or not if we get those ships! And I'm telling you the way to do it." He looked at Douglas. "Any questions, Douglas?"

"No sir. None at all."

"Very well. Remember what I said."

The crews filed out to the lorries which would take them out to the aircraft. "Sure different from what Westover told us, wasn't it?"

"They haven't made their minds up yet. I guess each flight commander works out his own tactics."

"It kinda shakes you. Peterson acted like we were written off already," Snow said.

"Let's survive and fool him."

"I suppose they'll find out who's right in the end," Tinline said. The lorry moved off.

They took off, and Peterson formed up with them as they made dummy runs on a Navy trawler. Douglas noticed that his turns were a little sloppy, and that he did not keep formation as closely or as crisply as the pilots he had trained with had done. They ran in on the trawler, the slipstream from their propellors kicking up a wake in the water, and pulled away at the time Douglas considered they had reached the approved 800 yards.

Peterson's angry voice cut through the static in Douglas' headphones.

"Damn it, didn't I tell you to get in to 800 yards? You dropped that torp at about fifteen hundred! You'll never hit a damn thing if you act like that! Now go in again and do it right and get closer to that bloody ship!"

"Yes sir. Sorry sir." Douglas kicked the plane into a turn and made another run at the trawler. This time he waited until it loomed in his windshield as if he were about to hit it, and then pulled away.

"That's a bit better. You dropped at about nine hundred that time. Try to get a little closer. Do it again."

Douglas made another run. "You still dropped too soon, but it's nearly acceptable. But don't jink on the run-in. How many times do I have to tell you that?"

"Yes sir."

"Come on back home. You've had enough for one day." Douglas shrugged his shoulders back and forth in his flying suit. He found he was wringing wet with sweat, although it was a cool day.

Peterson debriefed them after they had landed, his comments caustic and unflattering. Douglas said little. Snow and the gunners sat uncomfortably, angry at Peterson and sympathetic for what they considered an undeserved blast at their captain. As they returned to the parachute section to turn in their safety equipment Snow said, "Jesus, I don't see why he took out after you the way he did. I thought you were doing all right."

"It's his job, I guess—the son of a bitch."

"Maybe he figures he's doing it for our own good."

"If it's for our own good why does Westover tell us to jink? Westover has a better record than Peterson has." Douglas kicked a stone. "I know this—when I was shooting gophers out on the prairie it was a hell of a lot easier to hit them as long as they sat on their hills and looked straight at you without moving. A gopher that dodged around was a lot harder to hit. When we're dropping on a target I'm going to jink—I'll tell you that."

"Well, you're the skipper—I guess nobody can stop you doing what you want."

"Did you want me to do something else?"

"No—come to think of it, I'd just as soon you jinked. After all, I'll be in the kite too."

They turned in their parachutes, and then Douglas said, "I gotta go over to stores and get a new flying suit. The one I have has a big tear in it." He walked over to clothing stores, to stand in the rather dim, mothball-smelling area in which were stored the hats and coats and trousers which would be issued to the airmen and airwomen of the station, and the flying clothing that would go to the aircrew. A weedy, youthful Leading Aircraftman was standing behind the counter. "Yes sir?" he said as he looked up.

"I want a new flying suit," Douglas said. "This one is torn."

The LAC took it and looked at it. "Excuse me, sir, but this doesn't look like fair wear and tear. There'll have to be a charge to you."

"Charge? Whadda you mean, charge? I got that damn tear climbing up into one of your ropey aircraft? Now gimme another flying suit!"

"I'll have to call the sergeant, sir." The man disappeared, and a moment later a woman wearing sergeant's stripes appeared. She was stocky and grey-eyed, with her hair tied severely behind her head; a little older than Douglas perhaps. If they had met elsewhere Douglas might have found her attractive, but now she was all business. "Yes sir," she said. "What is the trouble?"

"Come on, sister," Douglas said. "Give me a new flying suit. I ripped this one climbing into one of your aircraft."

"The sleeve is torn, sir. However, stores regulations state that if the approved period of wear is not expired a pro-rata charge must be assessed against the wearer."

"Good God!" Douglas exploded, "D'you mean that you have to charge me for catching my sleeve on your pitifully-designed aircraft? My God, woman, you should have more sense than that!"

"There's no need to be abusive, sir. The regulations are quite clear."

"Damn it, get me another flying suit. I'm sure as hell not going to pay for another flying suit? That's one thing King George has to spring for? Damned if I will!"

"I can't give you a new flying suit until you sign the proper form, sir."

"There's nae need to be abusive sir," the sergeant said coolly. "I'll get the stores officer."

The stores officer, a balding flight lieutenant, appeared from an office. Douglas looked at him. "What do you mean I have to pay for this damned flying suit? I thought the government was supposed to issue me flying equipment!"

The flight lieutenant looked him up and down as coolly as the woman sergeant had. "I must ask you to sign this voucher, Pilot Officer. If you feel you have been unjustly treated you may submit a redress of grievance through the adjutant. In the meantime, do not curse my airmen and airwomen."

"All right, give me the damn voucher! But don't think you've heard the last of this!" Douglas signed the paper, and the sergeant brought him a flying suit. He tried it on, complained about the fit, and made her get another one.

14

He went back to his barrack-room seething. "Goddam store-bashers!" he complained to Snow. "What bloody right have they got to charge me for that flying suit?"

Snow shrugged. "They'll have a hell of a time collecting it. The voucher will have to be charged back to the Royal Canadian Air Force, not the Royal Air Force. It'll get lost before it gets there."

"That's one consolation, then. But I'd sure like to get sergeant bitch under my command for a while. I'd sure as hell make her jump!"

"You're aircrew. She's groundcrew. You'll never see her again."

"I hope not. The bitch!"

"Come on over to the mess and have a drink."

"Good idea. Got to have something to take the taste of that bitch out of my mouth."

That evening he wrote a letter to a girl he had known back in Valenby. "I sure don't like these English girls much. They're about as attractive as a bunch of—" He ran out of words. "Snow," he called? "how can I describe that English bitch sergeant in the stores?"

"She's not English. She's Scottish."

"That does it." He completed his letter. "—as a broken scotch bottle." He mailed the letter, and tried to forget the Scottish WAAF sergeant.

CHAPTER THREE

Douglas, Heathcote and their crews were sitting in the briefing room, listening to the operations officer outlining what the aircrew were to do. It was their first operation over hostile territory, and all of them were nervous.

"You're on Rovers today," the instructions came. "These are your areas." The operations officer pointed to two roughly triangular blocks outlined in red cord, stretched between magnetic markers on a map painted on metal. "Douglas to the more northerly one—Heathcote to the southerly. Your navigators have already laid them out on their charts. The weather's about right—bags of low cloud around. Don't get too far from it. Intelligence says there are several coastal vessels in the area. They may be escorted by German naval vessels, but the escort will be light. Avoid them. Attacking them is not your job. And your torpedoes cost eight thousand pounds apiece—don't waste one on a ship below about 4500 tons. Here are the recognition signals."

Pencils scratched busily on log-sheets and charts. The group looked up as Clifton stood up and walked to the dias. "Your first trip, gentlemen. Things should be comparatively quiet, if we can believe intelligence. Remember what you learned at OTU, and go through the drill. Good luck and good hunting."

Snow nudged Douglas. "That's what the Cubmaster used to say to us after a cub meeting back home. Maybe I better call the OC *Akela*."

Douglas nodded. "We're still tenderfeet in this racket. Let's hope we get to be full-fledged scouts before we finish."

The crews filed out and climbed into the back of a lorry. Douglas saw Snow lick his lips as he hoisted his navigation bag over the tail of the vehicle. The men sat down, fidgety and nervous, quiet. As they settled into their positions on the bench Douglas heard a single comment that grew into a babble of voices. "This is it, mates—"

"betcha old Adolph'll love this"—"the Germans'll never know what hit 'em." Douglas reviewed the instructions he had received during the briefing. Snow would be doing the same thing, he knew. It was easier for him; navigators were always working frantically, always with something to keep them busy, to keep their minds occupied. He hoped he would not have time to think.

The lorry stopped, and Heathcote's crew got out. Their Beaufort stood on an asphalt circle beside the taxi-strip. "Cheerio, chaps," Heathcote said to Douglas as he stepped out. The wireless operators waved to each other. "Ta-ta, old cock," Williams said as the lorry jerked into motion again, the gears grinding as usual, until it stopped a few minutes later. The four men of Douglas' crew climbed out to stand in front of their Beaufort, looking up at the perspex nose for a few seconds before they began their ritual walk around it, the visual inspection. Douglas pulled at the rudder and the elevators to make sure they moved, felt the propellor blades, kicked the tires. Snow rubbed a smear from his observer's window. Kitto pulled at an antenna wire. They climbed aboard.

Snow lugged his navigation bag into the nose. Kitto busied himself behind his radio dials. Williams climbed into the rear turret, at the end of the long hump on the back of the Beaufort. He would test the turret as soon as Douglas started the engines and gave him hydraulic power, and then crawl out again for the take-off. If the kite went in during the process of leaving the ground he did not wish to be trapped behind bent or crushed turret doors while the aircraft burnt.

Douglas went through his cockpit check. A Catholic priest had once told him how he dressed himself in his vestments, repeating a prayer as he put on each garment. This process of checking each instrument, moving each control, spinning trim-tabs, adjusting the seat to suit his length of leg, and flicking over the fuel gages, had become a ritual now, drummed into him by his instructors until he felt it would be fatal to skip a movement, whose faithful completion was a talisman for the flight's success.

Besides, it was his first operation, and everything had to be done right. He looked through the window at the airman holding a fire extinguisher beside the port engine, gave him the thumbs-up signal, and pressed the starter. The propellor moved sluggishly, the engine

17

coughed, and then the exhaust stack spat out a great dollop of smoke and the propellor turned into a shimmering disk. Douglas opened the throttle and then pulled it back to idle. The airman was already beside the second engine. Douglas pressed the starter. As soon as the starboard engine started the airman ducked under the wing to pull away the chocks. Douglas moved the throttles up and down the quadrant as he held the aircraft on its brakes. He flicked the magneto switches to check the drop in revolutions. Everything checked. He thumbed his microphone.

"Rear turret?"—"All okay, skipper."—"Wireless?"—OK, skipper."—Navigator?—"OK."—"Ready for take-off." A green Aldis light winked at them. Douglas looked at Snow, sitting beside him on the jump seat, and opened the throttle as he released the brakes. The Beaufort waddled off the hard-standing onto the taxi-strip. He taxied to the end of the runway in use, where he went through the engine run-up again, checked the fuel once more, and moved the controls and trim-tabs.

"Prepare for take-off!" He shoved the throttles forward, and the Beaufort moved, picked up speed, swung slightly, and straightened as Douglas shoved at a rudder pedal. The Taurus engines with their touted sleeve-valves bellowed in his ears. Douglas pushed the stick forward slightly to bring up the tail, watched the airspeed indicator, felt the aircraft's eagerness to fly speaking to him through the control-column. He eased back. The nose lifted and the bouncing progress down the runway smoothed as the wings took the load off the wheels. "Wheels!" Douglas snapped, and Snow brought up the undercarriage. "Brakes!" Snow touched the brake lever. The wheels jerked up into their wells, and the doors closed over them. Douglas levelled off at 500 feet to gain airspeed before he began the climb.

Snow unbuckled his seat harness, and slipped down to his navigation table in the nose of the aircraft. He spread out his map, made the take-off entry in his log sheet, and plugged in his intercom cord. "Navigator to pilot—your course is 083." "Zero eighty-three." Douglas had already set the course on his compass, but he checked the setting. The red end of the compass needle matched the red end of the compass dial. "Red on red," he told Snow. "I'll be staying at a thousand feet until we reach the coast," he continued. "Then I'll go down to two hundred."

"Roger."

Douglas adjusted the throttles, mixture controls, and manifold pressure until the engines were running smoothly at cruising revolutions. The countryside fell abruptly into the sea, and Douglas nosed down to lose height. The waves, which had made a netted pattern at a thousand feet, were distinct at two hundred. In the nose Snow was busy over his drift recorder, measuring how much the cross-wind was pushing them sideways. "Alter to zero eight seven—oh eighty-seven."

"Zero eight seven it is." Douglas set the new course on the compass and nudged the plane over with the rudder. Bursts of rain spattered against the windshield and shreds of low cloud flicked past. Visibility was poor, and Douglas wondered if he would see an enemy ship. The search depended on him, he knew. Snow would be so absorbed in his navigation that he would be deaf and blind to everything except his charts, his computer and his drift sight, and Williams would be scanning the sky for aircraft, not the sea for ships. A smudge came up on the horizon in front of them.

"Pilot to navigator—what are we approaching?"

There was a moment of silence, and then Snow's voice came. "Enemy coast ahead." Douglas felt a thrill run down his back, his feet growing suddenly cold as if he had looked over a precipice. Enemy territory, where he was fair game. He remembered how a duck he had shot, back in Saskatchewan, had tumbled out of the sky, and wondered if it would be that way for him too. He peered from side to side with hunted eyes.

"Alter course in two minutes, skipper," Snow ordered. "Next course is zero three three—oh thirty-three." "033 it is. Tell me when to turn." Douglas set the new course on the compass, holding the plane on the old course by the directional gyro.

"Start turning now." Douglas twisted the control wheel and pulled slightly back. The plane heeled over. Douglas watched the subdivisions on the gyro dial swing around, and straightened out. "On course." He knew Snow would be measuring the drift on the new heading and would give him an alteration of a couple of degrees. This was a short leg, ten miles long, twice visibility distance, before they set out to patrol the next east-west leg. Kitto was busy twiddling his wireless knobs and taking morse, but he was not sending any messages, since radio silence was in force. Williams kept swinging his turret. It was a nuisance, since the turret acted as a rudder to swing the plane off course, making Douglas tramp on the rudder to correct it. For the first half-minute or so he would take the pressure with his leg, and then he would reach to the rudder trim-tab and twirl it to compensate, and then Williams would swing the turret in the other direction. Douglas cursed to himself but put up with it. He wanted the turret swinging.

It was on the fourth leg of their patrol that Douglas saw the ships. Five miles ahead and to port, they were darker smudges on a dull horizon. He thumbed his intercom switch. "See anything over there on the port bow, navigator?"

Snow peered through his perspex. "Yes—yes—looks like two ships—or is it three?"

Williams chimed in from the rear turret. "It's three, skipper—two of them in line astern and the other off to the side."

"Probably two merchantmen and an escort," Snow said.

"You're sure they're enemy?"

"Oh sure," replied Snow. "We're too far east for them to be friendly."

"Okay," Douglas said, his voice hard. "We're going to attack. We'll come in from this side. Going down to seventy feet." He checked his airspeed—140 knots, dropping speed. Faster or lower, the torpedo would porpoise and head off in some unpredictable direction. Higher, it would dig in nose-first and head for the bottom.

"What speed do you estimate the ship is doing, navigator?"

"Probably about ten knots. Won't be going any faster."

"Okay." Douglas checked over the drill he had been taught at Chivenor. Come in quartering on the ship's bow, aiming just ahead of it, and drop at a range of 1000 yards—Peterson and Westover said eight hundred. He held his course until he was just ahead of the ship and turned toward it.

"Looks like they haven't seen us, skipper," Kitto said. He had deserted his radio and was crouched behind a waist gun. "Get the camera ready, navigator," Douglas ordered.

"They've seen us now," Williams said. Douglas could see the escort, a converted trawler, swivelling its guns at him. Red dots began to pump across the intervening water. Good God! Douglas thought, they're shooting at us!

"Tracer to port," Williams said. "I see it," replied Douglas, too intent on his job to let his voice rise.

"Bomb doors open," Douglas said, pushing a toggle switch. He felt the aircraft buck as the doors came open, and made a gentle turn. The nose of the aircraft slid along the horizon and settled just in front of the bow of the second ship. He saw the silhouette foreshorten as it began to turn toward him, and kicked the plane into a series of slicing S-turns. The larger of the two ships was leading, and Douglas saw with displeasure that his target was the smaller of the two. He was committed to the run now, and he flew on. The image in the windshield grew.

Black puffs of smoke suddenly appeared around them, and the aircraft shuddered to what seemed the blows of a giant smashing at them with a sledgehammer. The target ships added fire from their guns to the stream of tracers pouring from the escort.

"They've hit us!" Williams called out. "Holes in the rudder!" Douglas felt a difference in the way the plane handled, but it still answered to the controls. The ship was filling the whole windshield now. At OTU they had continually cautioned him, as Peterson had, about dropping too soon, but every nerve screamed at him that he had waited long enough. He shoved savagely down on the release button. The aircraft jumped upward as the torpedo fell away.

A stream of tracer flashed across the windshield. Douglas kicked the aircraft into a series of skidding turns. A column of water from an exploding shell rose abruptly in front of him. Water cascaded off a wing. The ship seemed within a hand's breadth away. Williams' voice came, "Torpedo running normally!" Douglas was in front of it, and could not see the line of bubbles that marked its passage. The aircraft vibrated to the savage jabber of Williams' guns as he swung the turret at the bow of the ship and blasted the gun position on its foredeck. The gun fell silent. Douglas turned the plane sideways and pulled up the nose. The ship swept past. A mile or so ahead the low clouds dipped almost to the surface of the water. Douglas headed for them, pursued by fire from the escort vessel. The ship was still turning.

"What did the torp do?" Douglas screamed at Williams. "Didn't see no explosion," replied Williams. His voice abruptly rose an octave. "Bandits! Starboard quarter!" His guns jabbered again. "Corkscrew

21

port—GO!" Douglas shoved the nose down and tramped on the rudder, at the same time shoving the throttles to the top of the quadrant. The engines roared and the aircraft dived and twisted, pulled out, entered a climb. Douglas saw an ME109 fighter, the black crosses ominous on its wings, flash past and pull into a turn to position it for another pass. Kitto fired at it with the waist gun. The cloud was nearing with glacial slowness. "Corkscrew starboard, GO!" The rear guns hammered. Douglas saw tracers flashing overhead, and then suddenly the wingtips were invisible as they were enfolded by the concealing cloud.

The guns fell silent. "Can't see a thing, skipper," Williams' voice came. "He's lost us."

"Bloody good thing too," Douglas replied laconically. "Keep your eyes open," He checked the throttles, bringing them back to cruising revolutions. "What's our course for home, navigator?"

"Steer 297," Snow answered. "I'll lay off a position and give you a better course in a minute." Douglas adjusted the manifold pressure and the propellor pitch. With a damaged rudder the aircraft flew roughly, but it held height and speed. They were in complete cover, and Douglas concentrated on his instruments. At intervals the aircraft fishtailed as Williams swung the turret. "Rear gunner from pilot—can you see anything?"

"Not a sausage, skipper. Can't even see the wing tips."

"Right. Keep a search going, though."

Snow spoke. "Alter to 305, skipper. Estimated time of arrival 1413."

"305 it is." Douglas turned the aircraft the requisite eight degrees. "How much longer over the sea?"

"Fourteen minutes."

"I'm climbing to six thousand feet. Wireless operator, call up base and tell them we're coming back."

"Can't, skipper. Wireless silence."

"Okay."

"Wireless operator, navigator here. Can you get me a bearing on an MF station?"

"I'll try," Kitto answered.

Douglas looked at his instruments. A gage flickered. He peered closely at it. "Dammit!" He pressed his microphone button.

"Navigator, how far to land?"

"Eight minutes. A little over twenty miles."

"We're losing oil pressure on the starboard engine... I may have to feather it. Where are we going to make our landfall?"

"Should be on track, but we could be ten miles either way. You threw her all over the sky when we were attacked by that fighter."

"Give Kitto a position. Kitto, if you hear an engine stop, send an SOS right away."

"Right, skipper."

" I'll try to get all the height I can."

"Don't get too high. That fighter may still be around," Williams put in.

The engine's smooth roar degenerated into a sputtering, coughing snarl. "I'm feathering," Douglas said. He shut off the engine and pressed the feathering button. The blades of the propellor turned toward the front to cut air resistance and stopped. As the aircraft turned toward the dead engine Douglas tramped on the rudder and twirled the trim tabs. With its direction under control, Douglas looked at his altimeter. They were starting to lose height.

"Sent that SOS yet, Kitto?"

"He can't hear you, skipper," Williams answered. "He's on the set."

Kitto's voice came a moment later. "Sent the SOS, skipper. Acknowledged."

"Throw your guns overboard, Williams, and your ammunition. Can't hold height."

"How about me?" asked Kitto.

"Throw out most of your ammo but wait until the last moment before you throw out the gun."

"Okay skipper."

"Navigator—how far to land now?"

"Five minutes."

"Holy Jesus—does time pass that slowly!" Douglas licked his lips. "Give me a course for the closest airfield." Douglas could feel sweat soaking his helmet brim. "I'm just figuring it out." After an agonizing wait Snow said, "Go onto 314."

"Three one four it is, three fourteen." Snow's calm voice was reassuring. Navigators were always so absorbed in their work that a little thing like a dead engine never worried them.

"How's our height?" Kitto asked.

"Three thousand. Still losing."

"We're out of the cloud now," Snow said.

"Yeah. Still sea beneath us, though."

"I think I can see land, Can you?" Snow asked.

Douglas' voice rose an octave. "Yes—I can see land! Four or five miles away. At least we won't have to ditch!"

The altimeter needle kept sagging. "Throw out that gun, Kitto—throw out your radios too if you can get them loose!"

Kitto set to work with a screwdriver, and in a minute was pushing his wireless set out a hatch in the roof. Snow struggled up from the nose with his machine-gun and drums of ammunition, which he tossed out.

"We're over land!" Williams cried.

Snow ducked back into the nose. He was quiet for a few seconds as he busied himself with his maps. "Skipper! We're ten miles north of track! Go onto 270 right away—there's an airfield that should be right ahead!"

"I can see it!" Douglas put the aircraft into a gentle turn. He called up the airfield on his radio-telephone set. "Fire the colours of the day, Kitto!" The multi-coloured blobs of light arced into the sky above them as Kitto shoved the Verey pistol into its chute and pressed the trigger.

"Strap yourselves in! I'm landing!" Douglas circled the field, lowered his undercarriage, and turned onto final. He saw the green light welcoming him in.

He landed almost normally, despite the dead engine. As he flared out he cut the throttle. With rudder trim on, the aircraft slewed. He touched down, stamped on rudder, and hauled the stick back into his stomach. The aircraft turned majestically and ran off the runway, to stop with a succession of shuddering jerks.

Douglas slapped the ignition switches and the engine choked to death. "Okay guys, let's get out of here!" The crew scrambled out of the plane and gathered a respectful distance away. The engine as it cooled was giving off crackling noises. Williams turned to Douglas to say, "Best landing you made all week, skipper."

"Ah, shaddup!"

A car drove up carrying the flying control officer and a sergeant. "Hello, chaps. Spot of bother?"

"Yeah. Shot up. Lost an engine."

"Hop into the old bus here. I'll take you to the tower. We'll have the aircraft fixed up for you. What do you think happened?"

"Probably flak in an oil tank."

"You've been torpedoing, I see. Wel, I'm afraid the intelligence officer will have to debrief you. Let's go."

They answered questions, filled out forms, had supper, and went to bed. None of them had any overnight gear, and the next morning, unshaven and grimy, they were told to return by train to Lower Lexington. It took them all day.

Westover commiserated with them in the mess. "Hard cheese, old top," he said. "I know those damn kites won't hold height on one engine—that Taurus hasn't enough guts. But I guess we'll have to live with them. You did all right for sprogs."

Peterson was a little less pleasant. "Results unobserved, you say. All right—you missed." He slammed a fist into a hand. "A single aircraft will always miss, and the damned Beaufort won't hold height on one engine! The smallest number of aircraft on a sortie should be three, and they should all attack together! And even if the kites are no damn good, we haven't enough of them!" His voice softened. "Welcome to the club, gentlemen. You've had your baptism of fire."

Two days later the adjutant called Douglas. "We've just received a letter from a fisherman. Says his boat was damaged by a wireless set dropped out of an aircraft. Do you know anything about it?"

Douglas checked the date and the position. "It would have been us, all right."

"Well, we hit something, even if it was only a fishing boat," Kitto said. "Let's go to the pub and have a drink to celebrate."

"We got lots to celebrate," Douglas said sourly. "We got shot up. We threw everything overboard. We landed away from home. We ran off the runway. We smashed up a fisherman's boat. And we didn't do a bloody bit of good."

"We need a drink to forget it," grunted Kitto.

"Ah, what the hell!" Williams put in. "We're still alive. That ain't bad these days." He headed toward his barracks to get his bicycle. "See you at the Coach and Horses!"

25

The celebration was beery and lengthy. The next morning they all had hangovers.

Douglas checked his flying suit. "Hot damn! It's got a flak hole in it! Now I'll got back to stores and get a new one! This time that damn WAAF sergeant won't have any smart cracks to make about fair wear and tear!"

He walked over to the stores section. The leading aircraftman was still there. "All right," Douglas said, "get the sergeant!"

The woman came, looking him levelly in the eyes. "Yes sir."

"Here's my flying suit? It's got a big rip in it—put there by flak from a German gun? Now get me another one!"

"Yes sir," the woman replied evenly. "I can remember your size." She brought him a flying suit. He tried it on, to find it fitted perfectly. "That's better," he said, "I'll take it."

"Now sign this," she said, handing him an indelible pencil.

"It's not one of your damned charge-back vouchers, is it?"

"No, it isn't. Now if you can be good enough to sign it we can go back to work."

Douglas signed the issue voucher. "Okay. I am glad to report, sergeant, that you were not so damned snippy this time. Congratulations." He bundled up the flying suit and left the building.

CHAPTER FOUR

The crew did not fly again until their aircraft was flown back from its diversion base and repaired. The faulty engine was changed, the flak holes were patched, and the guns and radios which had been jettisoned were replaced. While they were waiting for it to be made serviceable again they had little to do. Douglas lazed around the crewroom, while Snow rode about the neighbouring countryside on his bicycle, exploring the old churches and the paths and byways. On several of his excursions Harry Hobhouse accompanied him. Hobhouse turned out to be an entertaining companion. He had majored in history, and he was able to point out to Snow the sites of many of the battles which the Saxons and Danes had fought a thousand years before; a Roman road, a bridge which had been built by Cromwell's army, and a battlefield from the Wars of the Roses. Snow repaid him with tales of pioneer days in British Columbia, which he had heard from his father.

"You must come down and visit my family the next time we get leave together," Hobhouse said. "They'll enjoy meeting you."

"I'll enjoy meeting them. When you go on leave, do you go with your pilot?"

Hobhouse smiled. "Not dear old Ab Crossley," he replied. "Ab is rather a rough diamond. I'm afraid he's not much interested in Norman churches."

"Every man to his own poison. Thanks for the invitation, Harry—I'll take you up on it."

"Mum and dad will be glad to see you. I'll warn them to hide my sister."

Snow laughed. "I'll try to live up to my reputation."

The next day when Snow reported to the navigation section he

27

found his name chalked on as blackboard. "Here we go again," he told Williams and Kitto when he saw them.

"Another Rover," Williams grunted. He peered at the aircraft letter opposite the name. "Same kite we had last time. Hope it hangs together better than it did then. I was getting tired of throwing stuff overboard."

"They patched those flak holes in the tail and replaced everything," Douglas said. "The technical wallah from the engine company was here all last week, and maybe he made the engines run better."

"Or longer," said Kitto. "The kite doesn't hold height too good on one engine. Lose one and it turns into a submarine." Snow collected his navigation gear, stowed it in a brown canvas bag, and followed the three other members of the crew into the briefing room. Two crews were detailed for duty, the other captain being Crossley. He was a burly ex-policeman from Birmingham. His wireless air-gunners were an undersized Scot and a weedy Cockney. They were to patrol adjoining areas in the North Sea. The weather as usual was poor, with low clouds, rain squalls, and gusty winds. Snow made copious notes, and toiled over his flight plan, plotting his courses out on maps and working out his ground speeds and estimated times on each leg with his hand-held E6B computer.

The routine was not much different from their briefings at their Operational Training Unit, although the imminence of combat lent it urgency. Douglas looked at Snow and envied him. The involved and pressing tasks of a navigator kept him so busy that he had no time to think about the danger he was standing into. Snow was in introspective, dreamy fellow when he was not navigating, and Douglas shuddered to think of him as a gunner. Blind and deaf to his surroundings as he sat sunk in thought, the whole Luftwaffe would close upon him unobserved.

After Snow folded his maps and stowed them in his bag they walked outside to the waiting lorry. "Crikey!" the cockney gunner said as he looked up at the sky. "Ain't the weather ropey? Sure you can get the old kite in the air with all the clouds ahrand, skipper old cock?"

"You mind your manners!" Crossley grunted. "Aircraft don't have much trouble going through clouds if they don't have hard centres."

"Won't be able to see no ships, with visibility as bad as it is," the Scotsman put in.

"Fighters won't be able to see us either," said Kitto.

"You gotta take the rough with the smooth, Bach," Williams commented. The lorry stopped and Crossley's crew got out. Four minutes later Douglas' crew climbed out to stand before the Beaufort.

"Well, there she is, the ugly bitch," Williams said. "Hope she behaves better this time."

"I tried out my new wireless," said Kitto. "It ain't as good as the old one."

"Well, you will throw them out, you know," Snow replied.

From the next hard-standing they heard the cough, growl and snarl as Crossley started his *Taurus* engines. Douglas reflected as he walked around his aircraft, giving it the ritual external inspection that preceded every flight, that he did not like Crossley much. The beefy Crossley had the crude sense of humor, honed at the expense of the derelicts and criminals he had dealt with as a policeman, that made so many people in petty authority objectionable. Funny, Douglas thought; here was Snow thick as thieves with Hobhouse, and he and Crossley could not stand each other. Then he looked at the tail of his aircraft and saw the patches where the bullet-holes had been repaired, and forgot about Crossley and his crew.

The crew climbed into the aircraft, Snow last since he had stopped to wipe the window of his compartment in the nose. Douglas brushed water from the slight drizzle from his flying suit and started the engines. A green light flashed at them. They took off, Douglas and all his crew listening for any hesitation in the sound of the engines. All was normal. The unreliable, underpowered engines snarled away with all the authority in the world.

The flight was absolutely uneventful. They saw no ships in their area and no other aircraft. As they ducked from cloud-patch to cloud-patch Snow kept himself busy with his navigation, and Kitto absorbed himself with his radio. The air beneath the cloud decks, just over the confused sea, was rough, and shortly after they left the coast Douglas saw Snow vomiting into a paper bag. Snow was prone to airsickness, but after few minutes of misery he would go back to his navigation with his efficiency unimpaired, his course-changes passed in his usual unemotional voice and his ETA's correct.

After two hours the patrol became boring. They were making a formal search of the area, flying parallel tracks that stepped north a few miles after each sweep. Snow kept busy peering through his drift recorder, spinning his hand-held computer, drawing lines on his chart and making entries in his log. For him, the flight would not be much different from a cross-country training exercise. Now that his stomach was empty he was composed and happy, and in an hour he would have stopped feeling sick and would be able to eat a sandwich and enjoy it.

Williams kept swinging his turret. Looking out, controlling his attitude and his movement, he was as immune from airsickness as a pilot. Kitto twisted the knobs of his radio and copied morse. Douglas flew through the tendrils of cloud reaching down from the cloud-deck to the surface. The engines ran sweetly. Douglas cocked an ear at them and reflected that perhaps the factory representative had done something for them after all.

When they reached their Prudent Limit of Endurance Snow thumbed his microphone. "PLE in two minutes, skipper. Your course home is 243—two four three. I'll tell you when to turn."

"I didn't see a bloody thing," Williams said disgustedly. "No joy this trip."

"Whadda ya mean no joy?" responded Douglas. "I thought it was a real joy-ride."

"Navigator to skipper—alter course to 243—turn now."

"243 it is." Douglas twisted the steering yoke, pulled the control column back a little and touched the rudder. The plane swung around and Douglas applied opposite aileron and steadied into the turn. Douglas pulled it out onto the new course. Snow checked the drift, made a calculation, and called a course three degrees different. Douglas eased onto it. The plane flew on, the crew silent. Douglas kept swivelling his head. To be jumped by a fighter now would be a macabre anticlimax to their peaceful afternoon.

The English coast came up, surf making a creamy edge to the rocky beach. Douglas poured on power to climb to the 5000 feet which he had been briefed to fly home. He was in cloud at that height, however, so he let down to 3000 feet. Snow checked the landfall on his topographical map and altered course for base.

Douglas circled the air field, extended his wheels, pulled back the throttle, and glided down to a normal landing. He concentrated on making it smooth, bringing the wheels down to a few inches above the runway as he pulled the stick back to keep the plane from landing until it lost its last vestige of flying speed. The stall came and the wheels gently kissed the asphalt. The transition between flying and rolling was imperceptible. "You greased that one on, Eddy," Snow told him. "Couldn't 'a' done better meself, skipper, old cock," Williams' voice came. The plane waddled off, nose-high and tail-down, to the dispersal where a lorry picked up the crew. The intelligence officer debriefed them, looking disappointed as he heard they had seen nothing. "What did Crossley see?" Douglas asked.

"Crossley's crew is overdue," the intelligence officer replied. "We haven't heard from them."

Douglas pursed his lips. "Maybe he had to divert."

The intelligence officer nodded, avoiding their eyes. "I hope so." From his tone Douglas knew he did not think Crossley's chances were very good. The news cast a pall over the crew's elation at completing an operational trip on which everything went well, and the perfect landing which had completed it. The men's faces were serious, but Douglas knew each felt an unworthy joy that this other crew was lost while they were still alive. They avoided one another's eyes as they stood up from the briefing table.

The four men walked back to their billets, their steps dragging. Douglas and Snow shared a room in the officers' quarters, Nissen huts with partitions which did not quite reach the ceiling. Accommodation was spartan, patterned after that of an expensive English public school. There was a bed with a mattress which came in two portions referred to as "biscuits," a chair, a bookcase, and a contraption known as a "wash-hand stand," which had proved useful in the Boer War but had been made obsolete by the provision of ablution rooms fitted with washbasins and bathtubs. The bookcase was half-filled with books, most of them belonging to Snow, who never came back from leave without adding to their number.

Douglas' contribution to the shelf was mostly technical, about aircraft and automobiles. On the bottom shelf was a half-empty parcel from home, carefully packed by Snow's sister. The one Douglas had received the week before was long gone.

31

Snow and Douglas changed into their No. 1 5A Blue uniforms, hanging up their battle-dress on the length of pipe that did duty for a wardrobe. The station commander did not tolerate battle-dress in the officers' mess after six o'clock at night.

"One thing about this business of ours—we work decent hours," Snow commented. "Better'n Bomber Command—they work at night, like burglars."

"Can't see to torpedo ships at night," responded Douglas.

Snow looked at his watch. "We've got time for a beer before dinner. Let's go."

Peterson was at the bar, a tankard in his hand. Douglas nodded formally to him. "Crossley got home yet?"

Peterson shook his head. "No. If he's not heard from yet he won't be."

"Those engines again, d'you think?"

Peterson shrugged. "Maybe. Or fighters. One thing I do know— we're just pissing away our aircraft and crews using them in penny packets. There's only one ways to use anything—ships, infantry, aircraft—and that's in groups big enough to do some good." He took a pull at his beer. "Sending a single aircraft out—that's just asking for it."

Douglas nodded and edged away. Peterson had the reputation of a zealot who preached at everyone within reach. Douglas preferred to think that his commanders knew what they were doing. He ordered a beer from the barman and gravitated to a settee where Heathcote was sitting. "Hi Phil," he said. "How's things lately?"

"Nothing out of the ordinary. Hear you were flying today."

"Yeah. Didn't see a thing. Not a sausage."

"Just as well."

"Yes. That first trip was a little too exciting."

A woman approached them. She was wearing the uniform of a section officer, equivalent to a male Flying Officer or an army lieutenant. Heathcote and Douglas stood up. "How do you do, Lady Helena. May I present Ed Douglas?"

"How do you do, Pilot Officer Douglas," the woman replied in a cultured upper-class accent.

"This is Helena Compton-Morris, Ed."

Douglas took her hand. "Glad to meet you, Miss. I'm a new boy here—still a sprog, I guess."

"I've been here a year. Philip was telling me you've already done several operational trips."

"They put you to work pretty soon around here."

"Lady Helena is an equipment officer," Heathcote put in.

Douglas grinned. "That should be interesting. I've had my differences with store-bashers from time to time."

"Everybody has sooner or later," she replied. "We do the best job we can, I assure you."

Snow drifted up. Douglas introduced them. "Can I get you a drink, Helena?" Snow asked.

"Yes, thank you—a small sherry will do." Snow brought it. "You fly with P/O Douglas, don't you?"

"Yes. I'm his observer."

"Do you have an all-Canadian crew?"

"No. We have an Australian and a Welshman as wireless air gunners."

"There'll be quite a *melange* of accents aboard your aircraft. You and PO Douglas have broad Canadian accents, and the Australian and the Welshman have different accents, but just as broad."

Douglas nodded. "We get on all right. We all speak Air Force, after a fashion."

Snow looked at Helena. "A broad accent," he said musingly. "Tell me Helena—have you a narrow accent?"

"Narrow accent?" She turned to look at him. "Why—" Her brow knitted. "I've never heard it mentioned that way."

Snow cocked his head sideways. "Maybe you can measure accents by how wide they are. Do you use calipers, or just scale it off with a ruler?"

"A ruler?" She burst out laughing. "No. I always use a piece of string."

"Fine," Snow said. "You get the string, and we'll mark it off as broad, narrow or medium. Then we'll get a person to say something, and you hold the string up, and measure whatever they're saying."

"What a wonderful idea. I'll go right out and get the string."

"First we have to decide on the dimensions of the accent." Snow held up his finger and thumb. "You have a narrow accent, so you

33

should be about this wide. Ed Douglas here has a broad accent like me, so he'll have an accent this wide." Snow spread his fingers further apart. "As for an Australian accent, would you say it's as broad as a Canadian one?"

She creased her brow. "Yes, I think so—but it's not the same—maybe it's just not at the same angle." She held up her hands in the form of a cross. "It's like this, I think."

"Where does a Scots accent come in—or an Irish one?"

Helena twisted her hands. "Like this."

"I see. It's getting complicated though. For instance, which is broader—a Cockney accent or an Australian one?"

She looked at him with narrowed eyes. "How about a Canadian accent and an American one?"

Snow nodded. "I speak ordinary Canadian—which is standard Mid-Western American with some variations. It's the commonest English dialect. About ninety million people use it."

Her eyebrows rose. "I thought the King's English was that."

"No—not at all. You speak standard Southern English, which actually is a fairly restricted dialect—mostly upper-class Englishmen—and Englishwomen." He looked into her eyes. "My accent is the product of people I never knew—from Devon and the Midlands; the people who settled the eastern seaboard of what is now the United States. That's why I have the strongly-pronounced R and the flat A. Devon people still pronounce their R's, even if they use the broad A, and Midland people use the flat A the way I do, even if they can't be bothered with their R 's."

"You said the people in the eastern seaboard of the United States—"

"A lot of them emigrated to Canada after the American Revolution and came to Ontario—they called themselves United Empire Loyalists, and they took their speech with them. That set the fashion. And that's why I speak the way I do." Douglas edged away. He liked Snow well enough, and Helena was an attractive woman, but the conversation bored him. It bored Heathcote too, and before long Snow and Helena were sitting together discussing language and speech. They chattered amiably for half an hour, and then went in to dinner together. After dinner Helena left to return to her quarters, and Snow sought out Douglas and Heathcote, who were standing together holding pints of beer.

"You seem to have hit it off with Lady Helena," Heathcote said.

"Lady Helena?"

"Yes—Lady Helena. Her father's a duke, you know."

"A duke? Holy smoke, I never guessed—"

"Don't hold it against her." Heathcote grinned. "To coin a phrase, she's a real lady—in more ways than one."

"So I noticed."

"She usually keeps her distance. You're doing all right with her."

"Keeps her distance? Because she's a Lady with a big L?"

"Maybe there's a little of that. But she's had romances with two chaps, and they both went for a Burton. She thinks she's bad luck."

Snow pursed his lips. "Was she friendly with Harry Hobhouse?"

"A little."

"They speak with the same accent. She reminded me of him." He looked at the floor. "Tough about Harry."

"You get used to it."

"Yes, I suppose so."

"Have another beer."

The next evening Snow approached Helena in the mess. "Excuse me, Lady Helena," he said. "I have something for you—a present I am sure you will value."

"Yes—what is it?"

Snow took a piece of heavy cord from his pocket. "It's marked off in inches in red, and in centimeters in blue, so you can measure how broad a person's accent is. The blue marks are for people who speak with a French accent. I was going to mark it off in versts for the Russians, but I can't find out low long a verst is."

She laughed deliciously, taking the string and holding it at arms length. "I'll carry this with me, and measure everyone I speak to."

"You can write a book when you get enough data collected. Cut me in on the profits."

"I'll do that." She fell into step beside him as they walked into the dining room. They talked animatedly all through the meal, and then, as she had previously, she went off to her quarters.

Snow looked at her as she left the mess. She was an attractive woman, and he enjoyed her company, but he did not intend to press his acquaintanceship with her. As the daughter of a duke she was out of his league. Besides, those who had sought her favours had come to sticky ends. Maybe she was bad luck. It was probably academic anyway. During their conversations she had made it clear that she did not date aircrew.

When she left the evening was still young. Douglas came up to Snow to say, "Let's go to the Coach and Horses for a beer, and then maybe drop in at a dance they're holding in a local hall."

"Sounds good to me," said Snow. "Can't stay here all the time."

At the pub they found Williams and Kitto. "Thought we'd find you here, skipper," Williams said.

"You're getting to know me," Douglas replied. He and Snow sat down with the gunners at a scarred table.

"Rough do, Crossley getting the chop," Kitto said. "I was pretty friendly with one of his gunners, Syd Bell. He was a right dinkum bloke—we used to practice sending morse to each other in the crew room—had a lovely fist, he did—smooth and steady. I'm going to miss him."

"Harry McLaughlin, the other gunner, was a good drinking type— liked his beer," Williams put in.

"I'm going to miss Harry Hobhouse," Snow added. " I was going to visit his family next time we got leave together. Guess I won't be going now."

"No. Not now," Kitto agreed.

"I didn't know any of them very well," Douglas said. "I saw Crossley around the crew room but that was about all."

Snow lifted his glass. "Well, here's to them." They drank. There was a moment of awkward silence, and then Williams tossed back his beer and stood up. "Might as well get to that dance. See if there's any tail around."

"Righto," Kitto agreed. "Make us forget the occupational hazards of the business we're in."

After a few minutes Williams disappeared, and a friend of Kitto's had hailed him, leaving Douglas and Snow together. "Let's go to that dance now," said Douglas.

When they reached the dance hall Douglas nudged Snow. "Let's go check the trap line," he said as he looked at the girls along the walls. They wandered along the sidelines until Douglas suddenly stopped. "What the devil! There's that WAAF sergeant that gave me such a hard time!"

Snow looked where Douglas pointed and laughed. "I'll go and ask her to dance. Maybe she'll give me the lowdown on you."

He walked over to where she was standing near the door. "Excuse me, lady," Snow said formally, "but may I have the pleasure of dancing with you?"

"Thank you," she replied, and Snow stepped off with her. "You're with 842, are you not?" she asked.

"Yes. I've been with 842 a couple of months."

He found his steps blended well with hers. "You're a good dancer," he said.

"I studied dancing in Scotland."

"I didn't. The girls I danced with taught me."

"You learnt well."

"I never danced much until I came to England." He grinned. "Maybe that's why you think I'm a good dancer—my steps match yours, because I learned here."

"Very likely. I see you're a Canadian."

"The flashes on the shoulders of my jacket give me away."

"There are other ways of telling."

"Don't tell me we're as bad as all that."

"Some of you are."

"Well, you know how it is—innocent young fellows away from home—You're from Scotland, you say? Where—Glasgow, Edinburgh?"

"It's Edinboro—not Edinburg. That's the way it's pronounced." Then she smiled into his eyes. "But I come from Glasgow."

"Sorry I mispronounced Edinburgh. I never did learn to speak Scotch correctly."

"Scots—not *Scotch*. Scotch is a whiskey."

"That's why I thought you were Scotch."

"Why?"

"Because of your intoxicating personality."

She laughed. "That's good reason. But I prefer to be called Scottish."

"What's your name, then?"

"Moragh MacLennan."

"That's a lovely name. There was a family called MacLennan in Castleford, British Columbia, where I come from, and one of the

37

girls was called Moragh. I knew her quite well."

"I have heard that there are quite a number of Scots in Canada."

"Yes. As a matter of fact my skipper's name is Douglas—that's a Scottish name."

"Douglas?" Her brows knitted. "I know Mr. Douglas."

"He's my pilot."

"Douglas!" she spat. "That unlicked cub? I don't know how you stand him!"

"He's a good pilot. I like Ed."

"Well, I don't! He acted disgracefully when he came to me to get a new flying suit!"

"Yes," Snow laughed. "He told me about it."

"What did he say?"

"He said you had a very positive personality."

"I'll bet he didn't."

The music stopped. Snow said, "May I offer you a drink?"

"That would be very welcome," she answered, as they walked toward the bar. Snow went on, "I know you'd prefer Scotch, but they never have it. A gin and lime, maybe?"

"Thank you." They sat down together. She lifted her glass to him and said, "You know, you're really very nice."

"—even if I am Douglas' navigator."

"You're not like him at all."

"I admit I have much better taste than he has." He laughed again. "You know, Douglas pointed you out to me. I must admit I was agreeably surprised to find you such an attractive girl—besides having a positive personality. I agree with him there."

"Don't tell me you danced with me on a bet!"

"No. But if I had, I'd have thought myself lucky in at least two different ways."

The music started again. "Come, my dear lady," said Snow. "Let us forget our troubles in each other's arms—a dance floor is designed for that."

She stepped into his arms. "I don't know what a nice officer like you is having anything to do with that awful man Douglas!"

"I can't have good taste in everything, Moragh. And as for you, for a woman with a positive personality you're very beautiful."

"That's enough of that! I ken I'm no beautiful!"

38

"You're no judge of that, my dear. I'm the expert in that department. I can tell a beautiful woman when I see one."

She smiled. "If you want to say so, don't let me stop you."

At the end of the dance the orchestra played the home waltz. "May I take you home, Moragh?" Snow asked.

"Not tonight. You'll have to wait a little. You're not in the wilds of Canada now, you know."

"I can dream, can't I?"

"Yes, if you want to." He bent over and kissed her hand. She looked at him with eyes suddenly wide. "I always wanted a man to do that, but you're the first one that ever has. Maybe you did learn something in your mountains." She reached up and kissed his cheek. "Good night, Pilot Officer Snow." She smiled at him. "I saw your name on a crew list."

"When are you coming to another dance?" he asked her, before she left.

"There'll be another one here next week."

"Save me a dance, Moragh."

"I'll think about it."

Snow and Douglas rode home on their bicycles together. "You seemed to be cooking on the front burner with that WAAF sergeant," Douglas said complainingly.

"She's not all that bad when you get to know her."

"She's a bitch." Douglas looked at Snow. "How'd you make out with her?"

Snow shrugged. "You can never tell until the second date. I'll find out then."

"You're a smooth bastard with dames," Douglas went on. " You always know what to say."

"Well, it took my mind off Harry Hobhouse, anyway. You know, he told me he was going to introduce me to his sister. I saw her picture. She's quite a doll. I guess I'll never meet her now ..."

"No. You'd remind her too much of her brother."

"Well, that's the way the cookie crumbles. No sense crying over spilt milk."

They rode on in silence, and went to bed without further conversation, as if it had been an ordinary day.

39

CHAPTER FIVE

"You'll be flying with Flight Lieutenant Westover on a Rover," Peterson told Douglas as he reported for duty on a rainy morning. "One kite from each flight. You're going out as a pair. Maybe the brass has learnt something."

"Okay," Douglas nodded.

"You're getting reasonably experienced," Peterson went on. "You'll be able to stay up there with Hedley. He jinks around a lot."

"I know Flight Lieutenant Westover is pretty well known for the way he tosses his Beaufort around. He's got a pretty good record, though."

"Yes, he has. He'll be coming in to brief you directly."

Douglas and his crew sat around the table in the briefing room, where they were joined by the navigator and the two wireless air gunners of Westover's crew. Westover strode in, debonair and confident. Douglas looked at him and wished he could be more like him.

"Right, chaps, we'll take off and head for the Frisian Islands. We'll stay right on the deck."

"As usual," Snow observed.

"When we reach this little island here," Westover said, pointing out a point of land on a map with a forefinger, "we'll turn and go south. I'll play it by ear, and you follow me. Intelligence says there's supposed to be a tanker in convoy steering north. When we see it, I'll attack from head on, and you come in from the east. Go for the biggest ship. If I see a target I won't wait for you."

"Right," Douglas replied. Snow gathered his maps and the log sheet on which he had written his flight plan. With the gunners they filed into the waiting lorry.

They took off within minutes of Westover, and Douglas swung his Beaufort to a slot behind Westover, to the right and somewhat below. The distance between them was a hundred yards or so. He did not keep a tight formation, since it took less concentration in flying if he kept it loose; it gave him more time to look around him, and was also safer. Westover was a crack pilot, but he had a reputation for being inconsiderate of his formation mates.

They flew to the coast at two thousand feet, and then dropped down as the coast slid past beneath them. The broken clouds above them hid them from enemy fighters, and if they kept low they could avoid enemy radars. "Hold her steady for a drift," Snow said, and Douglas concentrated on keeping the plane straight and level. "Okay," Snow said at length, and Douglas relaxed, letting the plane's head swing back and forth a little. Ahead of him he saw Westover's plane bank to the right, and followed him. "Looks like Westover's getting a three-drift wind," Snow said. "Steady down again." Douglas turned the plane after it had swung through the regulation sixty degrees, and Snow measured the drift. After three minutes Westover's plane turned 120 degrees left, and Douglas followed him; another three minutes and it was sixty degrees right to the original course. Snow spun his E6B computer.

"What's the wind like?" Douglas asked.

"Three twenty-five at eighteen knots."

"That'll give us a bit of a head wind when we're coming home."

"If it doesn't change."

"What's our ETA for that little island?"

"Another eighteen minutes."

"Right." Douglas relaxed a little. Westover's aircraft was leading him, and by now he was able to average out the zigs and zags of his course so that he did not have to follow them so carefully.

A smudge of smoke appeared on the horizon. Westover's plane lost height until it was fifty feet above the waves, and Douglas followed him down and tucked in close to him. The smudge resolved itself into a line of ships, hull-down, with their top-hamper sticking up above the curve of the earth. Westover turned south to pull ahead of the convoy. Douglas, in accordance with his briefing instructions, stayed with Westover until they crossed over the convoy's intended track, and then pulled off toward the enemy coast. Westover swung into a wide turn to allow Douglas to position himself to the east, and then the two aircraft headed for the ships. "Just Westover's luck," Douglas said. "Finds the convoy without even having to start the patrol!"

Douglas flew north until the convoy was off to the side, on the port bow, and turned in toward it. Westover's aircraft appeared to be lagging somewhat. Douglas reached out a hand to open the bomb doors, and checked that the torpedo was armed. Lights sprang into brightness to reassure him. "Okay gang," he called, "We're going in." There was no answer from the rest of the crew.

A big cargo-liner was in the center of the convoy, protected by *sperrbrecher* flak-ships. Douglas estimated its speed at fifteen knots and framed it in his windshield, deliberately letting it pull ahead so that he could alter course for his final run. The guns of a *sperrbrecher* swung toward him, and black puffs of smoke suddenly erupted above him and to one side. He shoved down on the control wheel and kicked the rudder. Turn, steady on a new course, hold it for twenty seconds, turn a random number of degrees, hold the new course for another half-minute, and turn again, never staying on course long enough to allow the gunners a predicted shot. Shrapnel rattled off an engine cowling. Douglas hugged the waves even more closely. The ship's silhouette grew bigger as he dove toward it.

He flew past the stern of the *sperrbrecher* and heard the jabber of machine-gun fire as Williams raked it with his turret, and Snow fired his Vickers gas-operated gun from the nose. The cargo-liner was perhaps two thousand yards away now. Douglas pulled the plane up to dropping height, slewed the aircraft toward the ship, kicked rudder to aim ahead of the ship to compensate for the distance the ship would steam while the torpedo ran toward it, and felt for the release button. He should drop at 1000 yards; that would be another twelve or fifteen seconds. The ship plowed on, apparently unconcerned, although Douglas could visualize the frantic action, the flood of excited commands on the bridge.

Flak burst around him, and suddenly a great star appeared in the windscreen just to the left of his head. Douglas flinched, and the nose of the aircraft rose. He fought to regain control, shoved the nose of the aircraft down, and corrected his heading to swing the aircraft back to the aiming point. The ship was suddenly gigantic before him. He pressed the button on the control column, and the nose lifted as the torpedo fell free. The ship rushed toward him, and as he banked away he saw it turn toward him. It was swinging fast, presenting its head to him. "Damn it!" Douglas spat—the torpedo would miss, passing far ahead.

The ship had swung halfway round when a great stalactite of water sprang up behind it. The ship shuddered and immediately began to list. Douglas saw Westover's plane swing round the ship and dive down until it was skimming the wake of the stricken vessel. There was a deck of clouds a thousand feet above him, and as soon as they were a mile behind the convoy they both headed for it.

"Fighters!" Williams' voice rapped against his eardrums. Douglas swivelled his neck. The savage shapes of ME109's were slicing toward him. He swung away from them, clawing for height. The clouds were a few hundred feet above, and black with flak-bursts. "Fighters attacking!" Williams' voice came again, urgent but calm with the tones of one who was busy, knew what he had to do, and was intent on doing it. "Stand by to corkscrew!" Douglas' hands tensed on the controls. "Corkscrew starboard—GO!" Douglas kicked the plane to the right, nosed down, steadied, and then pulled up and to the left. Tracers streaked across the sky in front of him.

The cloud-base lowered to one side of them. He flew into it. As he turned he felt the aircraft shudder and saw a line of holes stitch across the tip of the wing, before they were shrouded in mist. "Lost the bugger," he heard Williams cry. "Go onto 290," Snow said unemotionally. Douglas turned onto the new course, and the aircraft flew out of the cloud. "Get back in there!" snapped Williams, "the fighters are still around!" Douglas hauled the aircraft around and flew back into the mist. He spun the tail-trim to gain height. At four thousand feet, still in cloud, he turned onto the homing heading. "Where are we, navigator?"

"I'm working out a DR position," Snow answered, "but Christ only knows where we really are. We've been flying in circles for the last half hour."

"Yeah—I know."

Snow reported a latitude and longitude. "I'm busy getting a radio fix. I'll have a little better idea where we are when we plot it."

"Let me know when we're twenty miles from land."

"Okay." The intercom was silent again. Snow came back with a time five minutes ahead, and Douglas waited for his watch to indicate it before he pulled the throttles back to allow the aircraft to descend out of the cloud. They broke into clear air over the sea. "There's the coast to port," Douglas said.

"Yeah—I can see it. We should be over the Wash."

"We are," Williams confirmed. "There's that lighthouse we passed last time."

Snow busied himself sighting on the lighthouse with his astro compass. "Okay. I've got a reliable fix now. Alter to 297—two ninety seven."

"Righto. 297 it is." Douglas set the heading on his compass, and a few minutes later they were over England again.

"We're over *blighty* now," said Kitto.

"Got the ship, didn't you?" asked Williams.

"Hell no! That was Westover's torpedo. The ship combed ours."

"All in the family," said Snow. "Anyway, that's one less freighter for Adolf."

"Too bad it wasn't our torp," said Kitto. The conversation died.

They flew through the gathering dusk back to base. Snow climbed up from the nose to sit beside Douglas and strapped himself in. Flying control called them—"Ploughboy Charlie— Mutton Chop—cleared to land."

The two crews met in the briefing room. Westover slapped Douglas on the shoulder. "Did damn well, Douglas old chap! That ship combed your torpedo, and presented her whole broadside to me—I couldn't miss!" He stood tall, good-looking, debonair. A twinge of doubt struck Douglas. Westover had lagged a little, enough to let Douglas come in first and draw the flak. But the tactics had worked; nobody could deny that. They had sunk a ship, and they were all still alive.

Snow was talking to Pat Hellyer, Westover's navigator, who had flown a year as a sergeant and had just been promoted to pilot officer. He was happy about his promotion, but happier about the successful flight. Crewmen of successful pilots got along better. The gunners were chattering away among themselves. They were all sipping at great stained mugs filled with coffee heavily laced with rum. Douglas did not like it very much; it was English coffee, and terrible. He would have preferred tea, and he would have preferred to leave out the rum. But it was ritual to drink it, and he did.

The intelligence officer debriefed them, with Westover dominating the affair, and the other seven men speaking only to agree with him. Westover, elated by his success, stood up to describe his attack, demonstrating his aircraft's flight with his hands, moving a cigarette package and a packet of matches about a table to illustrate the tactics of the target ship and the defending *sperrbrechers*. The intelligence officer scribbled away industriously, treating Westover with notable deference.

After the briefing the crews stood around the room finishing their coffee. Westover saw Douglas looking at the photographs of ships which lined the wall.

"That's the *Princess Marika*," he said, pointing to one of them. "She's one of the Norddeutscher Lloyd liners that used to ply between Hamburg and New York. She's tied up in Wilhelmshaven. I surely would like to get that ship."

"What for?"

"Because she's there, that's why! Think of the blow it would be to German morale!"

"Yes, I suppose so."

"Look at this." Westover took Douglas' arm and led him to a map of Wilhelmshaven tacked to a wall.

"This is the harbour entrance—there are flak guns on either side. But there's a hill here—" he pointed at the map with a finger that went straight to the feature—"where they must think they need no defences. A Beaufort could come in here—" he pointed again— "and clear the hill, and then cut the throttles, come down to dropping height here, turn starboard, and nail her."

"Yeah, I guess he could," said Douglas doubtfully. He questioned the whole concept. Tied to a dock, the *Princess Marika* was no threat to anybody. The German army was not going anywhere by sea, and the Marika wouldn't help it. And there were bound to be guns on that hill. The Luftwaffe wouldn't be stupid enough to leave them off.

"A determined crew could do it," Westover said earnestly. "A big ship like that—better than a measly little freighter, what?"

"Yeah—better'n a freighter."

"It'd be one in the eye for Hitler."

Westover shook his head.

"I hate to think of that ship sitting there laughing at us, with nobody doing a damn thing to bother it. Bomber Command's been there a few times, but you and I know they can't hit anything."

Douglas nodded. Bomber Command had been blasting away at the battleships Scharnhorst and Gneisenau in Brest harbour for months without doing them any damage.

"We're the only people who can do anything effective. With a ship as big as that moored to a dock you could put a fish into it with ease—you couldn't miss against a stationary target. It's just sitting there asking for it."

"It'd be a shaky do. The Germans have fighter airfields around there thick as fleas on a dog's back."

"The answer to that is to go in when the cloud base is low. You could follow the Frisian Islands, just under the clouds or just in them. Then make your landfall just north of the harbour mouth, pull up over the ridge and let fly at Aunt Sally."

Douglas nodded politely. The hazard of such a mission, which Westover had dismissed so cavalierly, was inconceivable. The flight to Wilhelmshaven and back would require eight hours at least, with the return journey taking place after a hornet's nest of fighters had been stirred up. The Beaufort, even before it launched its torpedo, would be in the midst of a fleet of enemy vessels, each bristling with guns. Douglas shivered, even as he mentally paid homage to this man who so cheerfully was laying plans to place his life in such danger.

"Yes," Douglas said, following Westover's forefinger tracing the possible paths of attack. It was an interesting concept, and many enterprises in wartime of equal risk had been undertaken, and some of them had even been successful. He just hoped that he would not have to take part in it.

Snow walked up to them. "Hi Ed. What say we bug off to the Horse and Buggy and hoist a few beers with Williams and Kitto."

"Sure thing," Douglas agreed. He turned to Westover. "How about coming along with us?"

"I'd like to, old chap, but I really have something I must do. I'm a married man, you know." He flashed his matinee-idol smile at Douglas.

"We'll go along if we're invited," Hellyer said. "How about it, chaps?" he said, turning to his two wireless air gunners.

The four men from Douglas' crew and the three from Westover's were sitting in the pub half an hour later, tankards of beer in their hands. Beer was cheaper in the messes, but the sergeants could not join the officers there .

"Good trip today," Snow said, lifting his tankard.

"I say, chaps," Hellyer responded, "let's drink to it. Jolly good show, what?"

"We done good," Douglas answered, deliberately mangling the grammar to contrast with Hellyer's upper-class inflections.

"Yayss," Kitto nodded. "We got one between us."

"Westover is pretty good," Williams said. "Comes in close. Got all the guts in the world."

"A little too close sometimes, for them as what 'as to fly with 'im," said Frank Gilmore, the Cockney gunner. "He's the tiger, and we're the tiger's tail."

"The skipper has a good eye," Charlie Pittman, the other gunner, put in. "Probably the best in the squadron."

"Yeah," Douglas assented. "He got the ship, not us."

Hellyer nodded. "Best of all, he's lucky." He smiled reflectively. "Today, for instance. That ship turned away from your fish and into ours. It could just as easily have been the other way round."

Douglas looked at him. "He waited just long enough for me to drop my torp. Actually it was pretty smart. Anyway, it worked."

"Westover's tricks usually work."

"What's he like to fly with?" asked Snow.

Hellyer grimaced. "Bloody awful, chaps. Never stays on course. Jinks all over the sky. It's horrible trying to navigate with him flying." He shrugged. "But he gets results."

"Where is he now?" asked Williams. "He didn't want to come and have a beer with us."

47

"Probably home. Ever seen his wife?" Pittman said. "She's the prettiest woman in the county."

"He's got it made," Snow said. "All the delights of flying all day, and marital bliss at night."

"If anybody has it made who's on torpedo ops," Douglas added.

"You're right there, cobber," Kitto agreed.

The publican banged on the bar. "Time, gentlemen, please." The men finished their drinks and drifted toward the door. Snow loitered behind to talk to Hellyer.

"Is Westover hot to trot about that ship in Wilhelmshaven?"

"I don't really know. He talks about it as if it's an obsession, but I think he's too smart to pursue it actively. Anyway, the wingco has told him not to go after it. It's too dangerous, and the chance of success is pretty slim."

"You can say that again!"

"And yet I don't know—if we could pull it off it'd be a real exploit—and Westover can do it if anybody can. It's just a matter of waiting for the right weather and the right time, and if you memorized the route—"

"Just as glad it's Westover thinking about it and not Douglas. Sure seems shaky to me."

Hellyer shrugged. Then he stopped suddenly and stood still and straight. "And how can a man die better than when facing fearful odds, for the ashes of his fathers and the temples of his gods." He stopped and looked at Snow, embarrassed.

"Yeah," Snow nodded. "Those old poets said it better sometimes. I know how you feel, old cock."

The men swung onto their bicycles. Snow and Hellyer rode off together, with the clannishness of their common navigator's trade. The other five men rode back to the air station in a gaggle.

Snow looked up at the stars. "There's *Betelgeuse*," he said, pointing at a star. "Funny—you work your butt off at nav school to learn astro, and when you get on ops you never use it."

"Let's see if I can still identify the stars," Hellyer said. They stopped and dismounted from their bicycles to trace out the stars among their constellations and talk about celestial navigation. The other five men pedalled off out of sight.

A cyclist rode up to them. Snow looked up, to recognize Moragh MacLennan.

"Oh, good evening, Sergeant MacLennan. You're out late."

"Oh, it's you, is it, Pilot Officer Snow?"

"May I present Flying Officer Hellyer, Miss MacLennan? Trev, this is Moragh MacLennan—she's the very attractive lady you may have met in clothing stores."

"How do you do," Moragh replied. "Now what are you doing out here so late at night?"

"Just at the moment we're looking at the stars. You know us navigators—always star-struck," Hellyer said.

"For a charming lady like yourself there should be a moon," said Snow. "I'll try to arrange things better next time. May we accompany you back to the base?"

"By all means, Mr. Snow, and Mr. Hellyer. I'll be glad of the company."

They rode off, making small talk, until they reached the guardhouse. They parted there.

As Hellyer and Snow rode toward their barracks, Hellyer said, "Douglas was telling me she's quite a battle-axe."

"Oh, she's okay once you get to know her. She's got a mind of her own, though."

"I like my women to be a little more feminine."

"Frankly, so do I," Snow said. They went to their respective barrack rooms, where both of them picked up books.

49

CHAPTER SIX

Kitto and Williams were sitting at a table in the sergeants' mess, drinking tea and eating rock cakes. "Been on the squadron six weeks now," Williams observed "We'll be due for a spot of leave."

"You're right, cobber," Kitto agreed. "Where will you be going—Wales?"

"Yes indeed, back home. Dad and mum want to see me. Why don't you come with me, Bach?"

"Thanks, cobber. Don't mind if I do. I've already been to London."

"No little bit of fluff there, then?"

Kitto grimaced. "I'm a married man. Got a wife and kid back in New South Wales, you know. It'd be better to go to Wales with you. Your folks will keep me on the straight and narrow."

"They'll keep me on the straight and narrow too."

"Where do you think Snow and Douglas will head for?"

"Douglas has relatives in Scotland. Snow has some in Lancashire. They'll probably go there."

"We've got to do one more training flight before we go on leave. Hope Douglas makes a good landing."

Douglas met them in the briefing room, where they gathered before making the flight, a cross-country that took them to Northern Ireland. "After this, we go on leave. We got a whole week off. Get a chance to spend all our hard-earned money."

"Where you going, skipper?" asked Kitto.

"I've got an aunt in Glasgow. I like Scotland anyway."

"So do I, as long as I don't have to go there," said Kitto. "Cold—it's worse than Canada."

"Don't be too hard on him," said Williams. "After all, Bach, he can't help bein' Canadian. It's better'n bein' a kangaroo like you, anyway."

"Shut up or I'll clobber you, matey," Kitto responded easily. "Mind your tongue or I won't go to Wales with you."

"Sorry, Bach," Williams replied. "A threat like that terrifies me." They filed out to the lorry, drove to the aircraft and made the flight. Snow worked desperately hard at his navigation, as usual, while the rest of them took things easy. When they returned Douglas made a rough landing.

"Last time we're going to let you go on leave before you bring it in better'n that, Skipper," Williams admonished him. "Come to think of it, though, the third and fourth landings weren't bad."

"Get off to Wales!"

"I will as soon as I get over my concussion from that landing." Williams dodged a blow and laughed.

The next day they went their separate ways. Snow went to Manchester, and the gunners to Wales. Douglas went to Glasgow.

Douglas climbed aboard the train carrying a bag of sandwiches he had cadged from the mess kitchen. The train, like all wartime English trains, was crowded to the doors, with every compartment filled, and the corridors populated thickly with people sitting on suitcases. Douglas weaved his way along until he gave up looking for a compartment with an empty seat and forced himself into one which was somewhat less filled than the others. All seats were taken by a group of women and their children, who like himself were going on holiday. They greeted him with frowns, since the compartment was already uncomfortably crowded.

Douglas leaned against the door-frame as the train hammered along, the wheels drumming out a rhythm that rose sharply in pitch each time they crossed a bridge. There was a trio of young boys sitting in seat corners, and who looked up at him with wide and curious eyes. "Are you in the Royal Air Force?" one of them ventured at length.

"Close enough," Douglas answered. "The Royal *Canadian* Air Force." He felt in his pocket. "Do you know what lifesavers are?"

"Course I do. They save people who fall in the water."

"Not this kind." Douglas took out a package of candy lifesavers and squeezed one loose. "Try this." The child popped it into his mouth. Cor," he said. "It's good."

51

Douglas offered lifesavers to the other children. "Where do lifesavers come from?" one of them asked.

"From Canada. My sister sends them to me."

"What's Canada like?" one of the children asked.

"I come from the prairies—it's mostly wheatfields."

"Are you a cowboy?"

Douglas laughed. "No—I'm an airman."

"Too bad," the child said, disappointed. "I know lots of airmen. But I never met no cowboys."

"What are they like? Do they shoot everybody?" asked another boy.

"No, they don't. The Mounties won't let them."

"That's a shame. Do you know any Indians?"

"Oh yes—I know lots of Indians."

"Did they ever scalp you?"

"No. I've still got my hair." He took off his cap. "See?"

"That's a shame. Canada doesn't sound like much fun—no shooting and no scalping."

"I guess not, young fellow." Douglas felt in the shoulder-bag he carried instead of a suitcase. "Here's a barley-sugar."

"Where'd you get that?" the boy asked suspiciously. "We never get barley-sugars no more."

"They give them to airmen to eat while they're flying. Only I always forget to eat mine."

The children accepted a barley-sugar apiece. One of the women spoke to her child. " 'Ere—git up on me knee. Let the young gentleman sit down." She pulled the boy over. " 'Ave a seat there, young man."

"Thank you." Douglas sat down and stretched his legs. The children subjected him to a barrage of questions, which he answered good-humoredly. By the time the train was entering Scotland Douglas was sharing sandwiches with the other travellers. As they left Douglas said to his first enquirer, "If I ever get scalped, I'll let you know."

Douglas referred to the letter and the sketched map his aunt had sent him, caught a tram, and rode out to her suburban home, changing to a bus after half an hour. The fare was only a penny, which left Douglas open-mouthed with amazement. His aunt was waiting for him, throwing her arms around him just as his mother had done when he came from the air station while he was in training. She sat him down in the living room, and plied him with tea and scones while his uncle broke open an obviously treasured bottle of scotch. They were not actually his aunt and uncle, being farther removed from that, but they were the closest relatives he had in Scotland. After supper he chattered away to them for an hour, telling them of his family back in Saskatchewan, of which they had scarcely heard, of his civilian job, and of his Air Force career. They had a son, Andrew, on a cruiser in the Mediterranean, and he could see that he was standing a surrogate for their own boy, who like him was in danger of his life far from home. He felt her hand linger on his arm, and saw the concerned, fearful, hopeful look in her husband's eyes. They avoided the subject of battles, sea or air, and concentrated on the absurd or comical adventures in their lives and his life and that of their son.

His uncle looked at his watch and snapped on the radio. There was a strain of music, and then the news. "There has been heavy naval activity in the Mediterranean." Douglas saw the glances his aunt exchanged with his uncle. They all listened quietly until the words came, "This is the end of the news."

"I must show you our pictures," his aunt said, as she took a heavy album out of a drawer. The pictures recorded happier days in peacetime, with people he did not know but to whom he was distantly related staring self-consciously at the camera. Douglas remembered his mother showing photographs in the same way, with the same comments, to visitors in Saskatchewan.

His uncle took an older album out of the drawer. It went back into the previous century. Among the pictures were those of a number of young men in Highland uniforms. "This is my grandfather—served in the Argyll and Sutherland Highlanders back in the Crimean War—he fought at the battle of Alma. This is my uncle Ian—he was with the Cameronians in India. Came back with a ruby he'd taken out of an idol's eye—loot, you know. And this is my cousin—a lot older than I am—he was in the Black Watch. He's living in Edinburgh now." He flipped over a page. "And here are the boys who were in the Great War—Neil, a cousin of mine—killed on the Somme. My brother, Alastair, killed at Paaschendael. Will

53

Henderson, who lived next door. He was killed at Ypres." He was silent for a moment. "And these pictures of Andrew—as a cub—as a scout. And this is of him as a sea cadet. He was always wild to go to sea. And here he is in his naval uniform. This a picture he sent us from Malta."

"He looks like his mother."

"Yes, he does," his aunt said, "but he has his father's build."

"You must be proud of him."

"Very much."

Douglas felt his aunt's eyes on him as he closed the photograph album. "You must have found some of those pictures boring," she said.

"No—not, all. After all, the people in the pictures are my relatives—a little distant perhaps, but still my relatives. Blood is thicker than water."

She nodded. "Yes. It's good to know the good Scots blood is still represented around the world."

"It certainly is in Canada. Our first prime minister was John A. MacDonald. Our present one is McKenzie King. Those are good Scots names."

"So they are," She was quiet for a moment. "What do you intend to do tonight?"

"I hadn't given the matter much thought."

"There's a dance at the local Women's Institute for lads like you—why don't you drop in? It may be interesting for you. Us old folks are out of your age class, laddie."

"That's is good idea," Douglas agreed. "Where is it?"

"Just down the street. You can't miss it."

Douglas grinned. "That phrase 'You can't miss it' has followed me all around Britain. I still manage to miss it, though."

"You'll no miss this one. I'll take you out the door and point you in the right direction."

After tea, Douglas walked along the street to the Women's Institute. Sure enough, there was a dance going on inside. He paid his shilling at the door and walked in. There would be somebody to dance with; there always was. With so many young Scots serving in the far corners of the world, there would be no shortage of nubile young women.

He danced with two different girls, and then blended back into the group of miscellaneous uniforms along the wall. Suddenly a face caught his eye. He started, and then went up to the girl.

"Well, as I live and breathe! My friend the fierce sergeant!"

The woman looked up at him. It was Sergeant Moragh MacLennan, the storekeeper from Lower Lexington.

She looked at him as coolly as ever. "How do you do, Mr. Douglas. I'm surprised to see you here!"

"I'm surprised to see you too."

"Why? I'm a Glasgow girl—why should you be surprised to find me in Glasgow?"

"You've got me there. All the same, I am surprised. Now, may I ask you if I may have this dance?"

"Why not?" She stepped into his arms. He was a little piqued to find her so unimpressed by him, but on looking back to their previous meetings he could hardly blame her. She was a good dancer.

"You're a good dancer," he told her.

"Thank you. Your navigator told me the same thing."

"My navigator?"

"Yes—Mr. Snow. He's a very nice man."

"Yes. He's a good navigator too."

"He's also a gentleman. They don't seem to make too many of them any more."

"No, I guess not. Anyway, I'm glad there is somebody in my crew you like."

"Mr. Snow says he likes you, although for the life of me I can't see why."

"He's a much finer man than I am. All navigators are, of course."

The dance came to an end. "May I get you a drink, my dear sergeant?" Douglas asked. "I must confess I don't know your first name. Hank Snow knows it, but I don't."

"Moragh."

"That's a nice name. I used to know a girl called Moragh back in Saskatchewan."

"Do all Canadians say that? Henry Snow told me exactly the same thing."

"It's true enough. The name isn't really very popular, though."

"You are most charming, Pilot Officer Douglas."

"Oh, I'm sorry." He laughed. "I should have Hank Snow here. For a quiet guy he sure knows the right things to say to a girl."

"Yes, he does. And now you may bring me that drink you promised. A Pimms Number One would be very nice."

Douglas brought her the drink, along with one for himself. They had just begun to sip them when a man in Highland uniform, wearing corporal's stripes, came up to them.

"Hello, Moragh," he said. "I see you've taken up wi' officers the noo." He stood beside their table, glowering. Douglas looked at him, silent."Oh, Ian!" Moragh smiled at him. "This is Pilot Officer Edward Douglas—he's from the air station where I'm serving. She turned to Douglas, "this is Ian MacDonald—we went to school together."

The man grudgingly put out his hand. Douglas stood up to take it, and then sat down again.

"Sit down, Ian," Moragh insisted, and the man pulled a chair roughly from another table and sat down.

"Care for a drink?" Douglas asked.

"Och aye, don't mind if I do."

"Scotch?"

"Ye'll no get it. A beer will do."

"Mr. Douglas is a pilot in a torpedo bomber squadron," Moragh said when Douglas returned with the drinks.

"Is that a fact?" the man glowered. "And how long have you been at it?"

"Six weeks," Douglas answered.

"No verra long. What's it like in them erryplanes?"

Douglas shrugged. "Not bad. A little scary sometimes."

"Ye're tellin' me ye're afeerd, are ye?"

"Damn right. Every time."

"Don't believe him, Ian. He's one of the best pilots on the squadron!"

"But ye said ye were afeerd, did ye not?" the man persisted.

"Put it this way—anybody who says he's not afraid is a fool or a liar."

"When I go into the fecht I'll no be afeerd."

Douglas looked at him. "That's fine. We need men in battle who are not afraid. Too bad I'm not among them." He glanced at the man's insignia. "You've been in combat, then. I suppose?"

56

The corporal looked at Moragh. "Ye know I didna get overseas because I broke me laig training—that's why. It wasna my fault!"

"Of course not," Moragh replied. "You're itching to get into battle—aren't we all?"

Douglas looked at him and shrugged. "You'll find out if you're afraid or not when you see the first gun fired at you."

The man jumped up. "So ye're sayin' ah'm a coward are ye? I'm no going' tae take that from any mon, officer or no? Ye'll see if I'm a coward or no!"

He reached into his pocket and pulled out a razor. "I'll show ye who's a coward, ye ken!"

Douglas pushed back his chair and stood up. The man ran around the table at him with the razor in his hand. He slashed at Douglas, and then fell forward. Douglas looked up from him to see Moragh standing with a beer bottle in her hand. She had felled him.

A pair of military police hurried up. "What's going on here?" one demanded.

Moragh turned to them coolly. "This corporal slipped and stunned himself when he fell."

"Yes, sergeant," the senior of the military policeman said. "We'll take care of him." They lifted him and hustled him out of the building .

"Good God!" Douglas said. "He was trying to kill me!"

"Aye, that he was. He's a violent man."

"I was safer in my Beaufort." He took her arm. "Let's got to a restaurant where we can have a cup of tea in peace. I need one to settle my nerves." They walked out. "I don't know what in hell to say to you!"

"Thank you might be a good start."

"Yes—thank you—but you—a girl—coming to my rescue like that? Where in hell did you learn to do that?"

"You can learn a lot in the Gorbals if you keep your eyes open."

"God yes! You'd never learn anything like that in Valenby, Saskatchewan!"

She laughed. "So the great pilot officer from the Wild West has tae come to Glesga for a wee girl to show him how to protect himself, does he?"

He smiled ruefully. "It sure looks that way. Well, here's a restaurant. May I invite you in for a snack?"

"Thank you."

They squeezed through a blackout curtain into la small eating-house, where they ordered Vienna steak, which appeared to be made mostly of sawdust.

Douglas shook his head. "Your friend didn't seem very friendly. We're supposed to be on the same side, aren't we?"

"Aweel, he's sensitive because he's in the Hielanders and he's spent all his time in Scotland. But he'll have his chance soon to see action. I hear they're sending more troops to the desert." She sipped her tea reflectively. "We used to play together when we were wee. He was always getting into fights then too."

"He seems bent out of shape now."

"That's what makes our Scottish boys such fine soldiers—they want to get at the enemy."

"That shouldn't be hard. I'll bet he makes a new enemy every day."

"Dinna be too hard on him. He has a tradition to live up to."

Douglas suddenly laughed. "I don't know how I'm going to live this down—a brave Beaufort pilot like me, and a little storekeeping WAAF having to come to my rescue! I'll look like thirty cents!" He took her hand. "I'll have to think of some lie." She laughed too. "Your secret is safe with me. I'll no mention the incident."

"Thanks," he replied. "Is there somewhere else you'd like to go tonight?"

"No thank you. Everything will be closed up anyway. Just take me to the tram stop and I'll find my own way home."

"That wouldn't be very gallant of me."

"No—but sensible. You'll never be able to get back here if you do take me home, and I hae no intention of inviting you to spend the night with me."

He laughed ruefully. "I hadn't got that far yet." He sighed. "Anyway, maybe I can see you again. Will you be in Glasgow tomorrow—or have you another date?"

"No—I have to go back to Lower Lexington. My leave is up."

"Too bad. Well, it's been nice knowing you—and exciting."

He rose and escorted her to the tram stop. As they waited for her tram she looked at him and smiled. "You know, Mr. Douglas you're no as stuffy as I thought you were. Now if you could only say the nice things your navigator says—"

"I'll have to take lessons from him." Her tram screeched up. She boarded it and left him standing, looking at her retreating back. He waited for the next tram, and took it to return to his uncle's house.

The next morning he set out for downtown Glasgow, to visit such places as Sauchiehall Street, of which he had heard so much. He was amazed at how jammed the street was as he wandered about the stores, visited a maritime museum, and then repaired to a small cafeteria for lunch.

The only vacant seat was at a small table where a young woman was sitting. Douglas bowed to her. "Mind if I join you?" he asked. "I hope I'm not bothering you."

"It's nae bother," the girl replied, and he sat down. Douglas looked at a round face beneath a shock of black hair, pleasant without being particularly pretty.

She peered at his shoulder-flashes. "You're from Canada."

"Yes. My ancestors came from Scotland, though."

"I hope you feel at hame here."

"Everybody is very nice to me," he replied, thinking with a twinge of the ferocious corporal.

"You're coming here to help us."

"It's our war too."

She nodded. "How do you like Glesga?"

"I haven't seen much of it yet. I think I'll buy a guide-book to tell me where to go."

"Dinna bother with a guide-book. I hae the afternoon off. I'll take you around to see all the old places that'll interest you."

Douglas looked sharply at her, surprised. "But I can't ask you to go to so much trouble—"

"It was more trouble for you to come here from Canada."

He shrugged. "If you put it that way—" He finished his tea. "Where shall we go first?"

"There's an old church just down the street." "That sounds like a good place to start." He offered her his arm. "By the way, I'm Ed Douglas."

"That's a good Scots surname—but a Sassenach Christian name. And I'm Margaret Reilly."

59

"Scotch-Irish?"

"Pure Scots. The Reillys have always lived in Glesga, my mum tells me. And her name was MacCallum."

She took his arm and piloted him down the street. He found her an amusing companion as they looked through the church, and then strolled through a park. Douglas suggested a cup of tea, and they found a secluded tea shop, where they sat opposite each other and discussed their several lives. He found she worked in a factory making aircraft instruments.

"Maybe I fly on a turn-and-slip indicator you made."

"I'll be more careful from now on," she smiled.

"It'll be more fun for me, wondering if you made the instruments, every time I fly a new plane."

They wandered about a little more, and then Douglas said, "I'll have to be getting back. My aunt will be sending out a search party." He looked at her sheepishly. "I'm sorry, I hadn't counted on meeting somebody like you."

"Dinna fash yourself, Edward. Your mother brought you up to be a good wee boy."

"Well," he said defensively, "she is my aunt—"

"Aye, and ye've had strict instructions from your mother to do what you were bid." She squeezed his hand. "Stay that way."

He coloured. "I wish I could do something to show you how much I appreciate what you've done for me—how much time you've given up for me."

She looked at him. "Come with me. I can show you one more thing." She led him to the brick entrance of a dimly-lit tunnel. "This is one of our air-raid shelters. It's no been used much since the raids slacked off."

"Yes. I've seen them before."

"I didna bring you here to admire the view." She led him inside into the dimness, and then her arms went round him and her lips sought his. Douglas hesitated a moment, taken aback by her eagerness, and then he responded as hungrily as she. They moved together toward a bunk in a dark corner and collapsed upon it, their lips exploring each other's faces. He cupped her breasts together, while she dug her fingers into his back. His hands fumbled with her clothes, hers with his. "Come to me, my love," she whispered urgently. Their bodies joined, first awkwardly, then triumphantly.

When it was over, and they were putting themselves together, Douglas muttered, "Jesus! I didn't expect anything like this!"

"I ken that, lover," she answered. "But ye're such a baby—I practically had to rape you."

"But—good God!"

"I know. You didn't think I'd be so forward, did you? Well, I'll tell you. I met two other RAF boys a lot like you. They took me to the pictures, and kissed me good night. And then they both went missing."

"I won't go missing if I can help it."

"That's what they said too. I thought I'd better get my pleasure before I lost the chance." She clung to him briefly. "I'm not a whore, you know."

"Oh my God! I never thought of anything like that!"

"You wouldn't, my dear boy." She took his hand and led him out into the sunlight again.

"But—holy smoke—I don't even know your address."

She gave it to him, and he noted it in a little book.

"Just put it there with all the others," she laughed. He coloured.

"And now yours."

"Pilot Officer Edward Douglas. RCAF, Military Post Office 274589."

"I'll remember. And now go on back home to see your aunt. Don't tell her what you've been up to."

"No, I won't."

"Here's your bus. Get on it, my wee laddie."

She practically pushed him aboard.

When he was back at his aunt's house he told her and his uncle of the places he had visited in Glasgow, taking care not to mention his meeting with Margaret. He left the next day to return to his station. His aunt made him a lunch to eat on the train. As he accepted it he was uncomfortably conscious that she, like Margaret, did not really expect to see him again.

CHAPTER SEVEN

Heathcote looked up as Douglas entered the crew room. "I see we have a new wingco," Douglas told him. "His name's Tenley. He was CO of a Service Flying Training School in Canada until a couple of months ago."

Squadron Leader Clifton left his office to join them. "What's that you're saying?"

"A knowledgeable corporal who apparently has a friend in the know in the Air Ministry tells me that we're getting a new OC— Wing Commander Tenley," Douglas answered.

Clifton's eyebrows raised. "Tenley? He's quite a man. Joined the Air Force in the early thirties. Got his squadron leader as soon as war broke out, and then got his wingco about a year ago. Used to be a pretty fair pilot."

"What does he know about torpedo work?"

"Took the course in 1935 or 1936 at Gosport—flying Wildebeestes."

"Wildebeestes? What are they?"

"Old open-cockpit biplanes—they used them on the Northwest Frontier in India. There's a picture of one of them hanging in the mess."

"Oh yes—they're older than Swordfish."

"Nothing's older than Swordfish," Heathcote put in.

"Wildebeestes were."

"That picture looks straight out of the First World War."

"Well, torpedo attacks are torpedo attacks. He knows something about them, anyway," Douglas said.

Douglas had just sat down to sum up his flying time for the month when Squadron Leader Clifton entered the crew room again. "All right, chaps, can you get your crews together and gather back here in fifteen minutes? Our new Officer Commanding has just arrived, and he wants to meet you."

"Yes sir," replied the more formal, while the breezier said, "Righto."

A quarter of an hour later they were waiting expectantly for their new leader. Clifton entered and snapped out. "Room—Atten-SHUN!" They stood up. A well-set-up man in his middle thirties, a little over average height, with a clipped moustache and a well-pressed uniform, looked them over for a long moment. "Stand easy," he said at length. "I'm Wing Commander Tenley, your new Officer Commanding. I am very glad to be here with you, and to be given the privilege of commanding your squadron. Squadron Leader Clifton has told me just how well qualified you are, and I can believe it. I know you will give me the same support and co-operation that you have given him."

"Welcome aboard, sir," Peterson said. "It is our pleasure to have you here with us."

"Yes sir," added Westover, in his easy tones. "I'm sure you'll find you've come to a good squadron."

"Thank you," Tenley responded. "I know I will get to know you all very well before long. I'll be flying with you—I believe in leading from the front. It has been my pleasure to have met you gentlemen. You may all stand down now." He turned and disappeared into the OC's office with Clifton.

The assembled group was just leaving in clumps, discussing their new leader, when the telephone rang insistently in the OC's office. Clifton emerged hastily a moment later to call "Attention!" at the top of his voice. The crews turned to look at him.

"I say, chaps, the squadron's on standby. Maximum effort." He looked around. "Who's missing?"

"Harris is on a day off," Douglas told him.

"Anstruther is orderly officer," Peterson said.

"Anybody know where Harris went?" Clifton asked.

"He's probably riding around somewhere on his bike. He used to be a bike racer," Snow said. "His navigator usually goes with him."

"His Wop-AG will probably be somewhere at one of the pubs," Williams said.

Clifton called to the sergeant in charge of the squadron orderly room. "Call the service police and tell them to start looking for Harris and his crew."

"What's up, sir?" Heathcote asked.

"I don't know, but we're to stand by to fly down to Norfolk. Get your overnight kits. It looks as if we'll be away for a few days."

The sergeant hurried up to Clifton. "The group captain just called, sir. He sends his compliments, and requests that you and Wing Commander Tenley report to him at once."

"Very good." Clifton and Tenley walked out of the building, heading for the Headquarters building and the station commander's office. They entered the office and saluted.

"Good afternoon, Clifton. And I'm glad to see you, Tenley. Sorry I won't be able to welcome you formally, but the Scharnhorst and the Gneisenau have been reported as having left Brest and are heading up the Channel."

"The Channel! Good God! The cheek of those Huns!" Clifton exclaimed.

"That's why you're on standby. We are to mount an operation against them at once—within hours. We are to fly down to Norfolk, refuel, and take off at once against them. You'll be briefed at East Coates. In the meantime I've told your armament officers to arm your aircraft with torpedoes."

"We'd better get started," Clifton said.

The group captain reached over and took Tenley's hand. "Good to have you here, Wing Commander. And you're getting your feet wet in a hurry."

"Who will lead the aircraft, sir?" asked Clifton.

"I should." Tenley's eyes met Clifton's." I'm the squadron OC."

Clifton took a long breath. "I know you are, sir. But are you confident you're familiar enough with the job? After all, it's a big operation—two major German ships, with escorts—several destroyers at least, and maybe a cruiser. We've been practicing the tactics for an attack like that for a month now. It requires formation flying, and if you're leading a formation you have to know the men who are formating on you. Some tend to get too close, some hang back too much. And of course you have to be familiar with the aircraft itself. With respect, sir, your experience on Beauforts has been limited."

"I am fully trained as a torpedo pilot, Clifton."

"Yes sir—but are you sure you can make the transition from a Wildebeeste to a Beaufort without a reasonable amount of flying time? And what about a crew?"

"I was going to take your crew."

"My crew!" Clifton's mouth opened. "Good God, you can't be serious? You know what a crew feels about one another? You can't take a whole crew at a moment's notice!"

Tenley looked at him. "Sit down, Clifton. Why shouldn't you turn your crew over to me?"

"But they're my crew! We've flown together ever since I've been on the squadron, and they're almost ready to be sent to a training school for a rest!"

"Are you telling me that you doubt my ability as an operational pilot?"

Clifton met his eyes. "I'm saying you haven't flown on torpedo operations before, and your recent flying experience has been in Ansons on a training station in Canada." He was silent for a moment. "I know you have pre-war torpedo bombing experience, but with a different aircraft, flying at much slower speeds, and never against active opposition. If you lead the squadron, you'll have the lives of all the crews in your hands—and God knows we have too few crews already."

Tenley clenched and then unclenched his fists. "Yes, I guess you're right. When I was commanding that SFTS in Canada, I wouldn't let a new pilot take up a student until he was properly checked out. You go, Clifton."

"Thank you, sir."

Tenley suddenly spun on his heel, to face the group captain. "Damn it, this is the crowning opportunity of my career—two big German ships—and I have to let it pass? Don't you muff it, Clifton!"

"I won't, sir."

"Well, you'd better go and help me brief the squadron. How many aircraft have you?"

"Twelve serviceable. Three unserviceable—shot up on our last operation. They won't be ready for a couple of days."

"Twelve it is, then." Tenley led the way outside, pausing to put on his overcoat. It was February, and cold. As they left he said to

Clifton. "I'll go along with somebody as second dickey. I have to get my feet wet."

"I'd advise you to go along with one of the more experienced pilots—Flight Lieutenant Peterson or Flight Lieutenant Westover."

"Are Westover and Peterson going to be leading flights?"

"Of course, sir."

"Then put me with a more junior crew. A flight commander will be too conscious of me along—he'll be trying to play things my way instead of his. I'll just get in his way."

"Very well, sir. How about Pilot Officer Douglas? He's a Canadian—got a good crew. Navigator is a chap called Snow."

Tenley grinned. "Snow? Is he a Canadian too?"

"Yes sir."

"God, I saw enough snow on those god-forsaken prairies to last me the rest of my life! But that's fine. Who are his gunners?"

"An Australian called Kitto and a Welshman named Williams. Both good men."

"Right. I'll fly down to Norfolk with you, and then fly on operations with Douglas."

The briefing was perfunctory. "You'll be briefed thoroughly when you get to East Coates, in Norfolk. We'll fly down in formation. The weather is ropey—bags of low cloud—so stay in close."

The crews left the briefing room. Snow turned to Douglas. "I picked up a special kind of protractor the other day, and I want to try it in the air. It's over at my quarters. I'll run over and pick it up."

"Don't take too long."

"I'll drop in at the navigation section on the way back and get the maps for the trip."

Twenty minutes later Snow was carrying his navigation bag into the aircraft. "Know what, Ed?" he complained. "They were all out of topographical maps for Norfolk. I'll have to do my navigation all on my mercator plotting chart. Won't be able to do any map-reading at all."

"No trouble. I'll stay with the formation. What happened to the maps you had when we flew down there the last time?"

"They were short of maps. I had to turn them in."

Douglas shrugged. "No big deal. We'll get there."

Snow grinned. "I'm a Coastal Command navigator. Always know where I am over water. Never know where I am over land."

66

"You can say that again. Don't worry—if you get lost I'll help you out." They took off, formed up, and headed out over the sea before they turned south. Snow spoke up querulously from the nose. "Hey, how about telling me when you change course? How'd you expect me to plot where we are?"

"Aw, lay off it. I'm just following Clifton's kite. Let his navigator take us there. Take it easy."

"Yes, Hank," Kitto put in. "Take it easy.   Just enjoy the scenery."

"Under 500-foot clouds! I've seen all the waves I want to already."

Tendrils of white straggled from the cloud deck, driving them lower. Snow was sitting in the nose, watching the whitecaps shooting past below him. Williams had the radio tuned to the BBC and was listening to dance music, and Kitto was sitting relaxed in the turret. He had blasted a few rounds into the tossing waves to test the guns, and Williams had done as much for the side-mounted Vickers gun. Douglas had switched the forward-firing gun to "Fire" and pressed the button on his control column. Since then the guns had been silent.

A high-pitched squawking invaded Douglas' earphones. A few seconds later Clifton's voice overlaid it. "Convoy ahead—I hear their balloon-barrage squawkers. A Flight break left and climb to five thousand feet. B Flight break right." Douglas swung his aircraft left and opened the throttles.

The squeakers still shrilled in his ears, growing louder, telling him that he was coming dangerously close to the barrage balloons protecting the convoy, with their trailing wires which could rip a wing off his Beaufort if he hit one. Naval gunners were notoriously trigger-happy too. He inched the stick toward him, moved the yoke sideways to put on bank, and pulled into a tight turn. "Turning 180." The altimeter spun. Levelling out at five thousand." They were still in cloud. "Going up another three thousand. Let's see if we can top the cloud deck. I'm not going to stooge around in clouds with a lot of other kites around." The plane broke out of clouds between two layers. "See anybody, Snow? See anybody, Kitto'"

"Not a sausage, skipper," came Kitto's Australian voice. "We're all alone," Snow said a moment later. "Nobody ahead."

"God knows where the rest of the formation is. Okay. Gimme a course for East Coates."

67

"I'll work one out." There was a moment of silence. "Go onto 213."

"Two one three." Douglas swung the Beaufort onto the new course. "We'll go to East Coates all by ourselves."

"I'll navigate you there, but you'll have to recognize the airfield by yourself," Snow told him. "I have no topographical maps, you know."

"No sweat. I've landed at strange fields before."

They flew on for half an hour. "My ETA is eight minutes from now, skipper," Snow said. "Better start looking for the field."

"Okay." Douglas looked at his watch. "Looks like it ahead."

He peered at the airfield and turned to join the circuit. As he looked past the edge of the wing he found something vaguely disquieting, but it was not until he had received permission to land and was on the final approach that he realized what the trouble was—there were no Beauforts on the field. He shrugged; maybe he was the first to arrive. The Beaufort flew over the end of the runway, and Douglas flared out and closed the throttle. The Beaufort's nose came up as the wings lost their lift and the plane stalled, to thump down on the runway. He tramped on the brakes and turned off at an intersection to taxi to the operations building.

An ascerbic flight lieutenant greeted Douglas as he climbed out of the aircraft. "All right, what are you doing here?"

"This is East Coates, isn't it?"

"East Coates hell! This is Market Hampton! East Coates is twenty-five miles northwest! Get back in your kite and get the hell out of here!"

"Sorry sir," Douglas said hurriedly. "I have no topographical maps—"

"Look, anybody can find East Coates! Damn it, you can see it from here! Get cracking!"

Chastened, Douglas scurried back into the aircraft, restarted the engines, and took off. He turned the aircraft to a heading of 315 degrees. "Twenty-five miles, ten minutes." He looked at his watch. "Tell me when ten minutes are up," he instructed Snow.

The English countryside, covered intermittently with snow, slid by underneath him. "Your ten minutes are up," Snow called. An airfield lay ahead of them. Douglas joined the circuit and called up the field.

"Cleared to land," came the reply. Douglas landed, taxied to the operations building, and got out. He was virtually chased away. "East Coates? Ten miles southeast."

"Give me a map."

"None to spare. We've been cleaned out."

"Damn it all," Douglas grumbled in embarrassment. "Airfields are thick as fleas on a dog's back here." He gunned the engines, flew the ten miles, and looked around him. There was another airfield beneath him. He landed. Again it was not East Coates.

Brushing aside the controller's objections, Douglas and Snow, who had accompanied him to the operations building this time, worked out a careful course and time to East Coates. This time they made it.

Crimson with embarrassment, Douglas reported to the operations building. The operations officer looked at him. "Douglas? Oh yes—from 842 Squadron. What in hell happened to you?"

"Got lost coming down here. We couldn't get any topographical maps."

"Not much of an excuse, is it? Oh well, your squadron commander will be glad to see you—he's around here somewhere. He thought you'd crashed." He lifted a telephone. "I'll call him now."

Wing Commander Tenley entered the room a few minutes later, his face a cloud. "You—Douglas? Where in hell have you been? Why are you so late?"

Douglas snapped to attention. "Just plain got lost, sir. Didn't have any topo maps."

"Why in Christ's name didn't you stay in formation?"

"Got separated when we ran into that convoy. Had to climb to avoid it."

"And you call yourself a pilot? Good God, a kid could have done better!"

"Yessir." Douglas replied miserably.

"Anyway, get your kite refuelled and ready to go. You've got your torp, haven't you?"

"Yes sir. What about the rest of the squadron, sir?"

"They left about half an hour ago. A squadron is coming from St. Eval. You can join them. I'm coming with you as second dickey."

"Oh Jesus!" Douglas burst out involuntarily. "I mean yes sir. Where do I rendezvous?"

"You don't seem to be overjoyed. Don't you want your Officer Commanding do fly with you?"

"Oh yes, certainly sir. It will be a privilege to have you fly with me, sir." Then, abruptly, he straightened up. "One thing, sir. When you're flying with me, I'm the captain. I'll give the orders. With due respect, sir."

Tenley smiled wintrily. "Of course, Mr. Douglas. You'll rendezvous with the St. Eval squadron right here. They're to pick up a fighter escort when they get here." Tenley turned to the operations officer. "Get the OC of the squadron at St. Eval on the phone. Tell him one of my crews will be joining him."

The operations officer lifted the receiver. A few minutes later he put the phone down. "The squadron's airborne, sir. I'll try to contact them by wireless."

"Do that. In the meantime, Douglas, get back to your aircraft. When you see the Beauforts coming take off and join them."

"What are we going after?"

The *Scharnhorst* and the *Gneisenau.*"

"Holy Jesus! The *Salmon* and the *Gluckstein*—the two biggest targets in the German navy!"

"That's right. Make sure you don't waste your torpedo when you go in. I can't tell you anything about tactics—Clifton tells me I'm hopelessly out of date. Just tack yourself onto a flight and make your attack with it."

Snow, who had been standing in the background, stepped quietly up to a map thumbtacked to the wall, removed it, and pocketed it. As they walked back to the aircraft he said, "At least we have a map now."

A bowser refuelling truck was standing beside the aircraft. Douglas walked around the plane, looking at the patches in the skin from enemy flak and bullets on previous sorties. They aroused no trepidation in him this time, as they had done in previous walk-arounds before other flights; his chagrin at losing his way and then at losing the squadron, and his uneasiness at having an obviously displeased wing commander with him drove out all other worries.

The crew climbed into the aircraft, with Tenley sitting in the jump seat beside the pilot, and Douglas started the engines and taxied to the end of the runway. After a few minutes his earphones crackled.

"The Beauforts are approaching the field. Cleared for take-off."

The aircraft from St. Eval circled the field. Douglas swung in behind the last Beaufort. He called up the flight leader to tell him what he was doing. "Very well. Stay in formation."

"Where's the fighter escort?"

"Blessed if I know. Should be here but we can't see them."

There was a gabble of agitated voices. "Goddam it, where are those bloody fighters? We can't stooge around here all day!" The voice of the leader became suddenly emphatic. "All right, damn it! we can't wait! Set course!"

"Jesus! No fighter cover!" Snow said.

"The clouds are so low fighters shouldn't bother us too much," Douglas said. Snow did not reply. Wing Commander Tenley said nothing. He was the rookie, the man with no combat experience; these battle-hardened junior comrades of his held the floor.

"Aren't we supposed to have Hudsons co-operating with us?" Douglas heard a pilot call over the radio.

"Can't see 'em neither," someone replied.

"Christ, what a fuck-up! No fighters, no bombers!"

"I see some Hudsons, but they're with Bomber Command, not Coastal Command, and their radio frequencies are different," a Canadian voice from another aircraft spoke. "Maybe they'll attack the same time anyway."

"Yeah. Maybe."

The formation flew on. "Ropey weather," Williams said from the turret.

"Old *Salmon* and *Gluckstein* would naturally choose the worst possible weather to make their move," Kitto commented.

"Trust them, the bastards," Williams said cheerfully.

They flew over the coast. Snow entered the time in his log sheet. The flight altered course for a wind-finding dogleg. The gunners tested their guns, and the aircraft was briefly loud with their jabber. The sky, despite the low ceiling, was full of aircraft—Spitfires, Hurricanes, Blenheims, Beauforts, Hudsons, and over toward the horizon German ME109's, Me110s, Heinkels, and Junkers 88s.

"Keep your eyes peeled for fighters," Douglas said.

"They're peeled, skipper," Williams replied. An order ripped through the ether. "Enemy in sight." Douglas and Snow saw the dim shapes of the two great ships slicing through the haze. The sea around them was a forest of columns of water as shells and bombs exploded. Douglas was surprised at how big the ships were. Enormous bones in their teeth, their castellated silhouettes black against the chaotic background, the ships zig-zagged between their zig-zagging escorts. Sparkles of light lined their decks as their anti-aircraft guns hammered at their attackers, and then enormous red lights flared at Douglas as the main armament fired.

The aircraft beside Douglas turned in to attack. Douglas followed him. Williams spoke. "Fighter on starboard quarter—he's coming in—prepare to corkscrew—corkscrew port—GO!" Douglas dipped the left wing and tramped on the rudder. He heard the turret guns hammer, and then Kitto's gun joined the chorus.

Tracer streamed across his wingtip and he saw the German fighter hurtle past him. He pulled the aircraft to the right again. The dropping angle was impossible now, and he saw he would have to turn much farther right to drop on the other ship. He tramped on the rudder again. The airspeed was too high now, and he pulled back on the throttle. Slowly the nose of the *Gneisenau* came into view, and then it suddenly sprang into frightening prominence. "Jesus, we must be within a thousand yards now!" Snow said. The sea beneath them was boiling with explosions. Douglas steadied the plane, touched the rudder, and opened the bomb doors. His thumb reached for the torpedo release button. Just as he pressed it a thunderous explosion rocked the plane, and his right foot went fully forward. The plane slewed madly sideways. Douglas pulled up the nose and slammed the throttles open. "She's not answering to the rudder!" he screamed.

Exploring the controls, he found he still had aileron control and that the plane answered to the elevators. He reached for the trim tabs and twirled them. Slowly the aircraft straightened. The compass swung, settling on northwest. Douglas reached the bottom of the clouds just as another German fighter dashed past underneath.

The aircraft flopped around the sky dangerously. Douglas adjusted the engines against the trim-tabs to bring the plane onto something approximating a constant heading and an even keel. As the plane steadied Douglas suddenly found time to be frightened, and his hands began to shake. "Jesus Christ, that was a close one!" Then, remembering his duties, he asked, "Everyone okay?"

"I'm okay," said Snow. "Nothing wrong with me," added Williams. "Got a nick on my hand," Kitto said. "Nothing serious."

"Okay, sir?"

"All right," Tenley replied. Douglas realized they were the first words he had uttered since take-off. "We got off lucky. Okay, we're going back to East Coates. Get that map out, Snow." He hesitated, and then ordered, "Put your chutes on, boys. The plane seems to be under control, but I don't know if it'll stay that way. I'm going home at 120 knots. The kite doesn't need any more stress on it than it's had already."

There was a brief silence over the intercom, and then Kitto's voice came. "My chute is unserviceable, skipper. I guess it must have got a piece of flak through it. It's spilled all over the wireless compartment."

"Oh Jesus! Well, you probably won't need it."

The Beaufort wallowed through the sky, with Douglas working at the controls and continually adjusting the throttles to use the varying pull of the engines to keep the aircraft straight. Sweat poured from his brow, making his flying helmet sticky and uncomfortable. He ran a finger around the brim of the helmet and the plane pulled to the right. Hurriedly he put his hands back on the controls.

"Map-read me to East Coates," he said, and Snow replied, "See that cathedral ahead and off a bit to the right? The airfield is just south of it."

"Okay. I know where I am now." Douglas checked the altimeter. "We're at four thousand feet. Snow, Williams, Wing Commander Tenley, prepare to jump!"

"Douglas—" Tenley began.

"Damn it, jump! I'm the captain! Jump!"

"Very well." Tenley pulled open the hatch above his head, pulled himself through it, and vanished.

"Okay, Kitto," Douglas said calmly. "Now we'll take her in. Fire a red Verey cartridge to tell them we're in trouble."

Douglas made a long, slow approach to the field, jockeying the throttles, and made painfully gentle adjustments to the trim-tabs. The aircraft staggered through the air, nosing and hunting, the engines out of synchronization.

When he was committed to the final approach, Douglas saw he was too low and would land short, but it was too late to do anything about it. The ground rushed up at him. He eased back on the throttles, and spun the trim-tabs. The plane flared out, too high. He cut the throttles and the plane dropped down onto the rough earth of the overrun, bounced, and groundlooped. A wheel caught in a rut and the undercarriage collapsed. With a rending crash the fuselage broke in half just forward of the shell-riddled tail. The plane came to a grinding halt amid a cloud of smoke and dust and torn-up soil. "Get out! Get out!" Douglas screamed as he slapped the ignition switches off. He turned to look at Kitto, to find him slumped over his set, still strapped in. Douglas unbuckled him and dragged him forward to the escape hatch over the pilot's head, open since Tenley had bailed out. Kitto was unconscious, and Douglas had to use every ounce of his strength to bundle him out of the hatch. He followed him, grabbed Kitto's shoulders, and dragged him away past the shattered wingtip. There was a ditch fifty yards or so away stretching across the field, and Douglas shoved Kitto into it and then dived into it himself.

He waited a few seconds, and then cautiously raised his head. The aircraft was lying with no signs of fire about it. "Looks like it isn't going to blow up," he said. He turned back to Kitto, who lay sprawled in the bottom of the ditch, unmoving. Douglas laid his head against his chest, and found he was still breathing.

An ambulance jolted up to them, and a doctor and two orderlies jumped out. The doctor rapped out a command, and one of the orderlies dashed back to the ambulance, to return with a stretcher. "Get into the ambulance, you!" the doctor ordered Douglas. The two orderlies rolled Kitto onto the stretcher and slid him into the ambulance. The doctor knelt by him as the ambulance jolted into motion.

"How is he?" Douglas asked.

"He's had a nasty crack on the head. He's in no immediate danger of death, though."

The ambulance stopped in front of the hospital, where another doctor gave Douglas a thorough examination, and then ordered him into bed. "You're cut and bruised and shocked, but there's nothing seriously wrong. No broken bones." An intelligence officer entered the hospital ward to question him about the raid.

"See what's happened to the rest of my crew, will you?" he asked him.

The door opened, and Tenley walked in. Douglas sat up in bed. "Good to see you, sir. How are Williams and Snow?"

"Williams broke an ankle, and he's in hospital at Market Hampton. Snow, your navigator, is all right—he phoned in from a police station. A car is being sent for him."

"How about Kitto?"

The doctor answered the question. "Kitto has a fractured skull, but he's out of danger."

Douglas smiled, relieved. As an afterthought, he said, "And how about you, sir?"

"Quite all right, thank you. Got a bit dirty when I landed in a pigsty, I must admit."

Douglas laughed. Then he sobered. "How'd we do?"

"No reports of any hits, damn it!"

"Too bad, sir," Douglas grimaced. "I lost my kite too." He shook his head. "Oh well, she was a cross-eyed old bitch."

"You did very well, Douglas, you and your crew, after your somewhat unfortunate start. You pressed home your attack very well." He looked at Douglas. "You were quite right, you know, to order me to bail out. After all, you were the captain."

"Thank you, sir." Douglas leaned back on his pillow, and a moment later he was asleep. Tenley tiptoed out of the room.

The next morning the doctor visited him, examined him again, and discharged him from the hospital. He reported to the operations room, where ten of the squadron's crews were gathered out of the twelve that had flown to East Coates the day before. Two crews had not come back; one of them had been seen to crash at sea, and the other had simply vanished. Two other crews beside Douglas were without aircraft, their Beauforts too badly damaged to be flown home. Tenley and Clifton circulated among them disconsolately for a few minutes, and then Clifton called them to attention.

"We'll fly home individually. You chaps who have no aircraft will have travel warrants given you by the adjutant. Any questions?"

"Yes," a slight Cockney answered. "What 'appened to *Salmon* and *Gluckstein*?"

"I'm afraid they got away," Tenley replied. "They were damaged but they got home."

A moan rose from the group. "Goddam it, now we gotta do it again!"

"We will—we will!" answered Tenley. The reaction he got was not as enthusiastic as he wished.

Williams was in hospital, and Douglas told Snow they would visit him before they returned to their own station. After the briefing the two men returned to the station hospital to visit Kitto. The medical officer would not, however, admit them to the ward.

"Sergeant Kitto is in intensive care," he said. "I appreciate your concern, but he must not be disturbed."

"What's the matter with him?" Snow asked.

"His skull is fractured. His life is not in danger, but he's pretty ill."

Snow nodded. "He must have got that crack on the head when the fuselage caved in on him. Too bad he couldn't bail out like me."

Douglas turned to the medical officer. "How can we find out how he's getting along after we return to base?"

"Ask at the station hospital at your station. The MO will find out for you."

They went on to visit Williams. His leg was in traction, but he seemed as cheerful as ever. "I'll be up and around before too long. Maybe the war will be over before they send me back on ops."

Snow nodded. "We'll miss you until you're flying with us again. We had a hell of a good crew, you know."

"Sure will," agreed Douglas. Both he and Snow knew they would never fly with him again.

The two drew their tranport warrants and caught a train back to Lower Lexington. Snow, as usual, had a book to read that he had bought at the station bookstore. Douglas read a newspaper and then dozed in his seat.

With the two men missing from their crew they were sent on survivors' leave, which they spent in London. When they returned they found they had been allotted two new wireless air gunners, a stocky Yorkshireman named Charles Harrington and a quiet New Zealander named Angus MacKenzie. Both had served in other crews; Harrington's pilot had been killed in a crash when he was air-testing a Beaufort, and MacKenzie had filled in for a while with a crew whose gunner had been injured in a motorcycle accident.

76

Douglas and Snow enquired about Kitto. They had intended to fly down to the base hospital to which he had been moved, but they never got around to it. Months later they heard that Kitto had been declared unfit for aircrew duties and had been sent back to Australia. None of them ever heard from him again.

Kitto had written two letters in case he was killed, one to his wife and one to the beautiful redhead back in Winnipeg. A clerk, going through his gear after he was wounded, mistakenly mailed the one to Winnipeg. Rumour had it that Thora Gustavson cried for a while, but more because she felt it was expected of her than from genuine emotion; in truth she scarcely remembered him.

CHAPTER EIGHT

Flight Lieutenant Peterson called Douglas into his office. "Help me update this training schedule," he said. He read out a record of the training missions each crew had flown while Douglas chalked them up on a blackboard. When they were finished he said, "Care for a cup of tea, Ed?"

"Thanks." As he sipped at the cup Douglas said, "Well, what do you think of the Scharnhorst do?"

Peterson looked at him savagely. "We did bloody awful, and you know it! Not a torpedo hit! We lost two crews and three aircraft, and another damaged! You lost your aircraft and both your gunners. We could scarcely have done worse! And then those six Swordfish that attacked the ships—all of them shot down! I tell you we put the cause of torpedo bombing back ten years!"

"The boys did their best," replied Douglas defensively.

"The boys? Of course they did! The crews are as good as any torpedo squadron anywhere. But they're not used properly!" Peterson stood up. "We're busy fighting a private war—every squadron attacking independently! The only way is to form torpedo wings—two or three squadrons, all attacking at once, and with fighter cover as well as fighters making strafing attacks to suppress anti-aircraft fire. This business of splitting up our forces into penny packets is ruining us!"

"We had fighter cover when we went in on *Salmon* and *Gluckstein*."

"Like hell we did. There were fighters around, but none specifically detailed to work with us; and you know why—because we'd never practiced with fighters. Why, we didn't even have the right crystals to let us talk to the fighters by wireless. Damn it, we can't get proper support from the Air Force because Coastal Command is controlled by the Navy, and we don't get proper support from the Navy because we belong to the Air Force! It's crazy, I tell you!"

Douglas, inured over the past months to what the other aircrew considered Peterson's intemperate ravings, listened to him with only half an ear. Out of politeness he said, "Well, what would you have done?"

"I'd have collected all the torpedo aircraft months ago and trained them to operate as a unit—as a team, not as flights of two or three. I'd have them attack a single target from every direction—one flight from dead ahead, one from one side, one from the other, and one from the stern. I'd mix light bombers like Blenheims with the force, and have fighters doing two jobs—one to give fighter cover, the other to strafe the ships. And we'd have better wireless—or at least sets we could talk to each other with torpedo planes, bombers, fighters, the whole bag. Then anything a ship might do to avoid one torpedo or perhaps a bomb would take it right into the path of another."

Douglas nodded. "Yeah—it sure shook me when I found I couldn't contact any of the fighters I saw flying around."

"We acted like a bunch of amateurs. We could be—we should be—professionals." Peterson began to pace up and down his office. "We could have done so much—and not a single bloody torpedo hit!"

"There's no argument about that."

Peterson swung around to face Douglas. "You're getting to be an experienced man on the squadron, Douglas. You've got some time under your belt. You and your crew have been around longer than anybody else except three or four—"

"We've stayed alive, you mean. And we haven't got a complete crew. Kitto and Williams both have been replaced. We don't really know yet how the two new bods will fit in."

"Be that as it may, you're going to be leading other crews pretty damn soon—you'll be a flight commander one of these days. And when you do, I want you to remember what I'm telling you now. We're wasting men and planes the way we're doing it—when you get more responsibility you've got to do things better. Remember that? if you don't we're likely to lose the bloody war!"

"Jeez, that's putting it pretty strong."

"Strong! Not strong enough. Look, Douglas, how long have you been on the squadron?"

"Five months."

"And how many torps have you dropped?"

"Five."

"And how many hits?"

"Maybe one."

"See what I mean? One possible hit in five months! And you've lost an aircraft, had another badly shot up, lost a wireless operator and a gunner, and come back full of holes time and time again. And your crew is one of the best in the squadron—you're a good pilot, and you have a good navigator. Time and again we train crews at ten or fifteen thousand pounds a head, and put them in a fifty-thousand-pound aircraft, and lose them on their first trip! I tell, you, Ed, we're not running this business at a profit!" Douglas, embarrassed, made non-committal noises. Then suddenly Peterson smiled. "Oh, by the way—I almost forgot—I have some good news for you. We've just got a letter from the Royal Canadian Air Force. You and Snow are both promoted to Flying Officer."

"Oh good!" Then Douglas laughed. "It's no big deal, though—it's supposed to come automatically after six months. It's six months overdue."

"Better late than never," Peterson said. "Now go and tell Snow. Don't get too drunk tonight when you celebrate it."

Douglas left the office and stood outside the door, reading some notices pinned to the wall. He saw Peterson returning to the reports on his desk. Viciously he jabbed at a sheet of paper with his pencil. "Results unobserved!" he snarled. "Missed, goddam it! And why—because he didn't get close enough!"

Tenley walked by, heard him muttering, and walked into the office. "Still grousing, Peterson?" he said conversationally as he entered the office.

"Yes, goddam it, I'm still bitching—sir!" Peterson added "sir" as an afterthought. "You know we're just spinning our wheels as well as I do."

Tenley made patting motions with his hands that a ground crewman used to call for an aircraft's engines to be slowed. He turned and shut the door. Douglas looked curiously at the closing door, and looked even more curiously when Tenley reappeared. Peterson was sitting at his desk, his head down, his hands compulsively clutching the arms of his chair.

Douglas walked down the room, avoiding Tenley, who strode purposefully toward the door. Another pilot was sitting leafing through a ship recognition manual on a bench near the door. Douglas sat down beside him and jerked his head toward Peterson's office. "Looks like Tenley just tore a strip off Derek."

The other man answered without looking up from the manual. "For being bloody-minded, I guess."

"Probably. His comments aren't always calculated to build up morale among the senior officers."

"Yeah. He says the brass are always doing everything wrong."

Douglas rubbed his chin, and then turned abruptly to the other man. "You know, I think he's right. We are doing everything wrong. I think he's the only one around here who has a clear idea of what he's trying to do."

"Clifton doesn't think much of his ideas."

"Clifton is a good man, all right, but I don't think he's thought this business out the way Peterson has. And Peterson has a good record—sank three ships."

"And cracked up three aircraft, put two navigators and six wops into hospital, and broke his arm as well."

"He's a ropey pilot—I often wonder how he managed to get through training without getting washed out. But he still has the right idea, for my money, about operational flying with torpedoes. The brass ought to listen to him."

"One day they probably will—if he lives long enough."

Douglas nodded and stood up. The comment reminded him of his mortality, and he wanted to forget it. He went off to the mess for tea.

That evening in the officers' mess Douglas saw Snow talking to Stanley Barton, Peterson's navigator.

"Hi, Hank," Douglas said. "Did you hear the news?"

"Good lord, is it out already?" Barton asked. "I only heard about it myself half an hour ago."

Douglas looked startled, but pleased. The news of his promotion had not struck him as of great import, even if he had been anxious to tell Snow. "Well, it's hardly a shock, you know."

"Yes, I suppose we all expected it. But when Derek told me he's been transferred to the OTU at Chivenor, you could have knocked me down with a feather," Barton said, "It was so dashed sudden!"

"Oh—uh—well, I guess," Douglas said uncertainly.

"It is a bit thick for me, you know—I've only done six trips, but with Peterson leaving I'll be on my third crew. My first pilot wrote himself off when an engine quit on take-off, and now Peterson's been sacked. I'll have to look for another pilot. It gets a bit wearying, I must say."

"Yes. That does get old."

"I've only done two trips with Peterson—I replaced Stevens, who broke his leg when Peterson crashed on landing. Maybe I'm not that unhappy after all," Barton added. "Peterson is a ropey pilot. Does his best to fly your courses, but makes ropey landings."

"Maybe Tenley will grab you. He's looking for a crew, isn't he?" Snow said.

"That'll be the day—the squadron OC with a navigator who's practically a sprog?"

"Oh, I don't know, Barton," Douglas replied. "Peterson seemed satisfied with you—and you know what a bitcher he is."

"Peterson isn't easy to satisfy," said Snow.

"No—considering what a ropey pilot he is," Barton answered.

"Anyway, Tenley didn't waste any time getting rid of Derek," Douglas said.

"You can get turfed out in a hurry if you cheese off the squadron commander once too often," Snow said.

"Well, I'll find my own fate tomorrow," Barton said.

"Good luck to Derek wherever he's going," Douglas said slowly. "You know, that man's got good ideas. We'd be wise if we listened to them."

Douglas turned as he heard his name called. "I say, Douglas!" It was Hedley Westover. "Are you busy tonight?"

"Not so's you'd notice, Hedley."

"Good! My wife's sister is visiting us, and they want to go to a play in town. I wonder if you'd care to come along to make up the party?"

82

"Sure. Thanks for the invitation. I'll come."

"Thank you, Ed. I'll come around in my car at seven o'clock."

"Why me, Hedley?"

"I've known you quite a while now—and you're reasonably presentable. My sister-in-law will probably enjoy meeting a real live Canadian."

"Thanks, Hedley."

Hedley arrived at seven, as promised, with his wife and sister-in-law. His wife, Beatrice, was a dark-haired, elegantly curved woman who had obviously been a raving beauty five years before and was still beautiful. Her sister, Charlotte, was taller and fairer, with more chiselled features. She was a little acerbic, as if she had never really become resigned to being in her lovely sister's shadow. Douglas squeezed into the back seat with her. "Charlotte," he mused. "That's a lovely name."

"I hate it—I've always hated it!" she replied fiercely. "It's a family name, damn it!"

"Still, it makes you Queen of the Islands, doesn't it?"

"What do mean—Queen of the Islands?"

"The Queen Charlotte Islands—on the west coast of Canada."

"I don't remember ever having heard of them.They can't be very famous."

"They're not. They're almost uninhabited, except for the Haida Indians." He laughed. "I'd never have heard of them either if we hadn't had a teacher who made us learn all the islands on Canada's coasts. I expected you to know more about your own islands—after all, they're named after you, aren't they?"

She turned to him. "I know there had been a Queen Charlotte about a hundred years ago."

"But not the islands. You should know more about your own empire."

"I guess so, but there's such a lot of it, you know. Still, it doesn't make me like my name any better."

"I could call you Lottie."

"Don't you dare."

"How about Charlie, then?"

"That's worse."

"I'd better go back to Charlotte then." Douglas looked at her

83

reflectively. "You know, I used to think Charlotte wasn't much of a name either."

"No?" she said frostily.

"But you associate names with people. Now that I've met you, I think Charlotte is a lovely name."

Her eyes opened with surprise. "What a nice thing to say!" She laughed. "All right—call me Charlotte."

The evening was pleasant, ending with coffee and cakes at the cottage in which Westover, his wife and his two-year-old son were living a few miles from the airfield.

"Must be nice, having a wife to come home to," Douglas said. "Civilized."

"It is very nice," Westover nodded. "After all, this is my career. Can't let a little thing like a war interfere with family life. In a while young Digby will be going off to school, and I won't be seeing much of him. I'd better enjoy him while I can."

"Yes, of course." Douglas looked around him, wondering how Westover could keep his life so normal, when he was engaged in such desperate enterprises. Douglas, like his fellow-Canadians, the Australians and the New Zealanders, had divorced themselves from their former lives. They were Overseas.

"What do you do when you're posted? I imagine they'll be sending you off to be an instructor with an OTU one of these days, like they did with Flight Lieutenant Peterson."

Beatrice answered for him. "I'll stay for a few weeks. My aunt lives in Chivenor, we can stay with her if we like. Hedley will look for a cottage."

"He was successful in finding one here. This is a nice place to live."

"Air Force wives are good at living anywhere they can," Beatrice laughed. "We were stationed in Hong Kong before the war."

"It must have been interesting," Douglas replied. "You've seen the world. I haven't."

"You're seeing it now," she said. "Now I must go off to the kitchen. Excuse me."

Douglas turned to Charlotte. "You work in London, Hedley was telling me."

"Yes. I'm a civil servant now, trying to do my bit."

"It's a bit warm in London, isn't it, what with bombing and everything?"

"You get used to it." She offered him more coffee.

Douglas looked at his watch. "Guess it's time to leave. Thanks for a lovely evening."

"I'll drive you to your billet," Westover said.

As they drove back to the air station Westover said, "You seem to have hit it off with Charlotte."

"She's a lovely girl."

"You seem to know the right things to say."

Douglas nodded without speaking. The phrase about her name that had caught her attention was one that he had heard Snow use one day when they had met two girls in a pub.

"I appreciate you coming with us tonight. Charlotte needs something to take her mind off living in London."

Douglas laughed. "I thought London was the centre of the world."

"The Germans seem to think so—they bomb it so much."

"The blitz has tapered off a bit."

"That's true—high time too. Well, here we are. Goodnight, Ed."

Douglas watched him as the car drove off. Hedley Westover lived so normal a life, and was at the same time obsessed with that ship in Wilhelmshaven that he wanted so much to sink. If he had a wife as beautiful as Beatrice he wondered if he would ever think of anything else. Well, maybe your ideas changed once you got married ...

He went to bed, and wondered when the day would come that he would fall in love.

CHAPTER NINE

Douglas flew two cross-country exercises to familiarize himself with his new wireless air gunners, and found they fitted in reasonably well. Neither of them was as cheekily familiar as Williams, or as skilled as Kitto, but they were good average men, and Douglas had nothing to complain about. After the shake-down flights they flew on three Rovers, which resulted in no sightings of enemy ships. On one flight they were attacked by a fighter, but Harrington saw him in time for Douglas to duck into a cloud bank, and they escaped without even being shot at.

After the third Rover they went on leave. Snow went off to visit his relatives in Manchester, while Douglas returned to Glasgow. Three days before he left he wrote a letter to Margaret Reilly, not really expecting her to accede to his request for her to meet him at the railway station. Her family had not succumbed to the temptation to install a telephone, so he could not call her.

When he left the train at Glasgow, however, Margaret was waiting for him, and they ran to each other, to become one of the thousand kissing couples in the station. She clung to him and said, "It's so good to see you again, Eddie!"

"Wonderful to see you, Margaret! Wonderful to kiss you, too," he smiled at her. He offered her his arm as they walked through the crowd to the street. After an abortive attempt to hail a taxi they took a tram to his hotel, where he deposited his shoulder bag, and the gas mask and steel helmet that the authorities insisted he carry with him. He washed his face, and then came down to the lobby where Margaret was waiting. "How about a bite to eat?"

"Wonderful," she said, and they had dinner together in a fairly posh restaurant, although the standardised meal was mediocre at best.

They lingered over drinks, and then went to a dance-hall, where they jitterbugged together for a while. Then the orchestra began to play a round of Scottish country dances, the Gay Gordons, Strip the Willow, and an Eightsome Reel. Douglas was reluctant to try them, but Margaret pulled him onto the floor and pushed him around until he got the hang of things, whereupon he found himself having a wonderful time. He grinned at her. "Too bad I'm not wearing a kilt."

"Dinna fash yersel'—you look braw in your uniform," she told him. He danced away from her, and danced back, suddenly the dance was over.

As the orchestras played the home waltz Douglas said, "Well, that's that for the evening. Fortunately, there's a bottle of Pym's Number One in my room. Would you care to share it with me?"

"Aye, that I would. Let's go." When they reached the hotel room Douglas poured two drinks. Margaret sipped hers slowly while Douglas chattered about the dance, and then put the glass down. "There's nae need tae get me fuddled first, my dear boy. I know what I'm doing. Here—help me with these buttons." As he stepped toward her she added, "You look braw in that uniform, laddie, but there's no sense in keeping it on all the time." They undressed each other, and collapsed laughing onto the bed. Their lips found each other, and then he was kissing her breasts and her abdomen and her shoulders. Their bodies joined.

"Och, ye're good," she sighed happily as she lay back after it was over.

"It comes naturally." His statement was not true. He was remembering what he had read in a book on the subject, but he was glad he had behaved adequately.

"So it does. Give me a cigarette."

"Gosh, I never carry them. I don't smoke."

You're a pure thing, aren't you now? Are you a virgin too?"

"You know the answer to that."

She laughed. "Get me my handbag. It has some fags in it." She took out a cigarette. "Did you every smoke?"

"I smoked heavily between the ages of seven and eight, until my father found out what was happening to his cigarettes. Then I stopped abruptly."

"Did you take your meals off the mantelpiece too?"

"Did I ever!" he replied feelingly. "Dad belted me good."

"He did it for your own good. Maybe my dad should have spanked me—then I wouldn't be smoking now. Started when I was fourteen."

"It hasn't stunted your growth where it counts."

"So you seem to think."

"Maybe I ought to start thinking about taking you home."

She laughed. "There'll be no buses running this time of night, my dear boy. I'm here for the night. Even if I didn't bring a night-gown."

"We don't need it all that much. I'll keep you warm." His face sobered. "But what about your parents? Won't they be worried?"

"I'm a big girl now. I'll say I stayed with a friend. It's no the first time I've stayed the night."

"No, of course not."

"Turn out the lights and go to sleep. I'll wake you when I need you." She needed him two hours later, and he complied with her request.

Margaret went to work the next day, and left Douglas to wander around Glasgow, visiting a number of places she recommended. She met him for dinner. "What do you say to a little pub-crawling?"

"Not tonight, my laddie. I want you to come home and meet my family."

He raised his eyebrows. "If you want to—sure."

"They won't bite."

They rode a tram into a dingy and unprepossessing section of Glasgow, with the raw scars of bombing obvious everywhere. Margaret's family lived in a small second-storey flat. It was warm and cosy, even if it was furnished in garish style.

Margaret's mother was small and plump, with the lined face and wrinkled hands of someone who has worked hard all her life. Douglas took her hand and repeated a line he had heard Snow use. "Now I know where Margaret gets her good looks from."

"Oh, ye're a big liar!" she said, pleased. "Awa' wi' ye a'!"

Douglas shook hands with her father. He was short and slight, stooped from his life in the shipyard where he had begun work when he was twelve. It was obvious that he had grown up in privation.

Margaret was their youngest child; a married daughter lived a few streets away, and a son was with the Royal Army Pay Corps at

Bradford in Yorkshire. Another son had died of scarlet fever a dozen years before. Margaret had gone to work at fourteen. The outbreak of war, despite air raids and rationing, had improved their status. John Reilly's work, previously intermittent, had become steady and better paid, and Margaret had received numerous raises.

Mrs. Reilly bustled about, pressing tea and scones on Douglas. She talked continuously, firing questions at him and not waiting for the answers. She gave Douglas a complete family history, including some gory details of the appetites her relatives had for alcohol and sex that left Douglas scarlet with embarrassment. Her stories of the privation suffered during the depression made even the poverty of the prairie farms in Saskatchewan pale in comparison. Douglas was acutely conscious of the fact that he was dipping into their meagre rations of tea and margarine and jam, and promised himself that when he next saw them he would bring some of the luxuries sent to him by his mother in her parcels. John Reilly sat silent most of the time, apparently overwhelmed by his wife's loquaciousness, although when Douglas and he were alone he spoke readily enough. His tales of scraping for pennies during the depression were as shocking as those of his wife, and the courage with which he had confronted his difficulties were as impressive, as was his open-handed hospitality now. He pressed glasses of excellent scotch on Douglas, who did not really appreciate it, and felt uncomfortable because he did not. The family was obviously close-knit and affectionate. Indeed the only jarring note was the profanity into which they casually descended. Douglas had been brought up in a straight-laced family, with his mother frowning even on the use of the word. "Damn." But except for that he soon found himself feeling at home.

"You're a braw lad in that uniform," Mrs. Reilly told him when she returned, to take over the conversation. Margaret came to his rescue a few minutes later. "We need some milk," she told him. "Walk over to the shop with me," she said, taking his arm.

"Mum and Dad really like you," she told him as they walked down the street.

"They're fine people—real down-to-earth people," Douglas replied feelingly. "Nothing phoney about them. The salt of the earth."

"I like them too," she answered.

They bought the milk, and returned to the flat. Just as they opened the door an air-raid siren sounded. "Och, we'll have to gae tae the shelter," Mrs. Reilly said. "They never drop any bombs here, but we have to gae anyway."

The air raid shelter was poorly lit and crowded. Margaret found a corner where she could chatter away to Douglas, while her parents huddled with others of their own generation. The lights dimmed. As Douglas looked at her enquiringly, Margaret said, "It happens all the time." She move closer to him. "So much the better. We can have a wee cuddle."

Their lips met. "I wish it was a bit darker," Douglas said as he lifted his lips away.

"It will be in a minute." It was, and they fumbled for each other, unperturbed by the nearness of their neighbours, some of whom Douglas could tell by the sounds were similarly employed. After their climaxes came and they had buttoned themselves up again she said, "The Germans have their uses."

"You can say that again," Douglas agreed feelingly.

The all-clear sounded, and they reassembled at the Reilly's flat. Mrs. Reilly fed them more tea and scones. "Guess I'd better catch the next tram," Douglas said at last. "Thanks for a wonderful evening."

"Och, come again, laddie," Mr. Reilly said. "It's no often that we had the chance to see a real live pilot—and a Canadian at that."

Margaret accompanied him to the tram stop. "Och, it's good to walk out with an officer," she told him. "And those wings of yours are bonnie too." They kissed, and he climbed aboard the tram. As he settled into his seat he reflected smugly that Margaret's pleasure at his status was quite natural. He could show her a better time than a private could, and his uniform fitted better.

He travelled back to his air station the next day, a half-smile creasing his lips. He was satisfied, happy and tired, and he had a ten-shilling note left.

A parcel from his mother was waiting for him when he returned to his barrack room. He packed up the chocolate bars and a can of butter with some Canadian cigarettes given him by the Cigarette Fund, and sent the parcel to Mrs. Reilly with a note of thanks. "Don't think I'm depriving myself," he wrote. "I don't smoke."

Margaret answered. Her letter was warm, misspelled, with all the sentences running into one another, separated only by commas, telling him she was looking forward to seeing him again.

He put the letter in his pocket, and reread it the next day. He liked her, and she satisfied the lusts of the flesh, but he felt himself getting in too deep. He answered the letter non-committally.

The following day four aircraft went out on a strike against a German convoy, and two of them failed to return. Douglas scarcely knew the missing men, but they were his comrades, and he felt their loss. His fingers closed around the letter in his pocket. He might as well enjoy life as long as he had it, and a compliant woman helped a lot. He made up his mind to go back to Glasgow during his next leave.

"If I live that long," he muttered, and began another letter to Margaret.

CHAPTER TEN

Derek Peterson had left when Douglas returned from leave. He was pressed into service to keep up to date the blackboard on which he recorded the squadron's training. Finding that he needed some information, he telephoned Westover.

The sergeant who answered the phone told Douglas that Westover was at his cottage. Douglas called the number the sergeant gave him. Charlotte answered the phone. "No, Hedley isn't here. I'll have him call you when he comes back."

"Thank you. I must say I'm surprised to find you still here."

"I'm here again. I went back to London, but my sister wanted me here to attend a wedding."

"Swell!" Douglas hesitated for a moment, and then said, "Say, how about having dinner with me tonight? I know it's short notice, but this is all the time I have."

"That's quite all right, Edward. We have been properly introduced."

"We can go to the Bull's Head, if you don't mind."

"That sounds lovely."

Douglas enjoyed the evening, and Charlotte obviously did so too. He kissed her goodnight very chastely as they parted; after all, she was Hedley Westover's sister-in-law. As rode back to camp on his bicycle, Douglas reflected on the difference between his evening with Charlotte and the ones with Margaret. Charlotte was prettier, in her cool, well-groomed way she was cleverer, better-educated, with far wider horizons. But Margaret, with her warm, welcoming arms—"You're a damned snob," Douglas said to himself as he cycled along.

Hedley Westover greeted Douglas the next morning in his

usual debonair style. "Good morning, Ed. See you've been squiring my sister-in-law around, m' boy."

"Yes," Douglas answered, a little defensively. "She's a nice girl." He wished he could have said something a little less lame.

"Damned attractive, too. I'm familiar with the breed. You're showing good taste, young Douglas."

"I think so, Hedley."

"I say, Ed, she'll still be here today—leaving tonight. Beatrice wants to introduce her to some of the people from the air station. How would you like to come and bring your navigator?"

"Oh thanks, Hedley. I'll be glad to."

"I'm inviting Helena Compton-Morris."

"Good. She gets along well with Hank Snow."

"I'll give you both a lift in my car."

"Thanks, Hedley. I'll go and tell Snow. I'm sure he'll come. Only— "

"Only?"

"Only the sweet-talking son of a bitch generally steals our girls when we're out somewhere with him."

Westover laughed. "And you want to keep Charlotte for yourself?"

"Well, you know how it is—" he got up. "I'll go hunt for Hank now."

They were sitting in Hedley's living room at four-thirty that afternoon. Snow, as Douglas had feared, had caught Charlotte's attention immediately by saying, "I'm delighted to meet you, Charlotte. You're every bit as charming as Ed said you would be." She had smiled and coloured slightly. Douglas turned to Snow. "I've already told her they named the Queen Charlotte Islands after her. You don't have to."

Lady Helena laughed. "Henry told me, the first time he met me, that they'd named Helena, Montana, after me. It seems to be the fashion in North America."

"We North Americans are famous for our good taste," Snow replied. "How could we possibly do better than to name a town or an island after a beautiful woman?"

"We can't possibly disagree with that sentiment, can we, Helena?" Charlotte said. Beatrice Westover pouted a little and put in. "How about me?"

Snow laughed. "As a matter of fact, there is a Beatrice, Nebraska."

Douglas turned to him abruptly. "How in the devil did you know that?"

"When I was at the University of British Columbia I was on a baseball team that played a team from the University of Washington. One of the men on it came from there."Douglas shook his head. "Never know when an odd bit of knowledge is going to come in handy."

Charlotte poured tea for them while Beatrice served sandwiches and cakes.

"Beatrice and Hedley live better up here than I do in London," Charlotte said. "It helps to live where the food is grown."

"Yes," Beatrice agreed. "Hedley cultivates his family friends."

"After they've cultivated the soil, of course," Snow said.

Charlotte and Helena laughed. Douglas wished he had made the remark, and was a little piqued. He sought for some equally clever observation to make, and not finding any, took a bite out of a sandwich.

"It's an interesting part of England we're in," said Snow. "All studded with castles and battlefields and chock full of history."

"You're a bit of a historian, are you?" Charlotte asked.

"Not particularly, but one of my friends, Harry Hobhouse was, and we used to ride around on our bikes, with him telling me about it."

"We must have him here one day," said Beatrice.

Helena cast her eyes down. "He went missing."

"Oh—what a pity," Beatrice said.

"Yes, it is a lovely countryside," Charlotte put in quickly. "It must be different from what you two are used to."

"Yes," Douglas nodded. "It's sure different from the bald-headed prairie in Saskatchewan."

"It's different from the mountains in British Columbia," Snow said. "I must say that I come from a rather more scenic part of the country than Ed does."

"I've heard British Columbia is rather like Switzerland," Charlotte said.

"The mountains are not as tall, however," answered Snow. "However, they're just as beautiful. It's like you and Ingrid Bergman."

"Ingrid Bergman?"

"Yes. You're not as tall as she is, but you're just as beautiful."

Charlotte laughed. "I must remember that when I ever go to Switzerland again. I went there a few times before the war, to ski."

"We had a wonderful ski hill practically in our back yard at Castleford, where I come from," Snow said. "I had a lot of fun— probably as much fun as I could have in Switzerland. But in Castleford, British Columbia, you can't get any of that good German wine you can get in Switzerland."

"Oh—what a pity! I have a confession to make—I've always liked German wine too."

"So do I—although I've scarcely ever drunk it. You tend to drink the wine of the country. In British Columbia the country wine is beer."

"The best families will drink it, then. I presume yours is one of the best families."

"Without a doubt. My father is a railway conductor. In Castleford that puts you pretty near the top of the heap. Railroaders are the aristocrats of labour, you know."

Charlotte laughed. "I've always wondered what a real aristocrat looked like."

Snow was suddenly serious. "You know, once our milkman came to our door to collect the milk-bill. He said to my mother. 'Mrs. Snow, whenever I come to you, you always have my money for me. I never have to wait for it—not like some of the people in the big houses up on the hill. You're good people, Mrs. Snow. Ever since then I've known I come from a good family."

"My mother did the same," Douglas said, glad to say something. "She never let a bill run overdue."

Helena nodded soberly. "So that is how tradesmen decide who is a good family, is it? A very good way, I must say."

"Well, you know what Robbie Burns said about it—'From scenes like this old Scotia's glory springs, That makes her loved at home, revered abroad; Princes and lords are but the breath of kings—An honest man's the noblest work of God.' The trouble is I'm not honest."

"I can see that," Charlotte replied. "Obviously dishonest. But then, dishonest people are always the most interesting."

Douglas sat sipping his tea, his mood becoming blacker. Here he was, sitting dumbly in his chair while Snow chatted away with Charlotte. In a few minutes he had let her know that he was cultured, a university man, familiar with wine, practised in the polite sports like skiing. Yet at the same time he had stressed an ordinary background, his undistinguished parentage. Douglas who had learned nothing about skiing or wine in the plains around Valenby, and who had never set foot inside a university, and was unfamiliar with the works of Robert Burns, was crushed.

He saw Charlotte smile at Snow, and felt jealousy swirl over him. Damn it all, Charlotte was his girl! He looked at Snow through narrowed eyes. Sure, Snow was a smooth talker, but he, Douglas, was the pilot, the captain of the crew, the man in command. For all his suavity Snow was only the navigator, a full rung below him in the Air Force pecking order.

As if Snow had read his mind he spoke to Helena and Charlotte. "I'm very lucky to be flying with Ed," he said. "He's unquestionably one of the best pilots on the squadron. You know he saved the life of our wireless operator, Sergeant Kitto, when he landed our plane after the attack on the *Scharnhorst* and *Gneisenau*. Our aircraft was badly damaged by flak, and Ed had no response from the rudder at all, but he steered the plane by the way he handled the engines. Kitto's parachute had opened in the aircraft when a piece of flak went through it. Anybody else would have told him to bale out with his parachute that had opened in the aircraft—but not Ed; he ordered all the rest of us to bale out, and then he went on to land an aircraft that was practically a wreck. During the whole show he was cool as a cucumber, fully in command of the situation, and one of the best pilots I've ever flown with. Yes, I'm glad I'm flying with him. It's a real privilege, I tell you. You know, he does most of the work— he flies the thing, takes it off, lands it, and then he aims the torpedo and drops it. He deserves a lot of credit. I still think he should have got a decoration for what he did at East Coates. He would have got one, if the operation had been successful, but they don't give out gongs for operations that are failures."

Douglas looked away. Such fulsome praise was a little embarrassing, even while he revelled in it. He saw Charlotte's eyes turn toward him, and Helena's. Beatrice nodded. "Hedley's often told me how good a pilot Mr. Douglas is."

"It makes a lot of difference to me," Snow continued. "A navigator's life is literally in the hands of the pilot. With Ed, I know the hands are sure ones." Douglas smiled self-consciously, happier. He was recognised again. He saw Charlotte's eyes on him, and pretended he did not notice.

Hedley looked at his watch. "Well, I must take Charlotte to the station in twenty minutes. Drink up, everybody." They finished their tea, and then Hedley and Douglas climbed into Hedley's car with Charlotte, while Snow drove back to the air station with Helena, who had brought her own car. As Charlotte walked toward the platform Douglas fell into step with her.

"Charlotte—tell me something."

"Yes. What is it?"

"Your telephone number in London."

She laughed. "Oh, very well. You deserve it—Hedley says you're a very good pilot, and so does Henry Snow." She told him the number. The train thundered into the station, and Charlotte climbed into one of the coaches. Douglas and Hedley waved to her as it pulled out.

That night, as Snow entered the room, Douglas was lying in his bed reading a magazine. "Hi Hank," he said. "You stayed out late."

"Yes, I know. Dropped in at the mess on my way here."

"I thought you were smooching with Lady Helena."

Snow shook his head. "Not a chance. She's out of my league—a duke's daughter, you know. Anyway, she doesn't date aircrew."

"I wish she did. Then you wouldn't spend your time shining up to my girl."

"Who?"

"Charlotte, that's who."

Snow pursed his mouth. "Helena told me Charlotte was quite impressed with you. I was just along for the ride."

"You and your smooth talk! You're a menace to have around anybody's girl."

Snow laughed self-deprecatingly. "Still, you took her to the station. Lady Helena left me early and went off to her quarters alone. Don't worry—Charlotte's far more impressed with a pilot like you than a mere navigator like me."

"Okay. That makes me feel better." Snow turned out the light and went to sleep.

A few days later Douglas was scheduled for a cross-country exercise. Just as they were finishing the briefing, Clifton took a telephone message and called to Douglas. "Your kite is unserviceable—got a cracked cylinder. It won't be ready for a couple of days. I'm standing your crew down. Beetle off somewhere for a day or two—get out of my sight."

"Good show, sir," Douglas beamed. London was only sixty miles away, and there were frequent trains. He'd seize the opportunity to see Charlotte.

He collected a pocketful of coins and sought out a telephone booth. He called her number, and after a long-drawn-out battle inseparable from British telephones, he reached her.

"Got a night and a day off," he told her. "Let's do the town tonight. Have dinner, take in a show, go dancing."

"This is rather short notice, Edward," she demurred.

"I know, but it's all the notice I had. You have to do things in a hurry these days."

"But it's so far for you to come—"

"You're somebody special, Charlotte. It's worth while coming this far for somebody like you."

"Oh, very well," she answered, a laugh in her voice. "If you put it that way."

"Let's have dinner at the Ritz," Douglas said. "Only the best is good enough for you."

"If you want to."

"Where shall I meet you?"

"I'll meet you at the Ritz." They agreed on a time.

When Douglas walked into the hotel lobby she was waiting for him. He took her hands. "You look absolutely smashing," he told her.

"Thank you."

"How is my Island Queen tonight?"

"You keep mixing me up with ships."

98

"Steamships have lovely lines. So have you."

"Next you'll be telling me that I have a foghorn voice."

"Well, maybe. Foghorns sometimes send shivers down your back. Your voice does too, sometimes, but in a different way."

"You do say some nice things," she said. They went into the dining room. He would have bought her an exotic meal, but all the exotic items had been stroked off the menu.

With Charlotte all to himself, Douglas had a much better time than he had had at Westover's cottage. Her attention was reserved for him, and soon he was telling her of his adventures growing up in his little Saskatchewan town, of his training as a pilot, of his operational trips. In return, she told him of her family, her schools, her present job, in which she found herself working with a number of stuffy and often incompetent civil servants. It was plainly apparent that she considered most of her workaday associates a cut beneath her in the social scale, but Douglas found this intriguing. They laughed at each other's sallies, made minor confessions, and enjoyed their mediocre meal. From the dining room they went on to a play. Douglas had managed to get tickets through the squadron adjutant, who knew people in the theatrical world, and this small feat impressed Charlotte.

During the intermission Charlotte met a friend of hers to whom she introduced Douglas. The girl looked up at him with eyes that were interested and respectful, and he saw a trace of possessive pleasure pass across Charlotte's face. Looking around, he saw he was taller than most of the men near him, and his Air Force uniform looked good on anybody. Charlottes took his arm as they walked away, and Douglas was flattered.

After the play they stopped briefly at a dance hall. Compared to the Ritz and the theatre it was plebeian, but they both enjoy the music and the dancing. After a burst of jazz the orchestra played some Scottish country dances, which Charlotte danced expertly. He remembered how Margaret Reilly had taught him how to dance the steps, and felt guilty as he thought of her warm arms. Charlotte was loftier, more distant, icier; more attractive too.

They drove to her apartment in a taxi, after the dance-hall had closed and they had had tea in a dingy cafe. He reached for her in the back of the taxi, but she fended him off. "There are certain things, my dear Flying Officer Douglas, that dinner and show do not entitle you to," she said icily.

"My mistake. It's hard to contain yourself when there's somebody as beautiful as you around."

"Flattery will get you nowhere, although it's still welcome," she said. "However, don't presume quite so much on the fact that you are an attractive man, that you wear your uniform well, and that you know how to dance."

"Okay, you win," he laughed. The taxi arrived at her apartment. She leaned forward. "Driver," she said, "Will you wait?"

He walked with her to her door. She turned to him. "You may kiss me once," she said as she reached for her key. Then she smiled. "Thank you for a lovely evening. You are very nice, you know." She lifted her lips to his, and then she slipped inside the door. Douglas went back to the cab.

He went back to his hotel, and returned to Lower Lexington the next day. He thought of her as he rode north in the train. She had rebuffed him, and he was glad. It was part of the established ritual. In Valenby, a man took it for granted that a girl he would consider marrying would refuse himself anything but a kiss until he put a ring on her finger. Marrying her? He thought of her cool, haughty handsomness and wondered if he were falling in love with her. He'd see her a few more times, and then he'd know.

Would she marry him? He was wearing an officer's uniform, but he felt himself an impostor. Underneath his military finery he was just a clerk in a drugstore. He shrugged. That was a bridge he would cross when he came to it.

CHAPTER ELEVEN

Douglas left the flight office and nearly bumped into Snow in the corridor. "Get your gear together, Hank," he said. "We're going to the north of Scotland—Wick."

"Wick?" Snow knitted his brows. "That's up at the very tip, isn't it?"

"Sure is."

"What are we going to do—hunt for the Loch Ness monster?"

"They won't tell us until we get there."

"Okay. When do we leave?"

"In three hours."

"I'll get my stuff together. Think I'll navigate up there on astro. Time I took some sights."

"Go ahead. Just get us there."

The next day they were gathered in a Nissen hut briefing room, listening to Squadron Leader Clifton giving them their orders. "A convoy is on its way to Murmansk. We expect the German navy to make a sortie against it. Our job is to attack those Jerry ships as soon as they put to sea." He turned to the map behind him. "You're to go out in two flights; A Flight will steer for this point here—" he touched the map with a pointer—"and turn south as soon as they're twenty miles from the Norwegian coast. B Flight will steer for this point and turn north. The track of the enemy ships is reported by Intelligence to lie along this line here."

The crews made notes, and then stood up to head for their planes. As they left Snow said to Douglas, "I wouldn't be surprised if those Jerries were further west than the intelligence wallahs put them."

101

"What makes you think that?"

"If they're heading for a convoy, they want to keep their position secret as long as they can. They'll try to stay out of sight of Norwegians watching on the coast."

"You could be right. Well, we'll have to stay with the other guys. If they miss the Jerries, we miss them."

"Fun and games if we find them."

"You can say that again."The aircraft took off, formed into two loose gaggles, and set course. Snow spread out his maps, made entries in his log, and peered through his drift sight. There were five aircraft in one flight, six in the other, all that could be made serviceable. Douglas adjusted his throttles to keep pace with his companions and relaxed. There would be no enemy fighters so far from Norway.

He looked at his engine temperature gage to see one of them higher than the other. "Starboard engine seems to run a little hotter," he grunted, and checked the cooling gills. "Maybe it's just the indicator that's a bit off."

The needle continued its climb. Douglas pulled back the throttle, and it steadied. Snow's voice came, aggrieved. "Hey, skipper, what're you doing with the airspeed? It's off a couple of knots."

"I know. Starboard engine's heating up." He pulled the throttles back a little more. "If I keep full revs we'll have trouble."

"We're dropping behind the other kites."

"Yes. I know. But I'm not going to chance an engine failure. These under-powered bastard's will put us in the drink if we lose an engine. If we fall behind we fall behind." He adjusted the throttle and pitch of the other engine to synchronise the two.

"We're losing five knots now. Can you call up the other kites and tell them what's happened?"

"No. Radio silence."

"We'll be ten or twelve miles behind by the time we get to the turning point."

"So be it. Goddam these engines anyway. After that *Scharnhorst* and *Gneisenau* do, I'm used to them, but I'll never like them."

The other aircraft pulled ahead. There were scattered clouds, and soon the formation skirted one of them and disappeared, and Douglas did not see them again.

"We're out to win the war all by ourselves again," Snow commented from the nose.

"How's your navigation going?"

"There's a layer of low cloud that keeps me from getting all the drifts I want, and the sun is behind a cloud so I can't get any sun shots. I'm going along on dead reckoning."

"You'll do all right," Douglas replied unconcernedly. If anybody could do a good navigation job, Snow could.

Douglas heard Snow call the wireless operator to ask him for radio bearings, and went back to his flying. A little later he called the rest of the crew, "We're getting close to enemy territory. Keep your eyes open."

"Roger," the replies came. They flew on, away from the setting sun, toward the gathering dusk.

"Seen anything of the other kites, Hank?"

"No. Haven't seen them for an hour."

"What's our estimated time of arrival?"

"Another twenty minutes. Say, Ed, I haven't got anything to navigate with but the forecast winds. How about keeping on going until we make a landfall on the Norwegian coast? I need a pinpoint to restart my air plot. The wind could have been doing anything for the last hour."

"Okay. We'll keep going."

The coast loomed before them. "I'm going to climb until I'm just below the upper clouds," Douglas said. He pulled the nose up a little.

"Roger." Snow peered at his maps. The plane crossed the coast, and Douglas swung into a gentle turn. The gunner's voice came, suddenly urgent. "Hey skipper! Ain't that an airfield just over to port?"

"Jeez, yes it is!" Douglas shoved the throttles wide open and climbed into the cloud, dipping a wing as he headed back to sea again. "Hey, what was that, navigator?"

"Musta been the fighter drome at Lister," Snow replied. "Okay, I got my pinpoint."

"Thanks a lot, Snow," Douglas replied sarcastically. "You navigated us right over a Jerry fighter base."

"That's the way the ball bounces, skipper. They weren't expecting us, anyway; no flak, no fighters taking off."

"So far as we know. Anyway we're out to sea again. What's the course to the turning point?"

"Want to go to the turning point? We'll never catch up with the rest of the boys. Why don't we go another twenty miles out to sea?"

"Might as well." He pulled the throttles back to cruising revs again. "We must have wakened everybody up in that air station, anyway, so we'd better fly along the seaward edge of that deck of clouds to starboard. How far do you want me to keep flying west?"

"Thirty miles or so."

"Okay. I'm going to alter course now to two seventy. Work out a course to parallel the one we were briefed to fly."

"It'll be three fifty-two compass. I'll tell you when to turn."

"Roger." They flew on. "Time to turn—Now!"

"Roger. 352 it is. Turning." They flew north, slipping in and out of cloud. The sea lay dark beneath them, now and then showing a bright path of moonlight when they flew briefly into the clear. Douglas looked at his watch. "What's our Prudent Limit of Endurance, Hank?"

"An hour and twelve minutes from now."

"Okay." He heard Snow and the wireless operator chattering about radio bearings. He called the gunner. "Concentrate on your search to starboard. I'll look to port."

"Roger. skipper. Ain't much to see so far."

"No. It's pretty lonely. Just as well."

Snow's voice came, "Hold her steady, Ed. I want to check the course on the stars."

Snow climbed into the astrodome behind the pilot and stood peering through his astro-compass. After a few minutes he scuttled back to his navigation position in the nose. Douglas told the gunner to swing the turret to make a thorough search of the skies.

A half hour passed. Douglas watched the temperature gage, found it creeping up, and pulled back the throttles a little. The airspeed fell off another couple of knots. "Airspeed 133, Snow," he called. "Roger," came the reply. "133." Silence reigned over the intercom.

He headed into cloud, flew through it, and broke out into the clear again. His eyes quartered the area. Far to the left he saw a

104

silver line on the sea, with another, smaller line farther west. With a start he recognised it as the wake of a ship, with a companion ship beside it. He swung the aircraft toward it and a little ahead. "Altering to 330," he told Snow. The plane dipped a wing, swung to its new course, and steadied.

The ships grew larger and clearer. A shaft of moonlight struck the larger one, and Douglas recognised the clean, lovely lines of the cruiser Gladbach that he had pored over so often in ship recognition manuals. He pulled back on the throttles, to descend to dropping height. Mentally he ran through the check he had memorised long before. Estimate the speed—she had a big bone in her teeth, must be making 25 knots—level out at dropping height; open the bomb doors; arm the torpedo; ease the nose of the aircraft to the left to allow for the deflection; check on the altitude.

A little too low; open the throttles a touch and climb twenty-five feet. Retard the throttles again. Straight and level. Check the machine gun switch is on FIRE. They were a mile or so away now. No sign of life from the cruiser as it tore along, an enormous battle-flag trailing from its gaff, its nose dipping into the fairly calm sea, rising again, dipping, its beautiful silhouette standing out against the dim horizon.

Three quarters of a mile. A touch of rudder to bring the nose of the aircraft a little farther left to give the ship a little more deflection. Half a mile—a thousand yards. No flak from the ship. Douglas chewed his lip as he estimated eight hundred yards, steadied the aircraft, and convulsively pressed the torpedo release button on the top of his control column. The plane lifted as the missile fell free.

"Hey skipper—you've dropped your torp!" the gunner's surprised voice came. Douglas suddenly remembered that he had been so intent on what he had been doing that he had forgotten to warn the crew. Snow could see what was happening, and was crouched in the nose with his camera; the other two could see nothing ahead.

Douglas jammed the throttles open and swung around to pass the cruiser's stern and fly down its wake. He kept his eye on the cruiser's greyhound lines, ignoring the track of the torpedo toward it. A great column suddenly reared halfway down the ship's side, remained for a second frozen like an inverted icicle, and then collapsed onto the cruiser's decks.

105

The beautiful ship staggered, slowed, and keeled over into a heavy list. Douglas pulled the plane up toward the cloud-deck. Not a shot was fired at them before the concealing tendrils of cloud gathered them in.

"Got the bastard!" Snow's delighted voice came over the intercom. "Jesus, skipper, you've torpedoed the bloody *Gladbach!*"

"The wireless operator shouted, "You lucky bastard!" The gunner cried out, "You hit her good! She's heeled right over!"

"Send an attack report," Douglas told the wireless operator. "Hank, figure out the lat and long. We can break radio silence now." Soon the intercom was underlaid by the muted bugle-notes of morse.

"Steer 243 for base," Snow said.

"Climbing to five thousand," Douglas said. "We'll fly on top."

"Roger."

"So we sank a cruiser!" the gunner carolled. "I knew I was joining a good crew!" His voice suddenly changed. "Why in hell didn't you tell us, skipper?"

"Sorry, chaps. I just forgot. I didn't expect to see the ship, and then everything happened so damn fast!"

"Don't do it again, skipper. Next time tell us!"

"Right, chaps. Sorry."

The crew was as elated as if they had been drinking champagne. "Whoopee!" Snow sang, and the wireless air gunners echoed him. "Steady down a bit," said Douglas. "The Jerries will be mad enough to send fighters after us."

The intercom fell silent again. A few minutes later the wireless operator passed Douglas a message from base. "Send complete amplifying report." Douglas, Snow and the other two men, Harrington in the turret, and MacKenzie on the radio set, collaborated in drafting the report. MacKenzie encoded it and sent it, the morse feeding through the intercom as always.

"Figure you sank her?" Harrington asked.

"I don't think so. It takes more'n one fish to put a ship as big as that one down. But she'll be in dry-dock for months—and she won't bother that convoy to Murmansk."

"No. The crew'll have other things on their minds."

"What's left of them," Harrington added. Douglas' elation sobered abruptly as he realised he had just sent some number of human beings to their deaths. He shoved the image of men struggling in icy waters or bleeding to death on a shattered deck back into the corners of his mind. What the devil—they'd tried to do the same thing to him, hadn't they?

"How's that engine doing?" Harrington asked.

"Still running too hot. But it doesn't sound too bad yet." Douglas chewed his lip. He would be better off to gain a little more height in case he lost an engine, but he should keep close to the top of the cloud deck so that he could duck down into it should a fighter attack him. He compromised by staying at his altitude and pulling back the power. "How far are we away from Norway now?" he asked Snow.

"About two hundred miles."

I'll stay down at this altitude for another fifty miles—then I'll climb."

"That'll take us another half hour at the speed we're going."

"Jesus, skipper, are we going to take all night to get back?" asked MacKenzie.

"Blame it on the engine. It's cold in the drink. I have to nurse it along."

"Nurse it. Don't put us in the drink." Douglas shivered again as he thought of the sailors dying in the frigid waters his torpedo had bloodied. Then he thought of the stalactite of water rising out of the dark sea when his torpedo hit, and elation surged through his veins again. With an effort of will he sobered himself. He must not spoil everything by forgetting some elementary task of airmanship, or by over-confidence like fighter pilots who crashed doing a victory roll. He checked each instrument, looked at every dial, checked every switch. Everything was normal, except for the engine temperature gage that was too high. He was too keyed-up to relax, but he had a grip on himself.

They were at the two hundred and fifty mile mark. Douglas touched the elevator trim. The aircraft slowed a little and began a gentle climb. "Climbing at a hundred feet a minute, Snow," he told the navigator. "The airspeed is down to one fifteen."

"Roger." A few moments later Snow's voice came again. "Your ETA is two seventeen hours."

Douglas looked at his watch. "A bit over an hour." The intercom

107

was suddenly loud with dance music. MacKenzie had tuned in the BBC. Douglas checked his dials again. He cocked his ear to listen to the engine. It was running a little rough, but he was used to that.

The Scottish coasts approached, and Douglas could see the line of breakers through gaps in the clouds. He nosed the plane down again. "Airspeed up to 125. Letting down at 200 feet a minute."

They approached the airfield as dawn broke. The engine was running unevenly now, and Douglas made a straight-in approach. As they taxied to dispersal they saw a knot of people waiting for them, Clifton among them. Douglas swung the aircraft into position and cut the engines. Before he could release his straps Clifton was into the aircraft, pounding him on the back.

"Good show, Douglas! You got her! Wizard show!" The crew climbed out onto the tarmac, Clifton leading them. A photographer was leaning backward, shooting at them as his flash popped. The station engineering officer, three intelligence officers, the padre, the station commander, and a dozen others fell upon them, shaking their hands and pounding them on the back. A couple of wireless operators hoisted Harrington onto their shoulders, and two more did the same for MacKenzie. Two navigators beat their hands on Snow's back. Laughter and shouts and cheers rose into the chill Scottish air. Somebody struck up "For He's a Jolly Good Fellow!" Douglas stood abashed as the station commander shook his hand. The crew was ushered into the CO 's car and taken to the briefing room to be interrogated. The group captain personally thrust a rum-laced mug of coffee into Douglas' hand, while the adjutant did as much for Snow, and intelligence officers served the gunners.

"I'm putting you in for the DFC for this, Douglas!" Clifton said, as he accompanied the crew to the briefing room and listened to their answers to the questions the intelligence officers asked. Group Captain Deveney, the Station Commander, nodded. "Jolly well deserved too, I might say."

Clifton rose. "I'm laying on another strike against that cruiser, now that we know where it is. Too bad Wing Commander Tenley isn't here—he had to go to London on some Air Ministry business. He'll be hopping mad he missed the fun."

"Are we in on that, sir?" asked Douglas.

"Why—anxious to go again?"

"It's not that sir—our aircraft isn't serviceable. The starboard engine is acting up. It runs hot, and for the last quarter of an hour it was farting badly. I think it needs an engine change."

"We're not sending you out in an unserviceable aircraft. Anyway, you've done enough for one night."

"Quite right," agreed the group captain. "Come with me to the mess—all of you—to have breakfast, and then you can go to bed."

They ate with the station commander—eggs, bacon, kippers, jam—all the delicacies. After the meal the group captain personally took them to their quarters in his automobile, and they tumbled exhausted into bed.

When he awoke that afternoon, Douglas walked to the mess with Snow. A cheer arose as they entered, and when they went up to the bar tankards were placed before them without them asking. They lifted them to their lips. Douglas looked around him. "Hey—where's my old pal Heathcote?"

The faces around him sobered. "Heathcote and Clifton didn't come back."

"Missing? For Christ's sake. Jeez, that's a kick in the teeth." He nodded. "They got there in daylight, I suppose, and the air would be thick with fighters."

"Which observers?" Snow asked, putting down his tankard.

"Stewart and Wilkins." "Oh Christ—Murray Stewart and Bob Wilkins. Son of a bitch."

"Did they get the cruiser?" Douglas asked.

"No results observed," a man answered, grimacing. "Didn't do as well as you did, Ed."

"They musta thought I was a Ju88 when I attacked—didn't have a shot fired at me. They wouldn't be that lucky. Well, I'll be god-damned. Clifton and Heathcote. Son of a bitch."

"We're going back to Lower Lexington tomorrow. Have another drink, Ed."

Again Douglas felt the unworthy glee at being alive while these comrades of his were dead. He got very drunk, vomited in the washroom, and had to be carried off to bed. He woke in the morning deathly ill, and had to wait a day before he was fit to fly back to Lower Lexington. His aircraft had had its engine changed by then.

109

The crew was happy once they got into the air. The starboard engine ran sweetly, the air was smooth, and visibility was unlimited. Douglas and Snow had headaches, but by the time they touched down at Lower Lexington the headaches were gone and Clifton and Heathcote and their crews were ancient history. They were greeted as heroes when they arrived, with Tenley calling for them in his car, to take them to his office to congratulate them there.

After tea Lady Helena walked over to them to add her congratulations. As she did so the orchestra on the BBC program playing on the radio broke into a waltz. Snow swept her into his arms and swung her into a dance. It was strictly forbidden, but the elderly squadron leader who was President of the Mess Committee actually applauded them when the dance was over. "After all, chaps," he commented to a wing commander standing beside him, "one doesn't torpedo a cruiser every day. And besides that, they danced beautifully."

CHAPTER TWELVE

Douglas entered B Flight office in search of a training form. Westover was leaning back in his chair, looking at a copy of "Tee Emm," the informal training periodical which was distributed at regular intervals to aircrew. He looked up.

"Hello, Douglas," he said. "How's the conquering hero today?"

"Haven't conquered much this morning. Too early." Douglas noticed that Westover did not smile. "Keep up the good work," Westover said, and returned to his perusal of Tee Emm. Douglas found his forms and left.

Later that day Douglas was talking to Snow and Hellyer, Westover's navigator. "What's wrong with your skipper, Hellyer?" Snow asked. "He seems pissed off about something."

Hellyer shrugged. "I think he's just jealous. He used to be the fair-haired boy on the squadron—more hits than anybody. Then you went and torpedoed the *Gladbach* and now he has to take a back seat. He doesn't like it a bit."

Douglas nodded, saying nothing. Snow laughed, and then said, "How is he to fly with these days?"

"Not bad. He isn't as pleasant as he used to be, but his flying hasn't dropped off any."

"He'll get over it," Snow said. "Same as we will. Hero today, bum tomorrow."

Hellyer laughed. "I'll never get used to that phrase. 'Bum' means something entirely different in England. You use it to mean 'tramp', don't you?"

"That's right." Snow broke into a song. "Hallelujah I'm a bum, Hallelujah bum again, hallelujah give us a handout to revive us again."

111

Hellyer nodded. "Your North American culture amazes me."

Just then Westover ambled over. "I say, Douglas, my sister-in-law is visiting us again. Care to come over tonight for a game of 'OH Hell?'"

"Glad to. Thanks for the invitation. I'll take my bike. I need the exercise."

"I'll see you at eight, old chap."

As he strode off Snow lifted his eye brows. "If he's all bent out of shape because you fished that cruiser, he's got a funny way of showing it."

"That's the way you act if you've been to the right school, old man. You're trained to love your opponent," Hellyer said.

"He's pretty decent. After all, that sister-in-law of his is quite a dish," Douglas said.

"He is, after all, a gentleman," Hellyer added. Then he sobered. "One thing worries me, though—he's been poking around with that damned model of Wilhelmshaven again. I thought he'd forgotten about it."

Snow looked at him. "Now that Ed has stolen some of his thunder d' you think he might go after it?"

"Yes, and I'll be sitting right there in the nose of the aircraft!" Hellyer rose. "What the devil! What is written is written! Let's have a drink." A moment later he asked Snow, "What are you doing tonight?"

"There's a dance on in the village."

"Your Scotch sergeant from the equipment section might be there."

"She might be. She's a good dancer. I like dancing with her."

"A little strong-minded for my taste," said Douglas.

Snow shrugged. "We get along all right, Ed."

After tea Douglas and Snow rode out on their bicycles, Snow turning off half a mile down the road toward the neighbouring village while Douglas continued toward Westover's cottage. Douglas leaned his bicycle against Westover's garden wall and knocked on the door. Beatrice welcomed him.

"Oh, good evening, Edward," she said. "Hedley will be back in a minute or two. Charlotte is here."

112

Charlotte extended a hand coolly toward him, as if his lips had never touched hers. He took it and bowed. "How is my Island Queen?"

"I'm still a ship, I see."

"I've been wondering if you've had any more islands named after you lately."

"I've decided to switch to mountains."

They turned as Hedley entered. "Hello, Hedley," Charlotte greeted him. Beatrice offered them sherry. Charlotte lifted her glass. "To you, Ed," she said. "Hedley tells me you're quite a hero."

"Lucky, I guess."

"There's more than luck involved, I'm sure."

"No. It was pure luck. We fell behind the formation because I had an overheated engine. Then we just stumbled on the cruiser. And then they must have thought we were a German plane, because they never fired a shot at us. It was pure luck."

"Perhaps, but you aimed your torpedo properly—and it does require a certain amount of skill to fly a torpedo bomber, so Hedley tells me." Charlotte laughed. "You know, it's seldom that I meet a bona fide hero."

"Oh, come off it!" Douglas said, colouring. "You know I'm no hero."

"Well, perhaps not. Very well, I'll treat you with contempt and disdain from now on. Come with me. Beatrice and Hedley want us to play 'Oh Hell.'"

They played cards for two hours, and then Beatrice served them supper. As usual, there were things to eat that city-dwellers never saw. Douglas enjoyed it.

"You set a good table, Beatrice," Charlotte said.

Beatrice laughed. "One of the farmers has a daughter with a frightful case of hero-worship for Hedley. She sells him anything he wants."

"So she should," Charlotte said.

Hedley looked at Douglas. "I say, Ed, aren't you supposed to be wearing the ribbon of your DFC?"

"I don't think so. I haven't been awarded one."

"You haven't been? But it's a sure thing after torpedoing the *Gladbach!*"

113

"Maybe. It hasn't come through though."

Westover's brows knitted. "But I'm sure I heard Clifton say he was going to recommend you for an immediate DFC."

Douglas nodded. "I heard him say that, too."

Westover slapped the table. "That's it then! Clifton went missing before he could do it! Then Tenley wouldn't do it, because he'd think Clifton had already done it! You know, Ed, I'll bet you were never recommended at all." He nodded sagely. "That's right! Well, Ed, I'm acting squadron commander for the moment, and I'll put in that recommendation myself!"

"That's mighty decent of you, Hedley."

"Least I can do, old man. You deserve it. After all, you did put that fish into the cruiser. By the way, I got word today about the *Gladbach*. She's in dry-dock in Bergen. You won't see her at sea again for six months."

Douglas shrugged unhappily. "I was hoping I'd sunk her."

"She's too big to sink with one torpedo. You should have had another kite with you to give it the finishing touch."

"Yeah. I know I couldn't put her down with just one torp, but I had dreams. Anyway, I was all alone—that wonky engine of mine."

"That was a stroke of genius, flying farther out to sea the way you did."

"Actually it was Snow's idea—my navigator, you know."

"I'll put him in for the DFC too."

"You don't have to. The navigation leader already has—you know how those navigators stick together. Went through the adjutant. You were away at the time."

"Did he?" Westover laughed. "He'll get his gong before you get yours."

"Good. He's a first-class navigator. Dreamy, of course—but a good navigator."

"Hellyer, my navigator, is dreamy too. He's a friend of Snow's—they go off on leave together."

"On duty or off it, navigators always travel in clumps."

Douglas rose. "Think it's about time I headed back for camp," Hedley. Thank you for a lovely evening, Beatrice." He turned to Charlotte. "Hope the lamp on my bike works. Walk me down to the road in case it doesn't."

She followed Douglas through the door. As he pushed his bicycle down the walk he said. "It was wonderful seeing you again, Charlotte. I wish I'd had you to myself, though."

She put her hand on his arm. "I don't want to keep you to myself, Edward—I want to show you off. After all, you're somebody distinguished now." He laughed. "I've been called a lot of things—but never distinguished before."

"But you are, Edward—you are. You're really somebody now."

"I'm glad of that, Charlotte. Somehow I had the idea you weren't too impressed with sod busters from Saskatchewan, even when they were masquerading as Air Force officers."

"Don't say that!" She squeezed his arm. "But anyway you're the man who torpedoed the *Gladbach*. Besides, I can't gush over someone the first time I meet him."

"No. Everything in its proper time and place."

She laughed. "You know something, Edward? Hedley's frightfully jealous of you now."

"Hedley? I don't believe it! Why, you just heard him say he was going to recommend me for a gong!"

"That's different. Hedley would recommend you for a DFC if he hated you, if he thought you deserved it."

"There's not a jealous bone in his body!"

"That's what you think, my dear boy. Hedley's always been used to being the star—the best cricketer, the best sprinter—the best pilot. Now you come from your godforsaken hamlet in Saskatchewan and steal his thunder by sinking that cruiser! He doesn't like it, Edward." She smiled. "It's funny, watching him pretending he's not put out about it! The great Hedley, taking a back seat to whatever you called yourself—a dirt buster?"

"A sod buster—and anyway I didn't sink the ship—just damaged it." He shook his head. "But I've got a lot of time for Hedley. He was even nice to us when we first arrived on the squadron, the rawest of sprogs."

"He's charming to everybody. It's his nature. But he's still jealous, and it's funny."

They came to the end of the walk. Douglas propped his bicycle against a tree. "Charlotte," he said, "in all the time I've known you I've managed to get one little kiss. I want a long one now." He

115

pulled her into his arms and sought her lips. At first she was stiff and unresponsive, and then her icy aloofness melted, and she crushed herself to him. Her lips were like hot cream, her body vibrant and demanding. Douglas felt his head swirl, his senses tumble into chaos.

When she pulled her lips away, he whispered "My God, Charlotte, you're a beautiful woman!"

"You're rather sweet yourself," she said, and then laughed. " To coin a phrase—my hero."

"I can't believe it—you—the beautiful Charlotte—Hedley's sister-in-law—"

"I prefer just to be your island queen."

"When can I see you again?"

"Just call me. You know my phone number."

"Yes—yes—of course I do."

She bent forward and kissed him again, and then walked back up the path. Douglas mounted his bicycle and rode back to the air station, his head still swirling.

Snow noticed his demeanour when he entered their room. "What in hell happened to you, Ed? You get smashed? You look like you had your nose in the brew for hours."

"No. Only had two drinks." Then, to change the subject, he asked, "How'd you make out at the dance?"

"Fine. Spent most of my time dancing with your fierce WAAF sergeant."

"That's better than being with me sweet-talking my girl." Douglas went to bed and thought of Charlotte. It was an hour before he fell asleep. He was muttering her phone number when sleep overtook him.

A week later Douglas travelled down to London again. Charlotte met him at the railway station this time, and when he reached to kiss her she came willingly into his arms. They had dinner at an expensive restaurant. Halfway through the meal she beckoned to a couple of friend of hers who were entering the dining room, a naval commander and his wife. "I'd like you to meet Edward Douglas. He's a friend of my brother-in-law, Hedley Westover."

"Oh yes, we know Hedley," the woman said. She peered at the "Canada" badges on Edward's shoulders. "I see you're from Canada."

116

"Yes, so I am. I'm pleased to meet you. This is my husband, Commander Horton."

"How do you do, sir."

Charlotte looked at the couple and said archly, "Edward torpedoed the *Gladbach*, you know.

"What! You did?" the commander exclaimed. "Why, we were chasing that ship for months!" He sat down abruptly.

"Tell me about it."

"Well, it was really due to my navigator—" Edward began. Charlotte sat beside him a little smugly, until the orchestra struck up. "Come, Edward, dance with me," she ordered. They danced well together.

"It's been very pleasant showing you off, Edward," she told him. "It's not too often I dance with a hero."

"Oh, stop calling me that! You know I'm only a sprog pilot from Saskatchewan!"

"I decide things like that," she laughed, and steered him near two more friends of hers, to whom she introduced him.

When he took her home she kissed him passionately in the taxi, but would not allow him to enter her apartment.

"Kiss me once more, my dear boy," she said, "and then go home. You're sweet, but you can't have everything at once. I don't want to spoil you."

As he climbed back into the taxi he said to himself. "She's quite a dish." Later that night, as he lay on his bed, he muttered, "I love her."

He rode back to Lower Lexington. Snow greeted him as he entered their barrack-room. "What'd you do in London?"

"Saw Charlotte—Hedley's sister-in-law."

Snow nodded. "Hope you had a good time."

"I did. What about you?"

"Went dancing with our fierce little Scotch sergeant storekeeper. She taught me how to do Scottish country dances."

"Yeah. They're fun." Douglas thought of Margaret Reilly, who had taught him. Well, that was a closed book now. He was in love with Charlotte.

"You like our little Scotch girl. What are you going to do—marry her?"

117

"I'm not going to marry anybody until this torpedo bomber caper is over."

"In the meantime, stay in good with her. It'll make it easier to get clothing."

"Here's a letter for you." Snow tossed him a letter from Margaret.

Douglas turned it over in his hands. Then he sat down and wrote on the envelope. "Return to sender. Addressee missing, believed killed." He signed an indecipherable name and put it in a post-box the next day.

CHAPTER THIRTEEN

Westover called Douglas into his office. "You and I are going on a Rover tonight, Douglas. Take off at five o'clock. I'll brief you myself at four."

"Roger, Hedley. I'll have my crew there."

Westover went over the planned patrol area with Douglas and the two navigators. It was off the Dutch coast, in an area they had often patrolled before. There was nothing new, and the crews took it calmly. "If we get separated don't take it too seriously. Fly out your Prudent Limit of Endurance and come home." He turned to face Snow and slapped him on the back. "I see you've got your DFC ribbon up. Congratulations!"

"Thanks, Hedley, but I can't understand why I got one and Ed didn't. I didn't push that bloody torpedo button—he did."

"Anybody who flies with a pilot as ropy as Douglas deserves the Victoria Cross! Well, come on, chaps. Let's go." They gathered their belongings together and filed out to the waiting lorry.

The two aircraft took off and headed toward the gathering darkness to the east. As usual Snow was frantically busy in his navigation compartment in the nose, while the gunner kept swinging his turret, quartering the sky, and the man at the radio listened to morse but sent nothing.

Snow's voice came over the intercom during one of his rare moments of rest. "Say, Ed, why do you think Hedley took off so late?"

"Dunno. Thought he could get a couple of ships steaming around at night, I guess."

"Do you think he's going after that bloody ship at Wilhelmshaven?"

119

"Gee, I never thought of that," Douglas replied, knowing he was lying. "Why d'you think so?"

"Because Hellyer gave me a couple of letters before we left. Told me to post 'em if anything happened."

"We've all done that."

"Yeah, but these were new ones Hellyer wrote."

"Oh Jesus! I sure hope he isn't trying anything as crazy as that!"

"You know Hedley. All the guts in the world, and no sense."

"Hope you're wrong, Hank."

"Hope so too." There was a brief silence. "Stand by for a three-drift wind."

"Standing by." Douglas reached forward to reset his directional gyro. "Alter to 065 compass—now!" Douglas turned the steering yoke on the top of the control column and applied a little left rudder. The aircraft turned.

When they entered the patrol area Douglas went south, Westover north, as he had briefed them. They were out of sight of each other. Douglas and his crew flew their mission without seeing any enemy activity, and returned with their torpedo still in the bomb bay and their guns unfired except for the practice rounds they always fired into the waves to test the guns. They flew a creeping-line-ahead search, like the rungs of a ladder, until their time was up, and then Snow gave Douglas a course for home. When they were safely over land again, Harrington as usual tuned in the BBC. An orchestra was playing "*Stardust*" and Douglas hummed along with it, thinking how Charlotte had been in his arms when he last heard it on the dance floor. When he had a couple of days off the next week he would go down to London to see her again. He smiled as he remembered the hot pressure of his lips on hers at the end of the walk in Hedley's garden.

He called up the field, received landing clearance, and brought the plane in, banishing all thoughts but his task while he approached, flared out, held the plane in the air while it lost flying speed and stalled gently onto the runway, and braked gently to a stop. He taxied the aircraft to its dispersal, jockeyed into it to the waved signals of the ground-crew marshaller, and cut the engines. The crew collected their gear and climbed out.

"Wasn't much to that," said Harrington. "They can send me on as many trips like that as they want to."

"Money for jam." MacKenzie nodded.

"Yeah, you gotta take the smooth with the rough," Snow said. "Talking of smooth, that was a smooth landing."

"For a change," MacKenzie said, and ducked Douglas' fist. They climbed into the lorry to go to the briefing room.

"Westover back yet?" Douglas asked as the crew entered the room.

"No," the duty officer replied, handing Douglas a rum-laced cup of coffee. "Not yet, anyway."

Douglas looked at his watch. "When's his endurance up?"

"Ten minutes ago. He probably landed somewhere else. It's a habit of old Hedley's. He stays out too long and then has to land at the closest airport to the coast to refuel."

"Hedley's a boomerang. Couldn't get rid of him if you wanted to," another officer said.

"Hope not." Douglas led his crew into the debriefing room. They sat down at the table, opposite the intelligence officer. "When did you last see Flight Lieutenant Westover?"

Snow looked at his log sheet, and reported their position the last time they had seen the other aircraft. "Didn't see him again after that," Douglas said. They had their post-operational meal and went to bed.

When they awoke the next morning Douglas went as usual to the flight office. "What about Westover?" he asked.

"Missing," the operations officer told him laconically. "No word."

Douglas shook his head. "He didn't divert?"

"No."

"Rough."

"All in the game," the operations officer said. "I'm sorry."

"You don't think he went to Wilhelmshaven, do you?"

"God knows. Only the Germans know. Maybe he's a prisoner."

Douglas laughed bitterly. "What a hope!"

"There's always some hope, Douglas."

"Prisoner! From a torpedo bomber! Yeah—there's always some hope."

121

Douglas turned to see Snow enter the office. "What you been doing, Hank?"

"Posting Hellyer's letters."

"Bit early, don't you think?"

Snow shook his head. "No, I don't."

"Why not?" asked Douglas sharply.

"I checked with the intelligence officer. He showed me a transcript of a German communiqué. It reported that a British aircraft was shot down in Wilhelmshaven harbour last night. There was no official raid on Wilhelmshaven, and no other aircraft was detailed to fly over that part of the country."

Douglas nodded soberly. "Did they say what kind of an aircraft it was?"

"No."

"Then there's no proof it was Hedley."

"Stop trying to kid yourself, Ed. You know damn well it was."

"Yeah. I guess so." Douglas chewed his lips. "I guess I should drop in on Beatrice Westover. It's the least I can do."

"Better make sure that she knows he's really gone. You don't want to go there, knowing what you know, if she still thinks he's just missing."

"I'll see Wing Commander Tenley. He should know."

Wing Commander Tenley told them that he had informed Beatrice Westover of the German communiqué.

"She took it well," Tenley said. "It was as if she had been expecting it."

"Maybe she was. She knew him pretty well, you know."

"Why did you ask?"

"I thought I'd call on her, to tell her how sorry we are about it."

Tenley nodded. "Yes, of course. Is Snow going with you?"

"Gosh, I knew Westover, but not very well, and I only saw his wife once," Snow demurred.

"Come on, Hank. I need somebody with me."

"Okay then." They saluted and left Tenley's office.

The pedalled their bicycles to Westover's cottage and knocked on the door. It was opened by Charlotte.

"Charlotte? I didn't expect to see you!"

"I came up here when I heard the news. I thought my sister might need me."

"It's good you did. Beatrice will appreciate it."

Charlotte turned to Hank. "Flying Officer Snow—it's good to see you too. Come in."

"We came to pay our respects," Snow said, "and to tell you and Beatrice how much we sympathise with you in your loss."

Beatrice entered the room. "Edward—and Henry. It's good to see you. Will you have a cup of tea?"

"Thank you. It's very kind of you." Snow sipped his cup. "We wanted to tell you what a privilege it has been to serve with Hedley—he was a splendid officer, a wonderful leader. Knowing him has been one of the high points of our lives."

"Thank you so much," she replied. "I thought he was wonderful too." She nodded her head slightly. "Anyway, I have Digby to remember him by. He will live on in his son."

Douglas, ill at ease, made a few more conventional remarks and then edged toward the door. Snow, more self-possessed, finished his tea and made a formal farewell. As Beatrice escorted them to the door Charlotte followed her and stepped outside with them. Douglas turned to her and took her hand. "Gosh, there isn't much to say—"

"No—not from you!" she spat at him poisonously.

"From me!" Douglas stepped back, shocked.

"Yes, from you! You killed him!"

"Me? I killed him? How can you say that?"

"Because he was all set to leave the squadron and go to a training post—all safe and sound—when you torpedoed that cruiser! He couldn't leave the squadron as the second-best pilot—he's always been the best, everywhere he's been, at everything he's done! You knew what he was going to do, didn't you? You knew he was going to try to sink that German liner. You flew out with him, and you let him go on alone! All alone, and he never came back!"

"Good God, Charlotte, I had no idea what he was going to do! I had my orders—he gave them to me—and I obeyed them—to patrol my area and then come home!"

"You didn't know? I knew—Beatrice knew—Michael Hellyer knew. Everybody but you—and you had flown with him time and again!"

"Gosh, I'm sorry you feel that way—" Snow spoke. "It's terrible for all of us. Charlotte. You know we all loved him. What we must do now is to try to be worthy of him."

"You loved him?" Charlotte suddenly dissolved into a flood of tears. "You loved him? What about me? I loved him more than I've ever loved anybody in my life—and now he's gone!"

"It's this damned war," said Snow. He put his arms around her as she sobbed on his shoulder. "We must be brave, Charlotte. I know you are."

She pulled herself together and stood upright. "I'm frightfully sorry I behaved as I did," she said. She extended a hand to Douglas. "Good-bye—and thank you."

"Good-bye, Charlotte." Douglas and Snow turned away and mounted their bicycles. Charlotte walked slowly into the cottage.

As they rode off Douglas turned his head to Snow. "Good God! What was eating her?"

"What she said." Snow replied. "She was in love with Hedley."

"But he was her sister's husband!"

"Sure. But Hedley was the hero—the Beau Sabreur—the star. And stars go around screwing everybody they can find."

"You figure he was screwing Charlotte?'

"Yeah. Hellyer told me."

"How in hell did he know?"

"Hedley told him one day they were on temporary duty somewhere and they got tanked up in the mess."

"Jesus! I'da' never thought it—"

"She's a good-looking doll. Can't say I blame him."

"But she was his sister-in-law!"

"That wouldn't bother old Hedley a bit. Guys like him don't take things like that into consideration. He was one of those guys that everything comes to—he figured he was entitled to it."

"Jesus—I never thought—"

Snow looked at him closely. "Say, Ed, are you in love with Charlotte?"

"No—of course not—she's just a friend—God damn it, yes. I am—or was—in love with her. I don't know what in hell to think now."

"I'm sorry I said—"

"Not your fault, Hank. Jesus, Jesus, damn it, Beatrice didn't seem nearly so broke up as I thought she would be..."

124

"No. A Beau Sabreur can get on your nerves if a woman is married to him—especially if he's screwing around."

"But with Charlotte. Her sister. Jesus!"

"Charlotte sounded as if she was in love with him. She couldn't help that."

"No. He was a good-looking son of a bitch. But I thought—or hoped or something—that she might be in love with me!"

"Sorry, Ed. I wish I'd kept my big mouth shut."

"This is a crazy world we're in," Douglas muttered. So Charlotte had been sleeping with Hedley while he had fancied himself in love with her. He had considered asking her to marry him. And he had abandoned Margaret Reilly for her. He felt cheated. He thought maybe he could exhume his relationship with Margaret, and then angrily tossed the idea away. What was done was done.

In his heart he knew Margaret was shrewd enough to see through him.

"You know what I'm going to do, Hank?" he asked suddenly.

"Yeah. Get drunk."

"You're bloody right." He pedalled back without further conversation, and headed for the officers' mess. He had four quick beers and a scotch, got sick, vomited, and felt like a fool.

CHAPTER FOURTEEN

The crew kept flying, taking off to make patrols along the Dutch coast. Douglas made one drop against a freighter, the Beaufort beside him making a drop at the same time. One torpedo hit, and Douglas was sure the torpedo was his. When they returned, however, he found that his companion pilot had claimed the hit also. Tenley decided to credit it to the other pilot. "You've already got a cruiser, Douglas," he said. "Let somebody else have some of the glory."

"Okay by me," Douglas replied, but the injustice rankled. He looked at his chest, still innocent of the purple-and-white diagonal stripes of the Distinguished Flying Cross, which shone on Snow's jacket. He shrugged and walked back to his room in the Nissen hut barracks beside Snow. "I feel ropy," he said.

"You don't look so good," Snow replied. "Better go see the medical officer."

The doctor examined him, gave him some pills, and told him to go to bed early. Douglas did as he was told.

The next morning the adjutant called the flight office to tell Douglas that the Officer Commanding wanted to see him. "What've I done now?" Douglas said, a frown creasing his forehead. "Don't remember anything. Haven't cracked up a plane lately."

Douglas walked into Tenley's office and saluted. Tenley nodded to him and looked at him quizzically.

"Have you been complaining about your health lately, Douglas?"

"A bit. I've been off-colour for a while."

"Did you have glandular trouble a while ago?"

"Yes sir—I did. I thought it was a cold. Maybe I caught it from Snow, my navigator."

Tenley looked down at a paper on his desk. "Well, I've just received a memo from the medical officer. He says he's checked with the Command medical staff, and they say it isn't glandular trouble at all—it's nervous exhaustion. All torpedo crew members with more than thirty trips are to be taken off operations."

"What!" Douglas' mouth fell open.

"That's right, Douglas. You've got thirty-three. But you deserve a rest anyway." Tenley walked round the desk. "Go and get your crew and bring them back here. I want to thank them all."

"How about Harrington and MacKenzie, sir? They haven't got thirty trips in—I lost my first two wireless air gunners, you know."

"Oh yes—I remember that only too well. But bring them in anyway; they're just lucky. I'm screening them too. After all, flying with a pilot like you is hard enough to justify anything." He smiled. Then his voice hardened. "Douglas—why aren't you wearing the ribbon of your DFC?"

"I haven't got a DFC, sir."

"What do you mean? After that cruiser—"

"Nobody recommended me. Snow got one, but I didn't."

"Well, I'll be damned! But I heard Clifton say he was going to put you in for one—"

"And then he went missing before he had a chance to."

Tenley nodded. "Yes—yes indeed." He reflected for a moment. "No—not a DFC! We can do better than that. I'm going to recommend you for the Distinguished Service Order! God knows you've put in some distinguished service. The Air Officer Commanding is coming here next week, and I'll approach him then. You know, maybe you were just lucky after all—a DSO has a much more handsome ribbon than a DFC."

"Thank you, sir. I hadn't expected anything like that."

"Go and get your crew. Come back in half an hour."

Douglas hurried to the crew room and rounded up his crew. "Snow! Harrington! Come here! Where's MacKenzie?"

"Out at the kite, skipper," answered Harrington. "What's eatin' you now?"

"Go get MacKenzie. The OC wants to see us all. Button up your jacket, Harrington. We've gotta look smart, just this once."

127

Harrington and MacKenzie appeared twenty minutes later, and the four men marched into the OC's office.

Tenley was standing, waiting for them. "I suppose Flying Officer Douglas has told you the story."

"No, he ain't sir," Harrington answered. "He didn't tell us nothing."

Tenley laughed. "Thank you, Douglas, for letting me tell your crew myself. Gentlemen, it is my pleasant duty to inform you that you are all screened from operational duties." Ceremoniously he shook hands with all four men. "Congratulations. You're a good crew, capable and competent. I'm going to be sorry to lose you. But you deserve a rest, and now you'll have one." He paused before Harrington. "The adjutant has confirmed that you have been promoted to flight sergeant. I'm sorry I can't say as much for you, MacKenzie, but we have to check with the New Zealand authorities. The recommendation has gone forward, however, and I'm sure it will come through in due time."

"Don't feel bad about it, sir," grinned MacKenzie. "The other news is quite good enough to go on with."

"Thank you sir," said Harrington.

"I hope you will do me the honour of joining me in a get-together in the officers' mess at five o'clock—all of you."

"Thank you, sir," said Douglas. " We'll be glad to go, I assure you."

"We'll be having a bit of a do in the sergeants' mess too," said Harrington.

"I would be honoured to drop in there too, if I could find a sergeant do invite me," said Tenley.

"We'll be right glad to have you look in, sir."

"Thank you for your invitation, sergeant. And now—Oh, my apologies! Flight Sergeant ! And now until five!"

"We didn't expect anything like this, sir," Snow said.

"Frankly, neither did I," said Tenley. "But the Principal Medical Officer has diagnosed nervous exhaustion in men who have simply been on operations too long. What I do know is that you've done enough. God bless, you gentlemen."

They saluted and left.

The officers' mess was tumultuous at five o'clock. The four men of the crew were seized, lifted onto shoulders, and paraded around the mess. Drinks were pressed into their hands. A man seated himself at the piano and began to pound out " For He's a Jolly Good Fellow," with everybody joining in raucously .

The wing commander entered, the group captain Station Commander with him. "Attention!" the adjutant barked. There was a sudden stillness, and the parade and the piano stopped. "Good evening, gentlemen," the station commander said. "We are all here on an auspicious occasion—the screening of Flying Officer Douglas and his crew. I am as happy as you are, and as I know Douglas is." He looked around him. "And now let joy be unconfined." He looked at the piano player. "I believe you were playing *For He's a Jolly Good Fellow*. Carry on." The piano player slammed his hands down on the keys, and the voices roared again, following it with the unprintable lyrics of Air Force songs. The station commander accepted a drink, and joined his voice with the others. He knew the words to all the songs.

After a decent interval Tenley sought out Douglas. "We have an appointment at the sergeants' mess."

He sought out Snow. "Come on Hank. We're going over to the sergeants' mess. Come on Harrington—come on Mac."

Snow turned to the man he was talking to, who looked at him suddenly with sober eyes, the way they looked when they came out of a cinema after an escapist movie into the cold glare of the real world where their lives were in hazard, where they were unlikely to live out the year. Snow and Douglas had overcome the odds, and now they were safe at least for a breathing spell; their comrades were jealous of them even as they were glad for them.

The station commander and Tenley escorted the four men to the CO's car. They drove to the sergeants' mess, where the Station Warrant Officer, a thin, ageing regular who was standing stiffly to attention just inside the door, threw them a Guards-type salute. The mess was subdued, with the sergeants standing respectfully in groups, none of them with glasses in their hands. The station commander returned the sergeant major's salute, called, "At ease, gentlemen!" and accepted the tankard a fat sergeant offered him. The men began to talk, and suddenly the room was loud with congratulatory words, with hands slapping the four men's shoulders and pressing drinks on them.

"We're certainly making a lot of fuss over one crew," said Tenley to the station commander.

129

"Yes. But Douglas' crew is the first one to leave the station relatively undamaged. We've graduated only five crews since I came here. One was shot down and spent five days in a dinghy out in the briny—they never came back here, but were screened from hospital. Another had every man in the crew wounded, and one of them died. A third crew bailed out and collected a bag of broken legs, and the pilot was so shaky that the rest of the crew wouldn't fly with him any more. The fourth crew wasn't screened—they needed an operational crew at some godforsaken place in Canada called Patricia Bay. Now we have Douglas—and even at that it is only Douglas and his navigator who have survived the tour—his two original wireless air gunners never made it."

Tenley nodded. "Yes. I should have remembered. Douglas is rather a rare bird, sir."

"You could put it that way. But I'm glad to see Douglas and know that he is here and having a good time. Maybe there's hope for us all." The station commander finished his drink. "They'll enjoy themselves more without us." He and Tenley left the mess. As they settled back in their car, the station commander said, "Douglas seems a good enough chap. What's he like?"

"An ordinary man, sir—nothing special. A good average pilot. Comes from some little village in Saskatchewan. But he's lucky. That cruiser—"

The group captain sucked a tooth reflectively. "Napoleon said the first quality he required of his marshals was that they be lucky. Douglas passes that test." He turned to his companion. "Why isn't he wearing his DFC?"

Tenley looked embarrassed. "Sheer bad luck, sir. Squadron Leader Clifton told him he'd recommend him—and then Clifton went missing. Then Flight Lieutenant Westover did the same thing—and went missing himself. I didn't find out about it myself until today."

"Now what?"

"Let's wait until the Air Officer Commanding visits us next week. I want to put him in for the Distinguished Service Order instead. But if we just put him in for it, it could be turned down. If we prepare the way for it, it'll be approved. It'll look good to have the station given a DSO."

130

"Good thinking, Tenley. A little wait won't do any harm. Douglas will appreciate the DSO more than the DFC."

At the sergeants' mess Douglas, Snow, MacKenzie and Harrington, arms linked, stood swaying as they howled out a series of unmelodious songs. There was no liquor in the mess, just beer, but they were all thoroughly intoxicated. The air of euphoria was all-pervading; even the old hard-bitten ground crew sergeants, who considered it unjust, immoral and shameful to promote men to sergeant's rank without requiring them to work up to it slowly and painfully through the rank of corporal, as they had done, were singing along with them.

A clutch of sergeants were grouped around the piano, waving tankards in time to the song they were howling out. "Salome, Salome," they chorused. "That's my gal Salome; she's a great big fat bitch twice the size of me, with the hair on her belly like the branches on a tree; she can run, jump, fight, fuck, wheel a barrow, push a truck; that's my gal Salome!" The song was followed by "The Bastard King of England," "Little Angeline" and "An Airman Told Me Before he Died." There was a brief lull, and then an Irish flight sergeant began "Cockles and Mussels" in a beautiful tenor voice, while all the others briefly fell silent to listen to him.

The crew lifted their tankards high and drained them. "Screened, by Jesus!" Snow roared. "Fooled old Jerry! Drink to the poor marksmanship of der Luftwaffe!" He waved his tankard. "Come on chaps—here's to Goering—can't hit fuck-all!" The tenor took over. "Hitler has only got one ball," he sang, to the tune of the "Colonel Bogey" march. "Goering has two, but they are very small. Himmler is very similar, but Goebbels has no balls at all!" The others roared out the chorus.

Harrington staggered away, to be found an hour later in a washroom, face-down in one of the toilet stalls. Snow went next, staggering outside to be loaded into the back of a lorry, to which Douglas was brought a few minutes later, to be carried off to their quarters. MacKenzie lasted the longest, remaining until the mess was closed, and falling asleep with his head on a cushion under the billiard table.

The station sergeant major found him the next morning. "If you was anyone else, you'd get the rough edge of my tongue," he said,

131

"but today you're in a state of grace. Now go and get shaved!"

The crew assembled in the crewroom the next afternoon, the morning having been written off as a dead loss by all concerned. All of them had monumental hangovers.

Flight Lieutenant Rattray, who had taken Westover's place as flight commander, called them in. "Well, my buckos, you're screened. Got over your celebration yet?"

"God no," Douglas replied. "I feel like the Black Watch marched through my mouth swinging their kilts."

"God, my head!" wailed Snow pitifully. "Sure glad we don't get screened every day!"

"I'll be okay in a month or so," said Harrington.

"It was a bonzer party," put in MacKenzie.

"I'm glad you enjoyed yourself," said Rattray. "I have some news for you. Douglas, you and Snow are going back do Canada on sixty days' leave. MacKenzie, it's back to New Zealand for you, on a training job. Harrington, you've got three weeks before you report to Chivenor. Travelling time to Yorkshire isn't so long."

"Them bloody colonials allus gets the jam." Harrington grinned.

"We're sorry to see you go. It'll be a few days before we get official orders, though. In the meantime it'd be appreciated if you could show up in the flight room, to help the new boys on anything you think needs doing."

"Yes sir," Douglas answered for them all.

Rattray grinned. "You all look in terrible shape. Take the rest of the day off."

"Righto!" The men returned to their quarters. After supper that night there was an informal gathering around the piano in the officers' mess, the pianist being a bald-headed fatherly accountant officer. Snow and Douglas joined in, since by now their heads were clear again. There were four women officers in the group, one of them Helena.

After a few songs Snow took his tankard and sat down across a small table from one of the women.

She looked at him. "I understand you're leaving."

"Yes, I will be. Want to go with me?"

The woman recoiled. She looked at him beneath lowered brows. "You're a bit forward, aren't you, Mr. Snow?"

"Oh, I don't know." He took a pencil, smoothed a cigarette package lying on the table, and wrote busily on it. He handed it to the woman. On it was a quatrain:

"Please accept my explanation
Even though it's made in haste—
You reject my invitation
But you must admire my taste."

He handed the paper to her, and she took it with a disapproving frown. Then, as she read it, she burst into laughter. She handed the verse to the woman beside her, who joined her in laughter, and then handed it to a third woman. She read it, and said, "You've written a verse for Anne—write one for me." She pursed her lips sceptically. "Did you write this yourself?"

"So you think I have a stock of verses I trot out on occasion, do you?" he said, his eyes twinkling. "Your name's Irene, isn't it?" She nodded. He smoothed out another cigarette package and worked busily for a few minutes, making several erasures.

She read the words, and a pleased smile came over her features. "Why, that's very nice! You even had my name in it!"

"Lucky for me Irene is an easy name to find rhymes for."

"You did it very well."

The other girl leaned over and took the two slips of paper. "It's my turn now."

Snow sucked his pencil for pencil for a few moments, and then wrote a limerick. The girls read it and laughed.

"We didn't know you were so talented," one said.

"I need the proper inspiration—somebody like you beautiful ladies. That brings out the talent in anybody."

Helena Compton-Morris approached. Snow stood up and sat down again.

"I see you have all the WAAFs clustered around you."

"He's been writing us all verses," said Irene. "They're very good too."

Helena picked up the papers and read them. "Yes, they are good, Henry. You never told me you could do this."

"You never asked me, my dear lady."

"Then write me one too."

He shook his head slowly. "No—your name's too hard to find

133

rhymes to. And I always get it confused with the capital of Montana."

"You keep telling me of that town."

"Yes, only it's pronounced Hell—een-ah, not Helen-ah, the way you pronounce your name. It'll interfere with the scansion and the rhyme scheme. I'll write you a limerick later. It'll take me a little time. Double-barrelled names take longer."

She nodded, looking faintly disappointed.

"Ever been to Helena, Montana? It's a nice town—not very big. You'd think you'd know about it—after all, it's named after you."

"Is it anywhere near Seattle?"

"Seattle is in Washington state. Helena's in Montana. It's five or six hundred miles from Seattle—about as far as we are from Berlin."

"Is it? I didn't realise America was so big."

"Helena is south of Alberta—on a line between Calgary and Medicine Hat, if you know where they are."

"Medicine Hat! That's a lovely name! I've heard of it, but I don't know where it is."

"They didn't name it after you. It's only a little place—I used to change trains there when I was going home on leave from Air Navigation School. The train used to back into the station and then leave town going the wrong way for a couple of miles. People used to think they were on the wrong train." He stood up. "Can I get you something to drink?"

"No thanks—not right now."

"Excuse me, ladies." Snow walked off.

An hour later Snow returned. As he entered Helena was just leaving. "Oh, Helena—I have your limerick for you." He handed her a folded paper.

She took it and read it quickly. Her eyes flicked to Snow's face, and then she sat down on a settee and read it again.

"But it's not a limerick, Henry!"

"No. It's a sonnet. A Petrarchian sonnet."

She looked at him with sober, unsmiling eyes. "It's beautiful, Henry. Nobody ever wrote a sonnet to me before." She caught his hand. "I didn't know you felt this way."'

"I know you didn't."

"Why didn't you tell me? And why didn't you tell me you could write these lovely poems?"

134

"I was waiting until I got off operations. Frankly, I was superstitious about it. I kept thinking of Rupert Brooke and Wilfrid Owen, the poets of the Great War who didn't survive it. I know I'm not in their class, but somehow I felt the gods of war don't like poets—even if Goethe survived the battle of Valmy."

She nodded. "I didn't know you were so cultured, Henry."

"I was afraid to mention it, for fear it would change my luck."

"I know. So many of the men are like that."

"But I've beaten the odds now. I can write all the poems I want. They're sending me back to Canada, far from the sound of the guns."

"When will you be leaving?"

"In a week or so, I guess. Long enough for me to write you another sonnet. Would you like a Shakespearean sonnet this time? It's a bit sneaky of me to suggest it, of course—the rhyme scheme is more flexible. The Italian style of sonnet is harder—but then finding rhymes is easier in Italian."

She folded the sheet of paper. "I really have to leave now, Henry. Meet me here tomorrow with another sonnet. And I don't care if it's only a Shakespearean one."

"I'll be here. Same time, same place." She left, and Snow walked slowly to the bar and ordered a beer. One of the women walked up to him and asked him to write her another verse. It kept him busy until he left the mess.

He was sitting reading a paper the next day when Helena entered the anteroom. Putting down the paper, he rose and walked over to her, taking a folded sheet of paper out of his jacket pocket as he did so. "Here's your verse, Helena."

"Sit down beside me while I read it."

A few moments later she lifted her eyes from the paper. "I've never been told that I'm beautiful—so beautifully."

"You are beautiful, Helena."

"I have no choice but to believe it when you tell me the way you do."

"Beautiful women should be told they're beautiful, even when they already know it." His face sobered. "Besides, I'll be gone in five days. This is my last chance to tell you."

She looked into his eyes. "Is that all you meant to say?"

135

He shrugged. "What else? Tennyson already has said everything for me."

"Tennyson?"

He looked down at the floor. "Yes. 'Dear as remembered kisses after death, and sweet as those by hopeless fancy feigned on lips that are for others—'"

"Yes. I remember the lines."

"I thought you would."

"Come outside," she said. He followed her to the little runabout she had parked outside the mess. "I'm going to take you for a ride." He got in beside her.

She drove out the main gate, past the guardhouse, and turned into a secluded lane. Beneath a tree she stopped the car.

She turned to him. "What makes you think my lips are only for others?"

"Don't be silly, Helena. You're a duke's daughter. My father is a railway conductor—a guard, you'd call him."

"You silly goose! Kiss me!" Their bodies melded. When their lips parted Snow whispered "I never thought it could happen."

"Those sonnets of yours—and that kiss—what do they mean?"

"That I'm in love with you. I've loved you for months."

"I love you too, Henry."

He kissed here again.

"You're not married, Henry."

"No, I'm not."

"I know. I looked up your next of kin. Your mother and father."

He laughed. "Maybe you were interested in me more than I thought."

"Silly of me, wasn't it?"

"It's funny—neither of us made a move."

She fell silent. "I was afraid to—I've had such bad luck with everybody I've been close to. It was like you and your poetry."

"We're both off the hook now, Helena. At last."

"You must come and meet father and mother."

"A real live duke and duchess?"

"Don't be silly! They're just daddy and mummy!"

"I'll be glad to. I'll just have time to do it before the boat sails."

136

"So soon?"

"Maybe I can wangle a week or so off—or longer. But in the meantime let's do something to celebrate—will you have a drink with me at the Farmer's Arms? They have a cosy little bar there."

"Of course, my dear."

As they drove to the inn Snow said. "I never thought the rewards for writing sonnets were so high."

"They'll get higher, Henry."

They sat opposite each other in a corner of the bar, their glasses neglected as they looked at each other. "You're very beautiful, Helena—a beautiful lady. Funny, you're a lady by title. I don't quite know how to act toward a real live lady." He smiled. "Maybe I should just await your orders. I'm just an ordinary guy, you know."

"Do you believe that ordinary people should obey the dictates of the nobility?"

"Seems to be the accepted thing, my lady."

"Then I will give you an order, which you will disobey at your peril."

"Your servant, my lady."

"Kiss me."

He obeyed. "My lady. My lady love."

CHAPTER FIFTEEN

The next morning the Tannoy public-address system blared, "Flying Officer Snow! Flying Officer Henry Snow! Report to your squadron commander!"

Snow walked to the operations building and knocked on Wing Commander Tenley's door.

"Come in, Snow," Tenley called to him. "Snow, we need you."

"Need me? I'll be glad to do anything to help."

"I want you to go on standby with my duty crew for two days."

"Standby? But I'm screened! I'm through!"

"Yes, I know. But my navigator, Flight Lieutenant Barton, has just come down with bronchitis. I—we need a navigator for the crew. I'm taking the standby myself."

"Jesus, I've been through it all. And I've done all my flying with Douglas—I don't want to change now."

"Now look, Snow, it's only for two days, until Flight Lieutenant Cathran comes back from leave."

"Well-l-l," said Snow doubtfully. "I still don't like it."

"You'll be flying with me, Snow, and you probably won't be flying at all. But if you do, you're a good navigator, and I need an experienced man."

"Damn it, it's tempting fate. You're a reasonably good pilot, but—"

A shadow of displeasure passed across Tenley's face. "Well, I am glad to hear that, Snow."

"It's tempting Providence. It'll change my luck."

"That isn't much of a reason, Snow. Besides, strictly speaking, I have the authority to order you to do it."

"Yes, I guess so. Well, it looks as if I haven't a hell of a lot of choice. Just make sure you fly my courses, and tell me when you alter the airspeed or the altitude. And hold her steady for three drift winds." He was silent for just a moment, and then he added the word, "Sir."

138

"Yes. I'll do my part, Snow," Tenley said brusquely. "You know the drill. That's all." Snow saluted, turned about and left the office. Flight Lieutenant Rattray saw him as he walked down the corridor. "Hello, Hank," he said. Looking at Snow's grim face, he rubbed his chin. "You don't seem too happy."

"Would you be—if you were put on standby after you'd been screened?"

"No, I guess no. Well, it's only for two days. Nothing will happen, Hank. You're a lucky bastard."

"Now I'm going to be shit-scared for two days. When I was on ops it didn't matter—it was my job. But to be told I'm off ops, and then put back on again—"

"After all, the wingco is the boss."

"I know," Snow agreed sourly. "But he's not a wingco in my air force, and I'll never see him again—or you—after five days from now. Damn it, I've paid my dues."

"Yes, I suppose you have. You've done your job well—I can't deny that."

"Anyway, I'm stuck now."

He went off to his quarters, and then joined Helena for lunch. "Can you come down to meet mummy and Daddy tonight? I can wangle a day's leave," she said.

"I'd love to, but I can't."

"You can't?"

"No. The OC's navigator got bronchitis, and they put me on standby in his place. It'll only be for a couple of days until F/L Cathran comes back off leave."

"But it's not fair! You've done your share! Why did they pick you?"

"They just ran out of navigators, that's all."

"That's nonsense! There are all kinds of navigators on the squadron!"

"Experienced navigators then. Tenley wants a man with some time under his belt. The other navigators available are all sprogs." He shrugged. "Besides, I probably won't fly anyway."

"I hope not." She toyed with the rest of her meal. "Come with me, Henry." When they were standing together outside the mess she turned to him. "Haven't you forgotten to do something, Henry?"

"Forgotten something?"

"You told me you loved me, didn't you?"

"Yes, I did. I love you."

"Then why don't you ask me to marry you?"

His eyes opened wide." But I'm going back to Canada in a few days—and you're a duke's daughter—I was going to give you a while to think it over—"

She stamped her foot. "Damn it, ask me!"

He took her hand. "Helena, will you marry me?"

"Of course I will!" She stepped into his arms.

They were interrupted by an outraged voice. "Section Officer Compton-Morris! What are you doing?"

Helena turned, to see the senior WAAF officer standing beside them. Helena smiled. "Oh—it's you!" She looked at the angular woman with the squadron leader's stripes. "Let me introduce my fiancé—Flying Officer Henry Snow—DFC."

"Your fiancé?"

"Yes, my fiancé. I believe it is perfectly acceptable to kiss one's fiancé, don't you think?"

"Well—well—" The woman's mouth closed. "Congratulations, Section Officer Compton-Morris. I take it you haven't been engaged very long?"

"About five minutes. Thank you." She inclined her head and took Henry's arm. "Let's go for a stroll, Henry."

They walked toward the hangars, and then returned. As they entered the officers' mess the Tannoy bellowed, "Standby crews report to the operations room!"

"My God!" Helena cried. "I hope it's just a drill!"

"So do I." Snow kissed her again and reluctantly released her.

"For God's sake be careful!" she said urgently.

"I will."

At the briefing room Snow found Wing Commander Tenley standing on the dias. Crews were coming in, navigators carrying their navigation bags.

"Sit down over there," Tenley told Snow pointing to a table where his two wireless air gunners were already seated. He waited until the crews were complete, and began." All right, men, we have the chance of our lives!" Turning around, he pointed to the map behind him, where a magnet shaped like a tiny ship, flying a swastika, was sticking to the painted metal.

140

"The cruiser *Prinz Eugen* is out, heading for northern Norwegian ports to have a bang at the Murmansk convoys. It's up to us to get her. We had a bash at her once before when we were attacking the *Scharnhorst* and *Gneisenau*, and we didn't get her, but I don't intend to miss her this time."

"Oh Jesus!" Snow said. Tenley ignored the interruption. "Ignore the cruiser's escort—everybody else and everything else. We have six crews. We'll attack in two groups of three, one from the east and one from the west." He carried on with the briefing. When it was over he said, "All right, out to the aircraft!" The men stood up.

Tenley continued. "I'll take off first. We'll form up over the church ten miles north of the field and fly in a loose formation. My navigator will do the navigation for all of us, but keep your own plots."

Douglas walked out to the aircraft to wish good luck to Snow. "Anything new in your life, Hank?'"

"Yes. Helena Compton-Morris and I are going to get married."

"Good! I'll come to the wedding." Snow climbed into the aircraft.

The aircraft took off, all within five minutes, circled the field and formed up on Tenley. They set off heading north. At Wick they landed to refuel, and took off again half an hour later.

Snow licked his lips as the Scottish coast fell behind him. If he could survive the next four hours, he would have his heart's desire. Now that he knew Helena loved him, he could look forward to being married to a beautiful and desirable woman. He had everything to live for now. Those poems he had written her had won her—but had they changed his luck? The fear and the question nagged at his brain as he got down to navigating the aircraft. It was an absorbing task, which drove out all other thoughts. He bent over his drift sight, worked out wind velocities on his E6B computer, checked the airspeed, worked out the deviation affecting the compass, made workmanlike entries in his log sheet, and on his chart drew lines, with triangles and crosses neatly labelled with times, to mark the progress of his flight. He was so busy that it came almost as a surprise when he heard Tenley call out "There they are!"

Snow looked through the perspex window in the nose and saw the lean, low shape of the big German cruiser, with its escort of

141

leaner, lower destroyers. Everything looked, as always in the early stages of an attack, peaceful and calm.

"Yellow flight break off. Red flight close up on me!" The Beauforts broke into two three-plane vics, one attacking from one side and the second attacking from the other. Snow wrote the time in his log, and picked up his camera. He snapped a picture of the ships. As he pressed the shutter release, he saw a sparkle of light from one of the destroyers. The defensive barrage had commenced.

The plane heeled over as Tenley turned onto the dropping course. "Steady, chaps," Tenley's voice came, cool and even. "We're going in. Don't drop too soon."

There was a flurry of "Rogers" over the radio, and then silence, except for the normal aircraft noises. Snow looked out a side window. The decks of the destroyer off to starboard was ablaze with light now as every gun that could be brought to bear fired at them. Lines of tracers curved gracefully in their direction. Snow snapped a picture of a destroyer—he knew the intelligence officer would want one when he got back, and then turned his attention to the cruiser.

The world suddenly dissolved in a shattering explosion. Red hot needles drove into Snow's legs. He dropped his camera and grabbed for the edge of a bulkhead. A second later the plane hit the water, skipped off it, and slewed sideways, water pouring in through the shattered nose. He pulled the toggle on his life-jacket, which swelled up as the carbon dioxide gas whistled into it, and bobbed to the surface.

The aircraft dinghy had inflated automatically, and Snow began to swim toward it. He kicked out, and screamed with agony as his shattered legs rebelled. Tenley was already in the dinghy, as was the rear gunner. There was no sign of the wireless operator. Hands reached out to pull him aboard. "You're wounded!" Tenley cried. He and his companion ripped open the legs of Snow's flying suit and began to apply bandages. As the first turn of the sodden bandage circled his leg Snow saw the wing tip of the Beaufort slide under the water. He lost consciousness.

Thirty minutes later a German launch approached them. A seaman hooked the dinghy and pulled it close to the boat, while another stood guard with a rifle. "For you the war is over," the man said in German. Tenley and the gunner lifted Snow's limp body aboard the launch and climbed in after him.

The boat sped away after the cruiser, gradually overhauling it.

The ship hove to, and the launch was hauled aboard, and Snow, still unconscious, was carried off to the sick bay. The other two men were put in the ship's cells. There were no signs that the cruiser had suffered any damage.

An hour later the German captain entered the cell. "Come with me," he told Tenley. "Your comrade has no hope of recovering, but he is conscious. You can see him before he dies." He led Tenley to the sick bay, where Snow was lying, ashen-faced, upon an operating table. Snow opened his eyes.

"Bad luck, old man," Tenley said, struggling to keep his voice steady. "You did your duty. You did it well."

"I never should have written those sonnets—the gods of war don't like poets," Snow whispered. "Helena—those sonnets—" His head fell back. The German doctor felt his pulse and pulled a sheet over his head.

"What did he say?" the German captain asked.

"I have no idea—something about the sun—maybe he wanted to see the sun again."

"Perhaps. He was a brave man."

"I was privileged to have him under my command."

The German led Tenley back to the cell again.

"How's the navigator?" the gunner asked.

"He's dead."

"Oh Jesus. Tough luck. We lost the plane and half the crew. Well, he went out like a man. Did he have anything to say?"

"No. Nothing that made sense. I think he was delirious."

"God rest his soul."

"God rest his soul."

Of the six aircraft which attacked the cruiser, three returned. They flew back to Wick and landed there, one of them so badly damaged that it was declared fit only for scrap. The crews were debriefed and sent to bed.

Helena called the intelligence officer the next morning. "When are the aircraft coming back?"

"Today, probably."

"When will Wing Commander Tenley be coming?"

"I'm sorry, but Wing Commander Tenley did not return. His aircraft was shot down in the attack on the cruiser."

143

"Oh God, no!"

"I'm sorry, Lady Helena."

"How about his navigator? How about Henry Snow?"

"He went down with Wing Commander Tenley. We don't know if he was rescued or not. The other crews have nothing to report as to what happened to the crew."

"Oh God!" The telephone dropped from her fingers. She walked about in a daze for the rest of the day. Out of habit, she appeared in the equipment section the day after, sitting at her desk automatically signing vouchers.

Two days later the intelligence officer called her. "We have some good news for you, Lady Helena. Wing Commander Tenley is a prisoner of war."

"What about Snow?"

"Unfortunately he died of his wounds."

"Died of his wounds?" She hung up the telephone and burst into tears.

The next day she found a voucher before her which was only half-completed. She called in Moragh.

"Sergeant MacLennan," she said when the woman entered her office, "can you see to this voucher?"

"Yes ma'am," Moragh answered. Helena looked up at her. "You've been crying? What's the matter?"

"Oh nothing, ma'am. Just something personal."

"What is it? Is there anything I can do to help?"

"There's nothing anyone can do. It's one of the men who didn't come back."

Helena nodded. Tears came to her eyes. "I know what you mean."

"I know things have to go on—there's a war on—that we have to expect these things. But I was in love with him."

"Yes—I know how much it hurts."

"Aye. He used to take me to the cinema and to dances. We had a wonderful time together." Moragh broke into heart-broken weeping. "You know, he never touched me—never even tried to. He treated me as if I was a duchess. Once I asked him why he was so shy, and he told me to wait until he finished his operations. And now he's dead!"

144

"The same thing happened to me, Moragh." She walked over to her and put her arms around her, and the two women cried together, their tears mingling. Moragh looked at Helena. "You lost someone on operations too?"

"Yes. Somebody I was in love with. We were to have been married."

"Och, you poor soul!" Moragh clutched Helena again, and again their tears flowed.

The flight sergeant entered the office, a sheaf of papers in his hand, and then left discreetly. "This bloody war!" he said. He put the papers down on his own desk. "We won't get much work out of those two today," he told a corporal. "Better make a pot of tea. They'll need it."

The corporal plugged in an electric kettle. "Moragh is all broke up about Flying Officer Snow."

"I never knew him."

"He was Flying Officer Douglas' navigator."

"Well, she better look for another laddie now." The flight sergeant made the tea personally, and few minutes later knocked on Helena's door. "Some tea, ma'am?" he took in the tray and turned to leave. Helena called him back. "Have a cup with us, Flight." She rose and poured it for him.

"I'm terribly sorry," he said. "I had a friend—slept next to me when I was a corporal—who romustered to air gunner—shot down over Essen. It shakes you." He looked at Moragh. "That last flight?"

She nodded.

"Please accept my sympathy," he said formally. He finished his tea, and left the office, closing the door quietly behind him. Moragh followed him a few moments later and went off to her quarters. Helena left a few minutes after that and drove aimlessly down the country lanes in her car.

The group captain station commander called in Douglas two days later, to say good-bye to him before he left for Canada. After a few conventional remarks he said, "Anything you want to say, Douglas?"

"Yes. I hope you're satisfied. You killed my navigator." Douglas spoke in measured, vicious tones.

"What do you mean, saying a thing like that?" The station commander got to his feet.

145

"I mean you threw away my navigator on a hopeless bloody effort you knew was doomed to failure. Tenley had no goddam chance at all. He was just a sprog—never been on a decent operation! He just went bull-headed at that bloody cruiser and got my navigator killed! My navigator!"

"You forget yourself, Douglas!"

"Forget myself hell! I was never more collected in my life. You had no bloody right to let Tenley take my navigator and get him killed! Jesus, he was screened! He was on his way back to Canada! He'd done his share—thirty-three trips with me! We already pranged one bloody cruiser, and you had to send him against another—with a sprog pilot, even if he was a wingco—and get him killed! Honest to Jesus! We were like bloody brothers! You might as well have murdered him!"

"Murdered? Douglas, this is intolerable!"

"It was a bloody sight more intolerable for Snow! He got killed! You're still alive. All right, goddam it, you know how I feel."

The station adjutant had entered the office. "Flying Officer Douglas—you're under—"

"No-no!" the group captain interrupted. "Let him go. He's not rational." Douglas threw the group captain a formal salute, turned militarily on his heel, and left the office. The group captain turned to the adjutant after Douglas had left. "Have you got a recommendation for a decoration for Douglas?"

"Yes sir. For a DSO."

"Bring it to me."

The group captain took the sheets of paper, ripped them up, and threw them in the waste basket.

CHAPTER SIXTEEN

A week later Douglas was boarding a cargo-liner at Liverpool. Because of its eighteen-knot speed, it proceeded independently without benefit of attendant destroyers or inclusion in a convoy. As he went out on deck the morning after his night departure, to see the green hills of Ireland slipping past, he looked around him with a professional eye. There were low clouds off to starboard, with patches of rain here and there—perfect for a torpedo attack. The ship heeled as its bow swung around fifteen degrees onto the next leg of its anti-submarine zigzag. "That's right—jink!" The ship would be a perfect target for one of Douglas' German opposite numbers, and he felt a shiver down his back. A German aircraft would have to cross England to get at him, and attack was highly unlikely, but he would not be comfortable until the ship was out in the open Atlantic, out of range of Heinkels and Junkers 88's.

An officer saw him walking about the deck and invited him to visit the bridge. Ships travelling east were crowded to the gunwales. Those going the other way carried only a few passengers, since most of those who crossed the ocean to Britain would stay there until the war ended, go further east, or stay there forever. There were only a dozen passengers, half of them time-expired aircrew like Douglas. The ship's officers were glad of their company as well as their assistance as lookouts.

Douglas revelled in the food, traditionally good in merchant ships, which stocked their refrigerators in North or South American ports untouched by wartime rationing. When the second day dawned and the ship was beyond the radius of action of questing German torpedo bombers, Douglas relaxed.

They were still menaced by submarines, but Douglas was unfamiliar with their tactics, could not assess whether the ship's progress was making it vulnerable or not, and stopped worrying.

One of the navigators aboard the ship taught him how to use a marine sextant, and Douglas thought wryly that Snow would have been jealous. The navigator, Douglas was interested to learn, used the Air Force method of intercepts to solve celestial sights, rather than the complicated logarithmic method used by the captain. Douglas kept his own counsel on the subject. "I'm only a pilot," he told them. "I always leave that to the navigator."

"Was your navigator a Canadian too?"

"Yes. He was killed."

"Sorry." The subject was not brought up again.

The ship docked at Halifax, where the full-throated wailing bawling scream of a locomotive whistle told Douglas, after the piping whistles of the English engines, that he was home again. A Railway Transport Officer gave Douglas a handful of meal tickets and loaded him aboard the *Atlantic Limited* for Montreal. He changed trains at Montreal and settled down for the three-day journey to Saskatchewan. The train was crowded, mostly with servicemen going back and forth from leave or to duty. Douglas, as an officer, had a lower berth, but he found when it was made up into a seat for the day that it was uncomfortable, and he took to spending his time in the day coach, where the seats were more pleasant. He met a girl there, but the train reached Valenby before he had time to do anything but make her acquaintance. He felt cheated.

When he got off the train he forgot her. His mother, his father, his sister and his brother, and what seemed half the town of Valenby were waiting for him. His mother's welcome was tearful, his father's more restrained but just as joyful. They took him home, where his mother had an elaborate meal waiting for him. They kept him up half the night, plying him with questions. When finally he went to bed his mother, and then his father, came up to tuck him in, as they had done when he was a child. He laughed, but enjoyed their fussing over him.

The next day they showed him off to their friends. They took him to church with them, where the Anglican priest took time to bless him formally as he knelt at the communion rail. His brother insisted that he visit his high-school class, in the same classroom where he had himself spent so many days, and his sister was careful to walk down the street arm-in-arm with him.

148

The local weekly newspaper interviewed him, and the Air Cadet squadron invited him to be the guest speaker at a banquet. The cadets overwhelmed him with questions, looking at him with youthful star-struck eyes. Douglas, only five years older than some of them, felt ancient and exalted and a bit of a fraud.

One of them asked him about his crew. and for a moment he felt a pall as he told them of Snow and Kitto. A moment later, however, he saw the young eyes light up with the certainty that no matter who else would fall to the grim mathematics of war they never would.

His father took him to the local branch of the Canadian Legion, an austere hall used also for dances and for meetings of the Loyal Order of Moose. It was decorated with pictures of the Royal Family, group photographs of regiments which had gone overseas in the Great War and in this one, an elk head at one end and moose head at the other, and recruiting posters for the army, the navy and the air force. The place was half full, mostly with men of the elder Douglas' generation, who had formed part of Sir Arthur Currie's "incomparable infantry" of an earlier war. His father showed him off, asking him leading questions, and the men listened attentively for a while until they were caught up in their own reminiscences of Festhubert and Passchendaele, and Douglas sat back and listened.

His own battles, dangerous though they were, were brief. These ageing men had spent weeks and months in muddy squalor, wet and dirty, always tired and hungry, watching their comrades being blown apart. They had had to live cheek-by-jowl with corpses, unable to take off even their accoutrements while they slept in the corner of a trench. A few minutes after an aircraft had been shot down the sea was clean again, and himself back on his way to clean sheets and the Officers' Mess.

His father introduced him to his friends, proudly but with a touch of deference. Douglas knew them already; they had been the adults he had seen in a different world when he had been a boy, talking man-talk to his father about concerns of which he had no interest and no knowledge. Douglas remembered some of them as those whom he had condemned as professional veterans, and felt a twinge of remorse, now that he knew what they had gone through.

"You remember my son, Edward?" the elder Douglas said to a thickset man whom Douglas remembered as a railway fireman, walking home in blue denim overalls and a jumper, with a lunch-bucket in his hand.

"Couldn't forget him, the way you talk about him," the man said, looking Douglas' uniform up and down. "He's got a prettier uniform than we had, back in the North Saskatchewans, eh?"

"Of course—he's an officer, Don. I never made it past sergeant."

"Glad to be back, Ed?"

"You can say that again."

"Your dad says you were on torpedo bombers. What kind of airplanes are they?"

"Beauforts, twin-engine planes with a four-man crew. "

"Your dad told us about them. Did the rest of your crew come home with you?"

No. Only the navigator was a Canadian, anyway. He was from B.C. A guy called Snow."

"He come home too?"

"No. He went on one more trip after he was supposed to be finished and was killed."

The engine man clucked his tongue. "Ain't that a bitch!" He shook his head. "The other two members of your crew—were they English?"

"One was Australian. He was bashed up in a crash-landing and invalided back to Australia. The other was a Welshman. He broke a leg when he had to bail lout. The men who replaced them were a New Zealander and a man from Yorkshire. They stayed in England when I left."

The engine man raised his eyebrows. "Holy smoke! You had bad luck with your crews! What do you think you'll think you'll be doing when you finish your leave?"

"I'll be an instructor at an Operational Training Unit, teaching other guys how to fly torpedo bombers."

"That'll be a change. Will any of your pals be instructing with you—ones that you served with on the squadron, or went through training with?"

"I don't think so. We were the only crew to be screened from the squadron—taken off flying as time-expired. And all the crews I went through torpedo-bombing training were lost."

150

"Good God! It's as bad as Passchendaele!"

"Clean sheets every night, though," said Douglas.

"Yes. We didn't have that. But you seem to be in a pretty rough game."

"It's not all that bad," said Douglas. "I'm still around." He looked at his father, whose face was suddenly grave, and laughed deliberately. "That's the way the ball bounces."

"Was your navigator a particular chum of yours?" his father asked.

"Not particularly. We liked each other well enough and he was a good navigator—but he was kind of a funny guy—always with his nose in a book—used to look at old cathedrals and things. Funny thing, you know—there was a girl—a woman officer—the daughter of a duke. She was crazy about him. Just about went bonkers when he went missing."

The engine man nodded sympathetically. "Too bad." He changed the subject. "I guess you saw a lot of England."

"Edward visited Scotland too. He told us about it in his letters," the elder Douglas said.

"Yes. Went to visit my relatives. Had a real good time in Glasgow."

"Yeah. The Scotch lassies are really something, aren't they?"

"Sure are," Douglas agreed enthusiastically, thinking of Margaret. "Come on. Let me get you another beer." The engine man brought him a bottle and Douglas settled back, drinking it slowly. He knew his mother disapproved of him drinking at all, and he had to go home sober.

As they walked home his father said "You won't have to go back on operations, will you, son?"

"No. Not for a while, anyway. They need instructors at the training school. Somebody has to do it."

"It might as well be you, son. You've done your share."

His mother had an elaborate meal waiting for them when he and his father came home. She also had a gathering of friends, all of whom professed great interest in his exploits, but soon wandered off into discussions of their own affairs. Douglas soon realised that they had no concept whatever of what he had been doing or what was happening in England. He sat back and listened to them talk of the homely affairs that had loomed so large in his life before he had

151

gone off to war. He would have been happier with a beer in his hand, but his mother saw no reason to relax any of her rules, and he was not about to rebel. She was his mother and he knew she was quite aware of the danger he was in. He was grateful that the structured world he had known as a child still existed.

The next day Douglas visited the drugstore where once he had clerked, and shook hands with the proprietor, who greeted him warmly but with a certain reserve. They had parted with coolness, which both of them professed not to remember. "Ed! It's good to see you again! I heard you were in town! You've been away quite a while."

"A couple of years."

"That's a long time. Where were you?"

"Overseas—England. I've been flying Beaufort aircraft on torpedo operations."

"Oh yes—you're a flier, aren't you?" Douglas saw that his reference to Beauforts and torpedo planes had gone unnoticed.

A girl appeared from the back of the store. Douglas had known her during his high-school days.

"Ed Douglas! I heard you'd come back."

"Yes, I'm back." He took her hand. She looked at him, and sensed he had forgotten her name. "I'm Elaine Mann," she told him. He nodded.

"My boy friend is in the army too—Joe Harleson—you know him." She looked at his sleeve, with the thin flying officer's stripe on it, and a pleased smile came to her lips. "I guess he's doing better than you are. He's a corporal."

"Yes, I guess he is. I'm glad to hear it."

They were interrupted by a woman who entered the store, Douglas recognised her as the mother of a boy who bad won his wings a few months after he had, as he had learned from a copy of the local newspaper that his mother had sent him.

"Hello, Mrs. Lockwood!" he greeted her.

The woman looked at him with eyes that were suddenly filled with pain. "Oh, hello Jim. You're Jim Hendry, aren't you?"

"No—I'm Ed Douglas."

"Yes, of course. Ed Douglas. You're in the army, aren't you?"

"No. The Air Force."

152

"Of course—the Air Force."

"How's Gordon getting along?"

"Gordon was killed. His plane crashed."

"Oh, I'm sorry to hear that."

She nodded. "I'm glad you're getting on so well. Gordon would have been glad too."

"Thank you."

"God bless you, Jim," Mrs. Lockwood said. "Your parents must be proud of you." She turned to the clerk. "I'd like a bottle of aspirin, please," she said, and did not look at Douglas again. Embarrassed, he edged away and slipped out the door.

After a few days Valenby began to bore Douglas. None of his friends were still around, except one or two to whom his military finery was a reproach, and the village's facilities for entertainment were strictly limited. There were a few unattached females, but he knew them and their parents, and by the code his mother enforced so thoroughly they were out of bounds.

"Think I'll go to Saskatoon for a few days," he told his parents. "A couple of the guys I went through Service Flying School with are instructing at the SFTS there."

"Oh, do you have to?" his mother said. "We've seen so little of you these last few years."

"I know, but I do want to see my friends. I won't be gone very long."

"If you want to go, go," she said, holding his hand a shade too long, and looking disappointed.

His father understood better. "Go on to Saskatoon and enjoy yourself. You're only young once."

He caught the train in the morning for the three-hour ride to Saskatoon. The car was crammed with riders, including a dozen student pilots on their way from an Elementary Flying Training School where they had learned to fly Tiger Moth primary trainers to the Service Flying Training School where they would progress to twin-engine Ansons. Douglas settled himself into a seat and opened a book he had brought. After a few minutes, however, one of the students, the white flash in his cap advertising to the world his aircrew status, came lurching down the aisle, friendly as a puppy.

153

He staggered as the train leaned into a curve and put his hand on Douglas' shoulder to steady himself. "Oh excuse me sir!" he said, abashed, as Douglas looked up at him.

"Okay kid, no harm done." Douglas returned to his book. The nineteen-year-old boy stood without moving on, and then cleared his throat to say, "You on your way overseas, sir?" as he motioned to the badges spelling out the word *Canada* on Douglas' shoulders. Only men warned for overseas duty or returned from overseas were allowed to wear them.

"Been over. Back on leave."

The boy looked at him with eyes that were suddenly awe-struck. "What were you doing over there?"

"Flying Beaufort torpedo bombers."

"Torpedo bombers!" The boy's voice was hushed and awed. "Beauforts!"

Another student pilot, about the same age, overheard their conversation and wheeled around. "Were you flying Beauforts, sir?" Douglas nodded.

"You were on operations?" the first boy asked.

"Yes."

"Did you torpedo any ships?"

"One or two. Put a fish into a cruiser once."

The two young men stood silent, overwhelmed. Finally one of them motioned to the rest of the group. They clustered about him, one of them slid into the seat opposite him, while the others stood in the aisle, paying court. One of them spoke eagerly. "Were you overseas long?"

"A little more than a year and a half."

"A whole year and a half!" The eyes were upon him wide and respectful. "You finished your tour, did you?"

He nodded. "That's right. They sent me back for a spot of leave after it was over."

"What's it like to fly with a navigator and gunners?"

"You get used to it. It takes lot of the load off you."

"Did your navigator come back with you?"

"No! He was killed."

A sudden pall fell on the conversation.

"How about the gunners?"

154

"One of them was hurt in a crash-landing and sent back to Australia. Another had to bale out when our plane was shot up and broke his leg."

"Well, uh, sir, were you flying the aircraft when your crewmen were killed and wounded?"

"I was flying the kite when the wop was hurt in a crash landing. We got shot up in the attack on the *Scharnhorst* and the *Gneisenau*, and I told the rest of the crew to bale out. The wop's parachute had opened in the kite, though—a piece of flak went through it—and I had to land it. The controls were unserviceable and I had to steer the kite by differential use of the engines. It didn't work too well. I ran off the runway and the kite broke in two. The wireless operator was pretty badly injured."

"Jeez!" one of them said reverently. "You've really seen some action, haven't you?"

"I got back. It couldn't have been too bad," Douglas said.

"How about your navigator?"

"My navigator was killed after we got screened—taken off ops, you know—because the squadron OC borrowed him for an attack on the cruiser Prinz Eugen and got shot down. He was already posted back to Canada—he'd be here now if he hadn't gone on that last flight—it really was his last flight. It really pissed me off—I went in and raised hell with the station commander about it."

"You mean you bawled out the station commander?"

"Yeah. Maybe that's why they sent me home to cool off. It sure didn't get me a promotion."

The group sat goggle-eyed, hanging on every word. Here was a man who had flown and fought, who had seen men killed around him, had torpedoed a cruiser and had—his greatest feat of all—talked back to a Station Commander.

"What was he—a wingco?"

"A groupie."

"Jeezez—a group captain!" It was like reproving God. One of the men brought Douglas a waxed paper cup of water and splashed rye whiskey into it. Douglas accepted it regally and began to describe an operational flight. The students sat round him, entranced, disciples at the feet of a master, daring to interrupt him only when he hesitated for a moment.

155

Douglas leaned back, sipped at his paper cup, and described the attack on the *Scharnhorst,* complete with the ritual, hallowed through thirty years of hangar flying, of hands manoeuvring to simulate aircraft.

The students hung on every word. Douglas enjoyed himself hugely, even as he told these neophytes quite truthfully of the deadly dangers they would face when they graduated to operational flying themselves. None of them believed that they would fall victim to enemy fire; they were all immortal, the flat Saskatchewan scenery outside proving to them that no such risks could possibly exist. They were young and skilful and they would never die. Douglas had survived, and so could they. His navigator had been killed, but he was only a navigator, and expendable. Anyway, combat was in the dim future; they still had to gain their wings, those magic badges that shone so brightly upon the chests of men like Douglas.

The train raced through the prairie while Douglas held forth. At last they entered the station in Saskatoon. The student pilots ceremoniously shook hands and parted, to report to an officious flight sergeant who was waiting for them on the station platform. Douglas walked across the street to the Bessborough Hotel, and checked in.

CHAPTER SEVENTEEN

Douglas bought a case of beer, which he placed in his room, and a small bottle of whiskey—a "mickey"—which he slid into his jacket pocket. His plan of action was simple; he would go to a night spot, look for an unattached girl, and then let nature take its course.

He started his search at the Moose Hall, which doubled as a dance hall, where Johnny's Woodbutchers held forth from the bandstand. He prowled around the line of girls standing on the sidelines until he found one was reasonably good-looking, although a little hard. She stuck her gum underneath a table when he asked her to dance and stepped off with him. He found his steps, learned in England to a different drummer, did not meld too well with hers. Her conversation was banal, and she smelled. He escorted her back to where he had found her and prowled further.

His next attempt was more fortunate. She was a rather plump girl who was impressed by his uniform, and even knew that he was an officer. "Are you an instructor at the school?" she asked.

"No—I'm on leave. I just came back from overseas."

"Oh," she nodded. He did not elaborate. Such details as Beauforts and torpedo bombers would mean nothing to her. He found her steps matching his better as the dance progressed, and for a few minutes he concentrated on his dancing. She smiled at him as she felt their feet fitting better.

"Do you think you'll be an instructor after your leave is over?"

"Maybe," he answered, "but probably not here. They'll send me back to England."

"Being an instructor here is real important," she said. "The fellows I've met from the school say it's the most important job in the air force."

"Yeah," he said, a a little miffed. "I guess it is."

"You've never been an instructor, then?"

"No."

"That's too bad."

The music stopped, and Douglas led her to one of the tables ranged in one corner of the hall. "How about something to drink?"

"That'd be nice," she answered. "I'd like a Coke."

"Coming right up." He made his way to the refreshment bar which sold only soft drinks, anything else being illegal. He carried two glasses of Coca-Cola back to the table, and laced both of them liberally with whiskey. She puckered her mouth as she tasted the drink. "Don't tell me you like this stuff!"

"You get used to it."

"That's what I'm afraid of," she replied, but she finished the drink. He invited her to dance again, and then brought her another coke, which he laced with more whiskey. She did not make such a face this time. They talked as they drank. He found she was a cashier in a restaurant, and that she was distressingly familiar with the ploys of airmen on the make. He was about to leave in search of greener pastures when a young man sat down at the table with him.

"Hello sir," the man said. Douglas looked up to see the fresh face of the Leading Aircraftsman, with the white aircrew-in-training flash in the hat stuck in a pocket, that he had met on the train. The boy turned to the girl he was with, a pretty blonde. "This is the officer I was telling you about," he said. "He's been overseas—flying torpedo bombers."

"Oh—are you?" the girl said, looking at Douglas. "Bill here has been telling me you're quite a hero."

"Oh, I wouldn't say that—"

The boy smiled. "You don't have to, sir. I know how important Coastal Command is, and what attacking enemy shipping means."

Douglas smiled embarrassed. "Well, it is interesting sometimes."

"You sank a cruiser, didn't you sir?"

"No—I didn't sink it. I managed to torpedo the German cruiser *Gladbach*, but they got it back into drydock. Took them six months to fix it up, though."

"It's a privilege to talk to an operational pilot like you, sir," the boy said.

The music started again. Douglas rose and asked his companion to dance. This time she was much more impressed, even going so far as to show him off a little. There were two other girls in the hall she knew, and she steered Douglas toward them and introduced him.

The boy leaned toward him when they were at their table again. "Tell me sir—what does it feel like to torpedo a ship?"

"It's just a job you're trained to do—you do for real what you've been doing in practice. Once you're committed to the run-in you have to keep going. Of course having the Jerries shooting at you introduces a little difficulty." He went on to describe an attack on a North Sea convoy, becoming animated and enthusiastic as he spoke. His audience, now grown to six, with another student joining them, listened intently, hanging on every word. Douglas revelled in being the center of attention, and was sorry when the Home Waltz was played and the dancers left the hall.

"How about something to eat?" he asked the girl. She nodded, and they sought out a restaurant where he ordered steaks, a half-forgotten luxury in Britain. She seemed impressed by his open-handedness. When the meal was over he said, "Care to have a nightcap? I'd like to invite you to a secluded bar, but the law of the land says I must ask you to accompany me to my room."

"Oh, very well," she said, and rose to follow him. When they reached the hotel she said, "We'd better go up by different elevators."

He poured her a drink from the remains of his bottle of whiskey, and opened a beer for himself. They clinked their hotel glasses, and Douglas put his arm around her and kissed her gently. She returned the kiss, and he put down his glass and moved his hand to cup her breast. "Done that before, haven't you, big boy?" she said. His mind slid back to Margaret Reilly, and he kissed her again with remembered passion. She sprawled back on the bed, and he began to remove her clothes. He fumbled with a condom and returned to her. Their bodies joined.

When they rolled apart he poured another drink for her and opened another beer. "That was good," she said. "As a real live hero, you're pretty good." She vanished into the bathroom, and he followed her example when she left it. When he emerged she was dressed. "Time for me to go home," she told him.

159

"I'll call a taxi." He dressed and accompanied her to the hotel lobby. When she had climbed into the taxi he paid the driver, and then suddenly he checked his wallet again. It was curiously light, and he found that thirty dollars were unaccounted for. He was suddenly blazingly angry, and then he laughed. He mentally translated the amount into English money. Seven or eight pounds—not too much for an evening's entertainment.

"Hope I didn't get a dose," he muttered, and then went back to his room and went to sleep.

The following evening he bought another bottle of whiskey and another case of beer, and sought out another dance hall and another girl. He was seated with his new companion when a young officer, also with a girl, walked up to the table.

"May I join you?" the man asked, motioning to the full tables near him,

"Join the crowd," Douglas replied. "The more the merrier." The man looked at Douglas' shoulders. "On your way overseas?"

"Been overseas. Back on leave."

His eyes widened. "You've been overseas? What were you doing?"

"Torpedo bombers. Beauforts."

"Beauforts? Torpedo bombers!" the man's voice became suddenly hushed. "You were on operations?"

"Yeah. Did a tour."

The man stood up and put out his hand. "I'm Len Cathcart—an instructor at the SFTS. It's sure good to meet you—somebody who's been overseas on operations."

"My pleasure." Douglas introduced the girl with him, whom he knew only as Cathy, to Cathcart and his date, a pretty, self-possessed young woman who was obviously a local glamour girl. Douglas tossed off a few remarks, carefully offhand, to underline his combat service, and to enjoy the frank admiration of Cathcart and his companion.

Two more officers joined them at the table. Cathcart introduced them as fellow instructors. One of them was a burly, fleshy flight lieutenant whom Cathcart referred to a flight commander at the SFTS.

"You've got a good job," Douglas said to him. "Hang on to it."

The man's face stiffened. "Yes. I am proud of what I have the privilege of doing for the war effort."

160

"You say you've been flying Beaufort torpedo bombers," Cathcart said. "I hear they're first-class aircraft, the best for their job in the world."

"You heard wrong," Douglas answered. "They're mankilling bastards, underpowered—won't hold height on one engine, and if you lose an engine you're in the drink. Too slow. Unmaneuverable. If a Jerry fighter takes after you you've had it."

Cathcart looked shocked. "We were told they're one of the best aircraft in service!"

"Underpowered, underarmed, no guts, too slow."

"Well," said the burly flight lieutenant, "what aircraft would you recommend if you don't like the best aircraft the Royal Air Force has?"

"The Ju88."

"The Ju88? That's a German aircraft!"

"Yes. Too bad the Luftwaffe gives their crews good aircraft. Not like the bloody RAF."

"But the RAF has Blenheims too! The fastest medium bomber in service! Why, we're making them in Canada!"

"Blenheims!" Douglas snorted. "They're worse'n Beauforts. Duck soup for Jerry fighters. Christ, one Blenheim squadron at a field I was on sent out twelve aircraft and got three back, in one sortie."

"But you survived!"

"You know how many pilots lasted for a year on my squadron? Five. One was picked up at sea from a dinghy, half dead from exposure. One bailed out and broke his leg. One was in a crew that was shot down and every man wounded. My own navigator was killed. Both my wireless air gunners were wounded. Everybody who was on the same OTU course with me is dead."

"Good God!" Cathcart cried, appalled. "I had no idea things were that bad!"

"They're bad enough. Well, let's forget about it. Have a drink!"

The burly flight lieutenant put down his drink. "What you're saying is absolutely disloyal! I don't believe it for a minute!"

Douglas looked at him. His face was beginning to grow a little fuzzy from the whiskey Douglas had been drinking. "What in hell do you know about it? The closest you've ever come to the sound of the guns is an Errol Flynn movie! Get some time in on operations and maybe somebody will listen to you."

161

The flight lieutenant stood up. "Look, flying officer, you're not allowed to talk to a superior officer like that! Watch your tongue!"

"Watch my tongue! Hell, I'm the only combat airman here! I should watch my tongue! When you get overseas you'll have the right to talk—and not until then!"

"So I'm a coward, am I? I volunteered to go overseas when I joined up. I won't take that from anybody!"

"Well, goddam it, get some time overseas under your belt and you won't have to. I know how bloody brave you'd be running in on a cruiser!" The big man caught the back of Douglas' head in one ham-like hand and smashed the other fist into his face. Douglas found himself on the floor, blood pouring from his mouth. Two men grabbed the burly flight lieutenant by the arms and pulled him away while another two helped Douglas up and took him to a washroom. He shook off his would-be helpers angrily and cleaned himself up as well as he could before staggering out of the washroom, holding a paper towel to his face and making his unsteady way to the door of the hall. Cathy was standing uncertainly near the table. He avoided her eyes, slipped out the door, and walked back to the hotel.

In his room he drank two bottles of beer, cursing at the bellicose flight lieutenant, his own incapacity in a fist fight, Saskatoon, the Royal Canadian Air Force pilots who had never been overseas, and his evil luck.

At last he drifted off to sleep, to wake in the middle of the night with a terrific headache, a nauseated stomach, a face that burnt like fire, and an eye he could scarcely see with. He lay miserably in bed until half through the morning, when he felt well enough to be hungry. Suddenly he remembered that the hotel provided room service. He ate breakfast in his room. After lunch he crept down to the lobby, bought a newspaper and a couple of magazines, and took refuge again his room.

He remained holed up for two days before he felt able to face the world again. He put on the shirt and sweater he had rescued from a closet in Valenby, and wandered about the city taking in the modest prairie sights that he scarcely remembered from infrequent visits he had made as a child to Saskatoon. There was not much to see, and the weather was unpleasant. He cursed the flight lieutenant again as he felt the golden days of his leave, when he should be receiving the plaudits of the neophytes as he had on the train, going to waste.

162

He returned to Valenby, sitting in the corner of the railway coach trying to hide his discoloured eye. His mother clucked over him, and his father nodded sagely. "Boys will be boy," he said, taking him again to the Legion. By the end of the week his appearance was normal again, and he returned to wearing his uniform. It was unfortunate that the RCAF had not advanced to the point of awarding medals for combat service, and the only mark of his dangerous past was his Canada badges. He wished he could have been awarded the DFC he had been promised.

His leave came to an end, a few days after the arrival of a telegram telling him to report to the Embarkation Depot at Halifax. He had a boisterous leave-taking at the Legion, and a tearful one with his mother. She handed him a big brown bag of sandwiches as he left, which he gave to a boy in the day coach after the train started, and ate in the dining car himself, on Lake Winnipeg goldeye. The dining cars specialised in goldeye, and Douglas loved it.

CHAPTER EIGHTEEN

Douglas returned to Britain aboard the vessel *Louis Pasteur*, travelling in rather more state than he had during his first voyage overseas. As a combat veteran he basked in the admiration of his fellows who had yet to experience their baptism of fire. He was still exposed to the irritations of troopship life, such as being fed only two meals a day, but the ship's officers allowed him on the bridge where did lookout duty. The trip was uneventful, as it usually was aboard a "monster" liner shuttling back and forth across the Atlantic carrying troops. They could outrun submarines, who concentrated on plodding convoys anyway. As they neared Britain Douglas kept an eye open for hostile aircraft, but they were not molested, and except for a friendly Sunderland flying boat and a lumbering Catalina which flew slowly past them the sky was clean of all save clouds. The ship docked at Liverpool at night, and Douglas travelled to London by train the next morning.

He reported to Canadian Overseas Headquarters in London, where he found a gaggle of sergeants and squadron leaders scurrying about carrying bundles of papers. As operational aircrew always feel when they visit headquarters which are inhabited by bureaucrats who control their lives without understanding them, he was intimidated by their proximity to the seats of the mighty even as he felt a casual contempt for clerkly pursuits far from the sound of the guns. The personnel officer who interviewed Douglas was indeed grand, although he was polite enough.

He informed Douglas that he was to go to a Flying Instructor's school for a course to teach others to fly, after which he would report to a Torpedo Bomber Operational Training Unit for duty. "Your course will be short," he told Douglas. "The OTU is having trouble getting enough qualified personnel, particularly time-expired

164

aircrew like yourself. The squadrons seem to want to hold on to them."

"I can see why. If you'd checked you'd find most of them being held in Davey Jones' locker."

The man nodded his head. "Yes—it is dangerous. At any rate, they'll be glad to have you. Sergeant Henderson will give you your travel warrants."

He had the rest of the day to himself before his train left. He telephoned Charlotte, thinking she would have got over her unrequited passion for Westover, and was somewhat chagrined when she told him she was busy. He went to a movie instead.

At Flying Instructor School he learned how to keep up a constant stream of comment to calm and encourage students, and was amazed at the number of things he had forgotten or never learned during his own training. It was a chastening experience, which reduced him from his initial stage of tour-expired cockiness to embarrassed hope that his instructors would not find out little he knew. His three-week tour was hardly long enough to give him back his self-confidence, and he was highly apprehensive when he reported to the Operational Training Unit. He reported to the Chief Flying Instructor, who started him off by sending him to teach student pilots how to fly Beauforts.

He then spent his time giving lectures on airmanship and on the fuel system of the Beaufort when he was on the ground, and in checking out pilots when he was flying. The students gave him the exaggerated respect which they felt a combat veteran deserved. Behind his back he often heard the words, "He's the man who torpedoed the *Gladbach*." Between classes, and in the officers' mess, they would gather round him to hear tales of his experiences, looking on him as an examplar or as a talisman: if he had survived so could they. Douglas saw their fresh young faces, looking up at him for the received wisdom, and was flattered even as he knew himself inadequate, owing his survival far more to luck than to good management. He looked at them, knowing how little chance they had of survival and was appalled, and fought to keep his concern for them out of his voice.

He found himself caught up in the minor administration of the OTU—scheduling exercises, completing assessment forms, administering examinations, and rating student pilots. It was interesting at first, but it became boring routine. Douglas found himself missing the frenetic excitement of squadron life, the pumping of adrenaline in his blood, the rush to the aircraft to take off for an attack, the search for the quarry, the exhilarating, terrifying torpedo runs. Sometimes at night the knowledge of the danger he had lived through took him by the throat, to leave him shivering and clutching at his bed-sheets, and when he woke up, sweat-soaked, he was glad that he was safe in his instructional job, but this was rare. Faced with another stint of coaching a pilot through "unusual positions" he wished himself back in the easy, carefree, dangerous life on a squadron, with its leisure when he was not flying. "I'm not made for an eight-to-five job, " he told himself.

Teaching other pilots to fly the Beaufort was simple and straightforward as long as both engines were running. When one stopped in mid-air, however, matters became instantly desperate. The plane would immediately begin to lose altitude. With new, well-kept aircraft held on the ground for days between operations with the mechanics tuning them, it was bad enough; with the elderly, clapped-out Beauforts the OTU kept in the air, with minimum maintenance, an aircraft with only one propeller dropped like a stone. Douglas had it happen to him once, when he was flying with a student pilot named Howard on a check flight, after which the man would be on his own.

When he heard the engine sputter and quit, his first impulse was to grab the controls, but when he saw they had a thousand feet of altitude and were only a mile from the airport, he simply said, "You have control. Let's see you do a single-engine landing." He tightened his safety belt and said nothing more. Howard made a good landing, and was loud in his praise of Douglas, as a cool and capable instructor. When Douglas said, "You could make a better single-engine landing than I could," nobody believed him, although Douglas knew it was the truth; the memory of his own single-engine landings would made his hands shake. The students intrigued to fly with him after that.

Douglas, when he first arrived at the OTU, had taken the aloof, condescending attitude toward the students that the other instructors took, calculated to show them their lowly place in the Air

Force pecking order. But soon his genuine concern for the students began to show through, and he forgot himself enough to treat the students as equals. It was not approved behaviour among the other officers, who had been trained in English public schools to keep their juniors in their places, but with Douglas' record he could get away with it. Douglas went so far as to accept rides to the nearby village on Pilot Officer Howard's motorcycle—twice. After that he found other means of transportation, since even combat flying seemed safer.

The base was a dozen miles from a market town. One of the staff instructors, a pilot called Harry Mansfield, was a native of the town, and invited him to a party at his house, to provide an extra man to balance a woman friend of the family.

She turned out to be a startlingly attractive woman, outrageously made up and dripping with jewellery, seven or eight years older than Douglas. Mansfield introduced them. "Good evening, Connie. May I introduce Ed Douglas. Ed, I'd like you to met Constance Davidson." He turned to her. "I told you I'd bring you a real live cowboy."

"Oh, I say, how frightfully thoughtful of you!" She gave Douglas a languid hand, holding a long ivory cigarette-holder in the other. "Connie's an actress—stage mostly," Mansfield told him.

Douglas licked his lips uncertainly, searching for something to say. "Can I get you a drink?" he asked at length. "Yes, please. Whiskey and a dash of soda." Douglas returned with it a few minutes later, to find her busily talking to the man beside her. "Oh thank you!" she said throatily. She spoke to her companion. "This beautiful creature here is Mr. Edwards. He's a cowboy, you know."

"Oh, I know Ed," her companion, another instructor from the OTU, said. "But if he's cowboy he's kept it pretty dark."

Douglas' sole experience of cows had been helping to muck out a stable at a farm where he had spent a summer. "Can't tell everything at once," he said.

"Tell us about your adventures riding the range," Connie demanded.

"Well, I was sitting on old Paint, my cayuse, when the herd was stampeded. There was a cliff just ahead, and I knew that they'd all fall over it and be killed if I didn't do something. They got nearer and nearer. Things were getting desperate. Then I did what I had to do."

"Yes? What was it?"

"I sang them Brahms' lullaby. That put them all to sleep."

She laughed deliciously. "I hope they made you a range boss for that!"

"No. I failed the cowboy test and was fired."

"Failed the test ? I don't believe it! What was it?"

"Rolling a cigarette with one hand while riding a bucking horse. I couldn't even roll a cigarette on the ground. The boss was good about it, though. Said he couldn't keep me but that I could kiss my horse good-bye. It was a sad moment. I was lucky old Paint was a mare. Nothing queer about me."

She laughed again. "Certainly not. We don't want any scandal, do we?"

"Seriously," Douglas said, "you've probably seen more real cowboys on the stage than I ever did on the prairie. The cattle country doesn't really start until you're in Alberta, anyway. I come from Saskatchewan. Wheat country."

"Saskatchewan? That's near the Rio Grande, isn't it? I'm sure I saw a film about it."

"Not exactly. A few thousand miles north. That's close enough for government work, though. Tell me, Connie—what's it like being an actress?"

"Divine—just divine. You meet fascinating people—and some dirty old men, and some old bores. It's all so interesting though— every part is new, and the directors keep changing, and there's always a new city. It's really corking fun!" As she continued she dropped her pose of langour and became animated and vibrant. Douglas, fascinated by her torrent of words, stood back and let her talk, encouraging her with the odd question.

During a brief lull, he referred to a comment she had made about her husband. "Your husband is a lucky man to have such a fascinating wife."

"Oh—dear Maurice? We haven't seen each other for over a year. He goes his way and I go mine."

"Too bad," Douglas muttered. "I'm surprised he lets you out of his sight." "How sweet of you to say that!" She bent forward and kissed his cheek. "But he does. He's found his consolations, I know."

"He's in show business too?"

"Of course? We always end up marrying one another—it's incestuous really."

"Incest is not exactly what I'd think of committing with you."

"So you have designs on me, then?"

"You're pretty well designed already."

"Thank you, my dear." She knitted her brows. "You haven't had much to say—not that I let you have a word in edgeways."

"I've been listening. I haven't met many people from the theatre—there aren't many living in Valenby, Saskatchewan."

"How do such people impress you?"

"You're the only one I've met ."

"Then how do I impress you?"

"You're a wonderfully interesting person. You have a good brain—you notice everything, and tell the most fascinating stories. You hold people's attention." He was silent for a moment. "You're not bad to look at, either."

She laughed. "So it's my mind that attracts you? I noticed you put my looks last. I didn't know I was such a scarecrow."

"I expected an actress to be beautiful. I didn't expect her to be smart."

She dropped a mock curtsy. "What kind of a brain did you expect me to have?"

"You'd have to have a good brain—you're in a pretty big league."

"You're absolutely priceless—I tell you that you look beautiful, and you tell me I have a good mind."

"Then you're lying and I'm not."

"But you are beautiful!"

"Thank you. And you do have a good mind. By the way, you are also a beautiful woman." He raised his glass.

"We have a meeting of the minds," she said. "And of the glasses." He clinked his glass against hers.

Another of the men asked Connie to dance. Douglas raised his glass to them, and moved off to mingle with the other guests.

Half an hour later Connie walked up to him. "I say, my dear, you certainly deceived me!"

"What, already? I only met you tonight."

169

"Yes. There I was, chattering away at you, and I didn't know you were a real live hero. Harry told me you sank a German battleship."

"Oh that? It wasn't a battleship—only a cruiser. And I didn't sink it. I put a torpedo into it, and it was laid up for a few months, but I didn't sink it."

She kissed him. "You're too delicious for words! A modest hero! I didn't think they existed any more!"

"I'm just a small-town boy, Connie."

"You're blushing! I love that, my dear boy—I haven't seen anybody blush for ten years."

Douglas gulped "I didn't know—"

She put her hand on his arm. "Don't ever change. You're the most refreshing person I've met all year."

"And you are the most unusual—not to mention the most attractive."

"Still low-key, aren't you?" she laughed. "Speaking of keys, take this one. It fits the door of my room at the Inn. I expect you to use it tonight, after the party." She tucked it into his pocket, and then moved gracefully away.

The party moved to its close, and the revellers left one by one. Douglas waited until Connie left, and then made his way to the Inn. He found the door, and the key fitted. Connie, still in evening dress, was waiting for him.

He stepped toward her, put his hands on her waist, and looked her up and down. "You have a wonderful brain," he said. He reached forward and kissed her shoulder. "You're a wonderful conversationalist." He kissed her cheek. "Splendid thinking." His lips met hers. When he lifted his lips she said, "What do you say now?"

"The power of matter over mind," he said. "I've got to get to the bottom of this intriguing investigation into just how beautiful an intelligent woman can be." He undid the zipper at the back of her dress. "That will strip some of the concealing camouflage from this important consciousness."

"I've always wanted to meet a man who was interested only in my mind," she said. "As for you—you look very well in that uniform—that silly uniform? Take it off!" He did. The next twelve minutes were wonderful.

They spent the night together. The next morning he borrowed her razor, cut himself while shaving, and made his way back to the air station late for work. He was reproved by the flight commander. The reproof rolled off his back as he stood, his face professional, solemn, and a smile in his eyes.

Connie left town that day, the play having run its allotted week, and moved on to Bristol. Douglas was disappointed but resigned. Well, Bristol was not too far away to be reached on a weekend pass. He found, however, that he did not know how to contact her. He did find the name of the theatre at which she was playing, but the doorman at the theatre made sure that his telephone calls never got through to her. After three attempts he gave it up a bad job.

CHAPTER NINETEEN

The weeks went by, with Douglas flying over the English countryside putting students through their paces, or lecturing to his awed pupils, most of whom he knew would not live another year. To the students he became a mystery man. He was the pilot who had torpedoed the *Gladbach,* but he had not been decorated or promoted. One day a student asked him? "Didn't your navigator get a DFC for torpedoing that cruiser?"

"That's right."

"And you didn't?"

"No. I didn't."

"Why not? It was you pressed the tit that dropped the torpedo, not the navigator? It doesn't seem fair!"

Douglas shrugged. "That's the way it is. You can't recommend yourself, you know."

"Where's your navigator now?"

"He's dead."

The man pursed his lips. "I guess his DFC isn't doing him much good."

"No. You know, he was flying with the squadron commander when he got it—they were shot down attacking the *Prinz Eugen.* I guess I'd sooner not have a gong but still be in one piece."

"It isn't fair at all!" the man repeated.

"The squadron commander had told me was going to recommend me for a gong, but he got shot down himself before he got around to it. That's how the ball bounces. Come on—let's have a drink."

The conversation left Douglas even more of local hero. He had been cheated out of a decoration by a quirk of fate, and did not complain about it. Douglas never mentioned the matter again, but he knew he was the subject of admiring conversation, and basked in the knowledge.

He gave Howard his final check ride and made out his report—like most RAF reports, it classed him as 'average', which meant entirely satisfactory. When he walked into the officers' mess for tea he found Howard and his navigator, Pilot Officer Reginald Crane, sitting around a table. He threw himself down into a chair and reached to pour himself a cup of tea. "Good day, sir," Howard said. "Looks like we're out of your hair—at last."

"You're all checked out now." He nodded toward Howard's navigator. "Hello, Crane. Take good care of Howard here. After all the work I've put into him somebody has to."

"The whole crew will do that, sir—you can count on us."

"You're not a bad crew. The navigation leader says you've done pretty well in your exercises, and your wireless ops aren't bad either."

"Oh, thank you sir," said Crane. "It's jolly fine of you to say so." He reflected for a moment. "I wonder where we'll be going."

"You'll find out pretty soon. They can't keep the secret from you forever."

"I dare say they will. I wonder if we'll torpedo a cruiser the way you did."

Douglas grimaced. The man's hero worship embarrassed him. He merely grunted.

"I suppose you were glad to get off operations," Howard said.

"I was at first—figured I was using up my luck. But instructing gets old—the same thing every day. I'd like something else."

"I didn't know instructing was all that bad. You get a lot of flying. You wouldn't think going back on ops was better."

"I'll have to go back on ops sooner or later, anyway, after this instructional tour is finished, Ops aren't all that bad, although I'd like a little quieter tour than the one I did."

"If you did go back on ops would you pick up your old crew again?" Crane asked.

"My navigator's dead. Lord knows where my wops are."

"Oh—hard luck." Crane fell silent, and Howard and Douglas took to discussing flying techniques.

Three days later Douglas saw the crew again. They were two days from graduation. "Don't know for sure," Howard told Douglas, "but rumours are we're going to India—actually Ceylon."

173

"Goodo," replied Douglas. "Better weather there than rainy old England." "Yes," Crane agreed. "The weather is beastly here, especially lately."

He looked at his watch. "Excuse me, Mr. Douglas. I must be off."

"That navigator of yours seems an awful kid."

"Don't let his looks fool you," Howard replied. "Besides being a good navigator, he has a will of iron when he wants to use it. He has a lot of influence too. His father has pots of money—you've heard of Crane's Potteries, haven't you?"

"Oh—that Crane!"

"Yes. His dad drove to the air station a couple of weeks back—in a Rolls-Royce. Treated the station commander like one of the help and got away with it."

"Let's hope he can use his pull in Ceylon."

Howard laughed. "Funny thing, but he never uses his influence—he's decent about it. Only time he ever showed his teeth was once when one of the boys on his navigation course was being kicked around by an instructor. The instructor heard about it in no uncertain terms, and changed his tune in a hurry."

"I guess it helps to have your old man rich."

"It's his mother too. She's as protective as a lioness, and she doesn't hesitate to go to the very top if she figures her darling is getting anything but the very best."

"Are you sure torpedo bombers are the best?"

"Crane probably told her they were."

"Yeah. That's what I told my parents."

Howard laughed. "Same here."

They parted. Douglas wished Howard and Crane well and dismissed them from his mind.

The day before Howard and his crew were scheduled to graduate from the OTU Howard rode his motorcycle to a neighbouring town to make a few minor purchases, and then spent an hour in a pub. On the way back, circling a roundabout, he lost control and skidded into a ditch, where he lay helpless for half an hour until a policeman found him. The medical officer who examined him diagnosed a compound fracture of Howard's left femur, and announced he would not be fit to fly for six months.

"Tough luck," Douglas commented to the flight commander, shaking his head. "He was one of the best pilots on the course. You know, when I first arrived in England that Jerry woman on the Calais One Radio station said, 'Another shipload of Canadian airmen has landed in England. We have nothing to fear. Half of them will kill themselves on motorcycles and the Luftwaffe will look after the other half.' She didn't know how right she was."

"His crew will have to wait for a new pilot. We've got too many headless crews hanging around already."

"It's a bind for them and us. We don't know what to do with them, and they get all the joe-jobs."

"Anybody that's slated to go back on ops could pick up a good crew there. Reg Crane is a good navigator, and the two wops are pretty good too."

"Any of you guys that wants a crew go right ahead," Douglas said. "Just now I've got no ambition to go on ops again. I want to hide in my hole for a while yet."

"Don't blame you. You'll get back on ops soon enough."

Douglas shrugged into his flying jacket and picked up his helmet. "Gotta fly with McGuigan's crew." He went off cheerfully, heading for the flight line where he knew Flight Sergeant McGuigan would be waiting for him.

Two days later the Chief Flying Instructor called Douglas into his office. Douglas made the ritual comment, "What've I done now?" and walked in, saluting casually.

The CFI looked at him and said, "I have some news for you. He handed Douglas a green copy of a signal form. Douglas ran his eye along the smudged lines. "J127480 F/O ED Douglas posted to Far Eastern Command. Subject officer will join crew formerly captained by P/O DC Howard."

"What in hell's this?" he demanded.

"You're posted overseas."

"Holy cow! I am overseas! And I'm here on my instructional tour!"

The CFI smiled sardonically. "You colonials say you're overseas— we Brits don't. Anyway, you're to take over Howard's crew and go to Ceylon."

"What! Good God, I've only been here three months! Jesus, I don't want to go back on ops so soon!"

The CFI shrugged. "I have received information that you have stated that you were bored with instructing and wanted to go back on ops."

"Christ, everybody says that! Sure, I'll go back on ops after a year or so—I know I gotta take my chances. But after only three bloody months—Good God! Hell, I could get killed!"

The CFI nodded. "To tell the truth, I wasn't too happy to see that signal either. We're short of experienced instructors, and you get on well with the students."

"Then—Jesus, why didn't you squawk?"

"Can't do a thing about it, old chap. I did squawk, as you put it, but the order came down from Air Ministry. It named you—nobody else would do."

"But why me? What's so special about me?"

"I don't know. But you are a good operational pilot with a good record."

"Yeah. That's why I'm getting such skyrocket promotion and a chestful of gongs."

The CFI looked away. "I had plans for you, Douglas, but you haven't been here long enough. I wanted you for a flight commander. It's a flight looey's job."

"I've been here long enough to get posted back on ops but not long enough for that. Big deal. Well, what now?"

"Meet your new crew. Fly with them a couple of times." The CFI stood up. "I know how you feel, Douglas, but I can't do a damn thing about it. Good luck."

"Thanks. It's been good knowing you." Douglas saluted and left.

That afternoon he met his crew. Reginald Crane hurried up to him and eagerly shook his hand. "We're most happy to have you as our captain, sir—it's positively top hole. We couldn't have done better."

Douglas nodded sourly. "Glad you think so."

"We hope we can live up to your former crew—we'll do our best." Crane stood there, a happy, welcoming smile on his young classically-handsome proconsular face.

"I'm sure you can. When you flew with Howard you were a good crew. No reason to change."

The two wireless air gunners shook Douglas' hand, "I'm Ray Hartley," the taller of the two said. He was a man of about thirty,

176

from Manchester, with a pronounced Lancashire accent. The other sergeant was broad-shouldered, stocky and well built, with curly light-brown hair and brown eyes. "Hi," he said as he shook Douglas' hand. "I'm Larry DesJardins—from Saint Boniface. Hear you're from Saskatchewan."

"We got a good prairie crew then," Douglas grinned. "You from Manitoba, me from Saskatchewan. We'll have to keep them in line."

"We got them outnumbered two to two."

"That's good enough." Douglas looked at them, "We'll fly a cross-country tomorrow. Take off at nine. Briefing at eight. Crane, go see the navigation leader and get the route. I've got to see the adjutant." He looked at Crane. "Do you write poetry?"

"No," Crane answered, surprised. "Why do you ask?"

"My old navigator did. He got killed. Just as glad you don't." He grinned sourly. "OK, guys, see you tomorrow."

Douglas walked into the adjutant's office. "Hey, why in hell was I picked to take Howard's crew? Lots of guys been at the OTU longer'n I have."

"The reason is that Crane asked for you."

"Jesus—do I have to be at the beck and call of any old pilot officer—and a navigator at that?"

"Crane's father has friends in the highest places—cabinet ministers, air marshals by the dozen. Crane told his father that you had told him you wanted to go back on ops. Did you say that?"

"Sure, but what the hell—it's what you're supposed to say—"

The adjutant shrugged. "You said it. But it's not that bad. Ceylon's not like the North Sea. Besides, you've got a good crew—Crane's a good navigator, Hartley and DesJardins are good wops. If you had to pick a crew to go east with you couldn't have done better. Anyway, Crane seems to have an attack of hero-worship about you. Thinks you're wonderful. Frankly, you'd better just go."

"Oh Jesus, me and my big mouth!" Douglas went to the mess and waited for the bar to open.

The next day, the cross-country mission went off successfully. Before they climbed into the aircraft, however, Crane called the two wireless gunners together and bowed his head. Douglas turned to him and said, "Wattin hell—?" when Hartley raised his hand for silence. "There's no way of gettin' Reggie into the air without he says his prayers first."

177

Douglas stood silently, annoyed, while Crane recited the Lord's prayer. "Okay if we get cracking now?" he said sarcastically. "Howard used to moan about it too, skipper," DesJardins said, "but it didn't do no good. We have to put up with it."

Douglas' annoyance dissipated, however, after they were airborne. Crane proved himself a good navigator, and the other two worked as a smooth and competent team. Douglas was the one who was the rustiest. He neglected to arm his torpedo when he made a dummy run on a target ship, he settled down on a course of 256 instead of 265, and he bounced on landing. After the flight he was reluctant to met his crew's eyes, and he was gruff and short with them. He went off to his room, his face a storm-cloud, and later headed for his favourite pub on his bicycle. Over the next few days, however, he regained his composure and his flying skill, and found himself on easy terms with his crew.

Crane welcomed him at the aircraft a day later with the words, "I say, Mr. Douglas, my pater and mater want you to spend the weekend with us. Ray and Larry will be coming too. I'd very much like to have you."

Douglas nodded. "Fine. Thanks for the invitation."

When Friday came, Douglas followed Crane to the front of the officers' mess. "My parents have come for us. I'd like you to meet them." Douglas saw a silver-gray Rolls-Royce, with the station commander standing beside it, talking to a man and a woman dressed in tweeds. The two wireless operators were standing self-consciously a pace away.

Crane and Douglas saluted. "This is Flying Officer Edward Douglas, mother," he said. "This is my father and mother, Ed." He bowed slightly to the station commander. "Of course you know Group Captain Darlington."

Douglas shook hands with all three, and then stepped back, scratching the back of his head.

"Quite a car!" he said to Crane. "Didn't see too many Rolls-Royces in Valenby, Saskatchewan. Doc Wilson who ran the garage had a 1936 Buick, but we went more for Model A Fords." He turned to Mrs. Crane. "I enjoy flying with your son, Ma'am."

"I'm glad you do, Flying Officer Douglas. My son tells me you're a veteran with a splendid record."

178

"Don't believe everything he tells you, ma'am," Douglas replied. Mr. Crane drove off. "We used to have a chauffeur," Reg told Douglas, "but we gave him up as an austerity measure." He laughed. "He joined the Royal Army Service Corps, and now he's the chauffeur for a general. Anyway, pater enjoys driving the car himself."

"I'd enjoy driving a Rolls-Royce myself."

"We'll arrange for you to have a spin in it tomorrow."

The house to which Douglas was driven was a mansion, and he was properly impressed. The evening meal, served by a butler, was complete with wines Douglas had never heard of, and there was a battery of knives and forks Douglas manipulated by copying Mrs. Crane. Douglas was less than surprised to find Reginald prefacing the meal by standing up and saying grace.

DesJardins, beside Douglas, brought him up to date. "Reg was studying to be an Anglican priest when he joined the Air Force."

"Huh! I didn't know that."

"Good thing. Don't have to worry about him getting into trouble in pubs. He keeps trying to save our souls, but I guess we're hard cases."

"We need all the help we can get."

DesJardins grinned. "Too bad God's a Catholic."

"Somebody told me he was United Church."

"Reg is a good head, though. Being loaded with dough doesn't seem to affect him. Being religious seems to help."

Douglas shook his head. "My last navigator was a poet. Now Reg Crane is a Bible-puncher. Snow was a good navigator. Crane seems to be one too. We'll see."

After dinner Mrs. Crane appropriated Douglas. "Reg tells me you've had a distinguished career, Mr. Douglas."

"I've done an operational tour if that's what you mean."

"You're much too modest, young man. We're very glad to have met you, after what Reginald has said about you. My husband and I are sure you'll look after Reginald." She paused, and Douglas saw her heart in her eyes. Her son meant everything to her, and she was pleading to keep him safe from harm.

"We look after each other, ma'am," Douglas told her. "We're all one crew, working together."

179

"Of course, my dear boy. Reginald told us how much you wanted to fly with him when he lost his former pilot, and we dropped a word in the ear of our dear friends, Tom Sullivan, who arranged things. Of course you're just as glad as Reginald is."

"Tom Sullivan?"

"Yes—Tom. He's in the Air Ministry. He's a Wing Commander or an Air Marshal or something. He was glad to help."

The name rang a bell. Air Vice Marshal Sullivan was the Senior Air Personnel Officer in Coastal Command, who controlled the destinies of forty or fifty thousand men who served in it. A request from a friend to make a pilot available so that a crew could go on operations rather than cooling their heels at a holding unit would obviously be sympathetically received. And Douglas had unquestionably told Crane that he wanted to get back on operations, which he would have to do sooner or later anyway. He nodded sourly.

"Yes, Tom Sullivan. Of course he could arrange things."

Mrs. Crane nodded. "Some wine, Mr. Douglas? It's pre-war port."

"Yes, thank you." He savoured the wine. It was good, though he was no connoisseur. He resolved to enjoy the rest of the evening. Mrs. Crane had invited a trio of local young women, and Douglas found them admiring and attractive. He chose the prettiest and obtained her telephone number. If he was still in England in the following weeks he would follow up.

The next morning they all went to church, where Reginald read the lesson. Even the Catholic DesJardins attended, after making everybody promise that nobody would leak the matter to the Catholic clergy. They all felt good about it.

On Sunday evening Mr. Crane drove them back to the air station. As they parted Mrs. Crane looked deeply into Douglas' eyes and repeated her appeal for him to look after Reginald.

180

CHAPTER TWENTY

They were slated for another cross-country the next day. When they got into the air DesJardins called up from the turret. "Say, skipper, how about letting me handle the controls for a while? You need a rest."

"Don't be silly!" Douglas snapped. "I belong up here in the cockpit—you belong back there!"

"Don't be so greedy, skipper. If two guys from the prairies can't get along who can?"

"Who's supposed to man the turret when you're up here?"

"I can," Hartley broke in. " We're on radio silence anyway."

"Okay? We're too far away from Jerryland to have any intruders in daytime anyway. Come on up."

DesJardins squeezed into the pilot's seat while Douglas sat in the jump seat beside him. The plane porpoised as DesJardins over-controlled, and Douglas laughed at him. "Not so easy as it looks, is it?"

"No, damn it!"

Douglas slipped automatically into his instructor's patter. "Wait for it—just centralize the controls now—okay, that's better—now remember to keep the nose on the horizon—don't bother about the instruments yet—okay, give her a little right aileron—you're skidding a bit; bit of right rudder now—" DesJardins stayed at the controls for half an hour, and left wringing wet with sweat.

DesJardins spent some time at the controls for the rest of the week each time they flew, and Douglas saw that he had the makings of an acceptable pilot. He was alert and quick, and his reflexes soon attuned themselves to the demands of piloting. He was neither too dreamy, as Snow had been, nor too unmechanical, like Crane. Douglas never entrusted him with anything as delicate or

181

dangerous as a landing, but before long he could maintain altitude, airspeed and heading very well indeed. On one cross-country Douglas actually went so far as to allow him to fly the aircraft for half an hour, while he climbed into the turret and diverted himself by swinging the guns at imaginary targets. He enjoyed it; it was something different, and flying had lost its first bloom for him.

The other two crew members made token protests, but neither of them were interested in taking over the pilot's seat. Hartley was older, and Crane was immersed in navigation and devoted to it. Realistically they considered that having another man able to bring the aircraft home with a dead or disabled pilot was a good idea.

At the end of the week the Chief Flying Instructor told Douglas he would be leaving in a week. "Your crew's as ready as it'll ever be. A ferry pilot will be delivering a new Beaufort next Sunday. You can fly a long cross-country to check its fuel consumption for the trip to to Malta, then on to Alexandria. Until then you're on your own."

Douglas' thoughts gravitated to London; plays, restaurants, pubs, dance palaces. He ran his eye through the theatrical section of a newspaper, looking for a play it would be amusing to see. The name of Constance jumped out at him.

He collected a pocketful of coins and sought a telephone kiosk. Getting through to her was a chore, but after many pennies and many moments waiting for the penny to drop, he was finally connected to her dressing room.

"Douglas Edwards? How nice to hear from you!"

"Good to hear you. By the way, it's Edward Douglas. I'm sorry to hear you think I'm so backward."

She laughed. "Not at all—if anyone is backward, it's not you. Why did you call?"

"I'm about to leave England. I wondered if I could see you before I went."

"Why, of course, my dear! I'd love to see you! Are you in London?"

"Not until tomorrow—but then I'll have a few days leave. If you have some time—"

"I can always make time for you, Douglas—or is it Edward?"

"No matter—if you remember either name I'll be happy. Where shall I meet you?"

"Why don't you come to see the play tomorrow night? There'll be a ticket waiting for you at the wicket. Come around to the stage door after the performance."

Douglas watched the play the next evening, seeing Constance moving about the stage competently and convincingly, clothed in the personality of someone completely different. He heard her speak in three different accents, saw her change from at uncertain, awkward girl in the first act to a suave, polished sophisticate in the third. He was mightily impressed.

When the curtain fell, Douglas walked to the stage door. The porter guarding it put up a token resistance, but motioned him towards Constance's dressing-room after a couple of minutes. "I shouldn't do it," he said, "but I've a lad in the RAF—go on in there, but look sharp about it."

Connie was seated before her mirror, removing her make-up. She sprang up when she saw him and threw her arms around him. "Douglas!" she cried, her voice full and vibrant as it had been on the stage. She kissed him, smudging his face with her make-up.

"Hello, Connie," he said as she leaned back in his arms. "You sure know how to make a guy feel welcome."

"You're a very special—guy, did you say?"

"Glad you think so, Connie. I forgot 'guy' means something different in England." He pushed her away from her far enough to look at her. "You're as beautiful as ever—as if that were possible."

"I thought it was my mind that attracted you," she smiled. "Tell me—how did you enjoy the play?"

"It was wonderful—and you were the most wonderful person in it. I still can't see how you can remember all those lines."

"It's my business, dear boy. Was I convincing?"

"Convincing? I should say. You were three people in one night."

"I'll try to be somebody else for you, my love. Now let me take all this make-up off and put some more on just for you." She returned to her mirror. "Go on and look about the stage—I'll tell you when I'm ready."

Half an hour later Douglas was sitting opposite Constance at a restaurant table. She was chattering away as usual, and her conversation was as interesting as it had been when he first met her. Her theatrical world was full of feuds and intrigues, jealousies

183

and liaisons, in some of which she was obviously implicated. Douglas sat fascinated. At intervals she said, "But I'm monopolizing the conversation. You must tell me what you've been doing."

"Not much. Yours life is a lot more interesting."

"Oh, it can't be!" Then, a second later, she went on talking excitedly and animatedly about her romantic, dramatic, sharp-edged illusionary world.

They finished their meal. "I'm not sure what I can invite you to do now. I can't very well invite you to go to a show."

"Come on up to my digs. I have a bottle of Spanish brandy there. It's hard to get French brandy these days." Douglas nodded. He had never drunk brandy in his life.

"Let us depart, my love," Connie said. Douglas offered her his arm, and she walked with him through the restaurant as if to show him off. "You're a lovely creature," she told him, and laughed. "You're blushing again."

After an irritatingly long wait they found a cab. Her flat—a tiny two-room affair littered with feminine frippery and theatrical magazines and newspapers—was close, and Douglas was a little outraged by the fare the cabbie charged him, but he was in enough of a hurry to pay for it without protest. Connie led him into the cluttered sitting-room, lifted a bottle from a cabinet, and poured stiff drinks for them. Douglas sipped at his glass and made a face. Connie laughed.

"I don't care much for Spanish brandy either," she said, "even if it is the king of drinks and the drink of kings."

"I didn't know what to expect. I'm a beer man myself."

"Do you drink whiskey in Canada?"

"Rye, mostly."

"Rye whisky?"

"It's not like Scotch at all. I guess you have to develop a taste for it. Like Spanish brandy, I guess." He put the glass down. "I was hoping I'd get to see double. With somebody as beautiful as you I'd have twice the fun."

"You're sweet." She sat down beside him. He pulled her gently toward him and kissed her.

"This chair is a little cramped," he told her. "We should go where we have more room for maneuver." He stood up, swept her into his arms, and carried her into the bedroom.

184

"You'll crease your dress," he said. "Don't you think you'd better take it off? I'll help you." He began to undo her buttons.

"You do have some wonderful ideas," she said langourously, "I must say you're a little overdressed yourself." She removed his tie. When they were both naked he ran his hot lips the length of her body, and cupped her breasts and buried his face in their hollow. She pulled him toward her, and a moment later they were joined in writhing passion. When at last they had exhausted their mutual lust, she threw an arm wide and reached for a cigarette. As she sucked in a mouthful of smoke she looked sideways at Douglas.

"You said you were going somewhere."

"I'm not supposed to tell anyone."

"Don't be silly! I'm not a spy!"

"You're beautiful enough to be one."

"It's overseas then."

"I'm overseas already."

"Nonsense. You're in England." She laughed deliciously. "Oh—I forgot—you're a colonial. It is overseas for you, isn't it?" She was suddenly sober. "You'll be going back into action again, won't you?"

"I suppose so."

She put her arm around him. "Look after yourself."

"I'll do the best I can."

She pulled him to her with sudden fierceness. "Now don't go off doing anything silly!"

"There's a war on, you know." He grinned at her. "You know, this isn't a bad war. If it hadn't been for the war I never would have met you. There aren't many girls like you in Valenby, Saskatchewan."

"And if there hadn't been a war I'd never have met you—I'd have been condemned to spending all my time with people in the theatre." She looked into his eyes. "You're real, you know. You're a funny combination of hardness and naivety. Your eyes can be cold, but you blush. You're blushing now."

"An operational tour grows a man up in a hurry sometimes. But the Air Force is a sort of a sheltered life—you've seen a lot more life than I have."

"Perhaps I have. Maybe that's why somebody like you attracts me. But you do look divine in that uniform. The other women tonight were green with envy when they saw me with you." She yawned.

"Now I'll have to get ready for bed properly."

"Guess it's time for me to go home."

"No, my love. Stay here. I may need you in the morning."

"Always glad to be of service to a lovely lady."

"Go off and use the bathroom. I'll take lot longer than you will."

The next morning he woke before she did. He found an electric kettle and made tea, which he brought to Connie in her bed. She struggled to open her eyes and reached automatically for a cigarette as he put the cup on the night-table beside her. She was not as glamorous as she had been the night before.

"Go on out and leave the flat to me," she ordered. "I'll see you again tonight after the show. Go on—I hate people in the morning!" He left.

The following evening was a repeat. They had dinner, with her doing all the talking; they returned to her flat, where they drank more of the brandy; they went to bed and made love. Douglas had his pyjamas, his toothbrush and his razor, and was able to make himself presentable in the morning.

Their third evening began like the others, in Connie's dressing room. Then, instead of having dinner with him in a restaurant, she took him to an expensive house in Belgravia, where a gathering of theatrical people was talking in a multitude of accents. All of them were talking and none of them were listening, except for those who were seeking better roles from producers and impressarios. A buffet was set up in a corner, boasting a variety of food that obviously stemmed from the black market.

Connie showed off Douglas to her associates, introducing him as "My wonderful young airman from Canada, who torpedoed a battleship." Douglas did not bother to make a disclaimer. Connie was immediately surrounded by a number of admirers, and Douglas found himself talking to an aging actress who had been famous twenty years before. After some initial uncertainty he found her very interesting, as Connie was, with a similar fund of maliciously-absorbing stories. They were sitting in a corner over drinks when Connie swept up and carried him off. "I got you just in time," she told him. "Heaven knows what that old trout was planning to do with you. You must take me home now—I need my sleep, you know, to do justice to my public."

186

They were familiar with each other now and slid into an easy routine of drinks, love and a cigarette for her after it was over. She was lying back on her pillow, puffing at her cigarette, both of them naked, when the door burst open and a flash exploded in their faces. Constance sat bolt upright, clasping her hands across her breasts. "Maurice!" she screamed.

One of the two men nodded his head sardonically.

"Yes—Maurice—your husband, my dear. I wondered if you'd remember my name."

"What are you doing? How did you get in?"

"With a key—I'm entitled to one—I'm your husband. But I won't be your husband much longer—I have all the grounds I need for a divorce. Thank you, my dear. I'm leaving." He turned and stepped toward the door.

Douglas, who had jumped over Constance to the floor beside the bed, moved toward him. The other man help up an arm. "No need for that, sir. I'm a private detective, going about my lawful pursuits." Douglas stopped uncertainly. The two men left, Connie's husband tipping his hat as he closed the door.

"My God? What was that?"

"My dear old husband Maurice," Connie spat. "The swine! Bursting in on me like that! Well, that makes it official. We haven't had a real marriage for years. He has his evidence now, anyway." Her face sobered. "You know why he did it? Because he didn't want to pay alimony, or give me a divorce settlement."

"My God? What a cad!" Douglas pulled on his clothes. "I'll go out and—"

"You'll do nothing of the kind, my dear. He's actually in the right, in a swinish sort of way." She lay back on her pillow. "Go on over and bolt the door, and then come back to bed. We might as well be hanged for a sheep as a lamb."

It was half an hour before Douglas was in the mood for love again, but then he responded adequately. Constance was tigerish in her passion. When it was spent, she sat up.

"That swine! He'll regret that for the rest of his life, I promise you! I'll even up quits with him if it takes me until I'm ninety!"

"Gosh Connie, I'm sorry I'm so much trouble for you," he said lamely.

"You? If it hadn't been you it would have been somebody else. I'm in no mood to live like a nun, you know." She laughed again. "It's funny—my name is Constance." She reached over and kissed his cheek. "You're a nice boy to be inconstant with, Douglas."

"My pleasure, my lovely. Well, in wartime you have to live dangerously."

"Yes. I know you're living dangerously in your aeroplane. Even I am, here in London. That's one reason to take our pleasure where we find it."

"I hope there's no air raid tonight."

"If there is, we'll ignore it. We have to get some sleep sometime, and what better place is there than in each other's arms?" He reached over to put out the light. "That was a hell of a thing to happen on my last night in London—my last night with you."

"Put it out of your mind, my love. Take me in your arms and go to sleep."

The next morning he made tea for her again. She took it from him and said, "I'm surprised you know how to make tea."

"My mother taught me."

"You'll make somebody a splendid wife some day." She yawned. "You look perfectly dreamlike in that uniform, Douglas, my love. You're good in bed too. No matter what happened, it was worth it. Now come and kiss me, my dear."

He kissed her. "You know, Connie, I think I've fallen in love with you."

She smiled. "You don't have to be as grateful as all that, my dear, or as sorry for what happened. Don't worry—I'll never marry you."

"Never marry me—"

"No. I don't want to live on some godforsaken RAF station—or in the frozen north somewhere in Saskatchewan or Wyoming or wherever it is you come from, either. But you are terribly flattering to say you love me."

"But Connie—"

"Thanks again. Now go back to your aeroplanes."

"I feel as if I'm deserting you—"

"Nonsense, my dear boy. I didn't find out where you're going, but things won't be much fun for you. I'm glad I made your last few days in England a little more fun. And I enjoyed them too."

188

He kissed her again and left. The sun was just peering through rain clouds as he walked back to the hotel he had not spent any time in, feeling satisfied and humiliated and ashamed and proud of himself. He licked his lips as he thought of Connie's svelte body, the urgency of her passion, and the warmth of her lips, and carried the smile that the memory brought him the rest of the day.

CHAPTER TWENTY-ONE

"Navigator to pilot— steer two zero three degrees compass."

"Two hundred and three it is," Douglas answered as he shoved lightly down on the control yoke and gave the aircraft a touch of rudder. A wing came down, and the directional gyro walked around its case. "On course."

"Our ETA for the first turning point is 2015 GMT," the navigator said. They had taken off at dusk from St. Eval, in Cornwall. The flight across the Bay of Biscay should take place at night, secure from the attentions of questing German fighters. The flight from England to Gibraltar should take some nine hours, and it was important that they should be off the Spanish coast when the sun rose.

Douglas fussed with his engine controls, easing back on the throttle, increasing the manifold pressure, adjusting the propeller pitch to squeeze maximum air-miles out of every gallon of fuel aboard. With the all-up weight high as they set out with fuel tanks full, they should fly fast, and then Douglas should gradually pull back on the throttles to slow down as the fuel burnt. They had none too much petrol aboard to take them to Gibraltar. At least he did not have to worry about computing the fuel needed to take them to an alternate airport, since there was none; it was Gibraltar or nothing.

Buried in the back of his mind Douglas could feel the nagging knowledge that an engine failure could bring them down, to leave them bobbing around in a life raft where they would probably die of thirst. But he had survived many such trips in the past, and there was nothing he could do about it anyway. Fatalistically he found a more comfortable position in his pilot's seat, relaxihg as much as he could while the engines droned on.

Crane climbed from his perch in the nose, carrying his sextant.
He bumped his head as he crawled through the bulkhead, and
Douglas saw his lips move. He wondered if Crane were swearing;
knowing Crane, he decided he was not. A minute later, with his
headset plugged into the jack at the astrodome, the navigator was
speaking.

"I'm going to take an astro shot, skipper. Hold her steady."

"Roger." Crane busied himself peering through the sextant at one
of the stars that hung above them, bright and slowly twinkling in the
clear ocean air, while Douglas concentrated on flying the aircraft as
smoothly as he could. "Okay skipper, relax," Crane said as he
readjusted his sextant. "Ready for the next shot, skipper." Douglas
concentrated on his flying again. They followed the ritual a third
time, and then Crane brought his sextant back out of the astrodome
and returned to his position in the nose at the navigation table. The
intercom was silent for the next ten minutes as Crane worked out
the sights and plotted the position lines for his three-star fix. Finally
his voice came. "Alter course three degrees port, skipper."

"Where'd those shots put us?"

"About ten miles off track. Our ground speed agrees with the flight
plan."

"So far so good."

"We'll be west of Cape Finisterre at the north tip of Spain in half
an hour. Old Jerry shouldn't have many long-range fighters that far
away from their bases."

"Sure hope not. We should be halfway down Spain before it gets
light."

"I want another astro fix in about half an hour."

"Righto." The intercom fell silent.

Crane crawled back to the astrodome with his sextant. Douglas
was impressed by his skill at so esoteric a skill as celestial
navigation. Snow had taken the odd sun shot, and during their
infrequent flights at night had bashed away at the stars, but his
sextant sights had never worked out very well, and he had usually
fallen back on dead reckoning or map reading, relying on his drift
meter to find out much the wind was pushing him sideways. Crane,
however, seemed completely master of his sextant, and used it
twice each hour to get an astro fix.

The sun came up, silhouetting the Spanish mainland to the left. "Hold her steady, skipper, I want to take a bearing on that headland," Crane said as he bent over the astro compass. "Skipper! Alter to one nine eight." Douglas swung the plane around.

They ran down the Portuguese coast, just out of sight of land, holding an altitude of ten thousand feet so that they did not have to use oxygen. Cape St. Vincent came up, and Crane altered course again. Douglas looked anxiously at the fuel gages. He would have enough fuel to take him to Gibraltar, but only just. The sun rose higher, and Crane climbed back into the astrodome to observe it with his sextant. Douglas kept swivelling his head, on the alert for prowling enemy fighters; if he could fly so far from base, so could a Ju88. The sky stayed blue and clear, however, until the coasts of Spain and Africa reached for each other. At length Crane said, "OK, skipper, there's Gibraltar. Take her in by yourself. I've done with navigation for one trip."

"Righto." Douglas headed toward the Rock of Gibraltar, towering over the airstrip at its base. As he came close he fired off the colours of the day, the bright red and green stars arcing up above the Beaufort. A Hurricane flew up to inspect him and then a green light winked from the runway. Crane climbed into the jump-seat beside Douglas and strapped himself in. Douglas made a straight-in approach and landed the Beaufort, rather roughly. They taxied to dispersal, where an RAF corporal prepared to refuel it. A lorry took them to the operations room for debriefing.

They slept the day through, woke as the late afternoon sun slanted through the barrack windows, and lazily got up. Crane drew up a flight plan while Douglas checked the weather, and at sundown they took off again on their journey east. Their course took them through the middle of the Mediterranean. Crane kept busy with his sextant, feeding small course alterations to Douglas to compensate for wind changes. The tip of Sardinia loomed to the north, and Crane altered ten degrees to the south to head for the narrows between the tip of Sicily and Africa. Douglas shifted in his seat and began to scan the horizon carefully, now that they were in hostile country.

The sun rose in their eyes, to reveal the blue waters beneath them. Douglas had never seen the Mediterranean before, and thoughts of triremes and Carthaginian galleys came briefly to his mind, to be banished by a reproof from Crane. "Skipper! Get back on course! You're ten degrees off!" Douglas swung the aircraft to line up the compass needle with the "railway tracks" on the top surface. "That's better," Crane grunted, and went back to his navigation.

As the sun climbed Douglas let down until they were flying a hundred feet off the wave-tops. "How're we doing, navigator?"

"Ninety miles or so to Malta—forty minutes. This kite is so slow—"

"Fast as I can make it, old cock. This is a long flight and we have to conserve fuel."

"Too long. I don't like being up here alone."

Douglas swivelled his head, peered in the rear-view mirror, and jinked one way and then other, looking back over his tail. The sky stayed as empty as the sea. He peered ahead. "Holy smoke! What's that?"

The sky ahead was suddenly spotted by tiny black puffs of cloud. "That's Malta," Crane answered. "It seems there must be a raid on."

"How far away are we?"

"Thirty miles. We're going to approach right into it. Think we'd better orbit for a while."

Douglas looked at his fuel gages. "Not enough petrol. We've got to go in."

"Twelve minutes. Hope it's over by then."

"So do I." He fish-tailed toward the island, while Crane stayed in the nose, his hands on his machine-gun, his navigator's tasks forgotten. Douglas heard the jabber of guns as DesJardins tested them.

The crown of flak-bursts was coming closer. Peering ahead, Douglas saw dancing dots that were aircraft attacking the island or defending it, and then concentrated his attention nearer. If danger came it would not be from the distant aircraft, but from some German or Italian fighter prowling the waters near the island. He let down lower until his propeller tips seemed almost to be flicking the wave tops.

"Skipper—bandit on our port quarter!"

Douglas turned his head, to catch sight of a lean shape behind him and to the left, rapidly overhauling him. There was no point in jinking too soon; he would have to wait until the fighter was committed to fire. He waited for a few interminable seconds, his ears straining to hear DesJardin's command. It came. "Corkscrew port!" Douglas kicked left rudder and pulled up the nose. A string of splashes, tiny columns of water where the German cannon-shells struck, stretched ahead of him. The fighter flashed past. Douglas reversed the turn and headed down for the water again. There was the snarl of another engine, and a Spitfire passed him in pursuit of the enemy fighter. Douglas was too busy to spare a moment for the fate of the combat which had rescued him.

Douglas found himself out of position to approach the landing strip and circled. The sky was suddenly drained of its aircraft as the Axis planes broke off and flew away to the north. He climbed to approach height, put down the wheels, and throttled back. The plane slid down the final leg, and he cut the throttles and pulled back on the stick. The plane flared and sank; the wheels touched, hit a depression in the bumpy runway, full of recently-filled bomb-craters, and bounced into the air again. Douglas pulled the stick back into his stomach and fought to keep the plane on the runway. The voice of DesJardins came cheerfully over the intercom. "Been flying long, Skipper?"

"Ah, shaddup!" Douglas snapped. He taxied the plane toward a revetment where an airman was motioning to him, swung the plane behind the sandbagged shelter, and shut down the engines, listening to the crackling and rumbling as the cylinders cooled. He slid a side window open and put his head outside, to find the air hot and dry. Crane unstrapped himself, climbed back into the nose to retrieve his navigation bag, and went back into the fuselage to get his suitcase. Hartley and DesJardins helped him to lift out their baggage, and the four men gathered in front of the nose.

Hartley looked up at the sky. "How long will we be here?"

"Just until tonight. If the weather's OK we'll be on our way to Alexandria by nightfall."

"That sounds good. Things look a little shaky here. This runway is ten-tenths bomb-holes."

The airman who had marshalled them to the revetment walked over to them. "The operations office is over there."

"Where's the lorry to pick us up?" DesJardins asked.

"Won't be none. No lorries—no petrol for them. You'll just have to hump it, sarge."

"Jee-sus! No lorry!" The four men reached for their bags. Crane put his navigation bag back inside the aircraft. They straggled toward the flight office, plodding wearily, when an air-raid siren shrieked. An anti-aircraft gun swivelled as they passed, its slender muzzle probing the sky. A voice barked at them.

"You there! Come here! We're short-handed and we need men to serve this gun!"

"Goddamit," Douglas snarled, "we've just got here from Gib! We've been flying all night! We're dead tired!" A man in a rumpled army battledress, wearing a captain's pips, appeared. "If you don't help you won't just be dead tired, you'll be dead! Two men to each of these two guns! The sergeant will tell you what to do!" The air was sonorous with the sound of approaching motors. A hand caught at Douglas' sleeve. "Here, help the loader!" Douglas found himself standing beside a pile of shells. "Hand me a shell!" a voice cried. Douglas grasped one of the projectiles and handed it to a man who rammed it into the breech of a gun. "Here they come again," the sergeant in charge of the gun said calmly. The gun muzzle swung gracefully toward the intruders and fired automatically under radar control. The whipcrack of the explosion half-stunned Douglas, who stood irresolute.

"Look alive!" the sergeant barked, motioning angrily toward Douglas. "Open your mouth! Put your hands over your ears when she fires!" The gun roared again. Douglas bent to hand the loader another shell. The day was a cacophony of anti-aircraft guns, aircraft motors, and the boom of exploding bombs.

"I thought the bloody raid was over!" Douglas gasped to Crane as he handed him a shell.

"They came back. Lucky for us we had a chance to land." Crane handed the shell to the loader, who stuffed it into the gaping breech of the gun. The gun-layer sat behind his console of wheels and switches, moving the gun to probe the sky in response to orders from a radar set nearby.

A fighter roared across the airfield, its guns blazing. Beside the big gun Douglas and Crane were serving a four-barrel light flak pom-

195

pom blazed away, and the fighter staggered, trailing a thin line of smoke. The men at the guns paused long enough to cheer.

A stick of bombs walked across the airfield. "Hit the dirt!" the sergeant screamed at them, and the gun-crew threw themselves down on the hard earth beside the gun. A tremendous crash seemed to erupt inside Douglas' head as the earth beneath him heaved and rocked. Stunned, Douglas squirmed as if to burrow into the earth. A hard toe stirred him. "Get up, get up!" the sergeant shouted urgently. "We gotta get the gun back into action!"

Douglas struggled to his feet. "Come on, Crane," he called, turning toward the navigator, who was staggering erect, brushing dirt out of his eyes. The loader lay still. "Hey, get up there!" Douglas called. The man did not stir. Douglas dropped to his knees and looked at his face. The eyes were open and unseeing. Douglas shook him, and his head flopped loosely. The sergeant knelt beside him.

"Poor bugger's done for, sir," he said, shaking his head. "Look at the back of his head." A fragment of a bomb-casing was sticking out of the base of the man's skull. The sergeant stood up. "We still need you. You, sir," pointing at Crane. "Get up there and load that gun!" Crane jumped to the gun's breech and slammed a shell into it. "Let me show you how to close the breech now," the sergeant said, and gave Crane a frenzied half-minute's instruction. The gun fired, the barrel recoiled, and the breech flopped open. Crane took a shell from Douglas and shoved it into its place. He closed the breech, and the gun fired. The deafening whip-cracks of the guns firing blotted out all other sounds.

The raid ended abruptly, and the Spitfires came in for a landing. A lorry, used as an ambulance, drove up, and two orderlies lifted the body onto a stretcher and covered it with a blanket. As they slid it into the lorry Douglas stood to attention and saluted. The sergeant saw his hand come to his cap-brim, and stood to weary attention. "E was a good lad, that one was. Good soldier. God bless him."

"Yes," Crane's voice came. "The Lord giveth and the Lord taketh away. Blessed be the name of the Lord." He turned to the sergeant. "Is the flap over, sergeant?"

"Yes, they're gone—won't be back today—not for a while, anyways. Thanks for your help, sir."

196

The crew gathered its baggage and continued its way to the stone hut near the runway which had been pointed out to them as the flight office. A sergeant greeted them, and detailed an airman to guide them to the mess and to show them their quarters. They dined on beans and tea, and then collapsed on their beds in a building labelled *Transient Quarters.*

They slept until noon, and then arose to find themselves midway through a hot and muggy day. Douglas and Crane walked to the officers' mess for lunch. There were only two other air force officers there. They were surprised to see that one of them was an Air Vice Marshal who was talking to a squadron leader. Douglas, who had never spoken to an officer higher than a group captain, tried to make himself inconspicuous as he walked into the room, and then, surprised, he spun on his heel to greet the squadron leader.

"Derek Peterson! What are you doing here?"

Peterson looked up, and then sprang to his feet, interrupting a sentence to the AVM. "Ed Douglas! What are *you* doing here?"

"I'm on my way to the Middle East."

Peterson turned to the AVM. "Let me introduce Flying Officer Douglas, sir—one of the very men I was telling you about. Ed, this is AVM Hugh Lloyd." The august officer put out his hand, and Douglas took it, standing uneasily at attention.

"Douglas is one of the most experienced and capable torpedo-bomber pilots in the Air Force, sir," Peterson said. "I knew him at Lower Lexington. He torpedoed the *Gladbach.*"

A smile came over the AVM's face. "It's good to meet you, Douglas; you have just been appointed acting flight commander of A Flight of 735 Squadron, based here."

"735 Squadron! Based here! But I'm on my way to Ceylon!"

"You were, Douglas, you were. But those orders have been superseded by new ones. You'll report to Squadron Leader Peterson here—he's in charge of torpedo operations."

"But holy smoke! My crew's as green as grass—never heard a shot fired—I need a while to shake them down."

"They'll learn fast. We need an experienced flight commander. Glad to see you here, Douglas. Look after him, Peterson."

Douglas stood open-mouthed as the AVM left the table. "Derek? Whattinhell's this?"

Peterson smiled sardonically. "AVM Lloyd is desperately short of aircrew. Whenever a crew flies through Malta he snatches it. You're the latest."

"Good God! Ops in the Mediterranean—against the bloody Luftwaffe and the Eytie navy—I'll be lucky if I last a week. And I've got orders for Ceylon!"

"The AVM has overruled them. Come on over to the squadron office. I'll brief you."

"Let me bring my navigator—Reg Crane. He might as well get the good news too."

Crane greeted Peterson formally and deferentially, his public-school good breeding putting him at ease at once. Peterson brought them up to date. "735 Squadron has seven aircraft and eight crews. Three of the crews belonged to the squadron when it came out here, two are reinforcements, and the others were appropriated by AVM Lloyd the way you were. Your aircraft and your crew bring the strength up to eight aircraft and nine crews. As you know, the position of Malta is critical—we sit between Italy and North Africa, right in the middle of all the transport routes, bashing at everything the Axis sends to reinforce Rommel and his Afrika Corps. We're the target for everything the Luftwaffe can throw at us from Sicily—that's why you've lived through two raids before you've been here a day. We've got to stay in action, and we've got to stop those ships getting to Rommel. That's what you're here for."

"Oh Jesus!" Douglas said. "I thought we were going to a comparatively quiet area—Ceylon—and we end up here. That's all we needed!"

"Don't look at it that way, Douglas. Consider it an honour. AVM Lloyd was overjoyed to get you."

"Tell Lloyd he's a damn sight more overjoyed than I am."

Peterson slapped Douglas on the back. "We'll work very well together—I know I can trust you, Ed. I've given orders for your aircraft to be made serviceable. You'll be on the battle order right away."

"Thanks, Derek. Thanks a lot." Douglas slumped in his chair.

"You're lucky to have such an experienced captain," Peterson told Crane.

"We know that, sir. We'll do our best. With Ed Douglas as skipper, I'm sure we won't disappoint you."

Peterson nodded. " You have all the earmarks of a good crew—keen and anxious to get into the battle."

Douglas looked up. "That's okay for the other guys—they don't know what they're letting themselves in for. They're keen. I'm scared shitless."

Peterson laughed. "You've always been a frank devil, Douglas. But you're a good pilot. We're glad to have you."

Douglas got up. "Okay gang, let's get out of here".

"Briefing's at eight o'clock tomorrow morning. See you then," said Peterson.

"Right. By the way, congratulations on your promotion. I hate to say it, but you deserved it—sir!"

"See? I told you we'd get along fine."

CHAPTER TWENTY-TWO

The crew appeared the next morning for their briefing. Derek Peterson sought Douglas out. "You're the most experienced torpedo man we've got," he told him. "We have five Beauforts serviceable and five Blenheims. The Beauforts will carry torpedoes and the Blenheims bombs. Intelligence tells us there's a convoy of a tanker and one or two merchant ships, escorted by up to five naval vessels—probably destroyers. Our job is to get the tanker. The Blenheims will go after the merchant ships."

"What about the destroyers?"

"They can look after themselves. Machine-gun their decks as you go in."

"As usual."

"The attacks must be co-ordinated. Three Beauforts attacking from one side, the other two from the other side, and the Blenheims from ahead or behind, depending on whether the tanker is leading or the merchant ships are. I'll leave the decision up to you."

"Okay," Douglas nodded. "We'll give it the old college try."

Crane settled beside Douglas in the jump seat for the take-off. "Our baptism of fire, Ed!" he said.

"Yup," answered Douglas laconically, simulating a confidence he did not feel. This was the first trip of his second tour, and he did not have the valour of ignorance that he had possessed during his own baptism of fire. He knew what to expect, and he was not looking forward to it. Crane and the two wireless air gunners were nervous and apprehensive, keyed up and too obviously jocular, but they did not believe that any harm could really come to them, just as those who had sat beside him at previous briefings and now were dead has believed themselves sacrosanct.

Peterson pointed to a map painted on the wall behind him, "A Baltimore reconnaissance aircraft found the convoy at first light. Its position is here. You'll take off and fly straight to it." He turned to a blackboard supported by an easel. "Here are the tactics." He chalked in the expected position of the ships. "Two flights of Beauforts,—Douglas, Flanagan, Moffat from the west—starboard of the convoy. Gilmore and Bisley from the east—port of the convoy. All of you aim at the tanker—then no matter which way he turns he'll run into a torpedo from somebody. The Blenheims will attack in a direction more or less at right angles to the Beauforts—ahead or astern depending on the circumstances. Douglas will make the decision. The Blenheims will attack at mast-top height. Don't get too low, though—I don't want any of you running into masts. Come home any way you want." He turned to Douglas. "Have you anything to say?" Douglas walked to the dias. "If I go in, you take over, Moffatt. Then it's Flanagan. The Blenheims will be in charge of Flight Sergeant Watson, with Sergeant Jones as his vice. For the Blenheims, don't try for any fancy tactics—just go in bald-headed for whatever merchant ship you're closest to. I'll call you up on R/T to tell you which way to attack—if you miss the order, attack from the stern." Douglas looked at the fresh faces watching him, hanging on every hard-bitten professional word. Two of the Blenheim crews had arrived two days before, ostensibly on their way to Cairo, and had been shanghaied by AVM Lloyd. Three planes had started from England, but one had disappeared before it reached Gibraltar. The other two Blenheim crews were the survivors of a twelve-plane squadron which had flown into Malta six months before. Douglas had been drinking Hop Leaf beer with them the night before at the Transit Mess, and he looked at them with his concern carefully blanked from his eyes.

Crane was working busily at his chart, drawing lines, measuring tracks and distances, and computing the courses he would ask Douglas to steer. Douglas felt a twinge of envy; navigators were always so busy with their protractors and dividers that they had no time to be afraid. AVM Lloyd walked into the briefing room. Peterson called the room to attention, turned to Lloyd, and saluted.

"Good day, gentlemen," Lloyd said. "I came here to tell you how important your sortie is today. Our army is heavily engaged in the

Western Desert and Rommel is pushing it back. But he can't operate without petrol for his tanks and lorries, and that is where we come in. When we disrupt his communications and sink his supply ships we save the lives of our men. God bless you, gentlemen, and good hunting!" He turned to Peterson. "And don't let me catch you flying on the operation. I need you here! No sneaking off into an aircraft, mind you!"

A cheer went up from the group. Lloyd walked out of the briefing room, followed by the crews. Peterson stood watching them leave.

Crane walked underneath the nose of the aircraft, set his navigation bag on the ground, and turned to his three companions. "A short prayer, gentlemen." Douglas looked at him, shrugged his shoulders, and bowed his head. Hartley put in," Righto, guvnor—all the help we can get."

Crane closed his eyes, folded his hands in front of him, and said, "O Lord, thou knowest how busy we will be this day. If we forget thee, do not thou forget us. In Christ's name, Amen."

"Amen," the others echoed. They climbed into the aircraft. Douglas started the engines. An airman unplugged the battery cart used to provide the starting power, and then pulled away the chocks from the wheels. Douglas taxied out of the revetment, bouncing across the rough taxi-strip with its crudely-filled bomb craters.

The ten aircraft took off and funnelled into a rough formation, Douglas leading. Crane was working as frantically as usual in his position in the nose, conscious of the responsibility thrust upon him of being lead navigator for the formation.

Douglas relaxed. As the lead aircraft pilot he did not have to worry about keeping formation—the others had to fight throttles and controls to keep position on him. He nosed the aircraft down to 200 feet and set course on the heading Crane gave him.

The sky above was brilliant blue, with a slight chop on the blue sea beneath them. The air was smooth and flying would have been pleasant if it had not been so hot. Douglas unstrapped his parachute, took off his battle-dress jacket, and put it on a ledge behind his head. He rebuckled his parachute and adjusted his seat-belt and shoulder-belt.

"DesJardins!" Douglas called. "Keep your eyes open! We're in Indian country, you know."

"That's enough of that, skipper. I'm part Indian myself. Let's just have the proper respect from you immigrants."

"Okay. Just keep that turret swinging."

After an hour and a half Douglas saw a thin smudge on the horizon, like the smudges he had seen so many times before. It was the mark of old marine boilers under the care of inexperienced crews. The captains of the escorting destroyers were undoubtedly cursing the elderly ships and their smoky funnels as they stood on their bridges, anxiously scanning the sky with binoculars for the hostile aircraft they knew would be sure to come.

Douglas wagged his wings and altered course toward the convoy. "Navigator, steadying on two thirteen. Keep your eyes open, gang. Letting down to fifty feet."

"Roger, skipper," Crane replied, his voice calm and a little annoyed that his navigation should be interrupted. "Two one three." Douglas shoved the stick ahead a little and let the nose drop, picking up a little extra speed. The tops of the masts of the ships came into view above the horizon that still concealed the ships' hulls. They flew on, the superstructure of the ships rising into view, and then the dark hulls.

"Maybe the bastards ain't seen us yet," said Hartley.

"No such luck," DesJardins answered. "There's the flak now." Black puffs of smoke appeared in the sky before and above them, like woolly black sheep. Flashes of light appeared from the destroyers, and columns of water erupted from the sea, off to the right. "Alter course to starboard," Douglas said over his R/T set, turning toward the explosions as he had been taught to do.

The destroyers which had been sailing along serenely, sleek and beautiful, suddenly grew great bow-waves as they leapt to full speed and dashed to combat positions. The merchant ships continued to plod along.

Douglas flew to a point behind the convoy, his thumb lingering on his microphone button as he waited to give the command to break into three sections for the attack. He fought down his burning impatience as he watched flashes of light from the destroyers as they signalled to one another, knowing that every additional minute he gave them for preparation increased his danger.

The escorting ships were ablaze with flashes now. A line of Bofors tracer snaked through the formation, and the aircraft beside Douglas staggered as scraps of metal flew into it. The plane flipped over on its back, nosed up, and then was suddenly flying upside down over the seas. The nose jerked upward, a wing dropped and shuddered, and then the aircraft dropped like a stone and disappeared into a mountainous upsurge of water.

Douglas visualized what had happened; the pilot suddenly collapsing over his control column as a shell-fragment smashed the life from him, his nerveless hands pulling one side of the yoke down to give heavy right aileron, the plane responding, turning over, stalling as the elevators gave lift in the wrong direction to a plane that was upside down, and the final sickening plunge into the sea. Douglas saw the other plane move in closer to him.

He waited until the aircraft ran in upon the wake of the convoy, looked over his shoulder at the shapes of the ships, and thumbed his radio switch. "Deploy—now!" He turned the nose of the aircraft to parallel the ships' track. His remaining companion followed him, while the other two Beauforts turned away to fly up the other side of the convoy's path. The Blenheims, higher, flew straight toward the ships.

A rattle of blows, like a giant hitting the aircraft with a sledge hammer, told Douglas of a gun aboard a ship hitting him, and he put the aircraft into a skidding turn, jinking as he knew the rest of the formation would be doing. He gaged the point, a couple of miles off to the side of the tanker and just ahead of it, from which he would turn in to make his attack.

An Italian destroyer, a white bone in its teeth, a great battle-flag streaming from its stern and black smoke pouring from its funnel, tore between the two Beauforts and their quarry as it laid down a smoke screen. All its guns were firing, and the sea was pocked everywhere with columns of water rising to signal the fall of shells. Douglas thumbed his microphone. "Up to dropping height!" he radioed to his companion, and pulled back the stick and the throttles to climb to 300 feet and slow to 140 knots for the drop. The destroyer dashed across his line of sight. The Beaufort to Douglas' right, which had pulled ahead of him, slewed slightly to the left and Douglas out of the corner of his eye saw the torpedo fall free. "Too soon, you clot!" he screamed into the microphone.

"You're a mile away!" Dropping distance was 1000 yards—half a mile, a quarter of a minute from the target. Douglas fixed his eye on the tanker, still visible despite the smoke, estimated the lead angle he would need to compensate for the ship's speed, and checked to make sure his torpedo was armed.

The whipcrack of an explosion shook the aircraft. Douglas' windscreen was obscured by a wall of water that rose from the shell-burst beneath him. He flew blind for a few seconds, and then gritted his teeth, kicked the rudder to line up the ship a trifle more exactly, centralized the controls to fly the aircraft straight and level, and pressed the torpedo release button.

A shell-burst blasted his port wing upward, almost ripping the controls from Douglas' hands. He fought to regain control as the plane dropped and he pulled it out of its dive scant inches from the water. The tanker was dead ahead. He jammed the throttles forward and pulled up frantically to clear the ship, and then turned sharply to the right to fly down its wake. With his engines leaving a trail of disturbed water he tore along, jinking violently. The aircraft was loud with the jabber of all four guns; DesJardins blasting from the turret, Hartley at one of the waist guns, and Crane firing from the nose. The engine was screaming at full military power and the aircraft was vibrating in every rivet. They flew away from the convoy, leaving it shrouded in smoke, with the destroyers still dashing about, their guns blazing. The columns of water blasted upwards by the destroyers' main armament were falling behind them.

"Report!" Douglas called.

"Navigator here. OK."

"Rear gunner OK except for having the shit scared out of me."

"Wop here. OK except for having a piece of flak through the radio. Otherwise OK."

"Give me a course for home, navigator."

"Go onto three forty two, skipper. I'll have a better course in a minute."

"Three four two. What did you see, navigator?"

"I took a picture during the run-in. After the drop you were doing aerobatics. I snapped a picture but it'll probably only show the sky."

"Yeah—I guess so. See any results, you two other guys?"

"Results unobserved," replied Hartley.

"Didn't see anything," DesJardins said. "I was looking back."

Douglas looked at the convoy. "One of the ships is burning—somebody must have hit something."

"Looks like one of the little merchant ships—the Blenheims were after them," DesJardins replied.

"Can you see the tanker?"

"I can't say for sure—there's so much smoke around," replied DesJardins. "But it looks like the tanker is still there."

"We probably didn't hit it then, damn it!"

"We came close," said Hartley.

"Close only counts in horseshoes."

"What did you say, skipper?" Crane asked.

"Oh, it just looks as if our torp missed."

"I thought it might have."

"God knows what happened when we dropped it—it probably didn't run true, or maybe the ship combed it."

He saw the other two aircraft ahead of him. "I'm going to join up with the aircraft ahead."

"Okay, skipper," Crane replied. "I'll restart my air plot when you settle down on your new course. Might as well stay on 342 until I find a better course."

"Roger." Douglas fell in with the other two aircraft, and within five minutes two more aircraft joined them Douglas called them on his radio to check the losses. One of the Beaufort pilots who had attacked from the other side reported that his companion had suffered a direct hit and had crashed. A Blenheim pilot told Douglas that one of the four aircraft which had attacked with bombs had struck a ship's mast and cartwheeled into the sea.

"Three out of nine—thirty-three percent!" Douglas said. "Par for the course." The two Blenheim crews who had been on their first operational trip were half gone now. Three aircraft—nine men—had left England a week before, and now six men were dead. Of the four-man Beaufort crews, one had been on its second trip while the other had been very experienced, with a year of operations behind them. Three aircraft, eleven men, and on the other side of the ledger one small merchant ship damaged. Douglas shook his head. The exchange rate was too high.

206

The aircraft landed back at Luqa airport on Malta. Peterson met them at the briefing room. "Welcome back, chaps," he said. "Your good work is appreciated."

"Good work hell!" Douglas spat. "Jesus Christ, we lost three kites, and all we did was damage one tiddler of a merchant ship. You call that good work?"

"Mr. Douglas!" Peterson snapped, and then his tone became more conciliatory. "That merchant ship carried enough tanks, guns and ammunition to equip a whole battalion for Rommel. It'll be slowed down if it isn't sunk. Torpedo-carrying Wellingtons will get it tonight if it's still afloat. Or else a submarine will sink it. We know where it is, and it won't be moving fast."

"But, good God, is it worth the losses? Three trips, and we're all dead!"

"A lot more of the pongoes will be dead if we don't keep the supplies from getting to Rommel."

"But we didn't even get the bloody tanker!"

"You can't expect 100% results every time, Ed."

"Yeah, I guess so. Well, might as well get on with the debriefing." He looked at Peterson's squadron-leader braid and added the word "Sir." Peterson smiled. "We'll just have to tough it out, Ed." He left Douglas to continue with the formal debriefing.

Douglas looked at his crew. They were tired, but their faces showed their elation at having survived their baptism of fire. Until today they had been unblooded warriors, their swords unfleshed; now they were veterans, battle-hardened aircrew, able to hold up their heads among fighting men anywhere. They were still shocked by the viciousness of their initiation, and by the losses of their comrades, but they gloried in their own survival and new-found confidence. In any case they had scarcely known their lost fellows, and they had seen enough crashes in training to have become inured to losses.

The debriefing over, the crew went to the Transit Mess for their post-operational meal of beans, Spam and bread. The meal was unappetizing but they were hungry enough to eat every scrap, knowing that they would receive nothing more until the next day. Douglas was uncommunicative, although he could see Crane, Hartley and DesJardins wanted to talk about the trip, and were a little hurt by Douglas's laconic responses to their comments. After the meal, when he had unwound, Douglas regretted his coldness and sought Crane out, but by that time Crane was busy bringing his diary up to date, and Douglas left. He went into Valetta on a rickety bus, had a beer at a grog-shop on Straight Street, the "Gut," and went back to his barrack-room. They could not fly for the next four days, because their aircraft was being healed of the wounds the anti-aircraft shell had caused. The radio was badly damaged, and had to be replaced by one cannibalized from an aircraft immobilized by a damaged engine. The crew was under orders to rest much of the day to compensate for the skimpy rations they received.

A soon as the aircraft was serviceable again Douglas was sent on another strike. There were only four Beauforts with no Blenheims. All of them attacked from the same side, and one of them was lost. A big merchant ship was torpedoed and left sending a greasy black column of smoke into the sky. It was impossible to decide whose torpedo had struck, although Douglas was quite sure it had been his. He made no complaint—he had become a fatalist by now, and on his restricted diet he had no energy to argue the matter.

A week later he flew a reconnaissance mission scouring the Mediterranean for enemy shipping. Baltimore or Maryland aircraft, faster and higher-flying, usually did the job, but one was not available and a Beaufort was pressed into service. Crane plotted out a creeping-line-ahead search pattern on his chart, and navigated the plane along the gridiron legs straddling the expected path of the Axis ships. He checked the compass headings Douglas was flying against the course indicated on his astro-compass set up in a bracket in the nose, and busily checked the drift.

At intervals Crane took sights of the sun with his sextant. The air was smooth, the sky was empty, and there were clouds to duck into. Douglas kept his eyes open as he searched the horizon, but he was reasonably at ease, except that he subconsciously kept listening for an unusual rhythm from the engines. Nothing occurred; the engines ran sweetly. Douglas popped a barley-sugar into his mouth.

After three hours he saw a smudge of smoke on the horizon. "Navigator—what do you see on the starboard bow?"

"Starboard bow—oh yes—looks like smoke, skipper."

"Better have a look at it." Douglas swung the plane around.

"Steady on 173," he told Crane. They neared the smudge on the horizon, which gradually resolved itself into a clump of ships. Crane picked up his binoculars and peered through the perspex enclosing him. "I make it a big merchant ship—a cargo-liner probably—a couple of smaller ones, and six escorts."

"Looks like the ones we're looking for. Hartley, send a sighting report on our wireless."

"Roger, skipper. What's the lat and long, navigator?"

"3515 North, 2117 East."

Douglas swung behind the convoy and lined the aircraft up with the wakes of the ships, and said, "Mean line of advance looks like 240 Magnetic. Speed ought to be about ten knots—that's all those little ships will be able to do."

"Roger." Hartley worked out his message from his Syko code sheets and soon the intercom was interlaid by the muted bugle-notes of his morse key.

"Keep your eyes open for fighters, DesJardins. Shouldn't be surprised if they've got a Ju88 fighter cover."

"Jesus—there's one now—port quarter!" DesJardins yelled.

"Finish sending your message, Hartley, and then get on your gun," Douglas said. "You too, Crane."

"Roger." Crane slammed a drum of ammunition on the Vickers gas-operated gun poking through a flexible mounting in the nose of the aircraft, and crouched behind it.

The morse ceased, and Douglas saw Hartley take up his position behind the waist gun on the starboard side. The gun jabbered as Hartley tested it.

"I'm heading for that cloud," said Douglas. He flew straight for it, jamming the throttles wide open. The engines snarled. The Ju88 was going considerably faster, and he knew it would overtake him before he reached the clouds, but it would be useless to take evasive action before the German aircraft got within gun-range.

DesJardins' voice came, cool and professional, his Canadian cadence welcome to Douglas' ears after the British accents which surrounded him everywhere else. "Range 500 yards. Prepare to corkscrew."

"Roger." Douglas licked his lips and swallowed.

"Corkscrew port! GO!" Douglas shoved the nose down and

tramped on the rudder. The aircraft dived and turned, and Douglas saw white blobs of tracer curving past him. The Beaufort was filled with the savage jabber of the guns in the rear turret, and then by the closer blasts from the waist gun as Hartley fired at the Ju88's slim, lump-nosed fuselage. Shells from its cannon exploded against the Beaufort's wing as Douglas hauled back on the stick, and then a shattering explosion beneath Douglas' feet blew out part of the side of the fuselage. The Ju88 flashed past, and Crane pounded away at it with his front gun.

"Jeez, look at that!" DesJardins' voice came. "That Jerry kite's on fire! It's going down out of control!"

Douglas slowed his turn and headed for the cloud. Crane's voice came, "Yes, it's burning! It's spinning! There it goes—into the drink!" The cloud reached out for then, and suddenly they were flying with no sight of the sea or anything beyond the wing tips. Douglas turned and flew out of the cloud again. "Congratulations gang! You've got yourself a Ju88! He hit us, though. Any of you guys hurt?"

"My jacket's ripped, skipper—damn it, I'm bleeding!" DesJardins exclaimed. "God, he musta hit me in the arm!"

"Get out of the turret and have Hartley check you over to see where you're wounded."

A moment later Hartley said, "Larry's got a flesh wound in his arm—doesn't look too serious. I've bandaged it up."

"Okay, good work. How about you, Crane?"

"I'm afraid I got hit too, Ed."

"Okay, Hartley, fix Reg up."

Hartley carried the first aid kit into the nose. Douglas saw him ministering to Crane. "Reg has a nasty wound in his left arm, skipper. I've bandaged it up and the bleeding has stopped."

"You in much pain, Reg?" asked Douglas.

"Some, skipper." There was a brief silence. "Your course to go home is 265 magnetic."

"Okay." Douglas bent down to set the course on the compass. "Holy shit!" he suddenly burst out. "The compass is smashed all to hell!" He looked up at the emergency compass above his instrument panel. A shard from the cannon-shell had gone through it.

"Reg—you got a compass down there?"

"Just my astro compass."

"Can you use that?"

"It's quite a job. I say—wait a minute. Head toward the sun. It's four fifteen—the sun will be in the west. I'll take a bearing on it, and tell you how much to turn."

"Jeez—that means we gotta get out of the cloud—if there's any more 88's around we're for it."

"No help for it, skipper. I'll work out the sun's azimuth now." Crane opened his air almanac and his astronomical navigation tables. "The azimuth of the sun is 254. Set your directional gyro to 254 when you're headed right into the sun and then alter eleven degrees starboard."

"Right." With the aircraft on an even keel again Douglas peered around him. The sky and the sea were empty. " Keep your eyes open, gang!"

There was a hole beneath his feet, with a hurricane blowing through it. A side window was shattered, and the compass was twisted into junk. "Better get an SOS out, Hartley. Give us a position, Reg."

"Won't do no good," Hartley answered. "The wireless set took a shell through it."

"It did? Say, are you hurt too?"

"Ray got a slug that creased his chest. I bandaged it up for him after he fixed me up," DesJardins said.

"Jee-sus! Everybody wounded, the kite a mess, no compass, no wireless—we're in shit!"

"How badly are you hurt, Ray?" asked Crane.

"Not too bad. Stings a bit."

"Can you come to the nose and help me? I need somebody to keep resetting the astro compass. My arm's not too much use to me."

"I don't know nothing about it—"

"Look, guys," Douglas said suddenly, "we need somebody in the turret. DesJardins, come up here and fly this plane. I'll go down and help Reg. Hartley, climb into the turret."

"Jeez—fly the plane—me? Whattinhell, skipper—"

"Goddam it, Larry, come up here. If we don't know which direction we're flying we'll never get home! The only guy that can

211

find out is Reg with his astro compass! Get on up here and take over the controls. You wanted that badly enough back in England!"

"Okay." Douglas climbed out from behind the control column, and DesJardins climbed gingerly in. "Okay! you have control."

The plane wavered and dipped. DesJardins overcontrolled, recovered, and then steadied out reasonably well. "Okay, you're doing fine. I'm going down to help Reg now. I took some navigation at Service School—now I'll find out if I remember anything."

Douglas slid down into the nose beside Crane. "Okay, Reg. Tell me what to do."

Crane flipped the pages of his Air Almanac. "I've set the latitude on the astro compass. Thirty-five north. Now set the local hour angle." Crane watched Douglas make the settings, and then peered at the astro compass as he twisted the shadow-bar. "We're steering 292 now," he called DesJardins. "Set your directional gyro to 292 and then turn seventeen port."

"Okay, Reg. I'll try." The aircraft turned and straightened out. "Thank the Lord the directional gyro is still working."

The plane staggered along, draft from the shell-hole tearing at DesJardins' leg. Strange noises emanated from the shell-torn wing, but the plane maintained height, and the engines sang sweetly. Every ten minutes Crane would work out new settings for the astro compass, and he and Douglas would check the course. DesJardins would turn the aircraft a few degrees to adjust.

"What's our ETA?" DesJardins asked.

"Six-twenty—just after sunset. Look, I'm going to alter to fly down a leading line. I'll take a sight through the window with my sextant— I won't have to hold it—and that'll tell me when we're at the same longitude as Malta. The sun-line will tell us whether we're west or east of Malta but it won't tell if we're north or south; we were all over the sky after we spotted that convoy. I'm going to turn south to make sure we're south of Malta, and then turn north to reach it."

"I've heard about those leading lines," said Douglas. "Hope they work."

Crane set up the sextant, called to DesJardins, "Hold her steady as you can, Larry," and took the sight. He worked it out and plotted it clumsily on his chart with one hand. Twenty minutes later he told DesJardins to alter course thirty degrees port, and after another half-hour told him to alter due north. DesJardins turned on command. They flew on, and then a dark smudge appeared on the horizon.

"Whadda ya know!" cried Douglas. "That's Malta! Your navigation worked, Crane!"

There was no answer. Douglas looked at Crane, to see him slumped over the navigation table. "Jeez, Reg's passed out!"

"We better get down as soon as we can," cried DesJardins. "Come on up and land this kite! I sure as hell can't!"

Douglas strapped Crane into his seat, and climbed behind the controls again. He approached Luqa airport, happy there was no air raid going on.

"Hartley! Fire off the colours of the day!" The red and green balls soared into the sky. It was dark now, and Douglas looked for the flare path. He found it, nursed the plane over the runway, and brought it in. The landing was rough, since the plane did not answer properly to the controls because of battle damage. The plane bounced and slewed when the wheels hit the pitted runway, but Douglas fought it to a stop just off the tarmac. An ambulance jolted over to it and men poured out of it. Douglas directed them to the nose, where they lifted Crane out as tenderly as they could, slid him onto a stretcher, and into the ambulance. The two wireless air gunners stood watching Crane until the medical officer noticed them and ordered them aboard the ambulance also. Douglas climbed into the front seat. "I'll go to the hospital too see what's happening to my crew."

Peterson entered the hospital, in an underground cave, a few minutes after they reached it, an intelligence officer with him. He waited until the two gunners had had their wounds dressed and then said, "I'm sorry, gentlemen, but I must debrief you. We'll be as quick about it as we can. By the way, you did very well. Your wireless messages got through intact, apparently just before your wireless went out." He smiled. "We were rather relieved to see you, Douglas. We'd more or less written you off."

"We more or less had ourselves written off. We were shot up by a Ju88 just after Ray sent the signal."

"I see you evaded the Ju88, though."

"Evaded it! We shot it down!"

213

"You did! My word! Top-hole! Wizard! Who did it?"

"The gunners and Crane all had a go at it, DesJardins with the turret guns and then Hartley with the waist gun. Reg had a crack at it with the nose gun. I really think Larry got it, though—the others just helped."

Peterson nodded his head furiously. "That certainly is a good show! Now tell me about the trip."

Douglas did so, with the intelligence officer asking questions of him and the gunners. At intervals he said, "Good show!" and "Well done!" When the debriefing was finished DesJardins spoke up.

"Say skipper, don't you think Reggie ought to get a gong? There he was, navigating the kite without even a compass, and him all shot to hell!"

"You're quite right, DesJardins!" Peterson agreed. "I intend to recommend Crane for an immediate DFC—and DesJardins and Hartley for immediate DFM's. Hartley, that signal you sent allowed us to send a strike against that convoy, and the cargo liner and one of the escorts were sunk. It'll be a bitter blow for our friend Rommel!"

DesJardins spoke up again. "Jeez, sir, ain't you going to do something for the skipper? He was the captain, and he landed that flying junk-heap, didn't he?" Peterson turned to him and smiled. "We have something special in mind for Flying Officer Douglas, DesJardins."

An orderly walked up to them. "F/O Crane is conscious now, sir. Do you wish to see him?"

"Sure do, " said Douglas. The five of them walked into the ward where Crane was lying, pallid-faced. "Hi Reggie," said Douglas. "You'll take any excuse to get outta work, won't you?"

"I'd just as soon be working, Ed, the way I feel."

"You did well," Peterson told him. "You and Hartley and DesJardins will be recommended for decorations."

"Ed did all the work on the way back," said Crane.

"We know," said Peterson, "but we're recommending you anyway. Now try and get some sleep."

"Take it easy, Reg. We'll be back tomorrow."

"Wait a minute, gentlemen. We must say a prayer of thanks for our deliverance." They stood up and pressed their hands together in

214

front of them. Crane said the prayer, and they said the Lord's prayer together.

As they walked away, DesJardins said, "You know, I think that prayer he made us all say before we took off fixed us up. If it hadn't been for that we'd be at the bottom of the Med now."

"Yeah, I guess so," Hartley agreed. "I'll tell you one thing—I'm never gonna complain about him saying them prayers again."

"Me neither," Douglas added. As they dispersed Peterson called Douglas back.

"Ed!" he said. "That was a wonderful show. I'm putting you in for the DSO. I'll see the Air Vice Marshal about it tomorrow."

Douglas laughed.

"What's so funny?"

"This is the second time around. I was supposed to be recommended for a gong after I torpedoed that cruiser, and you can see what happened." He gestured toward his empty chest.

"You can depend on me."

"Thanks, Derek, but I'll believe I when I see it. Anyway, I'll be taking things easy for a few days. My kite is all shot up, and my crew is all shot up too. They're all in hospital. They've kept DesJardins and Hartley for observation, haven't they?"

"Yes, they have. To tell the truth, Edward, you should be in there for observation yourself—after all, you were in that kite too. Go get your head down." He took a step away, and then turned on his heel. "I say, Douglas, I'm really dashed glad you got back—after all, you're rather a friend of mine."

"Thanks, Derek. I was glad to get back. I'll take your advice—I'm going to hit the sack. Good night Derek—sir." He saluted.

"Good night, Edward."

Douglas slept the next morning away, awakening in time for lunch—beans and bread again, with some indefinable meat. He ate it, and then walked over to the operations room.

"HI," he greeted the sergeant on duty. "Where is everybody?"

"Taking another bash at what's left of that convoy you found yesterday, Mr. Douglas," the sergeant replied. "They're due back in an hour."

"Who led them?"

"Squadron Leader Peterson."

"I thought he was not allowed to fly."

"He wasn't."

"I see."

Peterson did not return. Nobody knew what had happened to him—he and his crew had simply disappeared. Douglas waited in the briefing room until his limit of endurance had passed, and then walked slowly over to the hospital to visit Crane.

"There goes my DSO," he said to himself.

CHAPTER TWENTY-THREE

With all three members of his crew in hospital, Douglas would have had nothing to do had Peterson remained on duty. As it was, the Wing Commander Flying conscripted him to serve as briefing officer for torpedo operations, which in a week expanded to make him essentially Peterson's replacement. He sat in on meetings with the station commander, the Wing Commander Flying, the officers commanding all the varieties of aircraft on Malta—the Beaufort torpedo planes, the Wellingtons which operated as torpedo carriers at night or bombers by night or day, the Blenheim light bombers, the fighters, and the reconnaissance planes—and the Air Vice Marshal himself. He found himself planning torpedo tactics, since the commander of the Beauforts tended to defer to his experience, briefing the crews, and debriefing them after a strike. The tactics he used were very similar to those Peterson had used, since he was a firm disciple of his lost leader, and believed that a concentrated blow at a target was all important. Under his influence the strikes were no more and no less successful than they had been under Peterson, and losses were still grievous. His chief contribution was that he advised the pilots to jink during the approach rather than come in straight and level, as Peterson had always advocated.

Douglas, who previously had been contemptuous of the "brass," was surprised to find how much work had been thrust upon him. Ruefully he recognized also that he was beginning to think of crews as pawns on a chessboard, to be moved or lost as the fortunes of the game demanded. He knew what the danger was, but he closed his mind to it as he sent the aircraft against convoys sailing to reinforce Rommel.

Hartley and DesJardins were discharged from hospital after two days, but Crane, more seriously wounded, was kept in the spartan

217

sick quarters for two weeks. The piece of flak which had driven a clean hole through the biceps muscle of his upper arm had made a wound which was painful but not dangerous and would heal normally, leaving nothing worse than a scar. He was able to use his arm again after four days, after which he was living more or less normally, except that his arm was stiff. The doctor declared him unfit to fly, which left Douglas without a complete crew.

Their aircraft was still unserviceable after the battle damage it had received, and there was no spare aircraft—the air raids had seen to that. The Wing Commander Flying kept Douglas busy in his role as operations officer, and Douglas recruited Hartley and DesJardins to help him. They did not object, since except for the frantic excitement of the frequent air raids life on Malta was rather boring.

After the first week Douglas was familiar enough with the administrative machine, which ran regardless of bombings and strafings, to enquire if the recommendation for decorations for his crew, which Peterson had promised, had actually been made. He checked with the adjutant, who sat in a tiny office with papers that made the Air Force run in peace or war.

"Say, adj," he enquired, "did Squadron Leader Peterson put through a recommendation for gongs for my navigator and my wops?"

The adjutant riffled through a file. "No, I don't see one."

"Look again. Peterson told me he'd submit one."

The adjutant looked through more papers. "No record, Douglas."

"Jeez, that's a kick in the teeth! When he debriefed us Peterson told us he'd recommend Crane for a DFC and Hartley and DesJardins for DFM's!"

The adjutant shook his head. "He didn't."

"He went missing before he could do it. That's par for the course."

The adjutant nodded. "Well, there's nothing I can do personally. There has to be a proper citation written by the squadron commander."

"Yeah, I guess so." Douglas returned to the operations section. The Wing Commander Flying was sitting at his desk, checking a battle order, when Douglas walked up to him and saluted.

The Wing Commander Flying raised his head. "Good morning, Douglas. Something on your mind?"

218

"It's my crew, sir."

"Yes?'

"When S/L Peterson debriefed us after that shaky do of ours, he said he'd recommend Crane, my navigator, for the DFC, and DesJardins and Hartley, my wops, for the DFM. I checked with the adjutant, and nothing's been done. I think Peterson went for a Burton before he got around for it."

The Wing Commander pursed lips. "Your think they all deserve gongs?"

"I sure as hell do, sir, and so did Peterson. They all did their jobs perfectly on the flight although they were all wounded, and they shot down a Ju88. Crane only had the use of one arm, and it must have been hurting like hell, but he navigated the kite back home without a magnetic compass, using astro sights and figuring out the azimuth of the sun and astro sights and leading lines and all that stuff—dammit, half the navigators in the squadron don't know what a leading line is, let alone bringing the kite home on them. He did a real bang-up job, with never a peep about that piece of flak through his arm until we got in sight of Malta, and then he passed out. If anybody deserves a gong he does."

"He didn't do more than his usual navigation job?"

"Hell yes—he had no compass, I tell you. And he couldn't use one arm. I didn't know how bad off he was till he keeled over. Besides that he was using his machine gun against the Ju88 that attacked us."

The Wing Commander nodded, "Yes, it seems he did a very good job. How about the wops?"

"Hartley got his first sighting report out perfectly, and that led to the convoy being attacked and the big ship in it being sunk. After that he was wounded, but he bandaged up Crane and DesJardins before he told anybody he was wounded himself. Then he manned the turret all the way home. He helped in shooting down that Ju88. I sure as hell figure he deserves a gong."

"How about DesJardins?"

"DesJardins was wounded too, but he flew the kite home so I could go into the nose and help Crane. Crane couldn't handle the astro compass with his wonky arm, and somebody had to help him. I knew enough about navigation to do it for him."

"So DesJardins flew the aircraft home? Against regulations, what?"

"Regulations be buggered! I'd be dead if he hadn't!"

The Wing Commander smiled. "Rather a good point, I admit." He reached into his desk and pulled out a file. "Here are some previous citations for other wallahs who've been decorated. Write out citations for your crew, telling what happened, along the same lines. I'll forward them. By the way, Douglas, what were you doing during all those heroic goings-on? I presume you were acting in an advisory capacity and staying out of danger."

"Jeez, sir, a guy can't recommend himself!"

"No, of course not. That's why I intend to write your citation myself. Tell me exactly what happened on that trip."

Douglas told his story while the Wing Commander wrote busily. When he had finished he said, "Very well, Douglas. Now write up the citations for your crew—and then back to work."

Douglas had the operations clerk type the citations out, and took them back to the Wing Commander. He leafed through them, looked up at Douglas, and smiled. "You've got the details here all right, but you haven't got the right music. Let me revise these citations a little. Remember, the people who read these citations don't know beans about actual flying." He winked. "I've recommended several people for decorations, and they've always been approved. Let's give your crew the same chance."

"Okay, sir," Douglas replied, miffed that his literary efforts should elicit so little admiration. "If you think that'll do the job better, that's OK with me."

The clerk retyped the altered recommendations. The Wing Commander Flying sent them to the station commander, and then made sure they were taken to the office of the Air Vice Marshal. Two days later the Wing Commander called Douglas into his tiny office. "I've been speaking to the AVM. He has approved an immediate DFC for Crane and a DFM for Hartley. He has the authority to do that. For you and DesJardins it's different. Crane and Hartley are Royal Air Force—they're limeys like me. You're Royal Canadian Air Force. The AVM hasn't the authority to award decorations to RCAF personnel without clearing it through RCAF Overseas Headquarters in London. There will be some delay."

220

"Here we go again!"

The Wing Commander Flying looked at him sharply. "What's so funny?"

"This the third time I've been told I've been recommended for a gong, but every time something happened that got in the way. I hope we have better luck this time."

"I assure you, Flying Officer Douglas, that all the proper steps have been taken. You can have complete confidence in the process."

"I'm sure you're right, sir. Now can I congratulate Crane and Hartley?"

"The award will be published in Daily Routine Orders tomorrow. Wait until then."

"Yes sir. The news will help Crane get better."

"I'm sending a signal to Alexandria at once about you and DesJardins. It should be on its way tomorrow too."

"Thank you, sir." Douglas returned to his desk and began to select crews for the strike planned against a convoy which had been reported by the morning's reconnaissance flight. Would the citation for him call for a distinguished Flying Cross, or for the more prestigious Distinguished Service Order? Peterson had spoken of a DSO, but the Wing Commander Flying had not heard him say it, and probably the best Douglas could hope for was a DFC. After all, the Wing Commander hardly knew him and would be reluctant to recommend him for the second-highest gallantry award. Douglas shrugged and went back to work. The next day the awards to Hartley and Crane, properly approved by the Air Vice Marshal, appeared in Daily Routine Orders. The actual decorations would be presented in due time by the King at Buckingham Palace, but in the meantime they were entitled to wear on their jackets the medal ribbons with their diagonal purple and white stripes, wide for Crane's DFC and narrow for Hartley's DFM. Hartley took Crane's jacket into Valetta in search of one of the military tailors who still abounded in Malta to have the ribbon sewed on Crane's jacket and on his. The three members of the crew made a ceremony of awarding the decoration to Reg, with a clump of nurses from the hospital and fellow inmates of the ward forming an audience. After giving him the jacket the three called "Speech! Speech!" Crane, however, crossed them up by offering a brief prayer. A stern and frozen-faced matron, who had come on the double to damp down any unseemly celebrations, had no choice but to stand there with her hands folded and her eyes downcast until the prayer was finished.

"You can trust old Crane," Hartley said. "Always knows the right things to say."

The citations for Douglas and DesJardins were typed out and sent to the wireless transmitting station for transmission to Alexandria, from whence they would be sent on to London. Just before the ground wireless operator was due to tap out the message, an air-raid alarm sounded, and he went to a shelter. When he returned he found that a bomb had blasted the transmitter room. By the time he had cleaned things up the message about the decorations had been swept into the discard. The message was never sent. Douglas waited for a few weeks with his hopes high, and then gradually relegated his dreams of military decorations to the back of his mind. In truth, he had expected nothing better.

CHAPTER TWENTY-FOUR

As soon as Crane was declared fit to fly the crew was sent out on a strike against a convoy. The tactics were as before—three aircraft attacking from each side. The weather was cloudy, and the aircraft were able to make their attacks without being subjected to the vicious fire they had encountered on previous attacks driven home under cloudless skies. The tanker which was their target turned toward Douglas to comb the three torpedoes launched at it from the port side, and those torpedoes missed, but in so doing it turned away from the other aircraft, and two torpedoes hit. A towering column of black greasy smoke rose toward the cloud-base, and as they left the crews could see the ship ablaze from stem to stern. One of the aircraft was hit by flak from an accompanying destroyer, but it made a good crash-landing and DesJardins saw the crew clamber out of the sinking craft into a rubber dinghy. The ship had been carrying a full cargo of desperately needed fuel for the tanks and lorries of the Afrika Korps, and the two pilots who had scored hits were recommended for decorations. Douglas was not. His torpedo had missed.

A week later a flight of six Beauforts landed at Malta, destined for the squadron based there. The station commander called in Douglas and two other pilots, the captains of surviving crews who had been hijacked on their way to the Far East or the Desert Air Force, thanked them, and told them that they and their crews were to fly to Alexandria in Egypt as passengers in a Wellington that was to leave that night. The fact that there were more crews than aircraft, due to landing accidents on the bomb-pocked runways or to battle damage that left the crews alive, made his decision easier.

The crew packed their bags in ten minutes. The take-off was uneventful, although a raid began as soon as they were airborne. The Wellington climbed to 8000 feet in the darkness and headed for Egypt.

223

"Good-bye Malta," said Crane. "I won't miss you."

"Me neither," agreed DesJardins. "Bloody near starved to death. It'll be good to have a square meal again. You know, that place was quite well known before the war as a holiday resort."

"Oh, Malta has its points," Hartley said. "At least we got gongs out of it," and then looked stricken as he avoided Douglas' eyes. Douglas laughed. "It's OK, you guys—I'll shine in your reflected glory."

"How long is the trip to Alexandria?" DesJardins said quickly, to change the subject.

"About six hours. It's 900 miles," Crane answered.

"We'll be hungry when we get there," said Hartley. "No food on this kite."

"I'm going to get some sleep," said Douglas. He lay down, put his head on his parachute pack, and dozed off. When he awoke dawn was in the sky ahead of them, and the Mediterranean was still under them. They flew for another hour, and then the Egyptian coast appeared on the horizon. They landed at the airfield and climbed bleary and unshaven from the aircraft, to head for the transient mess. There they were served eggs—a welcome treat—and there was jam for their toast. Crane looked at Douglas and said, "There is a lot to be said for simple pleasures."

"What will we be doing in Alexandria?" Hartley asked.

"Pick up a new kite, I guess," answered Douglas. "They bring them in by ship and assemble them here or in Cairo."

"Good. We left our last kite in Malta—or what was left of it. It was patched up a few dozen times," said DesJardins.

"We'll get our quarters assigned to us and then report back to the operations room at nine o'clock or so. We'll probably be on our own after that."

The operations officer returned Douglas' salute. "Oh yes— Douglas. You're slated to take a Beaufort to Ceylon. We'll have a kite for you by the end of the week—it's being assembled now. In the meantime enjoy the delights of Alexandria."

"Roger," Douglas answered, "we'll take advantage of it. Every time we went downtown in Malta we got bombed."

Three days later their cheeks, gaunt from Malta semi-starvation, were beginning to fill out again, and they enjoyed bomb-free Alexandria to the full. Crane, of course, visited the churches.

DesJardins went to a movie and to a dance hall. Hartley sought out a brothel.

Douglas fell in with another pilot at the operations room. "Name's Steve Winters," he said. "I'm waiting for an aircraft too. Where'd you come from?"

"I was in Malta for a while. On Beauforts."

"I was on Sunderland flying boats flying out of Ireland. Submarine patrol. They sent me to Beauforts a couple of months ago. Picked up a headless crew at OTU."

"What d'you do that for? I thought Sunderlands were good aircraft."

"Oh, I bitched so loud about being on them they posted me out. They were driving me crazy—fly all day looking out the window and never see a thing. I didn't see a single submarine in all my time there. The boredom was killing me. I wanted to do something where I could see something of the war."

"You'll have a pretty good chance of doing that on Beauforts," Douglas said. "Where you from in Canada?"

"Kamloops, British Columbia."

"I come from a little place in Saskatchewan called Valenby. What you got in mind now?"

"Let's go into town and see what trouble we can get into," Winters said.

"Good idea." He and Douglas made the rounds of taverns and dance halls. Douglas enjoyed Winter's company. He was pleasant and humorous. Although Douglas considered his exchange of a safe if boring life in Sunderlands for torpedo bombers insane, he did not say so.

Douglas reported to operations two days later, to find a newly-assembled Beaufort waiting for him. A test pilot had put it through its paces, but Douglas needed to fly it on a consumption test to make sure it would not run out of fuel midway to its destination. The six-hour cross-country flight to the pyramids and up along the Nile was relaxed and routine, and the engines never faltered. After an hour, when he was satisfied that everything was going normally, Douglas invited DesJardins up to the cockpit to fly the aircraft, while he took his position in the turret, where he admired the view of the green fields sandwiched between the desert and the Nile. When they landed Douglas said, "The

225

kite works fine. Let's head out tomorrow. The weather'll be good this time of year."

The crew appeared at the operations building the next day to check the weather. Crane had just prepared his flight plan for the first leg, to Aden, when an officer hustled in. "F/O Douglas—come with me!" He led Douglas to the office of the Wing Commander Flying.

"Douglas—we've got a maximum effort on—a convoy is approaching Tobruk with fuel for Rommel. Intelligence says Rommel is planning an attack on the British line. He's low on fuel, and if we can get his tankers we can cripple him. We need all the experienced torpedo crews we can get. You're very experienced, with a good crew. We're calling on you to take part."

"Jesus Christ! I'm on my way to Ceylon!"

"Sorry, old chap. The AVM has overruled your departure. Briefing is in half an hour."

"Jesus? But we just got out of Malta—only just! We're supposed to go to Ceylon! Enough is enough!"

"Orders are orders, Douglas. Get your crew together."

"Goddam AVM's! AVM Lloyd hijacked us in Malta and we damn near got the chop flying torpedo strikes! We got shot all to shit on one trip—everybody in the crew was wounded but me! Damn it, can't you take it easy on us?"

The wing commander stood up. "You have received your orders, Douglas. Obey them."

"Okay, if it'll win the war for you."

Douglas went back to the room where Crane was finishing his flight plan. "You can scrap that," he told him, "we're flying on a torpedo strike instead. Briefing is right away. We might as well go over to the briefing room."

"Jeez, skipper, that ain't cricket!" Hartley protested. "We just barely got outa Malta. This is just plain asking for it!"

"Goddam it, I was looking forward to a rest—out in sunny Ceylon," put in DesJardins.

"If we must, we must," said Crane, bundling up his equipment. They walked to the briefing room, where they were surprised to find a dozen very senior officers already there. A group captain called the aircrew to attention.

"All of you know what is happening at El Alamein," he began.

"The Eighth Army is fighting a crucial battle against the Afrika Korps and their Italian allies. The Air Force is doing everything in its power to help. The most important thing we can do is to cut off Rommel's supplies of fuel. A convoy is heading for Tobruk, including one tanker. We know that Rommel is short of fuel. What we must do is to sink that last tanker. If we do, we'll make our soldiers' lives a lot easier—and we'll save a lot of lives."

He looked around the room. "This battle is all-important. We have to get those ships—if we don't, it'll make things immensely more difficult for the Army—not to mention us too. If we don't get them the first time, we'll have to lay on further strikes until we do, even if it means daylight attacks on Tobruk." A murmur rose from the assembled crews; they knew what a daylight attack on a fanatically-defended base meant. "So let's do it—press home our attacks, get close to the enemy before we let fly at him, and refuse to be deterred by opposition."

The attack was to be made by twenty-two aircraft—eight Beauforts carrying torpedoes, nine Beaufighters (twin-engine aircraft armed with cannon), and five Bisleys carrying bombs. The Bisley was a version of the Blenheim, and Douglas was glad he was not flying in one of them, even if they would maintain height on one engine. The Bisleys belonged to a South African squadron, whose crews carried army titles of rank and wore khaki uniforms. The senior South African was a tall, imposing major who looked the part of a fighting airman, and Douglas wished that he himself were as dashing. The torpedo strike was to be led by an English squadron leader, chosen by the wing commander commanding the squadron, who was flying himself as an ordinary pilot because he was less experienced. He briefed the aircrew confidently. "He's got Peterson's methods," Douglas said to Crane. "Everybody attacks the tanker—to hell with the little merchant ship that accompanied it, and don't worry about the escort."

"It's the accepted tactics now, " Crane nodded. "Too bad Peterson went missing before his theology became dogma."

"Maybe he's watching from up there. If he is, he'll be pleased."

"Yeah," put in DesJardins. "Hope we're not up there keeping him company."

Hartley laughed. "We won't be going to the same place."

"Anyway, let's go get that tanker. If we do they'll let us go to Ceylon," DesJardins said, "where every prospect pleases and only man is vile."

"Yeah," Douglas added. "Take me somewhere east of Suez, where there ain't no Ten Commandments or Ju88's."

"There may not be any Ju88's," admonished Crane, "but the Ten Commandments will still be around."

"We got Beaufighters to give us fighter cover," Hartley said.

"They'll probably be used as flak-suppressors though," said Crane. "It'll be better for us if we don't have to face heavy fire from the ships because they're too busy coping with the Beaufighters blasting them with cannon-fire."

"I hope so," said Douglas. "You know, those Beaufighters would make pretty good torpedo kites. Wonder why they don't use them?"

"I heard they were talking about it," said Hartley. "One of the Beaufighter navigators was talking to me in the briefing room."

"Well, let's get it over with," said Hartley. The crew gathered their gear and walked out to the lorry which would take them to the aircraft.

They shared the lorry with the crew of Steve Winters. "Looks like I'm going to get a little excitement this trip," Winters said. "A hell of a lot better than those boring Sunderland trips. You know, you got one sighting every thousand hours. I had five hundred hours, and I didn't even see my half of a submarine." He was rubbing his hands in anticipation and smiling broadly. "In the war at last!"

"How'd your aircraft check out when you tested it?" asked Douglas.

"Had a little trouble with the radio. They tested it on the ground and couldn't find anything wrong. It'll clear up when we get airborne."

"They usually do," agreed Douglas. The lorry stopped and the crews got out. "Good luck," Douglas said to Winters as the crews headed for their aircraft.

The crew boarded the aircraft, and Douglas started the engines. "Good to fly a new kite instead of those old wrecks we had in Malta," he said to DesJardins.

"Yeah. But it was you that wrecked them, Ed. No more crash-landings. This is a nice kite—we want to take it to Ceylon."

"A moment of quiet, gentlemen," Crane's voice interrupted them.

228

"Time for our prayer," Hartley said. "We're going to need a real good one this time, Reg."

"Almighty God, thou knowest how busy we will be this day. If we forget thee, do not thou forget us." They all said "Amen." Douglas was no longer impatient. Crane's prayers comforted him, as Crane's sober, religious personality strengthened the crew. The other two members looked on the prayers as good-luck charms; once, when Crane had omitted the prayer, they had refused to take up their positions until he said the words.

Douglas took off and formed into a loose gaggle with his twenty-one companion aircraft, the Beauforts in the center, the Bisleys on one side, and the Beaufighters ranging overhead, keeping their speed down to match their slower sisters. It was 350 miles to Tobruk, the first leg over the sea. After a little more than two hours the aircraft turned south and swung towards the Tobruk harbour. There was no convoy there. The flight leader radioed the Beaufighters flying above him, who had better visibility than he had, and received the report that there was a two-ship convoy, escorted by three destroyers, approaching the harbour. He climbed up to look for himself, and saw ships, even if he was not sure one of them was a tanker. The flight leader decided that they were there; they had torpedoes; they would attack. He fired the Verey lights which were the signal for the attack and streaked toward the ships. The Beaufighters were already raking the five ships with cannon as the Beauforts settled down for the torpedo run.

Douglas saw the yellow flares, but he did not attack with his companions. "Say gang," he called, "There's no tanker there!"

"Sure as hell ain't," agreed DesJardins. "No, there is no tanker," Crane confirmed.

"Damn it, we were briefed to attack a tanker, not some old rust-bucket! There ain't no tanker there—I'm not going to waste a torp on that boat! Whadda ya think, gang?"

"You're the skipper, Ed," Hartley said. "If you go looking for the tanker, we're with you."

"Which way are we going, skipper?" Crane asked.

"South. We've already been north."

Douglas turned the plane. Off to his left he saw two other aircraft—Bisleys of the South African squadron. Their commander

229

had read the situation the same way Douglas had, and was formatting on him.

Only a couple of minutes passed before they found what they were looking for—the tanker, escorted by another destroyer. They were both within range of the flak guns on the coast, and the sky was filled with black puffs from the shell bursts. Douglas flew on until he was abreast of the tanker and turned to attack it, as the destroyer dashed to get between him and his prey. The destroyer's main armament was blasting at him, and the decks of the tanker were ablaze with light anti-aircraft cannons. Douglas let down to his dropping height and slowed to 140 knots as the tanker turned toward him. "Good tactics," he muttered as he saw its bow swing. The two Bisleys dashed past Douglas at over 200 knots, going in on a bombing run.

The captain of the ship, seeing this more urgent danger, reversed his turn, leaving himself almost dead in the water. Douglas had almost a no-deflection shot at the ship as he closed to 700 yards and dropped his torpedo. As his thumb pressed the release, he saw four two-hundred-and-fifty pound bombs fall from the leading Bisley, and saw one of them blast the ship's bridge. The second Bisley dropped its bombs also, but the pilot, intent on his target, waited one fatal second too long before he pulled up. The tip of a wing hit the ship's mast and the plane slewed sideways, cartwheeled into the sea, and disappeared in a column of white water.

Douglas, mesmerized by the sight of the bursting bombs and the quick, final destruction of the Bisley, held his course almost too long, and then pulled up desperately, putting on heavy aileron to dip the wing between the masts of the ship. As he flew away he felt a jarring crash as debris from the explosion of a delayed-action bomb flew skyward and thumped into the root of the starboard wing. The aircraft staggered, and he fought to control it as it dipped perilously close to the water. With the propellers almost touching the wave-tops he flew back out to sea from the chaotic harbour, whose waters were a forest of columns from shell-bursts. The torpedo, outpaced by the plane which had dropped it, hit the side of the ship a glancing blow, ran along it, and then exploded underneath its stern. As Douglas flew away the crew could see the ship blazing from stem to stern, a towering column of smoke and flame climbing from it. "We got it! We got it!" DesJardins screamed. "That's a few gallons of gas old Rommel won't get!"

"Now all we have to do is get home," Hartley said. Douglas opened the throttles to rejoin the gaggle of planes now heading for the Mediterranean. There were only nineteen of them now—a Bisley and a Beaufort had been shot down on the attack on the other convoy, besides the Bisley which had crashed beside the tanker. The flight swung to the north, passing two diesel-driven barges which spat at them resentfully with light flak-guns. Above them Douglas saw Beaufighters engaging some Macchi fighters which had intervened, but the combats were inconclusive, and soon the strike aircraft were flying home, their crews still alert but relaxing a little.

The flight left the harbour area, the diesel barges, and the enemy fighters, and turned for Alexandria and home. They were still flying low, to evade detection from any German radar stations on the coast, but they were widely spaced. Douglas eased off to the side. As he did so he saw a Bisley drifting toward him; he dropped off a little height until he could see its tail above him, and then spoke to DesJardins. "I'm going to roll the plane a little. Take a good look around and make sure there are no other aircraft under me."

"Roger, skipper. Douglas rocked the plane. "Nobody here."

Douglas lifted his eyes to the Bisley in front of him. "Say, what's that crazy bastard doing?" he asked angrily as he saw the plane approach a Beaufort from below and to one side. "That's Steve Winters' plane!," Douglas said. The pilot obviously had not seen the other plane, while the Bisley was in the blind spot of the Beaufort. Douglas thumbed his radio. "Hey Winters! Look out! Bisley Peter! You're getting too close to that kite ahead!"

There was no answer. "Betcha the poor bastard has his radio out! Hey you! Winters! There's a Bisley right underneath you! Look out, for Christ's sake!"

There was a flurry of action in the Beauforts, but not soon enough, The Bisley, climbing slightly and drifting sideways, struck the tail of the Beaufort with a wingtip and flipped it sideways. The Beaufort, too low to recover, knifed sideways into the water, striking the Bisley as it did so. The Bisley reared like a bucking horse and stalled, and a wing fell. The plane knifed into the water and disappeared immediately.

231

"Good God!" Douglas cried, as he eased his plane another wing-span from his companions. "Looks like Winters got all the war he wanted," he said to the crew. There was no answer. The flight, now with seven Beauforts and Bisleys instead of twelve, continued on its way to Alexandria, the shaken crewmen vigilant and wary. They flew out of sight of land until they were past El Alamein, where a mighty battle was raging, and then angled in toward their airfield. When the buildings of Alexandria appeared on the horizon Crane said, "We're in sight of base, skipper."

"It's about time," said Hartley. "That was a shaky do, even if we did torpedo that tanker!"

"You did good, skipper," DesJardins said. "We've decided to keep you in the crew."

They landed. The crew got out of the aircraft. Crane whistled as he walked round the aircraft and peered under the wing-root. There was a great splotch of red paint smeared onto the bottom of the wing, outlining a crushed patch of distorted metal. Douglas looked at it, bending down under the wing and shaking his head. "Holy smoke!" That piece of the ship must have gone right through the propeller-arc!"

"We were sure lucky," said Hartley.

"Well, let's go to debriefing," said Douglas. They climbed into the lorry and were driven to the operations building. A South African general was present, who listened carefully to the reports made by his men and by Douglas' crew. Crane had taken a picture of the Bisley cartwheeling into the sea, and another one of the tanker on fire, which had been rushed to the photographic section to be developed. It proved conclusively that the tanker had been destroyed, which meant that Rommel's planned offensive had been crippled. The group captain station commander was overjoyed, and he and the general shook the hands of the crew. "Looks like us colonials did all right," DesJardins said to the general, and he grinned.

The squadron leader who had led the raid was there also, looking unhappy and avoiding the eyes of Douglas and the South African Bisley crews. He had attacked the wrong convoy with most of the aircraft, while Douglas and the Bisley crews, who had disobeyed his orders, had sunk the tanker. The Wing Commander Flying was

232

there, keeping his own counsel. At the conclusion of the debriefing the general held a brief conference with his men, and the next day a notice was posted stating that the major, the pilot of the other surviving Bisley, and the major's navigator had all been awarded immediate DFC's.

Crane was outraged. "But you torpedoed the ship!" he cried to Douglas. "Why weren't you mentioned?"

Douglas shrugged. "Your gong will have to do for both of us. He grinned sourly. "Let's face it, Reg—no matter what I do in this man's air force I'm not going to get a gong."

Crane was not satisfied. He complained to the adjutant of the squadron in which they had been pressed into service. That officer pleaded that the matter was out of his jurisdiction, and referred him to the officer commanding the squadron, who in turn referred him to the Wing Commander Flying. He told Crane, "There are only so many gongs to go around. We can't decorate everybody who takes part in a strike. It was the South Africans' turn this time. Besides, their general was here. It's a bit difficult to argue with a general who has his mind made up."

"But sir—this is monstrous! F/O Douglas actually sank the ship the South Africans merely damaged! For heaven's sake—a bomb only lets in air—a torpedo lets in water!"

"I appreciate your loyalty to your captain, but you are not competent to decide such matters, Flying Officer Crane. My decision today is final. If you wish to say anything further, I suggest you put it in writing—send a letter to Air Ministry."

"Very well, sir." Crane saluted and turned about smartly and left the office. The Wing Commander looked at his retreating back and said to his second-in-command, who had heard the exchange, "Now there's the kind of officer we need. Not like that other Wild West character, Douglas."

The other man sucked his lip and said, "He had a point, though. Douglas did sink the tanker."

"I never met anybody in my service who was so reluctant to go on an operational trip as Douglas was—I practically had to threaten him with a court martial." He shrugged. "But I might have recommended him for a DFC if he had used the word 'Sir' once in our previous conversation."

233

Crane returned moodily to his quarters, and sat down to write a letter. It was not to the Air Ministry, however; it was to his mother.

"I am furious," the words went. "My pilot, Flying Officer Edward Douglas, has just been passed over once again for a highly-merited decoration. During the strike we flew on just yesterday, he torpedoed an Italian tanker transporting petrol to Rommel's troops fighting at El Alamein. An officer of the Eighth Army who is here on liaison duties has assured me that the tanker was absolutely vital to the enemy, and its loss tilted the scales very much in our favour. Three South Africans who bombed the ship were decorated, but not Ed Douglas—they only damaged the ship, he sank it.

"This was not the first of Ed's exploits. He had completed a whole tour of operations before he crewed up with us, during which he torpedoed the German cruiser *Gladbach*. His navigator received the DFC for the action, but Ed received nothing. He also took part in the attack on the *Scharnhorst* and the *Gneisenau*, after which he brought home a badly-damaged aircraft and made a crash landing instead of bailing out, because his wounded wireless operator was trapped in the aircraft. During our stay in Malta he flew on the most dangerous missions with us. On the trip during which I was wounded he brought the plane home, showing exemplary courage, skill and leadership, which I am sure saved my life. The trip was recognized by decorations awarded to myself and to Ray Hartley, our wireless operator, but none came to Douglas.

"It is shameful that Ed Douglas' service should not be recognized fittingly. The very least he deserves is a DFC—a Distinguished Service Order would be more fitting. A word in the ear of our dear friend Tom Sullivan may very well rectify this shocking injustice."

Crane sealed the letter, considered mailing it, and then reflected that a prying sensor might very well delete most of it. He decided to send it by a faster, surer method. He gave the letter to the command chaplain, who was on his way back to England, and who of course Crane had sought out a few days before. The letter was placed in the hands of Crane's mother a week later.

Mrs. Crane invited Air Vice Marshal Thomas Sullivan to dinner a few days later, and handed him the letter. He took it, read it, and promised to look into the matter. With a scrawled recommendation it was fed into the slow-grinding mills of the military bureaucracy, where it was considered by the appropriate personnel, all of whom held that an AVM's signature authorized anything.

Crane never told Douglas what he had done. After all, it was really none of his business, and he did not believe in meddling with the personal affairs of others, unless it was to point out religious truths and unless he was asked.

The next day, as the crew waited for their aircraft to be cured of the wound it had received from the flying hatch-cover from the torpedoed ship, a Royal Canadian Air Force group captain visited the air station. He was a Public Information Officer who had been promoted to his sky-high rank in keeping with his civilian position as editor of a Montreal newspaper. He asked to see any Canadians at the base, and Douglas and DesJardins duly waited upon him. Crane and Hartley came along.

He was professionally affable with all the aircrew. There was good copy in these combat airmen, who had just come back from a strike in support of the Eighth Army. Douglas introduced him formally to the three men in his crew. His eyes narrowed slightly when he shook hands with DesJardins; he spoke in the plain standard Canadian accent of any other Winnipegger, but he had an undeniably French name.

The group captain essayed a few words in French, and DesJardins replied with a torrent. In a few moments he established that DesJardins was actually Metis, of French and Cree Indian descent, with Indian blood flowing in his veins. The group captain's eyes opened wide when he learned this. The RCAF needed publicity about French-Canadians who had distinguished themselves in battle, and here was one who was not only French-speaking but also partly Indian as well. He was perfect.

"I see two members of your crew wear decorations but you do not."

"Course not, sir," Hartley put in. "When Larry and Ed was with us on the trip we got gonged for, they climbed out on a cloud and watched us while we brought the kite home."

The group captain turned to him. "What do you mean by that?"

"We was on a trip out of Malta, sir. We found the Jerry convoy we was looking for, and we shot down a Ju88 that attacked us. When we got back to Malta, in a kite that was shot all to ratshit, with Larry wounded. Reg Crane and me got gongs. Larry and Ed never got nothing. I told them it was their own fault—they was only colonials, wasn't they?"

"I consider it a monstrous thing, sir," said Crane in his patrician voice. "F/O Douglas and Sergeant DesJardins deserved decorations ten times as much as I did."

"Tell me about that operation, gentlemen," the group captain said. He sat down to take notes as they spoke. Twenty minutes later he stood up, thanked the crew, and hurried off to the office of the commanding officer of the base. He telephoned Cairo, and then sent an urgent message to England. His subject was DesJardins. Douglas was deserving, but there were many heroes from the prairies, with names like Douglas. The propaganda value of DesJardins was far greater. Anyway, Douglas' turn would come. The details were in his notebook, to be processed at leisure.

The next day he returned, all smiles, to tell DesJardins he had been awarded an immediate Distinguished Flying Medal. Crane and Hartley congratulated him heartily, and so did Douglas.

"I sure got a heroic crew," Douglas laughed. "I'm very proud of you."

Crane looked at him shamefacedly. "I just don't understand—"

"Don't worry about it, Reg. Everything comes to him who waits. Let's go have a drink to celebrate it. Come on, Larry."

The group captain turned to Crane. "I would be delighted to offer you a ride in my staff car to one of the hostelries in Alexandria, where we can celebrate together. Be my guests, gentlemen."

They went off together. After a couple of drinks they forgot the group captain's exalted rank, and enjoyed themselves hugely.

CHAPTER TWENTY-FIVE

The crew waited while the mechanics worked on their aircraft—besides the crushed wing-root there were the usual flak-holes. Douglas did his compulsory air test, and then the crew was briefed for the first leg of the trip to Ceylon, which was to Aden. Crane had spent some of his time when he and his fellow crew members were waiting in Alexandria in teaching them to take sextant sights, browbeating them into doing it with his usual brand of sweet reason mixed with insistence, to which was added his rich-man's-son habit of command. He acted in such matters as if opposition was unthinkable, and DesJardins and Hartley complied.

"Good show," he told the two WAGs as he prepared his flight plan. "We'll have lots of time to practice our astro. The air is quite smooth over the Red Sea, I've been told, and we don't have to worry about the enemy."

"Okay by me," agreed DesJardins. "I want to find out how good my sun-shots will be in an aircraft. So far I've only done them on the ground."

The flight began uneventfully, with the crew in their proper places until they were well away from the possibility of interception by prowling Huns. Then Hartley and DesJardins alternated in the astro dome, sighting on the sun, and passing the altitude readings to Crane in the nose, who worked them out and plotted them on his chart. Douglas put DesJardins in the pilot's seat later and took over the sextant himself, to find he was not as good as either of his wireless operators. He decided not to tell Crane about his experience with the marine sextant on the ocean on his way across the Atlantic.

237

There was actually no great need to use celestial sights, since the visibility was good and they could follow coastlines all their way down the Red Sea to Aden, and from Aden to Muscat, and map-read from Muscat to Karachi, from Karachi to Bombay and from there to Colombo in Ceylon. Crane was anxious to polish his skill at celestial navigation, however, and the rest of the crew found sextant work a welcome break in the boredom of a long and tedious flight. They flew on, part of the time with DesJardins in the pilot's seat, Douglas in the turret, and Hartley in the astro-dome, all in flagrant disregard of regulations. By the time they landed at Colombo Crane was more experienced in celestial navigation than any other navigator Douglas had ever met, and both the wireless operators were good sextant men. The only man who had not noticeably polished his skills was Douglas.

Everything went well until the last leg of the trip to India. Two hours out of Bombay the starboard engine began to run roughly. Douglas pulled back the throttles to ease the strain on the motors, and retrimmed the aircraft. "Navigator from pilot!" he called sharply. "Give me a course to fly along parallel to the coast within gliding distance of the shore!"

"Why do you want that, skipper?" Crane asked.

"The damn engines are acting up, that's why. The starboard engine looks like it's going to give trouble."

"Is it? Good heavens, I hadn't noticed."

Douglas grimaced; navigators, immersed in their work, were blind and deaf to what went on around them. A moment later Crane said, "Steer one one three compass."

"One thirteen." Douglas turned the plane. The Arabian Sea, blue under the sun, rolled on beneath him as the noise of the engine grew less melodious and his apprehension greater. He resisted the temptation to widen on the throttles to bring him to land sooner. Chewing on nothing, he licked his lips. "Jesus, can't that bloody land come up!" he muttered.

"You say something, skipper?" DesJardins demanded.

"Nothing, but I wish the land would show up. I don't like the starboard engine at all."

"No sweat, skipper—we'll make it. You've always brought us through before." Douglas growled something in reply. The faith of

238

his crew embarrassed him, since he did not share it. He chewed at a imaginary cud and shifted uneasily in his seat as he listened to the uneven rhythm of the starboard engine, and realized that he was as frightened as he had ever been on the run-in against a hostile ship with shell-bursts everywhere around him; more frightened, indeed, since now he was not busy enough to occupy his mind with anything but his fear. He looked down at the waves and shivered. Convulsively he thumbed his microphone. "Get ready to throw out those guns and ammo if we lose this engine!" he commanded.

"Roger," DesJardins replied. "Jesus, skipper, are things that bad?"

"Can't take any bloody chances with this old cow of a kite," Douglas replied, trying to keep the hysteria out of his voice. "Crane? How far is the coast?"

"About fifty miles. Twenty-two minutes at our ground speed."

"Twenty-two bloody minutes! Jesus, why does it have to take so long?"

"Don't worry, skipper," Hartley put in. "The engines sounded worse coming back from that tanker strike in the Med, and we still got home." Douglas grunted. He looked at his watch and found two minutes had passed. Then suddenly he thumbed his microphone. "Crane!" he rasped out.

"Yes, skipper?"

"Say a prayer, Reg."

"What?"

"Say a prayer, dammit!"

" Very well, skipper. There was a brief silence, and then Crane's upper-class voice came. "Almighty God, mercifully grant that these thy servants may overcome the perils of this day and come safely to their destination, to the glory of thy Holy Name, and for the sake of Thy son Jesus Christ, Amen."

"Amen," DesJardin's voice echoed him, and then Hartley's.

"That's better." Douglas relaxed a little.

Crane's voice returned, "Steady down for a drift, skipper."

"Roger." Douglas touched the controls.

Hartley's voice came. "That's the ticket, Reg. Trust in God and keep your powder dry and your navigation up to date."

A line on the horizon announced the Indian coast. When the land was under his nose Douglas turned the plane and told Crane. "I'm

239

settling down on 171 degrees. Keep track of where we are."

"Roger," Crane answered. "It's going to add considerably to our ETA."

"I know—I know," Douglas answered testily. "We'll have to put up with it." Crane computed a new Estimated Time of Arrival and Hartley transmitted a message, adding an explanatory phrase, couched in the "Q" code" of three letters beginning with "Q" which quoted engine trouble. Douglas advanced the throttle again, only to pull them back as the starboard engine began overheating.

"This cross-eyed old bitch won't hold won't hold height on one engine better'n any of the others," Douglas complained. "Give me a course for the nearest airfield." Crane complied. Then Douglas heard him laugh.

"Hey, what's so funny down there? Let us in on the joke."

"Fifty years ago Rudyard Kipling wrote a poem about soldiers on the Northwest Frontier of India. One line went, 'If you find that your bullets go wide in the ditch, don't call your Martini a cross-eyed old bitch.' Things don't change a lot in half a century." Douglas was quiet for a moment, and then he said. "Yeah, you're right. You know, Hank Snow woulda known about that poem too." He cogitated for a moment. "Crane, do something for me."

"Yes. What is it."

"Fly with me. If somebody else wants you to fly with them, don't do it."

"That's a funny thing to ask."

"My old navigator, Hank Snow, was all right as long as he flew with me—when he flew with somebody else he got killed."

"I'll do my best, skipper."

"How about me?" demanded Hartley.

"No trouble with my wops. One of them is back in Australia, and the others are teaching morse in some wireless school. No need to worry about them—or you."

The intermediate aerodrome came up under the wing, and Douglas landed. He complained about the engine. The trouble was diagnosed as a fault in the lubrication system, which was put right in an hour. They took off again the next day, this time completing their flight without incident, although Douglas nervously watched the engine-temperature and oil-pressure gages the whole way.

They reported to the operations room and were issued quarters. Douglas and Crane cleaned up and walked to the officers' mess for tea. They were munching on a slice of cake when a voice came to their ears.

"Flying Officer Douglas! What are you doing here?"

Douglas jumped to his feet. "Moragh MacLennan! Good to see you!"

He caught her hands and looked her up and down. "And an officer now? Congratulations Section Officer MacLennan!" He turned to Crane. "This is Reg Crane, my navigator. Reg, Moragh MacLennan. We were together in Lower Lexington. She's a storebasher. Sit down, Moragh, and have a cup of tea, and tell us what you've been doing."

"How do you do, Miss MacLennan," Reg said. "I'm delighted to meet you. Ed and I have been flying together for six months now. He's a splendid pilot."

"Och, he is that." She smiled at Crane. "You've just come out here frae England, I take it."

"By a rather roundabout route. We were posted here, but on the way we were pressed into serviced at Malta. Then we were shanghaied again at Alexandria. But we got here at last."

"What were you doing during your stop-overs?"

"Flying on operations. As a matter of fact, some of the flights were rather dicey."

Moragh nodded. "I'm not surprised. Everything happens to Flying Officer Douglas."

"Yes. He's had a most distinguished career. I am most happy to be flying with him."

Douglas turned to Crane. "Moragh was a real terror in her storekeeping empire at Lower Lex. Used to give me us real hard time." He smiled reflectively. "Funny thing—Hank Snow, my old navigator, could always get round her, but I never could."

A shadow of pain crossed Moragh's face. "Henry Snow was a wonderful man—a real braw lad," Moragh said. She stood up suddenly. "I'm very glad to see you again, Mr. Douglas, and to meet you, Mr. Crane. You must excuse me". She left, her tea untouched.

Douglas watched her retreating form. "Wonder why she rushed away so fast. I didn't say anything, did I?"

241

"Nothing that I noticed, skipper," Crane answered. "She's an attractive girl. Has a lovely broad Scots accent—I've always liked that."

"She's quite a girl. Got a mind of her own, though. When I met her in Lower Lex she was a sergeant."

"She seems capable."

"She is. Don't tangle with her."

Crane smiled, "I don't intend to."

"Still don't understand why she left in such a hurry." Douglas scratched his head. "Oh well, next time I see her maybe I'll find out."

Crane looked at Douglas. "Tomorrow's Sunday."

"So it is."

"I expect to see you in church tomorrow, Ed."

"What?"

Crane looked at him with level eyes. "You wanted a prayer when you were in trouble, Ed. You got it. Now you can fulfil your part of the bargain. It's not enough to be a Christian when things are difficult—you have to be a Christian the rest of the time too. You believe—you wouldn't have asked me for a prayer if you didn't."

Douglas nodded his head resignedly. "You're right. Okay, I'll be there."

The entire crew was present at church, as Crane had requested. Even DesJardins was there. "A deal's a deal," he said. "God will understand. He's a Catholic, but he'll make an exception in this case."

CHAPTER TWENTY-SIX

They reported to their squadron the next day, adding their new but already-damaged Beaufort to the four old ones and another new one which flew in from England the following day. The squadron had been given the job of standing guard in Ceylon against a possible attack by the Japanese fleet, which a year before had wreaked havoc in the Indian ocean, sinking several cruisers and destroyers and an aircraft carrier.

It was a wartime station, but living conditions were almost peacetime, and in comparison to England and especially to Malta, luxurious. There was plenty to eat, including delicacies which the crew had all but forgotten, such as steaks and chops. Fruit was served at every meal, as well as a variety of fowl and fish in exotic guises. Douglas had eaten curry occasionally in England, but Indian curry was deliciously different. Their quarters were well appointed, and they even had native bearers as servants. The weather was hot, but after Malta the crew was used to that, and many of the days were no worse than Saskatchewan in the summertime. Best of all, there were no bombs.

There were, of course, flies in the ointment. The station commander was a disgruntled group captain who had been eased out of North Africa after several botched operations, and who now concentrated his efforts upon pettifogging insistence on cleanliness, military smartness, and proficiency in drill. Douglas appeared on parade the day after he arrived, and was promptly told by the adjutant to buy a new uniform and a new hat. There was no difficulty in acquiring either, since the air station was besieged by Singhalese tailors, but Douglas resented being arbitrarily ordered about by someone he considered a mere functionary, even if he did

243

hold higher rank. His squadron commander had welcomed him formally, but when the crew appeared before him he noticed at once that although the other three men wore decorations, there was nothing over Douglas' breast but his wings and his battle-dress jacket. When the crew had left he said to the adjutant, "That Douglas—he's a rum chap. All the other members of his crew have been decorated but him. I wonder why? Think he's a trouble-maker?"

"I'll keep an eye on him, sir," the squadron adjutant said. "There's nothing in his record to indicate anything like that, though."

The squadron commander riffled through the file. "Funny," he said, shaking his head. "It says here he torpedoed the *Gladbach*, but he hasn't even got a Mention in Despatches. Something must be wrong. Yes indeed, keep an eye on him."

"Very good, sir," the adjutant replied, making a mental note to do exactly that. Douglas, if he had been received in reserved fashion by the squadron commander, expected to be welcomed by his new squadron mates. Instead, he was chagrined to find them standoffish and distant, treating him as a new boy at school. Forgetting that he had treated newcomers in exactly the same fashion himself, he reciprocated by treating his new mates with the disdain a combat veteran reserves for those who have not shared his danger. There were two other pilots and a navigator who had been under enemy fire, but the others had served only on patrols which, however necessary, had not involved them in violent action, and soon Douglas found himself gravitating to these peers of his almost exclusively. It did not make him more popular.

Douglas was aware that he was the subject of conjecture as well as a certain amount of resentment. His fellow squadron-members soon found, however, that his prestigious, decorated crew was devoted to him. They deferred to him, they defended him vociferously against the most minor criticism, and they coalesced into a tight knot with him in the briefing room and in the flight room.

Off duty, the knot loosened. Hartley frequented the sergeants' mess, as regulations called for. Off the base, DesJardins sought out Hartley's company in preference to Douglas, since their shared duties and their interests melded better. Crane had gone to church as soon as he arrived, and the Anglican chaplain had pressed him into service as an acolyte, and then as a Bible-class instructor for the handful of devout airmen at the station. Douglas took to spending his time with the few combat-hardened aircrew.

After a week he found himself requires to make a pilgrimage to clothing stores to exchange his flying suit, which had drawn the criticism of his flight commander, naturally enough since there were a number of holes in it left by enemy flak. He made a point of checking to see that Moragh MacLennan was there. She was sitting in a small office when he entered.

He waved to her. "Come on over and say hello," he called. She walked out to the counter where a corporal was serving him. "So it's you again, is it?" she smiled at him. "What have you done to your clothing this time?"

"I haven't done anything to it—it was the Germans that did it—or maybe the Eyeties. The suit was all flakked up in Malta. Couldn't get it exchanged there—they had nothing there to give me."

She nodded to the corporal. "Very well. Give this officer a new flying suit."

He raised his eyebrows. "Not giving me a hard time? You're losing your touch."

"Try me when you're working a wangle!"

"I'm too smart to do that." He looked at her. "Since you're being so agreeable, how about accompanying me to the pictures tonight? You're the only girl I know in Ceylon."

"You have a gift for the gallant phrase, Mr. Douglas."

He shuffled. "I'm sorry, but I don't know a damn soul here, and it's as lonely as hell. Come on—I knew you before. Heck, I've even danced with you."

She nodded slowly. "Oh, very well, For the sake of auld lang syne."

"Dinner first?"

She nodded.

"Thanks, Moragh. See you at seven." Douglas took the flying suit the corporal had brought him, signed the voucher, and left the stores building.

Douglas took her into Colombo that evening, to a restaurant recommended to him by one of his fellow pilots. Compared to the austerities of England, the meal and the surroundings were lush, with hordes of deferential waiters and a lengthy menu, plus a wine list. Douglas leaned back after he had ordered and looked at Moragh. "Sure is good to see a familiar face from the old days."

"What do you mean by the 'old days'?" she bridled. "It was only a little more than a year ago that we were at Lower Lexington."

"Sorry—there I go again. I seem to have a genius for saying the wrong thing. Sure wish I had the talent for smooth talk that Hank Snow had."

Her face sobered. "I wish you wouldn't talk about Henry Snow."

"Oh—sorry. Yes—of course you knew him."

"He was a wonderful person—the most wonderful person I've met. He was sweet and thoughtful and flattering—he was good looking—he was even a good dancer."

"Yes—so he was. He was a good navigator too. I really liked the guy. Dreamy, you know—but a good navigator."

"But he's gone now. Let's talk about us. What have you been doing since you left Lower Lexington?"

He told her, omitting any reference to Constance. She listened to him, making the proper comments at the proper intervals. He found he was enjoying himself. "And what about you?" he said at length. She told him how she had received her commission, and then had been sent to Ceylon. She described her journey on a troopship around the Cape of Good Hope and across the Indian Ocean. "I'm surprised they'd send a girl out on such a trip," Douglas commented.

"I think they did it by mistake," she answered. "They thought I was a man. Somebody misspelled my name as 'Morgan' on some form or other. I must say I enjoyed the trip, though."

"Good Lord! That trip was dangerous!"

She smiled. "After what you've been through, you say it was dangerous!"

"Well, they shouldn't expose a girl to that kind of risk."

"I'm a member of the Royal Air Force too," she responded.

"Anyway, you're here, and I'm glad."

After they had finished their dinner they went off to see a movie. He took her home, kissed her sedately, and returned to his bachelor quarters. He was a little put out. He had become used to having women fall into his arms the way Margaret Reilly and Constance

246

Davidson had, and Moragh had treated him as just a friend. He went to sleep feeling unsatisfied and a little cheated.

The crew flew on a cross country exercise the next day. The navigation leader insisted on laying out a complex route, and demanded a carefully-completed log from Crane. Crane was annoyed, since he felt that his operational experience entitled him to more consideration than that, but he complied with the instructions, and came home with the proper number of astro sights, drifts, compass checks, and ground speed checks. The wireless operators were given tasks also, much as if they were still back at the OTU, and they complained; but the signals leader was a flight lieutenant, and they could not make their protests heard. Douglas sympathized with them, but he had to go along with the orders also. At any rate it gave them something to do, and without the gut-wrenching stress of operational flying, the flight could be pleasant.

The Beauforts were stationed at Colombo as a strike force, but the battle of Midway and the battle of the Coral Sea, as well as the desperate struggle for Guadalcanal, had kept the Japanese far too busy with the Americans to allow them to spare any ships to range the Indian Ocean. Colombo was too far west to be in much danger of attack, and after an initial period of uneasiness the air station lost its air of martial purposefulness and relapsed into an unwarlike routine, despite the group captain's efforts to keep it smart and airmanlike. Catalina flying boats flew out to escort convoys and hunt submarines, and at infrequent intervals one of them would find a submarine and attack it. Otherwise, however, everything was peaceful. What Douglas and his crew appreciated most, of course, was the absence of fighter opposition, although the fact that there were no hostile destroyers spitting curtains of steel at them was also welcome.

For a month Douglas was kept busy practicing attacks on the merchant ships that plodded up and down the coast, and then Far Eastern Headquarters, unhappy to see serviceable aircraft and trained crews doing so little that was useful, decreed that the Beauforts be used for anti-submarine patrol. This involved taking a number of classes given by the Catalina squadron on the approved method of searching the sea, flying esoteric patrols named after reptiles such as rattlesnakes, dropping depth charges on submarines if they found any, and communicating with the naval ships and the convoy commodores with whom they would work. None of the information was really new, but Douglas and his three companions listened as attentively as they could.

Loaded with depth charges instead of torpedoes, the crew flew out, joined a convoy, performed stately pirouettes around it, and returned to base when they reached their Prudent Limit of Endurance. The aircraft did not carry radar, and the naked eyes of the crew were the only detection aid they possessed. They never saw anything but the convoys and the odd fast liner which sailed alone. They had been told that their main task was to keep the submarines submerged, but if they were successful in doing this they did not know it. Crane was the only one who really enjoyed himself. Alone over the trackless wastes of the ocean, he worked out fascinatingly complex plotting problems to intercept moving targets, plotting celestial sights on the sun and moon and Venus in the daytime and on the stars at night, learning how to estimate the speed of the wind by looking at the surface of the sea, and playing games at forecasting the changing wind velocities and then seeing how his forecasts worked out. When he found a copy of a Canadian newspaper in the mess, which referred to a local man as "the all-important navigator of a coastal command crew" he preened himself. Over the sea, as on it, the navigator was in his element.

Douglas relaxed for the first few flights, allowing DesJardins to fly the aircraft while he sat in the turret, swinging it back and forth lazily as he looked out at the wide and blue and always-empty sea. On the fourth flight, however, he had engine trouble. He pulled back the throttles and nursed the aircraft along, abandoning his patrol, jettisoning his depth charges, and fighting to gain extra height. He warned the crew to throw their equipment overboard when he gave the word, and almost gave the command once when the engine sputtered worse than usual. Its beat smoothed somewhat a moment later, however, and he struggled home. He had been two hundred and fifty miles out to sea when it happened, and it took more than two hours to creep home at an airspeed twenty knots below normal.

248

It happened again on his seventh patrol. Douglas headed for home immediately as he had before, and landed two hours after he had taken off. As he had done before, he complained stridently to the engineering officer. "Change that goddam engine! If we're going out in the blue at least we want our engines to work!"

"I'd like to," replied the officer, "but we have no spare engines. We'll check everything over very carefully, and I'm sure you'll have no more difficulty."

The next trip went off without difficulty, but Douglas by now was sitting uneasily at the controls, looking out at the endless blue sky and sea with its crisp whitecaps, apprehensive each time there was the tiniest variation in the note of the engines. He stopped letting DesJardins fly the aircraft; if there was engine trouble he wanted to be at the controls himself.

When he was not flying there was not much to do, and he felt himself becoming bored. The only bright spot was that Moragh MacLennan consented at intervals to see him.

One night as they relaxed over drinks in a restaurant after seeing a movie, Moragh said, "I met your navigator again yesterday."

" What was he trying to do—swindle a new flying suit out of you?"

"As a matter of fact he was. Your crew is awfully rough on their clothes."

"Yes, I guess we are."

"He's an awfully nice chap. I must say I took to him at once."

"Huh! Competition, I see."

"He spoke very highly of you. He told me you were the best pilot he had ever known. He was quite emphatic about it."

"Guess I've got him fooled," Douglas replied, embarrassed. "He's a good navigator—one of the best." He nodded. "Very religious, you know—intends to become a clergyman when he gets out of the Air Force. Kinda cramps my style a bit, I must admit—I've had to clean up my language and everything since I've been flying with him."

She laughed. "My heart bleeds for you."

"Yes. I've been lucky in my crews, you know. My first crew was first-rate too." He twirled his glass in his fingers reflectively. "Reg Crane is every bit as good as Snow was, and Snow was one of the best. Reg is a bit of a dreamer too. I guess all navigators are." He looked at her sharply as he saw her expression change. " I'm sorry,

Moragh. Did Snow do something to you? When I mentioned his name in the mess when I first saw you here you took off like a scalded cat."

"No—he didn't do anything like that."

"Did you see much of him?"

"Yes. I saw a lot of him. I met him when he came in to change a flying suit, the way you did. And then we danced together at the village hall. After that he used to go there every week, and I would always be there, and we would always dance. Then after a month or so he asked me to go to a movie with him, and then we went on a picnic. He was always a perfect gentleman—damn him!" She sipped at her glass. "No. I didn't really see a lot of him. Just enough to fall in love with him."

"What? You were in love with him?"

"Yes. I was in love with him. I even know when I fell in love with him. It was when I expected him to kiss me—and he kissed my hand."

"Yeah. He was an old smoothie."

"A smoothie! Perhaps. But wonderful. If he had lived I would have married him."

"You would have married him?" Douglas looked up sharply. The name of Helena Compton-Morris came to his tongue, but he choked the words back. "Yes, of course. He was a wonderful guy. I don't blame you for falling in love with him. I know you must miss him as much as I do. You know, he would have made a wonderful husband."

"Yes I know. We talked about marriage once or twice. Once I asked him why he never made a pass at me—all the other men I went out with did. He told me that in the little British Columbia town where he was born it simply wasn't considered the thing to do to make a pass at your special girl friend. Then later he told me that he'd never ask anybody to marry him as long as he was on operations. I know what he meant, though—he was asking me to wait for him. I would have." She dabbed at her eyes with her handkerchief.

"It was rotten luck when Wing Commander Tenley grabbed him to fly with him on that last trip."

"He murdered him!" She was suddenly fiercely indignant. "He'd done his share—he wasn't obliged to do any more!"

250

"The wingco wanted him because he was such a good navigator."

"Aye—and now he's dead! There was nothing fair about it!" She began to sob.

"No—there was sure as hell nothing fair about it. He was slated to go back to Canada to be an instructor at a General Reconnaissance School,—he'd be there now, fat and happy and out of danger, if Tenley hadn't taken him on that last trip. Against a bloody cruiser, too!"

"He'd already attacked a cruiser—got a medal for it. Wasn't that enough?"

"I thought so."

She wiped her eyes and smiled at him. "It's no your fault, Edward. I shouldn't ha' carried on like this. Come on—let's drink up and forget the past." She looked past her glass at him and raised it to him. Then her lips trembled. "But when I hear that Canadian voice of yours I hear Henry."

"Sorry, Moragh. I didn't know." He looked at the table. Here was this woman, calm and confident and capable, as capable of deluding herself as he had about Charlotte. Moragh had obviously known nothing about Lady Helena and her engagement to Snow.

"Life kicks you in the teeth now and then, Moragh." He raised his glass. "To absent friends."

"To absent friends." She looked at him a little sheepishly. "I didn't intend to blather on the way I did. You must forgive me."

"There's nothing to forgive you for, Moragh. After all, he was my dearest friend, my comrade—my crew mate—my friend."

"That's what he was to me—my friend. I wish he'd been my lover." She sipped at her glass again. "Will you dance with me, Edward?"

"I'm delighted to," he answered. When the dance ended she said, "You dance like Henry Snow."

When he took her home he kissed her on the cheek and left her to enter her quarters alone.

He saw her again several times. During one of them he took her to a tea-dance at Colombo, after which they drove around the city in a *gharri*. They had dinner, and several drinks, and then, in a secluded corner of the restaurant, he pulled his chair closer to her. She looked at him with lowered eyes, and then he took her hand and kissed it, and moved away. She caught her breath. "Don't waste

251

them there," she said, opening her arms. Their lips met and her arms closed tightly around his shoulders.

"I have a little suite in the women officers' quarters," she said. "Take me there. We can have a drink in private." He stood up and had the waiter hail a taxi.

She invited him into her two-room suite, and offered him a drink. They kissed again, with more abandon, and then she reached up and unknotted his tie. He picked her up and carried her into the bedroom.

She was passionate and responsive, and he considered he had made a conquest until he leaned over to kiss her after she was lying, dreamy and satisfied, beside him. He heard her whisper a name.

"Henry!" she said. Douglas leaned back. So she was still in love with his dead navigator, and she had made love do him because his accents and his choice of words reminded her of Snow. He took her hand and kissed it, and then stood up to put on his uniform again.

"You're a braw lad," she said. "Now gang awa hame and be a guid wee boy for the rest of the night."

"Goodnight, my beautiful Moragh," he said, and quietly left the building. As he walked back to his own quarters he was happy and unhappy. He had enjoyed the evening, and the love-making had been wonderful. But he knew now what it meant to be jealous of a ghost.

He saw Moragh a few days later, and when he made the approaches to her he thought that now were conventional, she rebuffed him firmly, "I don't want you to get any ideas, Mr. Douglas! Our episode is no a precedent."

"But Moragh—"

"I lost my head, I admit, but I have it firmly screwed back on the noo. Now you be a guid wee boy now, and take no more liberties."

When they parted she gave him her lips but that was all. He went off disgruntled but in a sense happy. She didn't want to kiss him; she wanted to kiss Hank Snow, who was dead. At least there was nobody else. He wondered if he were falling in love with her. He had fallen in love with Charlotte, and she had cast him off too. If he did fall in love with her he would be very careful about telling her.

CHAPTER TWENTY-SEVEN

Douglas and his crew flew on operations as they were ordered, never seeing anything hostile. If there were any submarines in their path, they had all seen the aircraft before they had been seen, and dived. The danger he had run during his previous operations had been far greater, but paradoxically that very danger had taken his mind off the risk he ran from the unreliable engines. The danger from an engine failure was worse off England, since the water was colder and the weather rougher, but it was still minor compared to flak and fighters. Here, with the flak and the fighters far away, the fact that the aircraft was underpowered began to prey on his mind.

On his seventh patrol he cut his task short, and returned to base early to complain about the engine. A mechanic could find nothing wrong with it, and Douglas insisted that the senior flight sergeant check it personally. Again there was nothing that could be found wrong with it. Douglas' crew loyally reported that they also had heard a rough-running engine, but the engineering officer patently disbelieved them. He said as much to the squadron commander. "This man Douglas is beginning to be a bit of a nuisance. He expects perfection, and nobody's perfect."

The squadron commander nodded. "Yes. I've been keeping an eye on him. It's high time he learned he's not the only pebble on the beach."

"My men are under great pressure, you know, sir, and no one pilot can expect special consideration."

The eighth and ninth missions were performed normally, although his crew began to notice that Douglas was testy and short-tempered. "Goddam it," he snarled at Crane when asked to hold the plane steady while Crane measured the drift, "don't be so bloody long about it! Can't you take a drift after all this time?"

"I'll be as quick as I can," Crane responded. He had done nothing differently from what he had done a thousand times before, and wondered why he was being criticized. The two wireless air gunners got their share of criticism also, mostly undeserved. DesJardins tended to snarl back at him, and Douglas, out of deference to the egalitarian colonialism of which he was proud, forbore to pull rank on him, but he continued his criticism.

Part of his ill-temper, he recognized in his calmer moments, was due to Moragh's rejection of him, but most of it was due to his apprehension. The rest of the crew did not share either, and they were happy. He knew he was being unfair, and alternated bouts of testiness with intervals of consideration, and wished he could be more even-tempered.

The crews took off one morning after a weather briefing from a Sikh meteorologist complete with beard and turban. The forecast was completely predictable, as was the mission. A convoy had left Bombay some days before, and an anti-submarine sweep was to be made of the waters surrounding it.

The orders called for a 'rattlesnake' patrol, flying out to the convoy, steering out a hundred miles kitty-corner from it, turning at the end of the leg onto a course which was a reverse of the convoy's path for twenty-five miles, and then returning to the convoy for a repeat of the patrol on the other side. It would be strictly routine, and it was unlikely to be dangerous. The chance of meeting a submarine was minimal, and there were no Japanese ships in the area. The navigator, as usual, would be working frantically, but the rest of the crew would find things easy. In the briefing room they sat at their table looking bored.

The first three hours of the patrol were routine. Douglas sat slumped in his seat, sweeping his eyes around the horizon. The sun was high in the cloudless sky, glinting off the infrequent whitecaps. At intervals the navigator called for the gunner to drop a smoke float and sight on it with his gunsight as it fell behind them to measure the drift. Navigation was easy near the equator. The compass was steadier than over the North Sea, the visibility was better, and the air was smoother.

Crane kept sighting on the sun with his sextant, sometimes impressing Hartley and DesJardins into service, warning Douglas to concentrate on his flying to keep the plane steady while one of them peered through the sextant eyepiece. Douglas was skeptical as to how much of the navigator's work was really necessary in these languid latitudes, where they could always climb up to ten thousand feet to look for the convoy as they approached it. But good navigators were compulsive workers, and skill honed by practice would come in handy when things got tough.

They flew out at their standard five hundred feet, turned to fly the reverse course, and turned back toward the convoy. Douglas switched the fuel gages from tank to tank, added the readings, divided by 85 gallons an hour the engines were burning, and worked out how much endurance remained. There was a good hour and a quarter of fuel which would be left in the tanks after landing. Douglas nodded. He had expected it and planned for it, but it was reassuring.

The convoy came in sight, exactly where it should have been. DesJardins, who was operating the radio, flashed his Aldis lamp at the big liner in which the commodore of the convoy was sailing, and read the flashes that answered. "Nothing new," he said. "Go onto the next leg."

Douglas flew over the convoy, circled the commodore's liner, and settled onto the outbound course, which Crane had handed up to him, written on a cardboard slip. He had pulled up when he approached, since naval gunners were notoriously suspicious of low-flying aircraft, and now he let down again to the patrol height of five hundred feet. He had just adjusted the throttles and trimmed the aircraft for straight and level flight when an explosion rocked it, and smoked poured out of the port engine.

"Jesus Christ!" Douglas called, "what was that?" He pulled the left throttle back. "She's blown a pot!" Hartley yelled. "The whole of the bottom cylinder is gone!" The aircraft slewed toward the dead engine. Douglas saw the trail of oil and fuel the engine was leaving behind it, and switched it off. He cranked on rudder trim to straighten out the plane, and punched the feathering button. The propeller blades twisted to face the front and stopped. The racket stopped, as did the vibration which had been shaking the aircraft from one end to the other. He looked at his altimeter. The needle was slowly revolving. "We're down to 400 feet already!" he cried.

255

"I'm dropping the depth charges. Throw out the guns and ammunition!"

"Think we're going to ditch, skipper?" Crane asked.

"Bloody right. These kites never hold height on one engine. Okay gang, prepare to ditch!" He turned the plane toward the convoy. The navigator scrambled up from the nose and buckled himself into the seat beside the pilot, and the gunner left the turret.

"Goddam it," spat DesJardins, "just when everything was going so well!" Douglas aimed the plane at a spot ahead of the convoy, and settled down into a glide as if he were making a normal practice landing.

"Anyway, the bloody water'll be warm," said Hartley, and then the intercom fell silent. DesJardins broke in; "Notre Seigneur qui est en ciel..."

"Brace yourself!" Douglas snapped. The aircraft neared the surface, and Douglas saw that the sea was rougher than it had looked from aloft. He kicked the rudder to turn along the trough of the waves. The plane kept sinking. Douglas pulled up the nose and cut the throttle to the good engine. The plane stalled and dropped, just a foot or so, into the water.

"First impact!" The plane skipped like a flat rock thrown over the sea. "Second impact!" The plane settled into the water amid a welter of spray that rushed over the top of the fuselage and poured through the hatch.

"Get the hell out of here!" Douglas yelled. Crane unbuckled his seat harness, reached up and grabbed the sides of the roof hatch, and hauled himself through it. Douglas handed him his navigation bag, as the drills had taught him to do, and followed him.

The aircraft wallowed in the waves, steam rising crackling and spitting from the engines. The two gunners emerged from the hatch over the wireless operator's seat. "Everybody OK?" shouted Douglas. "OK—OK!" came the responses. Beside them the dinghy, automatically inflating as the salt water covered the Graviner immersion switch, writhed and fattened. Crane tossed his bag into it, and the four men jumped into it. DesJardins cut the painter, saying, "Don't want the silly old kite to pull us under." They paddled away from the aircraft, which slowly filled and then dived for the sea-bed with a flip of its tail.

"Never did like that kite," said DesJardins. "I didn't trust it."

"We're in the path of the convoy," Hartley said. "I say—that big freighter's lowering a boat."

"Guess I won't have to navigate this dinghy to the shore after all," Crane commented. The four men watched the ship's boat splash into the water, saw it swing round toward them, and heard its engine as it neared. The boat—actually a motor launch—eased up to them, and a sailor threw them a rope. Hartley grabbed it and pulled the dinghy to the launch. The four of them clambered over the bulwark, to be welcomed by half a dozen men, speaking English interspersed with Norwegian. Three of them hauled the dinghy aboard the launch. "We might as well keep this," one of the sailors said. Crane reached to rescue his navigation bag. "I'm attached to this."

The bosun in charge of the boat steered the launch back to the freighter and ran up beside it. Two men grasped the falls dangling from davits and hooked them to the shackles at the ends of the boat. The launch was hoisted up the side and swung inboard. The captain, a wizened, weather-beaten Norwegian, greeted them, saying, "Come below."

He led them to a small wardroom. "There's nothing wrong with us that a good stiff rum wouldn't cure. We've just been for a bit of a yachting trip, that's all," said DesJardins, as self-possessed as ever.

"We can help you there," replied the captain, and a steward appeared a moment later with thick mugs of coffee laced with navy rum. "This will take the chill out of your bones."

"Except for getting soaked, there's nothing wrong with us," Hartley said, raising the mug to his lips. " You made a pretty good landing, skipper."

"Thanks, Ray." Douglas took a pull at his coffee. "Holy cow! This coffee is actually drinkable!"

The captain laughed. "Yes. We Norwegians know how to make coffee. Too bad about your airplane, boys. You couldn't keep it flying, no?"

"No. We lost an engine, and they won't hold height on one engine. If you're low your goose is cooked."

The captain raised his eyebrows. "Unfortunate."

"They're underpowered bastards. They ought to scrap them. But we have to make do with what we've got."

257

"That is always the way of it. I sailed with a log instead of a deck gun on two voyages myself."

Crane laughed. "It must have been hard to fire it."

"Yes. Now get your heads down—have a nap. We'll feed you when you wake up."

"Good idea, sir," Crane replied. "It does leave a man a bit tired."

They were put to bed in bunks; the ship had been a cargo-liner in the piping times of peace, and there were a dozen bunks for passengers. A steward took their wet clothes. The three crewmen turned their heads to the wall and fell fast asleep, but Douglas lay awake for an hour reliving the ditching. His eyes closed as he drifted into an uneasy doze and then he was sitting bolt upright, grasping an imaginary control column, his feet on imaginary rudder pedals, screaming. "I'm parallel to the swell! Rounding out!"

"Take it easy, skipper," DesJardins called. "You're down now, and we're all in one piece. You're OK, Ed—take it easy!"

Douglas looked wildly around him. For a moment he thrashed about, still controlling the phantom aircraft, and then he lay back and raised a hand to wipe the sweat from his forehead. "Sorry, chaps," he mumbled. "Guess I musta been dreaming."

"You did all right, skipper. We hardly got our feet wet. You greased her on just like that water was a runway. Nobody coulda done better," DesJardins said.

Douglas collapsed back onto the bunk, gasping and twitching, and then abruptly he fell asleep as quickly as a baby. Three hours later, when a steward came to take them to their meal, Douglas was so soundly asleep that Crane said, "Leave the poor devil," and they trooped off without him.

"What's wrong with the skipper?" Hartley asked "During that ditching he was cool as a cucumber. Then when it's all over he goes apeshape."

DesJardins nodded. "He was sure cool during the ditching. I guess he keeps it all bottled up inside. He's been through a lot—more'n we have. I guess things just piled up on him, like. We're damn lucky we have him. He's good when things are tough—the way they were in Malta."

"Well, he'll have a rest now. Survivor's leave and all that," said Crane.

258

"He ought to get a gong for this," Hartley said.

"He shoulda got one a long time ago," DesJardins said. "Honest to God, it makes me feel stupid—all of us with gongs, and him without one, and everywhere we've gone, he's gone."

"If he didn't get a gong for pranging that tanker, he won't get one for a ditching," said Crane.

"It doesn't look like it," agreed Hartley, shaking his head.

They sat down, and the steward placed before them heaping plates of food, the like of which they had not seen for years. "Jeez, lovely grub!" Hartley said admiringly.

"Save some for Ed," DesJardins said.

"There's lots. These merchant navy types know how to live."

"Yes. As long as they keep on living," Crane said.

"Not much activity in these waters. We've never seen anything on one of our patrols."

"Lucky for us."

They finished their meal and drank the Drambuie the steward placed before them, and then returned to their cabin. Douglas was still sleeping. They went onto the open deck in the tropic night, under the blazing stars, and looked over the stern of the ship at the wake, flecks of phosphorescence dancing in the calm water. The dark shapes of the companion ships of the convoy loomed around them, blacker than the darkness.

"Sure nice here," said DesJardins.

"Better'n working," Hartley agreed.

"Why worry? Our pay goes on, the food's good, and we haven't much to do."

"Thank God for small mercies."

Douglas walked up to them. Crane turned to him. "You finally woke up, I see, Ed."

"Yeah."

"Get anything to eat?"

"Not hungry." Douglas looked over the stern at the wake. "Jesus, you can see this wake twenty miles."

"Who's looking for us?" DesJardins asked. "The Yanks are keeping the Japs busy a lot further east."

Douglas swung around to face him. "Goddam it, how do you know that? Think we'd been sent to patrol around this bloody convoy if there was no danger? Jesus, the Japs are just looking for a convoy like this when we've got our guard down! I wish to Christ we'd finished the patrol!"

"We haven't seen a submarine since we got here."

"Our job is mostly to keep them down—if we don't see anything we're doing it. These goddam ships—every one silhouetted against the horizon! And these phosphorescent wakes! Christ, we're sitting ducks!"

"There ain't much we can do about it, skipper," Hartley said philosophically.

"I don't like being on this bloody boat. We've pranged enough of them, and being on one of them now is just asking for it! Jeez, I wish I was in a kite right now, instead of being a bloody sitting duck!"

"Yes, I suppose so," Crane said slowly, and edged away. "I'm going up on the bridge to bother the ship's navigator. I want to see how he does it."

They sailed on for two weeks, the three others enjoying their voyage, the food, the weather and their idleness, while Douglas stomped about fretting. After a few days they took to avoiding him. Crane spent his time with the ship's navigator, learning how to use a marine sextant, and how to work out celestial observations using logarithms, while the two wireless air gunners made friends of the radio officer, and spent much of their time in the radio room. They took to keeping watch for him. The convoy kept radio silence, and they could not send messages, but they could keep a listening watch, hearing the talk that filled the ether from shore stations and from such ships as were happily neutral. Douglas wandered, helping to keep watch on the bridge, complaining about his inactivity, and repeating that they were terribly vulnerable to every sort of enemy action.

The crew of the ship was glad to see him go when a destroyer escorting a northbound convoy sent a boat over to pick them up and take them back to Ceylon. Douglas' mood improved when he was aboard a naval vessel, with guns and depth-charges and the appurtenances of war. "Sure glad that's over," he told Crane. "It was getting to me."

"Yes, of course. It's good to be in an active warlike role again."

260

Douglas spent much of his time on the bridge, acting as a lookout. The ship's crew was happy to have him; he was an extra pair of eyes and he knew what to look for. Crane made friends with the navigator, who discovered he was an embryo priest, and told the captain; the captain conscripted him to hold a Sunday service.

Later Crane, DesJardins and Hartley were hanging over the rail at the quarterdeck, looking as usual at the wake. "You know," Hartley said, "I think Ed's flak-happy."

"Yes," Crane nodded. "The pitcher has been too often to the well."

"We still have the rest of our tour to do, too. It's not going to be easy on him."

"He's okay when he's flying," said DesJardins. "He's just bloody-minded when he's on the ground."

"Yes." Crane looked at the sky. "Brave as a lion when he's flying."

"And shit-scared the rest of the time. He needs a rest."

Crane nodded his head slowly. "It's easier for us. We just go where the kite goes, and do our job. We can't turn back. He can. I'm glad I have my job and not his."

"You can say that again." Hartley looked at the wake. "Maybe they should turn off these phosphorescent wakes. Then Ed could get a good night's sleep."

CHAPTER TWENTY-EIGHT

The destroyer nosed up to the wharf at Colombo, and Douglas and his three companions, clasping their meager possessions, walked down the gangplank. As they left the ship they turned to the quarterdeck and came to attention. They would have saluted but their caps were now resting with their aircraft on the bottom of he Indian Ocean. They had razors, shaving brushes and shaving soap, courtesy of the crew of the Norwegian freighter, and Crane had his navigation bag, but that was all.

A car was waiting for them. They were surprised to see it, expecting the usual lorry, but as a recovered crew the squadron was putting itself out to welcome them back. At the air station they were welcomed by the flight commander and the adjutant. "You don't look bad—been out on as pleasure cruise?" the flight commander asked.

"Sure thing, sir," replied DesJardins. "Partly courtesy of the Norwegian Merchant Marine, partly courtesy of the old gray-funnel line. Lovely grub. I highly recommend it."

"We're glad to see you back," the flight commander continued, "but in the meantime, the adjutant has some good news for you." The adjutant handed copies of three signals from higher headquarters, which had been following them, making their laborious way through the clogged official channels, from one station where they had served to another.

The first one said, "Flying Officer Reginald Harwood Crane DFC is promoted to Flight Lieutenant." The second one, also through Royal Air Force channels, said, "Sergeant Raymond Arthur Hartley DFM is promoted to Flight Sergeant." The third message, from RCAF Overseas Headquarters, said, "Sergeant Laurent Emile

DesJardins DFM is hereby granted the King's commission, and is promoted to Flying Officer." There was no signal mentioning Edward Douglas.

The adjutant formally shook the hands of the three, and then Douglas followed his example. "My gosh, I sure have a high-ranking crew now," he said. The adjutant nodded. "It is most unusual to have one crew with three members decorated. The squadron is very proud to have you with us, and your promotions are well-deserved. But in the meantime, you'll want to get changed. Your clothes were all gathered up when you went missing and put into the lock-up at clothing stores, with your other belongings. I'll have the driver take you there." He turned to DesJardins. "I recommend that you go to a tailor in Colombo to get an officer's uniform. In the meantime just take the stripes off your airman's uniform. I welcome you to the officers' mess."

Crane was suddenly furious. "All this for us—but what about our captain? He deserves a promotion far more than I do—why, he's on his second tour! He's flown with us on every trip for which we have apparently been promoted, and he gets nothing! This is positively infamous!"

The adjutant nodded wearily. "Such matters are not decided here, but at higher levels. I recommend you see the station adjutant about it. But in the meantime, go on over to stores and reclaim your belongings."

The crew got back into the car, to be driven to clothing stores. Moragh was standing behind the counter, checking on some vouchers. When she saw them she dropped what she was doing and ran toward them. "Edward! Reg!" she cried. Douglas grabbed her and kissed her, and then passed her along to Reg, who kissed her more sedately. "Hey guys! Let us in on some of that," DesJardins called, and he and Hartley kissed her as well.

The grizzled flight sergeant beside her stood frozen-faced as Moragh disengaged herself and then led the crew to a lock-up in a corner of the building, where their belongings were stowed away in canvas bags. They retrieved them and carried them to the car again. The men returned to the quarters which had been allotted to them—their former ones had been given to others by now— changed into clean uniforms, and then walked to the flight office to present themselves to the squadron commander.

263

"Welcome back, gentlemen," the wing commander greeted them as they entered his office. "For a while we'd thought we'd lost you."

"We thought so too, sir." Douglas said. "Well, what's on our plate now?"

"Since you've survived, you're due for survivors' leave. When you come back, it's back on operations. How are you feeling?"

"We're all OK, sir. Life aboard a Norwegian cargo-liner isn't bad. The destroyer was nothing to write home about, but we've been in worse places."

"You'll have to report to the medical officer for a check-up. Then report to the adjutant for your leave documents."

Douglas nodded, and then cleared his throat. "Oh, one thing, sir. How about those engines? That's the third time I've lost an engine, and every time it's scared the shit out of me, and damn near got me killed. Isn't there anything you can do so the kite will hold height on one engine? New engines might do it."

The wing commander's brow clouded. "I know what you're thinking, but what can I say? We're at the end of a long supply-line here, and what we do get tends to be the tag-end of the equipment after everybody else has picked it over."

"Yes, I know, but I'm getting tired of ditching. Can't you restrict the anti-submarine patrols to the Catalina flying boats? You've got some here."

The wing commander shook his head. "They're worked to the limit. We have to use the Beauforts for something, and there's no torpedo work for them—thank God for that."

"Well, see what you can do, will you, sir? These Beauforts are simply unsuitable for the job."

"Yes, I'll look into it. Anyway, it's good to see you all back. We can always use an experienced crew."

"The men left the office. "I know what'll happen," DesJardins said. "Nothing."

"You said it," Hartley concurred. "We're going to be flying ropey old Beauforts for a good while yet. Where are you going for your leave, Larry?"

"Think I'll try Madras. Can't get to Winnipeg in the time I've got."

They discussed their leave destinations. Reg went to Kandy, which was a historic city, and Hartley chose Bangladore. "I'm going to hole up in a hotel right here in Colombo for day or two until I make up my mind," Douglas said.

The crew separated. Douglas found a telephone and called Moragh.

"Hello—how about celebrating our return by having dinner with me?"

"I'd love to, Edward, but I'm busy tonight. Will tomorrow do?"

"Guess it'll have to," Douglas answered. He returned to the officers' mess, to find Moragh sitting talking to Reg Crane. Douglas joined them. Crane greeted him warmly.

"I was telling Moragh what an excellent job you did in ditching that aircraft. If you'd botched it, none of us would be around today."

"Thanks, Reg." Douglas took a muffin and poured himself a cup of tea. Moragh turned back to talk to Crane, speaking animatedly while he made brief remarks in his cultured voice.

The padre joined them. "Delighted to see you back, my boy," he said to Crane, "and you too, of course, Mr. Douglas." He rubbed his hands. "I've taken the liberty of arranging a short service of thanksgiving in your honour, gentlemen. You'll come, of course, Mr. Douglas?"

"Gosh, I didn't expect anything like that—"

"With as valuable a member of my congregation as Reg Crane, a thanksgiving service is certainly in order, if only for myself. I thought Reg would have told you."

"I was just going to, padre."

"Do the other boys know?" asked Douglas.

"I'm going to chase them down and tell them. It'll be at seven o'clock," said Crane.

"I'll call the sergeants' mess," said Douglas. "Larry is an officer, so we'll look around the mess and tell him." DesJardins protested that he was a Catholic and that this was a Protestant service, but Douglas told him he'd go to a Catholic service to make up for it.

The service was short but impressive. Douglas, Crane, DesJardins and Hartley sat in the front row, and were startled to find out how many had showed up for it. There were all Crane's theological and technical friends, including his Bible-study class; the squadron commander and the flight commander, a dozen aircrew, a handful of sergeants who were friends of DesJardins and Hartley, members

265

of the crew's ground-crew, and four little dark men whom Douglas recognized as bearers. Douglas was touched and proud, and paid attention during the service. Crane knew all the responses, of course, and Douglas knew many of them from his boyhood days in the Sunday School his mother had sent him to under pain of her extreme displeasure. Moragh sat beside the senior equipment officer. Douglas stole glances at her, to find she was looking at Crane. Then she looked toward him, and he turned his eyes away.

The service came to an end, and the little congregation dispersed. "Let's head for that pub just outside the gate and have a beer, gang," said Douglas to his crew. "We need a little celebration after that."

"Yes," Crane answered dryly. "That'll be known as thirst after righteousness."

They walked past the guard house, had several beers, toasted each other. Crane, wearing his new flight lieutenant's braid, stood up and raised his glass. "On your feet, gentlemen," he said to the two gunners. "To our captain—Edward Douglas will always be our captain—do not let us forget that!" Douglas blushed as the three men said, "To our captain—Ed Douglas!" Half a dozen other aircrew joined them, and they spent an hour singing boozy songs, the lyrics of which Crane turned out to know. "I don't want to be an airman," they carolled, "I don't want to go to war; I just want to hang around Piccadilly underground and live off the earnings of a high-born lady." They enjoyed themselves hugely. Douglas got rather tipsy, and staggered back to his quarters after midnight with Crane helping him. DesJardins and Hartley never returned to the camp at all that night.

The next evening Douglas escorted Moragh to their favourite restaurant. He lifted his glass to her and studied her face. It had been a long time since he had the exclusive company of a woman, and her face was made more attractive by the suspicion that she might have found somebody else during his absence.

"Still footloose and fancy-free?" he asked her.

"Still fancy-free."

"Good. Did you miss me? I was hoping that absence would make the heart grow fonder."

"If you persist in going on extended sea-cruises, whatever happens to you is your own fault."

266

"I only did it to test you."

"It was an expensive way to do it, crashing an aeroplane."

"I know, and you were worth it."

"If you knew who much store keeping work you caused, having to strike that aircraft off charge!"

"That's what you get paid for. Every time I make you more work I add to your empire."

"You're always thinking of me."

"That's not really what I was thinking of you."

"I know," she replied, suddenly sober. "I was heart-broken when I heard you were missing—after all, I'd been through it before. And then I was overjoyed to hear that you'd been rescued!"

"You must have gone through a lot."

"Yes," she said fiercely. "A girl's a fool to get involved with aircrew—you're always scared silly or in tears."

"Yes," he said slowly. "I guess she would be. I'm sorry."

"Och, I didn't mean it like that, Edward. You're special—and I enjoy your company very much." She stood up, suddenly smiling. "Aren't you going to ask me to dance?"

"Why, of course—" He offered her his arm, and they swayed around the floor to the slow music of an Indian orchestra, playing songs from the Thirties. "Guess it'll be a while before they get the latest songs," Douglas said. "England is eighteen months behind North America, and India is two years behind England."

"It's still nice to dance to those tunes, even if they are old."

He held her close as they danced, and then they returned to their table for more champagne. By the end of the evening, they were both slightly befuddled. Douglas had intended making a pass at her, but suddenly he found himself taking her back to her quarters, and the opportunity had passed. He walked back to his quarters and lay down on his bed under a ceiling fan, wishing he had been more aggressive.

The next day he took a train for Kandy, where he stayed for a day, and then went to Jaffna, at the north end of Ceylon. He stayed at Jaffna for several days, and then returned to the air station, a day early. He telephoned Moragh, but she was busy, and he had to contented himself with a movie and then a few drinks in a bar. He felt lost and at loose ends. He was glad when his survivor's leave was over and he was back on operations.

267

The crew was given a new aircraft—actually an old one, the previous crew of which had been broken up when the navigator fell victim to malaria, the pilot had been promoted and transferred to a more prestigious post, and one of the gunners had broken his leg playing football. With it, the crew returned to the same anti-submarine patrols that they had been doing when they ditched. Crane, Hartley and DesJardins were fatalistic about the matter; they had always delivered themselves into the hands of their plane and their pilot, and this was simply the mixture as before. Douglas, however, who had been apprehensive before his ditching, was doubly anxious now. The dangers posed by the enemy he could face with steadfastness, considering them the normal hazards of war; but engines that failed were too much, since they were the proof not of enemy malice but of friendly incompetence.

When Douglas climbed aboard the aircraft for his first trip after they returned to operations, he shut the port engine down after performing his cockpit check, on the grounds that the revolutions were dropping too low when he tested the engine, first on one magneto and then on the other. A harried flight sergeant, obviously displeased with this reflection on his work, rode up on a bicycle, started the engine, professed to see no difficulty, and engaged in a heated, if respectfully-phrased, argument with Douglas. It ended with the flight sergeant calling up a mechanic to change the spark plugs. This caused a fifty-minute delay, and when Douglas arrived at the convoy it had been unescorted for half an hour, which the convoy commodore complained about.

The patrol went off uneventfully, and no submarines were sighted. The air station did not take the objections of the sailors too seriously, since more acute aircraft unserviceabilities had interfered with air cover in the past. The flight commander made a routine answer, filed the yellow message-form, and forgot the matter.

Two days later Douglas delayed another flight for what seemed a trivial fault in an engine, a minor oil leak. The mechanics had seen it occur a dozen times before in that aircraft, and it had never caused more than a dirty oil-smudge on a cowling which the engine seemed to ignore. The flight sergeant pointed out this fact as forcibly as he could, but Douglas was adamant. He insisted on placing the aircraft unserviceable, and flatly refused to fly it until the oil-leak was repaired.

268

The repair meant another hour and ten minute's delay, and another complaint from the convoy commodore. The patrol was performed in exemplary fashion, with no sightings of any hostile submarines.

The next two patrols went off routinely. Late during the second Douglas saw a suspicious object which might have been a conning-tower but when he flew over the scene there was nothing to see. He reported the incident, which was plugged into the intelligence jigsaw as another piece, its importance decaying rapidly as the hours passed. Whether there had been a submarine remained problematical.

Two days later Douglas put another aircraft unserviceable, and this time the flight sergeant complained to the engineering officer, who drove up in a car. Breathing fire and brimstone, he led off by threatening Douglas with the ominous words 'disciplinary action.' Douglas stood his ground. "The regulations are quite clear. If an aircraft is not serviceable the pilot is forbidden to fly it. That kite's not serviceable. I won't fly it until it is."

"Who says it isn't serviceable?"

"I say it is, and I do not intend to fly it until it is serviceable."

"Impertinent young pup!" the engineering officer sputtered, and then climbed into the cockpit with the flight sergeant, who started the engine. The propeller spun, the engine roared and faltered briefly as the flight sergeant cut the switches for the magneto test. He shut the engine down and the two climbed out onto the hard-standing again.

"As far as I'm concerned this aircraft is serviceable!" the engineering officer said flatly. "It's perfectly ready to fly!"

"Let's climb aboard and take another look at those engines," said Douglas. The three of them entered the aircraft, and the engines roared into life.

"There you are!" the engineering officer shouted. "Serviceable!" Douglas cut the switches. "Ten revs low."

"Goddam it, you can't U/S an aircraft for ten bloody revs!"

"Yes I can—and I have. Now get your troops and fix the bloody thing. I'm not flying this clapped-out old kite until at least the engines are right!"

"Goddam it, man, you're ruining the operational effectiveness of this station!"

269

"Operational effectiveness be screwed! I've done all the swimming around I want to after one of your ropey old engines has quit working! Remember—I have to fly in these aircraft! You don't!"

"The station commander will hear about this!" the engineering officer shouted. However, he did make another aircraft available, fresh out of the shop. Douglas and his crew got into the air two hours late. Again the patrol was routine.

The next day the flight commander sought out Douglas in the crew room. "C.O. wants to see you."

"He does? Can't say I want to see him." He reported to the adjutant, who ushered him into the group captain's sanctum. Douglas saluted and stood facing the Commanding Officer, who looked up testily from his chair.

"What's all this about you refusing to fly, Douglas?"

"Who, me? I've never refused to fly I just want my aircraft to be serviceable, sir."

"My information is that you have been placing aircraft unserviceable for completely trivial reasons."

"Trivial to you, perhaps, but not to me. I have to fly in those kites, and to think of my crew. A Beaufort won't hold height on one engine. I want to make sure that both engines are fully serviceable before I take off."

The station commander leaned forward. "Look here, Douglas, we can't have one man ruining the operational record of this station. Before you started on this campaign of yours—which I interpret as nothing less than sabotage—we had a splendid record over convoys and we were known throughout Coastal Command as a capable, efficient organization! Now we're the subject of constant complaints, and whenever we trace down the reason, you're at the bottom of it!"

Douglas looked at a spot on the wall above the group Captain's head. "If the aircraft are completely serviceable I'll fly them, sir. But if you want your record to be impressive, may I suggest that you clamp down on your technical staff."

The group captain jumped to his feet "Damn it, Douglas, they're working as hard as they can! They're under great pressure, under severe handicaps! There's a shortage of mechanics, a shortage of aircraft, a shortage of spares! Your complaints, compared to theirs, are trivial!"

"They have their reputation on the line—you have yours. My crew has their lives."

"Your lives! Of course you have your lives on the line! You're an officer, man! You're here to risk your life!"

"Of course, sir. I'm willing to risk mine, but to enemy action—not to mechanical failures."

"Mechanical failures! These aircraft are perfectly serviceable! You're just making excuses! Other pilots aren't cancelling flights like this."

"The other pilots make their own decisions—I make mine."

"Maybe there's a different reason for what you're doing. I think you're just afraid."

"Afraid!" Douglas took a step forward, and then halted with a visible effort. "Yes, you're right, I was afraid when I torpedoed the *Gladbach*—and when I torpedoed that tanker off Tobruk!"

"You haven't shown any signs of heroism since you've been here."

Douglas stiffened. "In view of your own distinguished record, sir, you have of course the right to make such comments."

"What do you mean by that, Douglas?"

"What do you think I mean, sir?"

The group captain stood up. "When you first came here, and I saw that everybody in your crew was decorated but you, I had you tabbed as a trouble-maker. Now I know exactly why. Go back to your duties—and if I hear any more about your trivial complaints about perfectly serviceable aircraft I'll have you court-martialled!"

Douglas stood scarlet-faced, searching for words, when a respectful knock sounded on the door, and the adjutant entered.

"Sorry to interrupt, sir, but I have a signal here I believe you should see."

"Can't you see I'm busy?"

"Yes sir. But I still think you should read it—now."

"Oh very well." The group captain took the sheet of coarse teletype paper. As his eyes scanned the lines his face changed from belligerence to dismay and then to outrage. He threw the signal back to the adjutant. "All right, Douglas! Get out! Get out!" He sat down heavily in his chair and stayed there, panting, while Douglas saluted and followed the adjutant into the adjoining office.

271

The adjutant handed Douglas the signal. "Here you are, Flight Lieutenant Douglas."

"Flying Officer Douglas, you mean—or is it sergeant?"

"Read the signal."

Douglas read it.

"A. Flying Officer Edward David Douglas, Royal Canadian Air Force, is awarded the Distinguished Flying Cross for gallantry, skill and determination over and above the call of duty, in pressing home a successful torpedo attack against heavy enemy opposition upon the German cruiser *Gladbach*, which kept this vessel out of service for three months. Flying Officer Douglas' successful attack prevented the cruiser from delivering attacks upon a convoy to Murmansk, thus saving numerous lives as well as much valuable war material being delivered to our Allies the Russians.

B. Flying Officer Edward David Douglas, Royal Canadian Air Force, is awarded a bar to the DFC for gallantry, skill and determination over and above the call of duty, in torpedoing the tanker *Atalanta* in the harbour of Tobruk, thus depriving Axis forces of vitally-needed fuel, and thereby contributing greatly to the success of British arms in the battle of El Alamein.

C. Flying Officer Douglas is promoted to the rank of Flight Lieutenant, effective 15 January 1943."

Douglas' mouth dropped open. He read the signal again, and then reread it. "Well I'll be goddammed! Flight Lieutenant Douglas! Whadda ya know!" He slapped the adjutant on the back and burst into laughter. "If this happens every time the Old Man tears a strip off me, he should do it every day! Well, that puts things in the proper light, doesn't it? I'll be setting them up in the mess tonight— gotta wet that extra ring! Hope you'll be there, old boy!" He folded the copy of the signal and put it in his pocket.

"I say, Douglas, that's my copy."

"So it is. Well, ask the signals section for another one. I'm keeping this. But don't take a copy into the CO now—I'm not his favourite Canadian at the moment." Douglas raised his hand to the adjutant and walked out, whistling.

The news preceded Douglas to the flight office. Crane, Hartley and DesJardins seized him as he entered the building, swung him to their shoulders, and paraded him up and down the crew room. The

272

flight commander joined in singing, "For He's a Jolly Good Fellow!" and the other aircrew bruised his shoulders slapping them. Within minutes the din was deafening, and was reinforced when a case of beer appeared. The celebration continued at the officers' mess. Crane asked permission of the mess president to have Hartley join them, and the mess president thought it politic to agree.

DesJardins and Hartley stood beside him, singing a chorus of "Dear Little Angeline", when DesJardins looked at Douglas' uniform. "Damn it, Ed, you're improperly dressed! Come with us!" They dragged him out of the mess to one of the huts outside the gate, occupied by a Singhalese tailor.

It was late, but they made such a racket that the man appeared. DesJardins thumped on the counter. "Come on, you tailor-wallah, fix up Flight Lieutenant Douglas' uniform! DFC and Bar, and Flight Lieutenant's rings!" He threw down a handful of rupees. The tailor perked up at the sight, and within half an hour medal ribbons gleamed in purple and white newness and the new second ring on the shoulder of Douglas' battle-dress jacket outshone its weathered companion.

The celebration lasted until midnight, proceeding to a hostelry near the station gate. At one stage Crane stood up to give a short and dignified speech congratulating Douglas, which was cheered to the echo. When the crew was finally poured into bed it was to the accompaniment of a group of carolling aircrew, frightfully out of tune, who woke up everybody in the officers' quarters.

The flight commander mercifully did not order the crew to fly the next day. Two days later, when they were warned for a routine patrol, they were reasonably recovered. When they reached their aircraft Douglas found one of the engines exhibited a magneto drop, but Douglas cocked his ear at the changed rhythm, said, "Fuck it," and taxied out.

"It'll clear up once we get into the air," he muttered as he opened the throttles. He took off, held the nose down to pick up flying speed, and then eased back on the stick. The engine promptly quit.

"Okay gang," he said calmly. "We're going to make a wheels-up landing in that field ahead." Turning back to the airfield, as had been stressed during his training, could be lethal. He concentrated on the landing, and although there was a great crashing and

273

banging as the bottom of the Beaufort hit the dirt and the propellers bent, nobody was injured and minimal damage was done to the aircraft.

Lorries raced up to the scene, and the engineering officer climbed out of one of them. "Okay, Douglas, what did you do now?"

Douglas looked him up and down coolly. "Had a mag drop, old boy, and the engine took it seriously. See to it, will you?" The crew climbed into one of the lorries. Another crew and another aircraft had to be hastily dispatched to make the patrol.

CHAPTER TWENTY-NINE

The Commanding Officer sat in his office that evening, his mood blacker than the tropical night outside. Another complaint had come to him because of a delayed escort to a convoy, stemming from the accident to Douglas' aircraft. He cursed as he reflected that there was nothing he could even say to him. Whatever Douglas did now, he was sacrosanct; to court-martial a holder of the DFC and Bar was unthinkable.

The next morning he reached for his telephone and called a friend of his at Far East Headquarters.

"That bloody man Douglas!" he said in a strangled voice. "Get him off my station!"

"But he's just got the DFC and Bar!"

"I don't care if he's got the VC! Get him the hell off my station!"

"I'll do the best I can. Wait a minute—we've just got a signal requesting names be submitted of experienced torpedo-bomber pilots for staffing a new Beaufighter torpedo wing."

"Put his name in—right away!"

"What about his crew?"

"To hell with his crew! I'll screen them—take them off operations. I'll find some excuse for doing that."

His next step was to call the officer commanding the torpedo squadron and tell him to screen Douglas' crew. The man did not object—Douglas was getting to be a nuisance to him too, and with his decorations Douglas was outshining him. To a crew with all four members wearing medal ribbons he had to defer, and both DesJardins and Hartley were becoming too outspoken in briefings to please him. The excuse he made was that after the crash landing of the Beaufort they needed a rest.

Douglas was elated when he heard the news. "Beaufighters! Good. They're not underpowered, they're a hundred miles an hour faster, and they're much better armed. Sure sounds good to me."

"That's what we need," said Hartley, and then his face fell. "Hey, there's no room in a Beaufighter for a wop! It's only got a two-man crew! What's with us?"

"Yeah, I guess that's the way it is," said Douglas soberly. "I'll check with the adj to see what they have planned for you."

"How about Reg? A Beaufighter needs a navigator wireless op, not a straight navigator."

"Maybe I'll have to learn morse," Crane put in, "or else you'll have to learn navigation."

"That'll be a bind," DesJardins said. "Think I'll stick to radio operating and gunning. It's more fun, and you can see what's going on."

Douglas returned from his visit to the adjutant with news of their future. "We're all to go back to England. Reg is to go back to England to take a radio course. Larry, you're heading back to Canada. Ray will be going to be an instructor somewhere—we don't know where yet."

"That sounds good," said DesJardins, smiling broadly.

"I'm the bloody orphan," complained Hartley. "Joe jobs, here I come!"

"Morse!" spat Crane. "I've always hated it!"

"Better'n all that sextant-bashing you made us do," said Hartley. "We'll get our own back now."

"You've got a good start," put in DesJardins. "You already know the morse code from A to B."

"Larry, I do not usually indulge in Canadian slang, but I will this time. Don't be such a smart-ass."

"You're learning, Reg, you're learning." DesJardins slapped his back and left with a wave of his hand. "Gotta get a few souvenirs of Ceylon. Nobody in Saint Boniface will believe me I was here if I don't get them."

Douglas telephoned Moragh to tell her the news, and to ask her to have dinner with him. "I'll be leaving in a couple of days," he told her. "Somehow I have the feeling the C.O. wants me off the station as fast as possible."

At dinner that night Moragh asked, "Why did you say the C.O. wants you to leave?"

"I told him he was risking his men's lives by having them fly those ropey old Beauforts. He didn't take it too kindly, and he told me I wasn't brave enough for the job. I can't really disagree with him, but I did remind him that he'd never seen any real action himself, and now something tells me that I'm not his favourite Canadian, not that I ever was."

"No—but such an accusation wouldn't sit very well with somebody wearing the DFC and Bar."

"He didn't know about that when we having our little conversation. The adjutant told me about my gongs and my promotion just after the C. O. had finished tearing his strip off me. Kind of left the old man with egg on his face."

She smiled a little sadly. "You're always giving your C.O.'s a piece of your mind."

He sat back, grinning. "This time I don't think I'll lose anything by it."

She nodded without answering. He looked at her sharply. "Say, Moragh, is something wrong?"

"My sister's husband is missing. He was with Bomber Command."

"Oh gosh, Moragh, I'm sorry! What rotten luck!"

"Yes." She raised a handkerchief to her eyes. "I liked him."

"Damn this bloody war!" Douglas exploded. "It spoils everything!"

"We could have had a nice celebration if I hadn't got my sister's letter."

"I can't tell you how sorry I am—"

"You get used to it, I suppose—you've lost so many of your friends. But it's different with a man. No matter how friendly you may be with another man, you aren't in love with him. It can't hurt a man as much to lose a friend as it hurts a woman to lose a lover."

He shook his head apologetically. "I guess that's the way it is—but we can't afford to brood about it."

"No—and neither should I." She stood up. "Let's dance."

He took her in his arms, finding her remote from him despite her nearness. As they sat down again he looked at her, waiting a moment without speaking, and then said, "Still thinking about Hank Snow, aren't you?"

277

"That was a long time ago," She fell silent. Then she looked up at him and said, "It's that voice of yours—that Canadian accent. Every time I hear you I hear him."

"I'm still running second to a ghost, I see. If I spoke the way Reg Crane does would I have a clearer track?"

She sighed. "Reg Crane is very nice." Then she spoke with sudden venom. "A girl's a fool to get involved with aircrew."

"You said that before." He lifted his glass. "Well, drink up. That's one way to forget about the war." They danced, and drank, and danced again, and drank again. Douglas held his glass up to the light and looked at her through it. "You're very attractive, you know, especially when I look at you through a wine glass."

"That's the best way to look at me, I know."

He swirled the wine in the bottom of his glass. "Too bad you made yourself so clear earlier in the evening."

"I made myself so clear?"

"Yes. When I asked you to have dinner with me tonight I planned to ask you to marry me."

"What! You—were going to ask me to marry you?"

"Yes. But you made your position clear enough—you don't intend to tie yourself to anybody in aircrew. It's obvious there's no point in asking you. I just thought I'd tell you what I was thinking—you have a right to know."

"But Edward—you never told me you loved me."

"If I asked you to marry me I thought you'd guess."

"I do." Her face sobered. "You're wonderful, Edward—but I'm just not ready for it."

"Are you in love with somebody else—like Reg Crane, for instance? My navigators have all the luck."

"No—I'm not in love with anybody."

"Just Hank Snow."

She nodded, and then reached over and took his hand. "I won't forget him, I know—but you're sweet, Edward—I hadn't dreamed—I thought we were just friends—" She stood up.

"Do you want me to take you home now? I know I should never have brought the matter up."

"No. Don't take me home. I won't marry you, Edward—not now, anyway. But if you want me to go to bed with you, I will."

278

Douglas stood bolt upright. "What? You will?"

She smiled at him. "Take me back to the WAAF's barracks, then go around to the back ten minutes later. I'll be waiting for you."

"I'll bring along a bottle of champagne. Let's do it in style." Douglas called the waiter to order the champagne. As he paid for it Moragh looked at him. "Och aye—Edward—you're right bonny with that DFC ribbon up."

CHAPTER THIRTY

The crew flew back to England more or less the way they had come. A Catalina took them to Bombay, a weary Hudson carried them to Karachi, an American DC3 Dakota took them to Aden. A Wellington took them to Alexandria. DesJardins, wearing a khaki shirt without insignia, walked up to the cockpit, and offered to spell the pilot off for a while. He accepted the invitation, and DesJardins settled into the pilot's seat and flew the aircraft for three hours, smoothly and competently. When the pilot came back to the cockpit he had Douglas with him. "Is Larry here your co-pilot?" he asked Douglas.

"No," Douglas laughed. "He's my WAG."

"Your WAG? Good God! I let him fly the plane."

"Don't worry, I used to let him fly mine."

The pilot, an Englishman, looked at both of them. "You goddam Canadians!" he said, and took his seat back at the controls.

A converted civilian aircraft, an Ambassador, carried them to England by way of Gibraltar. The journey took them ten days.

They reported to Coastal Command Headquarters when they arrived, and from there DesJardins went to visit RCAF Overseas Headquarters in London. He was told he was to report to a wireless school in Montreal, where a French-speaking combat veteran with a decoration would be in his glory as well as being highly useful. He returned to Coastal Command Headquarters to say good-bye to his three colleagues, and they had a beery farewell a day later. They promised to keep in touch. Neither Crane nor Douglas expected to hear from him again.

As Crane and Douglas were walking down a corridor the next day, a man rushed up to them, his hand extended.

"Good God!" Douglas exclaimed. "Derek Peterson! I thought you'd gone for a Burton!"

"I did. Got picked up by an Italian destroyer after I was shot down. Then I was a prisoner of war in Italy four months, but managed to escape while we were being transported north after the invasion of Italy. I joined up with a bunch of your chaps—the Canadian army—and here I am."

"Am I glad to see you! You remember Reg Crane, my navigator?"

"Would I ever forget you?" He peered at Douglas' chest. "I see you're wearing a DFC ribbon. I took steps to recommend you for a DSO when we were in Malta."

"I guess the brass didn't think I deserved it." Douglas looked at Derek's uniform. "Wing Commander now—congratulations!"

Peterson looked at Crane. "We've been expecting you too. How's your morse?"

"Standard eight words a minute, sir."

"We'll have you up to eighteen in no time. You'll go to a wireless school for a crash course in wireless-bashing, and then to 947 Squadron with Douglas here. We're re-equipping with Beaufighters, and Douglas will be working with me to set things up, organize the squadron, shake it down, and get things going."

"Very good," Crane nodded, "but I'm surprised that you're willing to wait for me to take the wireless course. Surely you have qualified wireless navigators in the pipeline, sir."

"Oh yes, but none with your operational experience." Peterson jabbed a finger in Crane's chest. "Besides, we want somebody with a gong—makes it a lot easier with the sprogs, you know. Anyway, your job will mostly be navigation, and you're good at that."

Douglas grinned. "With only you in the kite, you'll have to take your own sextant shots for a change."

Peterson's eyebrows raised. "What do you mean?"

"Reg used to make the WAGs take his sextant shots for him. He even taught them to work the sights out. He was a terrible bully about it."

"He did, did he? What did you say your wireless operators' names were?"

"Larry DesJardins—another Canadian—and Ray Hartley. They were with me in Malta—surely you remember them. They came back

281

here with me. Larry's slated to go back to Canada to a wireless school."

"I think we need him worse than Canada does. A member of Douglas' famous crew—"

"Oh Jeez, Derek, don't grab him! You know what happened to Hank Snow! He was slated to return to Canada when Tenley grabbed him for that last trip and he got the chop!"

Peterson's face sobered. "Yes. I see what you mean. Maybe we can get your man Hartley instead."

"That'd be a better idea. Of course he'll need a navigation course."

"Very well." Peterson pencilled a note to himself. "I remember him. When can you report to the squadron?"

"When do you want me, sir?"

"I'll be able to get out of Headquarters here in a week or so."

"That's fine with me. I'll be there. By the way, Derek—sir—where did you say the squadron was?"

"Spokington—on the Wash."

"Where do I pick up my orders?"

"Come with me to the postings section—we'll lay something on right now. Come along with us, Crane—we'll get you fixed up too."

"Flight Lieutenant Douglas will be spending the next week at my parents' home, sir," Crane told Peterson. "My mother has everything arranged."

"You both deserve some leave—there's no doubt about that," agreed Peterson. "Very well. I imagine I can give the necessary instructions."

"Can you look after DesJardins and Hartley as well, sir? We'd like them to spend some time with my parents too."

Peterson nodded, and then his brow creased. "I was sure I had recommended you for a DSO at Malta, Ed. I'm surprised it didn't come through. I see Crane and Hartley got their gongs."

"It was something about them being RAF types and me being a member of the Royal Canadian Air Force. They said they'd have to contact RCAF Overseas Headquarters. I guess the message never got through. And then when you went missing there was nobody to push it the way you did."

Peterson shook his head. "Well, with a DFC and Bar I guess we'll have to leave it at that." He shook hands with them. "Report back to me when you come back from your leave." They saluted him, and he hurried off.

Douglas found himself two days later at the baronial Crane home. It was as impressive as he remembered it, and Crane's mother was as regal as ever. She and Crane's father welcomed the crew warmly, telling them she had arranged a formal dinner that night, with appropriate representation from the neighbouring estates.

The dinner was a festive occasion which Douglas enjoyed, although he was somewhat embarrassed by the way Crane's mother fussed over him. DesJardins lapped up the attention, obtaining Mrs. Crane's attention by responding to a few words from her in French in the same language, and discussing the difference between her Parisian French and his Canadian pronunciation, explaining it by saying that his version of the language was three hundred years old. He was actually from a Winnipeg suburb, but he made an elaborate pretence of being a Manitoba frontiersman, telling stories he had heard from his grandfather. He was well into the buffalo hunts before the dinner was half over, and Douglas found himself both interested and wondering why he had never been told the stories before. He reflected that his own tales of derring-do should not be told here; Crane's mother and father did not want to hear of the danger their son had faced and would face again. DesJardin's stories had happened to others in a strange and half-mythical land, with the dangers past and the enemies long gone. He could chatter away without worrying anybody. Douglas was glad he could.

At intervals Crane entered the conversation, usually with a laudatory comment about Douglas or DesJardins or Hartley. Hartley had been overawed at first to be among so many of the gentry, but after Crane told how he had bandaged both Crane and DesJardins before attending to his own wounds, he found himself the centre of admiring attention, and was soon chattering away to a baronet on one side and a dowager, almost as grand as Mrs. Crane, on the other.

Crane's praise of Douglas did him no harm with the local belle, Valerie Coningsby, who was seated next to him, and who was obviously taken with his uniform, his wings, his medal-ribbons, and Crane's deference to him. Douglas made a date with her to go on a walking tour of the neighbourhood beauty-spots the next day.

283

After dinner Crane's father collected the males and took them into the library for brandy and cigars. Douglas liked the brandy, but could not stomach the cigar; DesJardins attacked both with gusto, as did Hartley. It soon became evident that Crane senior, although he began by telling them he wanted them to tell him of their experiences, really wanted to recount his own memories of the First World War, when he had been an artillery officer in Flanders. Douglas was glad of it. It took the ball out of his court and let him savour his brandy and relax, without fearing he might be making a gaffe. He had no need to tell of his exploits; Crane did it for him.

They all slept late the next morning. After breakfast Douglas went for the walking tour that had been planned the evening before. He enjoyed the walk, with Valerie giving him a guided tour. She was witty and interesting, and she knew the area like the back of her hand. She also had a wealth of slightly-scandalous tales of the inhabitants, and of the Londoners who came to visit them. Douglas found her intriguing, and told her so when they sat down together on a bench in a shady grove, where she led him for a rest after an hour of strolling. Briefly they found themselves alone.

"You're fun to be with, Valerie. You sure know the countryside, don't you, Valerie?"

"Yes. I know a little about it."

"You sure know how to make it interesting. Where'd you learn it all?"

"Oh, reading about it—listening to all the gossips."

"It's lucky for me that you're so well-informed. Doesn't hurt a bit that you're so pretty either." He squeezed her hand. She swung toward him and raised her lips to his. Douglas was kissing her before he realized what he was doing. "Holy smoke!" A slow smile spread over his face. "That was nice. Do it again."

She complied. "I've always wanted to kiss somebody with a DFC and Bar."

"Kiss me again like that and I'll go out and win a Victoria Cross." Their lips met again.

"Is there anywhere I can meet you tonight?" Douglas said urgently. "The others will be around in a minute or two."

"I'm staying with the Cranes. My shoes will be outside my room. Knock on my door after dinner—I'll be expecting you."

"Marvellous! I'll be there." He stepped away from her just as the others came into view around a path among the trees. She made a laughing remark, and they took up their walk again, Valerie carrying on with her talk with utmost sangfroid. Douglas looked at her with respect; she had the poise that had made the Empire great.

That night, as she had arranged, he knocked on her door, to be welcomed by Valerie in a negligee. She motioned him to a bottle of champagne and two glasses on an end table.

He poured the wine and they drank it, their arms linked. He put down his empty glass and pulled her down onto the bed. She twined her arms around him as their lips met, and then they began to undress each other. She arched her back as he kissed her body, and lay back with her eyes closed as he ran his face up and down her legs. Their coupling was explosive and simultaneous.

"Jeez—you're good at that!" he said as they fell slowly apart, exhausted.

"You are highly skilled yourself, my darling," she replied. She hugged him briefly again, and then said, "And now—go on back to your own room. That's where you are supposed to be sleeping, you know." She lay back. "You know, Edward, you talk just like Robert Taylor."

He laughed, a little sourly. "So I remind you of Robert Taylor, do I? That's fair enough—you remind me of Helen of Troy." He left the room quietly. As he walked back to his own room he reflected that at least Valerie had never met Hank Snow. Just before he reached his room he met Larry DesJardins in the corridor, obviously returning from just such an excursion as he had just completed. They nodded conspiratorially and passed without speaking.

Nest morning the four men had to catch different trains. Douglas was to report to his squadron, Crane was to report to his wireless school. Hartley was to report to a navigation school, and DesJardins was going to an Embarkation Depot at Barrhead in Lancashire, from whence he would be sent somewhere to take ship for Canada.

Mrs. Crane parted from Douglas emotionally. "It has been pleasant seeing you again, Edward. Reginald has kept us fully informed of your conduct while you were together, and we are

285

delighted that you will be together again when he completes his wireless training."

"I sure hope he didn't tell you everything."

"He told me quite enough, Edward. We are looking forward to seeing you at intervals again, now that you are back in England. By the way, I must thank you for the way you took Valerie Coningsby's mind off her troubles—she's in a very emotional state, you know, with her fiancé in Italy."

Douglas swallowed. "It was my privilege, Mrs. Crane. There are others who have done so much more than I have—"

She took his hands. "I know you'd take that modest attitude, my dear boy. But we, who know the real story, won't be taken in by it." She nodded. "Now go with our blessing, Edward. Remember, we are always your friends, as Reginald is."

Valerie was with her. Douglas took her hand and said "It has been very pleasant knowing you, Valerie. I'm most grateful to Mrs. Crane for introducing us."

"Yes indeed," she replied coolly. "It has been nice for me too. I hope we may meet again some day."

"I hope so too," he answered, feeling her address in the pocket of his tunic. Mrs. Crane put her hand on his arm. "It's been wonderful having you with us. You must be sure to visit us again. And of course it's good in another way too—we can always use an extra man at a dinner party; with this wretched war on, there are so often ladies for whom we simply can't find a proper escort."

"Glad to be of help there too," Douglas answered. The station-master blew his whistle, and Douglas stepped aboard the train. The engine coughed into motion. Douglas leaned out the compartment window and waved at Mrs. Crane and Valerie.

As he leaned back he reflected that Reginald Crane was strait-laced, and his mother was a tyrant, but they had some accommodating friends. He fingered the piece of paper with Valerie' s name on it in his pocket. With her fiancé in the Italian mountains, he should not pursue the matter further. Maybe he wouldn't. And then, maybe he would.

CHAPTER THIRTY-ONE

Douglas reported to his new squadron the next day. During previous receptions at a new unit he had been processed by formally polite but disinterested sergeants, who shoved forms at him to be filled out, and then escorted to a shared room in a Nissen hut by a sleepy orderly officer, since trains always arrived in the middle of the night. At No. 976 Squadron, however, the adjutant personally welcomed him at the civilized hour of three o'clock in the afternoon, and he was shown to his quarters, which consisted not of half a room but of a two-room suite. The adjutant implied that Peterson had made it clear how he was to be treated.

The next day he was introduced to the Beaufighter aircraft he was to fly. He had operated from the same airfields as Beaufighters, at Luqa in Malta and at Alexandria, but he had never flown one. The Beaufighter was the only really good aircraft of the Bristol family, which included the Blenheim, the Beaufort and the Bisley, all of them standing invitations to German fighter pilots to fatten their scores. It had been designed originally as a twin-engine fighter, as its name implied, but it had proved unable to hold its own against such German opposite numbers as the single-engine Me109, and it was redesignated as a night fighter, where it proved itself murderously effective. It was also used as a ground-attack machine. Then, because it was far more manoeuvrable than a Beaufort, much faster, and capable of carrying a similar load, Peterson had seen its possibilities as a torpedo-plane, and had pestered his seniors until they had given him his head. It had taken six months of lobbying, but the heavy casualties in Beauforts in the North Sea had forced officialdom's hand.

287

Douglas reported to Peterson and was warmly welcomed. Peterson did not waste any time in putting him to work; he was checked out in a Beaufighter that very afternoon, and when tea-time came he had soloed. Two days later he was pitch-forked into the administrative world of commanding a flight. It was not totally unfamiliar to him, since he had been an operations officer in Malta, but it was wearing and demanding at first. It was a bare-bones organization, with only two other pilots, a radio-navigator, and an orderly-room staff of a sergeant, a corporal, an airman and an airwoman. He was a little embarrassed by the deference shown to him by his staff, but he soon grew accustomed to that and to expect it; formal respect and quick response to his orders he found very pleasant.

His brief euphoria, however, soon evaporated. Peterson, although he treated Douglas like a comrade after hours and swapped drinks with him in the bar, was a martinet during working hours. Douglas found he was expected to command, not merely lead others into battle. This involved gaining a complete grasp of all Peterson's tactics, understanding how he intended to deploy his forces to meet a host of different challenges; how he wanted his orders passed, how he wanted to have command handed over smoothly to the pilots of each aircraft in the flight, and how he wanted a combination of stereotyped responses to definite commands mixed with flexibility to cope with unforeseen circumstances. Douglas found he was expected to drill his men constantly so that response was automatic, with each aircraft answering instantly to a two-word or three-word command.

Before a week was out Douglas was beginning to feel like a private in the Guards, expected to obey instantly and never to think for himself. After a month, however, he felt himself promoted to a Guards sergeant, demanding instant obedience from others while giving it himself to his superiors. His task was complicated by the fact that the flight was far under strength, and was reinforced by dribs and drabs, so that he found himself continually repeating the lessons with new men who were unfamiliar with Petersons' tactics and unsympathetic with his methods. Some of them were experienced, who took reluctantly to this Prussian discipline. Douglas, with his record of challenging authority, felt uncomfortable as he berated them, thinking that the risks they had already taken entitled them to more consideration. But Peterson left him in no doubt as to what he was supposed to do, and Douglas passed on his scathing comments after having cringed under them himself.

Most of the training was tactical. The pilots kept the formations, dropped the torpedoes, and handled the voice communications. The navigators, for all their double-barrelled skills as navigators and radio operators, had little to do. Unlike the all-important observers of the long-range anti-submarine aircraft, who were always alone and far out to sea, torpedo navigators flew in tight formations where they had only to follow their leader. On the way out to the target radio silence was always in force, so that the morse keys were seldom used. The navigator had a machine-gun, pointing to the rear, but it was used in an attack only after the torpedo had been dropped, as an harassment.

The navigators did not complain. Those of them who had flown in Beauforts or Hampdens saw the Beaufighter as a new lease on life. Consciously or unconsciously the experienced torpedo-bomber men had written themselves off, having abandoned all hope of survival, and to find themselves on fast, manoeuvrable aircraft which could hold height on one engine and were armed with cannons as well as machine-guns, left them dazed with their good fortune. They occupied themselves with making sure their compasses were properly swung, and practicing overwater navigation whenever they got the chance. In the crew-room they practiced morse, although they had to drive themselves to this tedious chore. Few of them had their hearts in it; they were basically navigators, not radio operators, and navigation was their first love. But they showed up on time for flights and kept their navigation equipment in good order, and were content to let their pilots take Douglas' and Peterson's bullying.

Coastal Command Headquarters kept chivvying Peterson to use his squadron on operations. He kept fighting them off, raising one objection after another. When he finally was forced to give in he selected targets as easy as he could find, aiming to blood his men as inexpensively as possible. He insisted on proper fighter cover, and forced the fighter commanders to drill their men with his before he would take them out together against German shipping in the North Sea, meanwhile complaining vociferously if the fighters did not

289

show up on time, escort his Beaufighters as Peterson expected, and stay with them until the last moment.

Crane showed up on the squadron three months after Douglas had reported to it. He had a new-found but still uncertain knowledge of the morse code, had a tendency to forget exactly how to tune his radio set in which he had nothing more than a forced interest, and considered himself first and foremost a navigator. Douglas welcomed him and made him the navigation leader.

As he had done with DesJardins, Douglas insisted that Crane learn to fly the aircraft. Crane was not particularly keen to do so, but Douglas insisted. "You don't have to learn to take it off or land it—just fly it when we're cruising. If something happens to me I want you to be able to fly it home."

"Very well then," Crane assented, and climbed into the pilot's seat during the long cross-country exercises that Peterson insisted they fly. At first Crane's piloting was terrible; he was rough, he overcontrolled, he did not centralize his controls before they were at the top of a climb or at the end of a turn, so that the plane porpoised and wavered back and forth. Once or twice Douglas had to reach over from the jump seat where he was sitting beside him and grab the controls, to pull the plane out of a diving spiral. Crane was depressed. "I'll never get the hang of it, Ed," he said.

"Hang in there, Reggie. You'll get it—just don't quit." Douglas insisted that Crane spend time in the Link trainer, flying imaginary aircraft over imaginary courses, where Crane at first did equally poorly.

Then, just when he was about to rebel and refuse to take part in so unrewarding an exercise, when he climbed into the pilot's seat at twelve thousand feet over England everything clicked. His turns were suddenly smooth, his climbs and glides crisp and controlled, his handling of the engines smooth and competent. Whereas before he had found himself sweating and harassed, with the urgent moments crowding in on him with too much to do for the time to do it, now thing were almost peaceful and lazy. When the nose rose a little he reached over and cranked on elevator trim without thinking, and was surprised to find things at last coming automatically and naturally.

Douglas smiled broadly when he saw the confidence in Crane's eyes. "Knew you could do it, Reg—of course I was praying for you." "Fine," Crane replied. "You did something right, and I did something right."

"DesJardins would have been proud of you, Reg." They flew along for another hour, with Crane's piloting quite satisfactory. At the end of the time they found they were completely lost, and Crane had to desert the pilot's cockpit for his radio set and ask for a homing bearing. Ordinarily he would have been humiliated; today he did not care.

Peterson was in his glory at last. He was commanding an airborne task-force consisting of Beaufighters, some of them armed with a noseful of cannons and a torpedo, while others were armed with cannon and rows of rockets slung underneath the wings. He had been suspicious of the rockets at first, considering them a new and untried weapon which would only dilute his beloved torpedoes, but when he found on an experimental attack on a German *sperrbrecher* how successfully the rockets demoralized naval gun crews, leaving a comparatively clear field for the torpedoes, he changed his mind.

His concept now was to throw his aircraft in a compact, concentrated blow at enemy shipping. Covering the strike would be fighters, but they were there to keep enemy fighters from interfering with the Beaufighters. The rocket-armed Beaufighters would go in first, blasting the enemy decks to suppress anti-aircraft fire, and the torpedo-carriers would follow them, adding their own cannon-fire to the storm of steel lashing enemy decks. Shipboard gunners, blasted by cannon-fire, would find their accuracy plummeting even if they survived, while some of them would simply take cover instead of manning their weapons. The torpedo planes would then be able to come closer and suffer fewer losses before they dropped their deadly loads. Besides the changed tactics, Peterson had greater numbers to work with. Instead of six or seven Beauforts to fly on a strike, he could count on thirty Beaufighters, all of them trained to operate as a team.

That was his plan. Unfortunately he was pushed into action too soon. A juicy convoy was detected sailing from Norway along the Danish coast and then down the German coast to Holland, and orders came from Coastal Command to attack it.

291

"But the squadron's only half-trained," Peterson objected. "They know how to drop torpedoes and shoot cannons, but they don't know how to work together; an attack on a convoy shouldn't be just a bald-headed cavalry charge with each pilot going for the first ship he sees, but a properly co-ordinated attack in which each piece drops into place at exactly the right time. If we wait until we're ready, we can annihilate the whole convoy, escorts and all—if we go off half-cocked, we'll take a beating and we won't get the results we want."

His objections fell on deaf ears. The attack was made.

Douglas shared Peterson's misgivings. Peterson had detailed him to lead the torpedo attack, but half his pilots were newly arrived on the squadron, and their formation exercises had been sketchy. The rocket-armed Beaufighters were new to the squadron also, and the pilots were unpracticed in their use, while they had simply not had enough time to put the tactics under bullets to make sure they worked.

The attack involved aircraft from three different bases, including a fighter station, and although they were carefully briefed the fighter escort was early in making its rendezvous, and the short-legged single-engine fighters had to turn back after only a few minutes near the convoy, leaving the attack planes to return alone. The rocket-armed Beaufighters mistimed their attack, so that they came in for their flak-suppressant runs too late, and the torpedo planes had to face heavy fire from the unmolested vessels for a few frightful seconds.

Two torpedo Beaufighters and two rocket-armed Beaufighters, as well as a Spitfire fighter, were lost, and only one ship was left sinking.

Peterson was furious. At the critique of the operation he said flatly, "I told you so!" For a few minutes it was touch and go whether the group captain who had ordered the attack would rise in his wrath and order Peterson's court-martial, but he contained himself. Peterson received authority for four weeks of intensive training before the force was to be thrown into action again.

During that time Peterson made himself unpopular, even with Douglas, as he blasted each crew for each mistake it made, for each deviation, however small, from his orders. He insisted on split-

292

second timing, immediate response to orders, a careful hierarchy of command to be taken over by the next senior man if an aircraft came to grief, visual signals if radios failed, and a set of emergency procedures if weather changed, unexpected fighter opposition materialized, or intelligence was faulty. He also demanded constant practice with guns, torpedoes and rockets. The crews were razor-sharp when he declared them ready and every man hated Peterson and condemned him as a tyrant.

In June a German convoy, including two brand-new ships just launched from a Dutch shipyard, left the mouth of the river Scheldt. It was protected by a dozen *sperrbrechers*, and the decks of the ships themselves were bristling with anti-aircraft weapons. Peterson planned his attack, using aerial photographs and naval advice as to the route the convoy must take, and launched it in full daylight. Douglas led the torpedo bombers.

The aircraft took off, made a smooth rendezvous first with other Beaufighters and then with Spitfires, and flew out in formation, fighters above the twin-engine craft. They approached the convoy, and Peterson gave a two-word command. The formation wheeled like a battalion of Guards on parade and plunged down on the ships. The rocket-armed Beaufighters went for the escort vessels, with the pilots tearing in at maximum speed, opening fire with their cannon, watching as the shell-strikes hit the water, lifting their noses to walk the strikes into the ship's sides, and then letting the rockets go. Other cannon-and-rocket armed aircraft ran in at top speed against the merchant ships, passing the torpedo carriers approaching at their sedate 140 knots, and blasted the decks with shells and rockets that silenced the ships' guns. Six torpedoes snaked toward the frantically-maneuvering ships, but avoiding one torpedo led each ship into the path of another, and three torpedoes hit. The larger ship sank at once; the other was left ablaze from stem to stern with only an hour or so to live.

Rocket and cannon-shells sank one escort and damaged all the others, two of them so seriously that motor torpedo boats came out that night and finished them off. The whole attack, from take-off to landing, took only twenty-seven minutes. There were no casualties among the aircraft at all.

Peterson received a DSO and was promoted to group captain. Douglas would have received a DFC if he had not already had two of them. "We 're saving up for a DSO for you," Peterson told him.

"Thanks Derek—I mean sir," Douglas replied. "Don't go to any trouble. I'm doing a lot better than I ever thought I would already."

The next day, as he entered the officer' mess he saw a familiar face. He hurried over, to be greeted by a woman's voice. "Why Flight Lieutenant Douglas! Is that a DFC and Bar I see?"

"Lady Helena! How good it is to see you! What are you doing here?"

"I'm stationed at Command Headquarters now. I make periodical visits to the stations."

Douglas turned to Crane."Helena, I'd like you to meet my navigator, Reg Crane. Reg, this is Lady Helena Compton-Morris. We're old friends from Lower Lexington."

Crane bowed. "I see you're a squadron officer," he said, looking at her squadron leader's rings. "I'm flattered to be in such exalted company."

She blushed faintly. "Edward says you fly with him."

"Yes, indeed. We were together in Malta and in Ceylon, and now we're crewed up again here in England. We're almost as old friends as you are."

They walked into the dining-room. As they sat opposite one another at a table, Helena and Douglas chattered about their experiences at Douglas' former squadron. Crane noticed that as she looked at him an expression of pain crossed her face. He wondered what he had done or said to make so bad an impression, and then mentally shrugged his shoulders. "I presume you like flying together," she said to Crane at length.

"Oh, Ed is a terrible task-master. He's even gone to the length of making me learn to fly the plane, since he's much too lazy to fly it himself all the time. Yet he steadfastly refuses to help me with my navigation."

"Oh come on Reg! You made me do half the navigation that time we were coming home to Malta!"

"That was an exception, skipper. Flight Lieutenant Douglas has always abused his navigators shamefully, Lady Helena."

294

Douglas looked at Helena seriously. "I've always had good luck with my crew members—present company excepted, of course."

"I have to work pretty hard to live up to the standard reached by his previous navigator." Crane said. "Ed speaks very highly of him. Did you know him?"

"Yes, I did." She bit her words off, and Crane fumbled for a reply. Then, before he could speak, she said, "Yes, I knew him. We were engaged to be married."

"What—I didn't know—"

"Yes. We became engaged the day he flew on that mission from which he never came back."

"I'm frightfully sorry."

She went on as if she had not heard him. "He was a poet—an engineer who could write beautiful sonnets." She raised her eyes to Crane's. "Douglas' navigator. Tell me—do you write poems too?"

"No—no. Actually I intend to take holy orders—I was studying to be an Anglican priest when I joined the Air Force."

She looked at Douglas. "You choose unusual navigators, Edward."

"They are—they were—both good navigators. Both good men to fly with. Crane here is the best man with astro I've ever met."

"I knew you'd pick a good man."

"Reg and Hank are a lot different—but a lot alike too. Both kind of dreamy."

"Yes, I guess I am," Crane assented. "I've always been glad I'm not a pilot—I'd start dreaming and let somebody shoot me down. I'm in the right job as a navigator."

Douglas nodded. "We work well together."

Crane smiled. "Actually, Ed didn't pick me. I picked him. Our crew at OTU lost its pilot, and I managed to get Ed to replace him. Had to pull a few strings—my father has a number of friends in high places. Ed wasn't too happy about it at first, getting such a ropey crew, but after all he's only a colonial and doesn't deserve any better."

Douglas looked at him open-mouthed. "You never told me this before!"

"You never asked me, Ed. I don't tell you everything I know."

Helena looked at them both. "You're quite a pair. And yes, you do remind me, now that I think of it, of Flying Officer Snow—that

295

same quirky kind of humour. And then when I hear that Canadian voice of yours, Edward, I hear Henry."

Douglas jumped. "Uh—yeah—I guess so." He thought of Moragh MacLennan's comments and shuddered faintly. Anyway, he was not in love with Helena; he was not in competition with a ghost. He changed the subject. "What do you think of Derek Peterson making group captain?"

"Highly deserved," she said, and they talked of other things for the rest of the meal. After lunch they parted, and she went back to her duties while Douglas and Crane went back to theirs.

The next day Crane told Douglas that he wanted him to spend another weekend at his home. Douglas was agreeable. "Perhaps we can ask Lady Helena to join us," Crane added.

"She'd probably like to," Douglas replied.

Crane asked her that evening. She looked at him and shook her head. "Thank you very much—it's very kind of you. But it's quite impossible."

"To use one of Ed Douglas' phrases—take a rain check."

"Thank you again," she said, and walked away.

CHAPTER THIRTY-TWO

Peterson's task force ranged up and down the coasts of occupied Europe, smashing at the shipping the Germans were sending to Holland, to reinforce their troops in the Pas de Calais and Normandy for the invasion they knew was inevitable. Placing so many tempting targets in Peterson's way would have been unwise if there had been another way to move men and material, but the European rail system was subjected to hammer blows from Bomber Command, and trains moved slowly if at all. For the Germans there was no choice; they had to bring in supplies by water. Some of the ships got through, but the attacks hurt badly. Sweden refused to continue shipping iron ore to the western German ports, putting an even heavier load on the battered railways. As the war went on, German soldiers were pulled out of Norway on troopships, and torpedo planes smashed at them, slaughtering the troops. Douglas tried not to think about it, and Crane said, "Those who take the sword must perish by the sword." It made Douglas feel a little better.

The Beaufighters did not have everything their own way, of course. After a month the Germans thickened their defences, and the attacking planes began to fall victim to them. But the losses were never as severe as in the old, hopeless Beaufort days, and the damage done to the enemy was far greater. Douglas drilled his troops and polished his tactics and kept himself from thinking about the danger. In his moments of reflection he was amazed at how little it worried him.

A couple of months later Peterson called Douglas into his office. "Ed, we're forming a new squadron of torpedo Beaufighters, and I want you to command it. I know you'll do well. You've always been on the same wavelength with me, and while you've been working for me you've never torn a strip off me, as you usually do with your commanding officers. It's high time you were promoted anyway. Besides, as a squadron leader you'll have a chance at that DSO you so richly deserve."

"Holy smoke, Derek—I mean sir—I don't know what to say to that—heck, I'm not that important—"

"I'm the best judge of that, Ed. All you have to do is to stay alive for another week or so." He smiled, and shook Douglas' hand. Then he was all business again. "Oh yes—I have one last job for you. There's a convoy coming out of Hamburg now—we know it's headed for Antwerp, and it's our duty to stop it. I'm putting you in command of the whole show—one last bash before you go on to your new job."

"I can handle it, sir."

"I know you can. Off with you, then. And bring me back the news that the convoy's been smashed."

"We'll do our best, sir."

"I know you will." Peterson dismissed Douglas, and sat down again at his desk.

Douglas briefed the strike crews carefully, without omitting anything, even though he had done it so many times before that the words came as automatically as those of a priest celebrating communion. He questioned the newest crews on some minor points, and repeated the commands that would be given, and the maneuvers that must follow them.

Satisfied at last, he fell into step with Crane and headed to the parachute section to pick up his Mae West and parachute, as well as the escape kits that were mandatory, even if they were of little use while floating in a dinghy in the North Sea.

Crane and he climbed into the Beaufighter, Douglas feeling the regulation butterflies in his stomach as he settled himself into the pilot's seat and adjusted its position to suit his leg length. A mechanic stood by with a fire extinguisher as Douglas gestured with his thumb and started the port engine, and then the man walked around to the other side of the aircraft as Douglas started the starboard one. Douglas made the run-up, and then waved away the chocks. A green light winked at him from the control tower, and he shoved the throttles forward to start the aircraft on its waddling, ungraceful progress to the end of the runway. "Stand by for take-off, Reg," he said, half-listening for Crane's curt "Roger, skipper." He shoved the throttles to the top of the quadrant and the Beaufighter began to roll, accelerated, lifted its tail to Douglas' forward nudge on the stick, and then took to the sky as Douglas pulled the stick back.

The rest of the flight formed up behind him, a rather straggling echelon right, the planes staggered one behind the other and offset to the right side. Douglas did not bother them about the loose formation; there was no need to tire them unnecessarily on the outward flight, and they would close up when the enemy ships were sighted. With Crane navigating him, the convoy showed up on schedule, the naval craft scurrying around the merchant ships like sheep-dogs around their charges.

Douglas gave a curt word of command, and the aircraft peeled off into their formal airborne arabesques, the rocket-firing aircraft accelerating as they ran in for the attack, the torpedo aircraft slowing. Douglas checked that his torpedo was armed, let down to dropping height, checked his airspeed, and said, "Here we go, Reg."

He heard the word "Roger" and then gave the Beaufighter a little left rudder to get the larger of the two merchant ships in his sights. On both sides of him he saw his companion Beaufighters out of the corners of his eyes, their pilots, anonymous in helmets, intent like him on their torpedo sights. He allowed for the deflection required for the ship's forward speed, waited for the range to close to 800 yards, and pressed the torpedo release button. The torpedo dropped free, hit the water cleanly, and began its run toward the target. Douglas tramped on the rudder and shoved the throttles forward as he turned to parallel the wake of the ship. As he kicked the plane level again he saw the decks of the ship crowded with field-gray figures, and then he saw the torpedo strike. The ship rocked and shuddered as a great stalactite of water rose from its side, and then slewed to a stop. The soldiers aboard the troopship began to jump overboard into the cold North Sea waters.

Douglas cast a glance at them and then turned his attention back to his flying. The ship was listing badly, but the gun at the stern, still manned by a crew of surpassing courage, continued to fire. Douglas wasted no plaudits on them, and no compassion on the soldiers struggling in the water, thinking briefly that he took his chances and they took theirs. Then, just as he straightened out for a climb away from the battered convoy and the sinking ship, a shell exploded beneath the Beaufighter's nose.

The explosion blasted the aircraft upwards so that it reared like a bucking horse and almost stalled. Douglas shoved the stick forward frantically, and kicked rudder as it slewed sideways. He levelled the wings, and then felt the plane jump as it skimmed the top of a wave. He forced himself to pull back slowly, and the plane gained a little altitude. When he looked out toward the convoys, he found himself looking through a windshield starred with a thousand shatter-cracks. The convoy was off to the side, and Douglas noted fleetingly that its guns had been silenced. He turned the plane away from the ships it had attacked and called to Crane, "What's our course home?"

"Two sixty-seven." Douglas looked at the compass to turn the plane onto course. As he bent forward to set the heading on the compass-ring he saw with disbelieving eyes that blood was running down his fingers. He moved his arm, and screamed as an agonizing pain knifed through it.

"Crane!" he yelled. "Look at my arm!" Crane unsnapped his seat-belt and moved forward.

"Good God, you're wounded!" Crane undid Douglas' harness and ripped off his flying jacket, and then tore the sleeve off his shirt. "I've got to put a tourniquet on it!" he shouted in Douglas' ear, and quickly improvised one from the sleeve of the shirt. He twisted it closed, and then tore open the first-aid kit to slap a field-dressing on Douglas' arm.

"Oh Jesus, it hurts!"

"Can you cope?" asked Crane.

"You'll have to fly her home," Douglas answered. "Here—we'll climb to four or five thousand feet, and then you get me out of the seat and you take over." He peered at the instruments through fogging eyes. "Christ, what's that draft?"

"We've got a hole in the nose of the aircraft."

300

"The kite seems to respond to the controls well enough," Douglas muttered.

"We're at four thousand, skipper," Crane said. He took an ampoule of morphine from the first-aid packet and jabbed it into Douglas' shoulder. "Okay skipper, get out of the seat." He lifted Douglas out and laid him on the floor beside the navigator's position, and then slid into the seat himself. The plane lurched and fell off onto one wing, and Crane yelped as he fought to recover, which he did not manage until he had lost two thousand feet.

He muttered a prayer as he finally succeeded in flying reasonably straight and level.

Douglas saw Crane intent on his instruments, and closed his eyes as his head spun. He felt himself removed from his body, and drifted into unconsciousness. "Don't try too hard to fly well. Reg," he muttered, "you're over-controlling," and then his head lolled sideways.

Crane flew toward the English coast, pausing at intervals to wipe blood out of his eyes from a cut on his forehead. For a moment the plane began to porpoise, until Crane, gritting his teeth, forced himself to smooth his movements, letting the plane find the way it wanted to fly. He reached out a hand to adjust the throttles, and found that the handles were sticky with Douglas' blood.

He was too occupied with his flying to look around him, although he knew there might be enemy fighters stalking him. If they came, they came; he was too clumsy a pilot to avoid them, and they would find him a sitting duck. He climbed to six thousand feet, to give himself time to recover if something went wrong. After ten minutes he began to get the feel of the controls, and ten minutes after that he was able to trim the aircraft so that it flew hands off. He slid carefully out of the seat, inspected the dressing he had put on Douglas' arm, loosed the tourniquet and tightened it again, and got back behind the wheel, sweating with exertion and fear. He licked his lips and muttered another prayer as he fought to keep control of himself.

The radio jabbered in his ears when he plugged his helmet-cord into the socket from which he had jerked Douglas' head-set. He searched for the push-button that allowed him to transmit and jabbed it. The cacophony of voices ceased abruptly as Crane yelled,

301

"Mayday! Mayday!"

"Who called Mayday?" a voice asked over the radio, quiet now except for static. Crane jabbed the button again. "Beaufighter S-Sugar—headed west—north of the Wash—pilot wounded—navigator flying—give me an escort back home!"

"Can't see you—we'll keep looking. Good luck!" Crane saw he was flying in lonely splendour. He checked the compass and looked down at Douglas in his torn and bloody flying suit.

The English coast appeared ahead, and Crane pulled out a map and checked his position. A town lay ahead, and he avoided it, and then saw an airfield a little to the south. As he neared it he fired off his Verey pistol, arcing the colours of the day into the sky, and then knelt beside Douglas.

"Ed—wake up!" He shook him. "Look—I can't land this kite. We'll have to bail out!" He lifted Douglas and checked his parachute harness to make sure it was tight, and then as he looked at the seat-type parachute itself his eyes widened in horror. Flak had slashed through it so that it tumbled out in a shapeless mass onto the aircraft floor. "Good God! You'll never get out with this!" Crane shook Douglas again. "Can you land her, Ed?" Douglas opened his eyes. "What—what do you want?"

"Your chute's unserviceable—can you land the plane?"

"I can try." Crane half-bundled, half-lifted him into the pilot's seat. Douglas made an abortive attempt to adjust the throttle and screamed, "Oh God—that hurts! No go, Reg. Look—you'll have to handle the throttles while I handle the stick. When I move my finger back, retard the throttles, when I waggle them forward, advance them. When I close my fist close the throttles—when we flare out."

"Okay, old man. We're in this together."

Instruments wavered before Douglas' eyes. "How high are we, Reg?"

"Three thousand."

Douglas made a patting motion with the hand of his useless right arm, and Crane pulled back on the throttles. The aircraft began to sink slightly, and Douglas turned to circle the airfield, to make as normal an approach as he could.

"How high now?"

"Twenty-two hundred."

"Take off a little more power." Douglas steered the plane into a long lazy turn that ended with them a couple of miles from the base. "How high?"

"One thousand."

"Extend the undercarriage. We'll take her in." Douglas fought to keep control of his sense, forcing himself to concentrate on the landing. He motioned Crane to retard the throttles a little more. They approached the field. "Are we lined up all right?" he asked.

"Good enough."

"Put on carburetor heat." Crane extended a hand, flipped a switch. Douglas moved his fingers again, and Crane pulled off more power.

The runway was ahead of them. He corrected the heading a little, and saw they were too low. "Add power," he said, motioning with his fingers. Crane responded. The engines roared a little more loudly. The threshold of the runway lay just ahead of them. Crane took off more power. The plane came in over the airfield boundary. Douglas pulled back slightly on the stick and the airspeed fell. He clenched his fist and yelled, "Cut the power—now!" Crane reached over to the throttle quadrant and pulled both levers savagely back. The engines were suddenly quiet. The plane ballooned a little, dipped, swayed, hit on one tire, bounced, touched again, and caracoled off into a spectacular ground-loop. The starboard wing bit into the ground and broke off.

"Cut the switches!" Douglas yelled as the groundloop began. Crane slapped them off, and then hugged Douglas to him from his position behind the pilot's seat. The plane stopped in a great pillar of dust as fire-trucks and ambulances screamed toward it. Crane unsnapped Douglas' harness and shoved him out of the hatch over his head and followed him out. Flames began to lick out from an engine nacelle. Crane tumbled Douglas into a depression and jumped on top of him just as the fuel tank exploded. A piece of the fuselage slammed into him and he fell over Douglas' limp form, unconscious.

An ambulance jolted up and figures jumped from it, bringing out stretchers. Doctors had begun working on Reg and Ed before the driver had put the ambulance into gear. They were hurried into the emergency room at the station hospital.

Crane recovered consciousness four hours later, to find himself bandaged and splinted, able to see out of only one eye, and with his left arm in a cast. A nurse hurried over to him as soon as she heard him mutter, and a doctor answered her summons.

"Where am I?"

"Here in hospital. You're a very lucky man, my boy. You have a broken arm, multiple bruises and concussions, and a rather spectacular gash in your forehead. But there's nothing we can't cure. In a few weeks you'll be as good as new."

"How about Ed—my skipper?"

The doctor's brow clouded. "He's in intensive care. He's lost a lot of blood, he has a badly-broken arm and a broken leg, and he has quite a bit of shrapnel in him—at least he did, before we took it out. It'll be quite a while before he's up and about again, I'm afraid."

"Is he out of danger?"

"Not quite, my boy, but we're doing everything for him. He's young and strong—that's a help."

"Will I be able to see him?"

"Not for a day or two. He's still unconscious."

Crane nodded and lay back. The nurse took his temperature and gave him a sleeping pill. He went back to sleep.

When he woke up his mother and father were at his bedside. His mother threw her arms around him, and he yelped in pain. "Mater!" he gasped. "Be careful!"

"Oh!" she said, stricken. "I'm so sorry!"

Crane reached for her hand. "It's wonderful to see you, Mater. And father too. How are you, Pater?"

"We're fine, son. It's you we're worried about."

"The doctor says I'll be quite all right again before too long, but I want you to find out how Ed Douglas is getting along. Can you tell me anything?"

"I'll see what I can do, son." When he returned five minutes later he said, "Flight Lieutenant Douglas is still on the danger list, Reginald. He has not regained consciousness yet, and it may be a day or so before he will, according to the doctor."

"I'm worried about him. We've been flying together a long time, you know."

"We'll pray for him," said his mother.

304

"So will I. Can you make sure he gets the best of care?"

"I'm certain he already is getting it, but I'll put in a word anyway," his mother said.

Crane had other visitors. Derek Peterson came to the hospital, accompanied by a number of aircrew including three who had flown on the mission in which Crane and Douglas had been wounded. The Pokington station chaplain, who had come to know Crane well, arrived in his vestments and gave Crane communion, which Crane's mother dragooned all the other visitors to share.

Douglas opened his eyes the next day. He was completely immobilized, with a badly-broken leg in traction, a broken arm in a cast, dressings on his wounds from shell-splinters in his arms, legs and chest, and another dressing on a gouge in his head. Late in the afternoon Crane was pushed in a wheel-chair to see him, but Douglas' speech was scarcely intelligible. Crane said a prayer over him and returned to his ward. The next evening he returned, this time in a wheel-chair pushed by his mother. Strictly speaking she was not allowed to visit Douglas, but she had bulldozed all opposition aside. Douglas had only a few words to say, and they were shooed out shortly by a nurse who pulled a screen around his bed and took to performing various esoteric things upon his dressings.

The day after that Crane's mother, who had taken up lodgings in a nearby village to be near her son, visited him again, this time with Air Vice Marshal Tom Sullivan in tow. She had commanded him to come with her as regally as she commanded everyone else, and he had obeyed her, knowing that a visit to a wounded airman was politically wise. As he left his office he called a Public Relations Officer of the Royal Canadian Air Force, who was stationed at the Air Ministry, to tell him of the visit. "Must see a young officer—I know his mother—who stopped quite a packet on an attack on a German convoy. He and his pilot were both wounded. The pilot is one of your boys—a Canadian called Douglas. Might be an idea for you to come along."

"Excellent idea," the PR man agreed enthusiastically, looking forward to associating with an Air Vice Marshal whom he might impress with his competence and devotion to duty. "Ed Douglas will appreciate a visit," Reg said when they arrived. "Wheel me in there, mother."

The PR man made a few notes, and then asked him how he had been wounded. Douglas made a few non-committal and embarrassed remarks.

Crane stepped in. He told the whole story of the flight, praising Douglas at every step of the way. His skill as a pilot, his bravery in the attack, his determination, his leadership, his devotion to duty, were set out in the most glowing terms. The story of the attack was followed by the tale of the operations off Malta, the attack on the tanker at Tobruk, and then of the ditching off Ceylon. Douglas tried to interrupt, but Mrs. Crane firmly silenced him.

Crane was far more informative than Douglas would have been, and much more articulate. The incidents which Douglas would have credited to others Crane monopolized for Douglas alone. At the end of an hour the PR officer had a thick booklet of notes, and a dozen photographs of Douglas, of Crane, and of the hospital staff.

"Absolutely marvellous," he said. "This copy will get national coverage." He referred to a list in his pocket. "At first I thought only the Valenby Herald would be interested, and maybe the Saskatoon Star-Phoenix, but this will get national coverage. All Canada will hear about it."

"I'm glad of that," Crane said. "Douglas deserves recognition—the service he's seen, the dangers he's faced, and now the wounds he has received. And incidentally he saved my life by landing the plane as he did. How he managed to retain consciousness long enough to do it I'll never know."

Douglas, who had been lying with his eyes closed, suddenly spoke up. "You're a bloody liar, Reg. You know it was you saved my life. Goddam it, you know you coulda bailed out—your chute was in good shape. But you stayed in the kite to get me down. After all, you handled the throttles. Look, Crane's the bloody hero, not me. For Christ's sake put that in your paper."

The PR officer smiled beatifically. This was more than he had hoped for—an authentic hero, whose only words were to try to shift the spotlight to one of his comrades. "Yes, Flight Lieutenant Douglas, I'll make sure that Mr. Crane gets the proper credit."

A nurse entered to tell them their visit was over. Air Vice Marshal Sullivan pushed Crane back to his ward in his wheel-chair, while the PR officer made some final notes in his book. "I want to get this on the wire right away," he said.

CHAPTER THIRTY-THREE

Douglas reached for her hand. "It's getting better all the time now. Thanks for coming to see me."

Helena looked up as Crane rolled into the room in his wheel chair. "Oh—Flight Lieutenant Crane! I'm so glad to see you."

"I'm pleased to see you too, Lady Helena. Thank you for coming. Most kind of one of your exalted rank visiting us mere flight lieutenants."

She laughed. "Yes—it is very noble of me. I'm so glad you've survived that crash."

Crane nodded. "So are we."

"We wouldn't be here if Reg hadn't saved my life, you know," Douglas said.

"Oh nonsense," Crane countered. "You saved mine."

"Don't you two quarrel about it. I really believe you must have worked together. But I'm most awfully bucked up to find you both back—if not exactly in one piece."

Douglas smiled. "I guess I won't have to work for a living for a while, and neither will my navigator."

Her face was suddenly sober."Yes, of course. Reginald is your navigator, isn't he?"

"I'm bad luck for my navigators. Reg is lucky he got off with a broken arm. That's a lot better than Hank Snow did. Oh hell—sorry, Lady Helena."

Crane quickly said something to change the subject. "Did you hear the news this morning? The Allies have taken Antwerp. The war can't last much longer. There won't be much more for us to do."

Douglas looked at his extended leg. "I doubt if I'll be flying again for six months. Maybe longer."

"The war will probably be over by then. You've done your share, Ed," Crane said.

"Yes, certainly," Helena nodded. "The war can't last forever." They were interrupted by three more visitors. One was Derek Peterson; the other two were pilots from the squadron. Douglas greeted them warmly. As he looked at one of them he said, "Say, you've got your scraper ring; a squadron leader now! Congratulations!"

"Yes," Peterson said. Bob will be taking over the new squadron."

"Hey, that's the one I was going to take over!"

"I know, Ed, but you're not exactly fighting fit just now. Somebody has to do it."

Douglas burst out laughing. "Me and my luck! Of course I can't get my skew-ell now—I won't be filling a squadron's leader's job in this hospital. That's the way the ball bounces."

"I'm frightfully sorry, old chap," the new squadron leader said. "I hadn't intended to—"

"Don't feel bad about it. That's the story of my life. Anyway, I've still got that life. That's better than a scraper ring any day."

Douglas looked toward Helena. "Oh—I'm sorry. May I present some friends of mine, Helena. You know Derek Peterson, of course. And this is Bob Wreford and Bill Shearer. They're from my squadron—my new squadron—or maybe it's my old squadron now. This is Lady Helena Compton-Morris."

"How do you do, gentlemen," she said formally. "Flight Lieutenant Douglas and I are old friends. He was stationed at Lower Lexington when I was there."

Just then a nurse bustled in to interrupt them. Helena looked at Crane. "Perhaps I can push your wheelchair for you."

"Splendid idea,"agreed Crane. The group left Douglas' bedside. "Awfully decent of you, Lady Helena," Crane said as she pushed him along the corridor. "Can I offer you a cup of tea? There's a canteen on the ground floor."

"That would be very nice." A few minutes later they were sitting at a table in the austere and rather dowdy canteen.

"It was most considerate of you to come to visit Ed, Lady Helena. It's a long way to come."

"He's an old friend, you know."

"Did you know Ed well at Lower Lexington?"

"Yes, I knew him fairly well. Of course, I knew Henry Snow a lot better."

Crane nodded, and went on quickly to say, "I've been flying with Ed a long time now. You know he saved my life by landing our aircraft when it was mostly scrap metal."

She smiled. "That's not what Edward says. But I won't worry about it."

"You know, Lady Helena, you've unbent quite a bit since I met you at spokington."

"Yes, I suppose so. But circumstances are different now. You're not on operations any more."

"Not on operations? What do you mean?"

She looked down. "It seemed to me somehow that I brought bad luck to the aircrew I met. I knew several men at Lower Lexington—men I grew very fond of—and they were all killed. The last of them was Henry Snow. You know, at Bomber Command stations there are women who get the reputation of being 'chop girls'—they go out with a man, and then he goes missing. I got to thinking I was a jinx like them. And then when I met you I found you rather an attractive man—and I didn't want you to get yourself killed too. That's why I didn't want anything to do with you."

"Oh, bad luck! I'm sorry you feel that way!"

"That's why I was distant with you. I didn't to want to ruin your luck too."

"There isn't much danger of anything worse happening to me now. I think I've had my bad luck."

"I hope so."

"You know, Lady Helena, you're really a most attractive woman, now that you've stopped being so distant."

"Thank you. And there's no need to keep calling me Lady Helena—just plain Helena will be fine."

"Thank you—Helena. You have a lovely name, you know."

"I'm glad you like it."

Crane bent toward her. "You came here to see Ed, didn't you?"

"Yes, of course."

"I'd very much like it if you were to come back again to see me."

"That could be arranged." She touched his hand. "You're very

309

flattering." Her face fell. "But then Douglas' navigators always are."

"I'm sorry that I bring back unhappy memories."

"It's not your fault, Reginald. It's what your friend Ed Douglas would call the luck of the draw."

Crane nodded. "In any case, I'm frightfully glad that you came to visit Edward, and that I had the chance to see you again."

"It's my pleasure. It's more of a pleasure because you're still alive." She was quiet for a moment. "Do you expect to keep flying on operations?"

"No. Group Captain Peterson told me that we were both screened. Said the words about going to the well too often. I think he's right."

"I think so too." She stood up. "Time to take you back to your lonely hospital bed." She pushed him back to his room. "I'm glad I can do you some small service."

"You can do a big service for me."

"Yes. What is it?"

"Come back to visit me again."

"Of course, Reginald. I'll be glad to."

She was as good as her word. She returned each weekend for the next month.

On the fourth weekend Crane no longer needed his wheelchair. He and Helena spent half an hour with Douglas, who was still confined to his bed. When visiting hours were over Crane took Helena's arm and said, "Now we must go for a walk in the park across the way together. It'll be good for me, you know."

They sat down on a park bench. "Helena," he said, "there is something I must ask you."

"Yes, Reginald?"

He looked at the ground in front of him. "When I first met you, you told me that you had been engaged to Henry Snow."

"Yes, I was. I was engaged to him for one day."

He lifted his eyes to hers. "Are you still in love with him—with his memory?"

She looked away. "I was very much in love with him—but he's gone now—it's in the past—I don't know—"

"I want you to know that I have fallen in love with you, Helena. It may be presumptuous of me—you are a duke's daughter—but I want you to know it. I love you."

"Then kiss me." He took her gently in his arms, and their lips met. When he lifted his face from hers he repeated, "Yes—I love you."

She nodded, and then smiled, a little sadly. "It's funny—you're Douglas' navigator."

"Does that matter?"

"No—of course not." The smile left her lips. "It's just funny, that's all. Edward Douglas is just another pilot—but I fall in love with his navigators."

"Does that mean that you love me too?"

"Yes. I love you."

Crane pulled her toward him again, and kissed her, passionately this time.

"I love you, Reginald." She stood up, and he got to his feet to face her.

"Now there is something I want you to do."

"What is it?"

"Ask me to marry you."

"Marry you? Of course—but I thought—"

"I know what you thought, my dear. Now ask me to marry you."

"Helena—will you marry me?"

"Yes." They kissed again.

When their lips parted she said, "Come with me." She led him to the office marked "Hospital Chaplain", knocked, and entered. The chaplain, who was by now a close friend of Reg's stood up. "How do you do, Lady Helena." He turned to Crane. "Hello, Reg—glad to see you. Can I do something for you?"

Helena answered. "You're Flight Lieutenant the Reverend John Davis. I want you to marry me to Reginald."

"Why—of course! Reg, I'm utterly surprised—you never said a word—My heartiest congratulations! When do you plan the ceremony?"

"Today," Helena said. "Right now. You have the authority, haven't you?"

"This is impossible—there are laws—a waiting period—blood tests—"

"Those are man-made laws. We'll go though all the formalities later. We'll have a wedding in a church. You must marry us now—you must!"

311

"Reg—what about you?"

Crane, who stood looking stunned, without a word, sputtered, "Why, I must say—"

Helena looked at him and stamped her foot. "You said you love me. Do you want to marry me or not?"

"Yes, of course I do!"

She took a ring from her right hand and handed it to Crane. "This will have to do— you can get a proper ring later."

The priest looked back and forth from Helena to Crane. "But why this hurry? Surely you can wait—"

"No, I can't. I was engaged to a man once before, for one day! Then he was killed! Now I've found another man to love, I won't waste a moment. I can't trust luck any more. I want you to marry us—this very moment!" The priest shrugged his shoulders helplessly, and then donned his canonical robes. Crane looked at Helena and smiled. She was acting just as his mother would have, and Crane felt at home with her assertiveness. The priest opened his prayer book and performed the ceremony. Crane and Helena kissed.

Helena smiled at the chaplain. "Now not a word to anybody. My mother and Reg's mother will have a splendid time planning the second wedding that everybody will know about. Now, may I use your telephone?"

She called the station motor transport section and calmly ordered a staff car to be sent to the hospital. When it came she bundled an unprotesting Crane into it, and took him to a hotel in a nearby town. In their room she turned to him and said, "And now, my dear husband, let us consummate our marriage." When at last they were lying together, their passion spent, Crane looked at her with unbelieving eyes.

"Good Lord, Helena, I can't believe my luck! But it happened so fast! Do you always act so quickly?"

"No. You're the only man I've ever married."

"My only comment is the conventional one—'This is so sudden.' But why—"

"I wanted to defeat the nemesis that has followed me. I didn't want the cup dashed from my lips again. When I saw you, and found you were Douglas' navigator, and found myself in love with you, and

312

then when you told me that you loved me too, I made up my mind that I wouldn't waste a minute."

"I'm very glad you did, Helena." Suddenly he burst out laughing.

"Yes? What's so funny?"

"Now I know how your ancestors got to be earls."

"Earls knew what they wanted. I know too. I won't lose you now."

"No. There's no danger of that. Besides, I won't be fit to fly again for quite a while. You'll have me all to yourself."

She rose, bathed, dressed, and then helped him into his uniform. "Now I must take you back to the hospital. The nurses will be raising the roof."

"So they will," he smiled. "But I can trust you to carry things off. When will we do it all over again in style?"

"In a month or so. My mother and your mother will arrange everything."

"I'd like Douglas to be my best man."

"I'm sure it can be arranged." She kissed him, and looked contrite as he winced when she squeezed his wounded ribs.

CHAPTER THIRTY-FOUR

Douglas was sitting up in his bed when Crane and Helena entered his room the next day. "Hello, Ed," Crane said. "Helena and I have something to tell you, and something to ask you."

"Go ahead. I'll do anything that doesn't involve getting out of bed."

Crane looked at him without smiling. "Helena has consented to marry me. I want you to be my best man."

"Marry? Holy smoke, that was fast—sure—I'll be glad to be your best man. Congratulations to both of you. When's the big day?"

"Next month," Helena answered. "My mother and Reginald's mother will make the necessary arrangements. We want to be married as soon as possible." She smiled. "We've checked with the doctor. He thinks you'll be on your feet in a few days, and quite fit to take past in the ceremony in a month."

"I'm glad to hear that—he hasn't told me yet. Will there be a rehearsal or something like that so I'll know what to do?"

"I'm sure our mothers will take care of all such details."

"Are you going to invite some of the boys from the squadron?"

"Certainly. Reginald has many good friends there."

"It's too bad Moragh MacLennan won't be around to attend the wedding too, Reg," Douglas said.

Helena creased her brow. "Moragh? But she's just come back to England—I'll get in touch with her."

"Ask her to come and see me, will you?"

"Of course. She probably doesn't know you've been wounded and are in hospital."

"Thanks. I'll appreciate that. By the way, I'm awfully glad Reg is getting a girl like you—you've always been my favourite WAAF, you know."

314

"I thought Moragh was that."

"You never gave me a hard time in clothing stores."

Two days later Moragh MacLennan visited the hospital. Crane welcomed her in the lobby and took her to Douglas' bedside.

Douglas was sleeping. Moragh looked at him, and her hand flew to her mouth. "Edward!" She turned to Crane. "He's so—wasted!"

"He's been badly wounded, Moragh. A broken arm and a broken leg—concussion—bits of shrapnel in him. He's only been allowed out of bed since yesterday."

"He must have been through something terrible, the puir wee laddie."

They stood by his bedside until he opened his eyes. "Moragh!" he exclaimed when he saw her. "You're here! I was hoping you'd come!" He reached out his arms for her. She stooped over and kissed him.

'What a wonderful way to wake up!" he said. "I was dreaming of you—and when I woke up here you are!"

"Och, I'm glad to see you too! You look as if you've had a hard time, Edward."

"I had a little bad luck I'm coming back to life, though."

"Feel like a spin in your wheelchair, Ed?" Crane asked. He and Moragh supported Douglas as he swung his legs gingerly out of the bed and then slid into the wheelchair. Moragh spread a blanket over him, and Crane wheeled him out of the ward onto a balcony. A member of the Women's Voluntary Service was distributing tea from a cart, and Moragh brought Douglas a cup.

"You're always taking care of me, aren't you?"

"It's little enough I'm doing for you, Edward," she replied. "I'm so glad to see you getting better—I hadn't know you'd been wounded until Lady Helena told me."

"Lady Helena will be along in a few minutes," Crane said. "I'm going to the lobby to meet her now." He left the ward.

"Did you know that Reg Crane is going to marry Helena Compton-Morris?" Douglas said.

"No. I hadn't dreamed of it!"

"He's asked me to be his best man. They'll be married next month. I hope I'll be able to walk around well enough to do my duty."

"What did the doctor say?"

"He said I'd probably be all right. Duchesses and such make a big thing out of a wedding, and it has to be done in style."

"If I were a duchess I'd do things in style in style too."

"I'm glad you came, Moragh. I miss you." He smiled faintly. "Seeing Crane so happy with Helena made it worse. Every time she came to see him I wished you were here seeing me."

"It's awfully sweet of you to say that, Edward."

"I've known you for quite a while, you know—in fits and starts."

"For three years."

"Yes. Funny how we met. You wouldn't give me a new flying jacket. Can't say I blame you—I always ruin my flying clothing."

She laughed, "Aye, that you do. It's people like you who keep people like me in business, though."

Crane and Helena appeared, hand-in-hand. Moragh held out her hand to Helena. "Lady Helena! Edward has told me that you and Reg plan to marry! I'm so happy for you!"

"Thank you, Moragh," Helena replied. "We are looking forward to our marriage very much."

Crane nodded. "We are indeed."

"Edward says you're waiting for him to be up and around so that he can be your best man."

"Yes," Crane replied. "Ed and I have been through so much together that it's eminently fitting that he should be present at the most important event in my life."

"I hope that you will be able to attend the wedding too, Moragh," Helena said. "Indeed, I wanted to ask you to be one of my bridesmaids."

"Oh, I'd be delighted! I'm very flattered that you asked me."

A nurse entered, looking at her watch. "I'm afraid your time is up," she said. "Flight Lieutenant Douglas must have his dressings changed."

The next day he was sitting in his wheelchair, waiting for her. "Hi, Moragh. Maybe I can talk you into taking me for a spin."

"Of course, Edward." As she pushed him along he said, "I got some news today. The doctor told me I wouldn't be fit to fly again for at least six months—probably longer. And an officer from RCAF Headquarters came here to tell me I'm being sent back to Canada."

316

"You are? When?"

"When I'm walking around. It'll be a lot easier for me to go back across the Atlantic in an ordinary troopship than a hospital ship, anyway. Besides, I have to be best man at Reg's wedding."

"What will you do in Canada?"

"I'll probably get some desk job, since I can't fly. Or maybe they'll just discharge me—they have aircrew coming out of their ears these days, and they won't need me."

"If they discharge you what will you do then?"

"I've pretty well made up my mind I'll go to college. They have allowances for things like that, I've heard." He smiled. "I think I'll take a degree in pharmacy. Then I can run a drugstore and make the life of some clerk miserable the way my old boss used to make mine."

"The war is nearly over. You've done your bit, Edward."

He did not answer for a moment. Then he said, "Moragh, I've got something to ask you."

"Yes, Edward?"

Just at that moment three officers came tramping along the balcony. "I say, Ed old man," one of them cried. "So this is where you've got to, is it? We had the very devil of a time finding you!" He hurried forward and took Douglas' hand

"Trev Williams, my old wop! I thought you'd gone for a Burton!"

"I thought you had too—you nearly did, mate." He looked at Moragh. "I say—don't I know you?"

"Yes, you do," Moragh replied. "I'm Moragh MacLennan—I used to be in clothing stores at Lower Lexington."

"Oh, so you were! You were a real tough stores sergeant too!" Williams bent over and kissed her. "Never thought I'd get to kiss you, so I mustn't miss the opportunity."

"What have you been doing since you left the crew? You were lucky to get out of it when you did," asked Douglas.

"When my ankle healed they sent me to a wireless school as an instructor, because I couldn't pass the aircrew physical with my gimpy leg. I changed over to a ground wireless officer—they even gave me a commission."

"Gosh. it's good to see you again, Trev. We had the odd good time together when you were in the crew."

317

"So we did, bach, and I'm glad to see you're still in one piece and not likely to go looking for more trouble for a while. It's good to see you again, Moragh, now that I'm an officer myself, and don't have to bother you for uniforms, we can be friends."

"I'm sure we've always been friends—Douglas' crew, you know." A shadow passed over her face which he never noticed.

Douglas looked at the other two men. "Rattray! So you made it off the squadron too! That's wonderful! And you too, Hawkins!"

"We thought we'd drop in on you when we found out about you getting pranged. Can't let you have all the fun here without making sure you're staying in line, you know." Rattray reached into the patch pocket of his tunic. "Here's a wee something for you." He took out a small flask of Scotch whisky. "Have a wee drappie, my lad. It'll have you on your feet in no time." He unscrewed the top of the flask and poured out a dollop of whisky. Douglas tossed it off and made a face. "There are times when a guy appreciates his friends."

Rattray retrieved the metal cup, refilled it, and proffered it to Moragh. "And you, my dear lassie! My apologies—I should have offered it to you first! Will you do me the honour?"

She accepted the cup. "Thank you, Mr. Rattray. As a Scots lassie, I'm just a wee bit familiar with the dew of the Highlands." She sipped, and handed the cup back. "Just a wee bit—even on an occasion like this."

They stood laughing and talking until a nurse bustled up, trim and prim and efficient. "Flight Lieutenant Douglas!The very idea! You must come back to the ward directly! It's time for your medication!"

She grasped the handles of the wheelchair and rolled him along the balcony to the door leading to the corridor. "Now the visitors must leave. They've been here far too long!"

"Orders are orders," said Hawkins with a grin.

Douglas grasped Moragh's hand. "Come back and see me soon, Moragh!" he said urgently.

"Of course, my dear." The nurse wheeled him away.

Two days later Douglas was sitting in his wheelchair when he heard a tap of high heels on the floor. He pushed the chair around to look, and saw a tall woman, dressed in the height of wartime fashion, sweep up to his bed.

"Constance Davidson!" he cried. "I never thought—why, this is a surprise—"

"Of course it is!" she said, dropping artistically to one knee, throwing her arms around him, and kissing him hotly. "Douglas Edwards—you naughty boy! You never even told me you'd been wounded! As a matter of fact, you never told me you were back in England!"

"Heck, I'm sorry, Connie, but I thought I'd caused you enough trouble already—"

"Nonsense, my dear boy! Anything that ever happened to me with you was worthwhile—wonderfully worthwhile!" She kissed him again, with lips that were hot and soft, like warm cream, and he pulled her toward him. "Gee, Connie, you're just as beautiful as ever! You sure look good!"

"I rushed over as soon as I heard about you. One of my air force friends told me."

"Lucky for me!" He shook his head and smiled. "You sure know how to kiss, Connie!"

"That's not all I know how to do—remember?"

"How could I forget?"

"We've had our memories, haven't we?"

"Say, Connie, I don't want to pry, but what—well, you know—"

"Everything's just fine now, Douglas. I'm free again, of course. No more worries about jealous old men! I can't say I miss our Maurice much. Not with you around, Douglas. Douglas Edwards—that's a nice name."

"Still think I'm your backward lover, don't you? It's Edward Douglas, you know."

"Oh, so it is. But who cares? You kiss as well as ever. Tell me, Douglas, when are we going to spend a little time together? You're a real live hero, you know. Pictures in the paper and everything."

"That's up to the doctor, Connie. He's kind of narrow minded."

"I know. So let's make the most of today." She kissed him again, enthusiastically and he responded. "You haven't forgotten a thing," she told him.

"Neither have you. Just like the old days." He looked up. Moragh MacLennan was standing in the doorway.

"Oh!" He blushed. Connie stood up, smiling sweetly.

319

"Connie, this is Moragh MacLennan—"

"And I'm Constance Davidson. How good it is to meet you. You're one of Douglas' friends, I believe."

"I was," Moragh replied. "I've seen you on the stage, Miss Davidson. It's a great pleasure to meet you, I'm sure." She turned to Douglas.

"I see you're busy. Flight Lieutenant Douglas. I just came here to bring you a book to read. I'll be leaving now—I have only a few minutes." She left.

Douglas called after her. "Moragh! Don't go!" Her retreating back ignored him.

Connie laughed. "She wasn't as glad to see me as you were, my dear boy."

"Not exactly."

"She must mean a lot to you, Douglas."

"She does."

"I can mean a lot to you too, Douglas. You won't be in this terrible hospital forever, you know." She kissed him again. He put his good arm around her and crushed her to him.

She stood up and smoothed her dress. "Here's my telephone number, my dear. Give me a ring as soon as you're up and about."

"Yes. Thanks, Connie." He ran his eyes up and down her. "You're just as beautiful as ever."

She pirouetted. "And you're just as handsome, Douglas. Hurry up and get on your feet. I'll be waiting for you."

"I won't forget."

A gaggle of nurses and nurses' aides gathered at the door of the room, attracted by her movie-star fame. One of them rushed up with an open autograph book. She smiled at the girl and signed her name, and then signed another half-dozen books which suddenly appeared.

"And now I must leave you." She danced back to Douglas, kissed him, and left, blowing a kiss to him as she disappeared down the corridor.

"Oooh! She's so pretty, isn't she?" one of the girls said. "Just like her pictures! And so sweet, too!" One of the girls came closer to Douglas. "Is she a friend of yours?"

"Yes," he replied smugly. "A close friend."

"Ooh!" they chorused admiringly. Douglas smiled, and then the. smile faded as he remembered Moragh's hasty exit. He suddenly realized that it was Moragh's smile that he remembered, not Connie's thousand-volt one. He wheeled himself out into the corridor, looking for Moragh, but she was gone. He shook his head and wheeled himself back into his room. The book that Moragh had brought him lay on the table. He leafed through it, desolate.

"Goddam it!" He felt an overwhelming sense of loss.

He waited for Moragh to return, but she did not. He wrote to her, but did not receive an answer. He tried to telephone her, but could never get through to her, and when he asked whoever answered the telephone to have her call him back no calls came to him. He was hurt and lonely. After a while his sense of loss turned to resentment. If Moragh would have nothing to do with him, at least he could count on Connie to come to see him.

He basked briefly in her reflected glory as nurses and nurses' aides clustered around him, asking him about her, and enquiring when she would return to visit him. Here again he was disappointed; the days passed without her return. At length he admitted to himself that she had struck him off her list, and when he was able to look at himself in a full-length mirror he sourly recognized the reason. In his shapeless hospital uniform he was no longer the dashing warrior she had known two years before. His face was drawn and thin now, with lines in it he had not noticed before. He was encumbered by casts and his body was lumpy with dressings, and he had to be pushed about in a wheelchair. There was nothing dashing about him now, nothing debonair. Connie liked to make entrances to posh restaurants on the arm of a handsome young officer, one that she could show off as a conquest. Haggard men in coarse hospital uniforms did not enter into her calculations. She wanted to dance, to be swept up in strong young arms. Pushing a half-helpless companion in a wheelchair did not suit her requirements at all.

He had resigned himself to not seeing her again when she unexpectedly visited him once more. This time she was accompanied by a flying-boat pilot who treated Douglas with the deference he would have accorded an elder statesman.

Connie brought Douglas a bunch of grapes grown at Torquay on England's south coast, and a bottle of wine the young pilot had brought from Gibraltar. She entered the ward dramatically, the glamorous actress bearing gifts to the wounded hero, but as she introduced him to her escort Douglas knew that quite literally she was kissing him good-bye.

Nevertheless he was glad to see her. She was beautiful and exciting, she attracted a bemused gathering, and she flattered him with her caresses. He was sorry to see her go, even if she went on the arm of the young and mightily-impressed pilot, who looked just as Douglas had looked when he first met her.

He had more to occupy his time now. The physical therapist, a young and sturdy WAAF corporal, put him through an extensive series of exercises, and showed no sympathy for him when he complained about the effort or his discomfort. He progressed from his wheelchair to crutches as soon as his arm had healed enough to allow him to use them, and the walks the corporal made him take took his mind off his other worries.

When he was able to stump about he extended his travels until he was walking in the hospital grounds. Helena and Crane came upon him there as he made his way to a bench and sat gratefully down.

"Ed, old boy!" Crane exclaimed. "I say, it's good to see you up and about! You're doing wonderfully!"

"Yes, indeed." Helena said in her usual formal manner. "Do you think you're up to attending a wedding soon?"

"Any time now," Douglas answered. "I won't have to walk very far."

"That's very good," Helena said. "After all, it's high time Reg and I regularized our liaison."

Crane laughed. "Yes indeed—high time."

"Our mothers suggest three weeks from now," Helena said. "They've been champing at the bit for weeks now."

"I'll be there," said Douglas.

He did not see Moragh until he appeared, limping and helping himself along with a cane, at the rehearsal for the wedding. Moragh appeared in her uniform, as he was in his, and at first she treated him with icy reserve.

They went through the rehearsal with Douglas forgetting several important details and Moragh giving a flawless performance. When it was over he grinned. "I knew I'd goof and that you'd do it perfectly. That's par for the course."

322

"I'm sure you will perform satisfactorily on the day, Flight Lieutenant Douglas," she said.

"Is that all you can say to me?"

"I am sure my behaviour to you is quite correct."

"Yeah. That's what's bothering me."

"Will your other lady friends be present at the wedding?"

"I have no other lady friends."

"That is not the impression I got."

"Damn it, Moragh, you're jumping to conclusions!"

"Jumping to conclusions! I've never been so humiliated in my life! When I left you the day before, I thought you had something important to tell me. Then when I came back, I find you in the arms of another woman!"

"That was Connie Davidson—"

"I know perfectly well who it was! Don't you think that I read the papers or go to the theatre?"

"She's just somebody I knew before I went to Malta! When she found out I was in hospital she came up to see me. It was good publicity for her, taking goodies to a poor old wounded airman. I tell you I didn't have anything to do with it!"

"You were kissing her a lot too enthusiastically to suit me."

"She kisses everybody like that—she's an actress—kissing people is her stock in trade. I just happened to get in the way, that's all."

"But kissing her the way you did—in front of me, too!"

"All right, damn it, I'll kiss you that way too!" He reached for her, but she fended him off, and retreated icily to a far corner of the room.

Just then Crane and Helena entered the room. "Ed!" Crane cried. "You've earned a libation! Come with me for a beer while the ladies talk things over." Douglas reached for his cane and stomped out.

"Come with me for a cup of tea," Helena said. When they were sitting opposite each other, Moragh looked at Helena and frowned slightly. "You know, somehow you don't seem as impressed by the ceremony as I thought you'd be. It seems as if it's old hat to you. Have you been holding rehearsals on the sly?"

Helena smiled. "No, not exactly." Then she leaned confidentially closer to Moragh. "Let me tell you a secret. Swear you'll never mention it to a soul—at least not for several months."

323

"Of course not, Helena!"

"Reg and I have actually been married for a month."

"What! Why—I'd never have guessed—"

Helena looked at the wall, over her cup. "I shouldn't tell you this, but you are one of my best friends. I was engaged to be married once before, and my fiancé was killed before the wedding. When Reg asked me to marry him, I didn't want to waste a minute. I couldn't let another chance for happiness slip through my fingers. We were married secretly."

Moragh's eyes opened wide. "Oh my! Where were you married—in a registry office?"

Helena smiled. "Heavens no! Reg would never stand for that! We were married by a proper Church of England priest, using exactly the same ceremony we rehearsed today."

"When you make up your mind, you certainly act fast."

"I'd had such rotten luck with the other men I'd been close to—they all seemed to go missing as soon as we got to be friends—that I didn't intend to take any chances with Reg."

"I'd never have guessed. It couldn't have been when we were at Lower Lexington. You acted so—normal, all the time we were there."

"Yes. it was. But I was only engaged for one day—less than a day. My fiancé was killed less than a day after he asked me to marry him."

"That must have been awful!"

"It was. I never mentioned it because it hurt too much to talk about it." She smiled sadly. "It's funny—my husband is—or was—Douglas' navigator. So was my fiancé—the man I lost."

Moragh sat bolt upright. "Edward Douglas' navigator?"

"Yes. Henry Snow. You may have known him."

"Yes," Moragh answered in a strangled voice. "I knew him."

"I knew him for months, and he never showed anything more than ordinary friendliness. And then, after he thought his operations were over, he wrote me a beautiful poem—a sonnet—telling me he loved me. He said he'd loved me for months but had been afraid to say so."

"He'd loved you for months?" Moragh half-whispered.

"Yes. I'd noticed him, but we'd been nothing more than friends. And then when I read the sonnet he wrote for me I realized I loved him."

"Then did he ask you to marry him?"

She smiled sadly. "Yes—after I bullied him into it. He was so aware that I was an earl's daughter—as if that mattered. I would have gone anywhere and done anything for him. And then I lost him."

Moragh nodded her head slowly. "At least you didn't lose him to another woman."

"No—for all the consolation that was. But the time has come for me to make a new life, with Reg. At least I am staying faithful to Edward Douglas' navigators. I love Reg Crane, but I'll always remember that once I loved Henry Snow."

"I will never forget him either," Moragh said slowly. "We danced together a few times." She stood up. "It's been nice to see you again, Helena. I wish all the best for you and your husband."

"Thank you, Moragh," Helena said as they parted.

Moragh walked away slowly, and then retraced her steps. She saw how she had deluded herself—she was so sure that Snow had loved her, and he had considered her only a friend—a dancing partner. She admitted to herself reluctantly that he had never made a pass at her—he had always been a perfect gentleman—too perfect.

She suddenly turned and sought out Douglas. "Edward," she said with no preliminaries, "did you know that Henry Snow had asked Helena to marry him before he went on that last trip of his?"

Douglas nodded. "Yes, I did. I guess I was the only one he told. He didn't have much chance to spread the word around."

"When we were at Colombo, you never mentioned it."

"No. I gathered that you didn't know Hank and Helena were going to be married. I knew something else about you, though."

"That I was in love with him?"

He nodded. "I guess that's it."

"You mean when you asked me to marry you in Ceylon, and I wouldn't because I was still in love with Henry Snow, you wouldn't even tell me then?"

He spread his hands. "It would have been an awful thing to say—"

She stepped back. "You know, Edward, you're really very decent after all." She hesitated for a moment. "When we were interrupted in that balcony when those three officers came and then the nurse hurried you away, what were you going to say to me?"

"You know damn well. I was going to ask you to marry me."

"Very well. I accept."

325

"Really! That's wonderful!" He reached for her, caught her by the shoulders, and pressed her lips to his. Just as they were about to touch his wounded leg gave way and he tumbled in a heap to the floor, pulling her down with him. Douglas writhed in agony, gritting his teeth to keep from screaming.

Moragh disentangled herself and knelt beside him. "Edward! Edward! Are you hurt?"

He caught his breath. "I don't think I've broken anything new, but it sure smarts. Here—help me to my feet."

"No—lie down until we get a doctor to look at you."

Helena and Crane, attracted by the sound of Douglas' fall, hurried over to them. "Whatever's happened?" Helena asked.

"Just lost my balance, that's all—not too steady on my pins these days," Douglas answered. "I'll be all right. Just help me up."

"Heavens no! You must be looked at properly before you move! Terrible things may have happened!"

"Forget about a doctor! There's nothing wrong with me!" Douglas tried to struggle up.

It was then that Helena's mother appeared on the scene. "What's happened here?"

"Flight Lieutenant Douglas slipped and fell, Mother," Helena said. "His leg isn't properly healed, you know."

"Then he must stay right where he is without doing anything foolish!" she ordered. "Reginald, go at once to fetch a doctor!" Douglas looked at her and realized resistance was impossible. He relaxed and pillowed his head in Moragh's arms.

The countess looked at Douglas and then at Moragh. "You're this young man's fiancee, aren't you?"

"Yes, my lady, I am."

The countess nodded her head. "Very good. When have you planned your marriage, young lady?"

Moragh coloured. "We're not sure, we've only been engaged for five minutes."

"Perhaps we can be of some assistance to you. My daughter's husband-to-be and your fiancé are very close. We must discuss the matter at your convenience."

Douglas looked at Moragh and laughed. "Well, that settles that." He reached for her hand. "I hope you'll like Valenby, Saskatchewan."